Peter Henry Bruce

Memoirs of Peter Henry Bruce

A Military Officer in the Services of Prussia, Russia, and Great Britain

Peter Henry Bruce

Memoirs of Peter Henry Bruce
A Military Officer in the Services of Prussia, Russia, and Great Britain

ISBN/EAN: 9783337170059

Printed in Europe, USA, Canada, Australia, Japan

Cover: Foto ©Raphael Reischuk / pixelio.de

More available books at **www.hansebooks.com**

MEMOIRS

OF

PETER HENRY BRUCE, Esq.

A MILITARY OFFICER,

In the SERVICES of

PRUSSIA, RUSSIA, and GREAT BRITAIN.

CONTAINING

An Account of his Travels in GERMANY, RUSSIA, TARTARY, TURKEY, the WEST INDIES, &c.

AS ALSO

Several very interesting private ANECDOTES of the CZAR, PETER I. of RUSSIA.

―――――――――――――

LONDON,

Printed for the AUTHOR's WIDOW; and sold by T. PAYNE, and Son, Mewsgate; and all other Bookfellers.

MDCCLXXXII.

ADVERTISEMENT.

THE following Memoirs are taken from the manufcript of an officer of great merit and undoubted honour. It is immaterial to add, that they are genuine, as they bear fuch internal marks of authenticity, as will admit of no difpute.

Any anecdotes that relate to the character of fo extraordinary a perfonage as the Czar Peter, cannot fail of being acceptable to the reader; who will of courfe enjoy an additional pleafure in receiving them from the pen of a man who was in his fervice, and in his confidence. It is this circumftance that will render it unneceffary to apologize for any deficiency in point of ftyle, as it is entirely difregarded in this narration, the chief merit of which confifts in a ftrict regard to truth, without the leaft pretenfions to embellifhments.

As

ADVERTISEMENT.

As the manufcript leaves off abruptly, in the middle of the Rebellion, in 1745, it may be necefíary to mention, that the author was, about that time employed in fortifying Berwick ; and after having finifhed that work he retired to his houfe in the country, where he died in the year 1757

CONTENTS.

BOOK I.

BOOK II.

a
tions

CONTENTS.

BOOK III.

BOOK

CONTENTS.

BOOK IV.

BOOK V.

     service.

C O N T E N T S.

B O O K. VI.

C O N T E N T S.

B O O K VII.

B O O K VIII.

Occaſion

CONTENTS.

B O O K   IX.

B O O K   X.

C O N T E N T S.

CONTENTS.

MEMOIRS

OF

PETER HENRY BRUCE, Esq.

BOOK I.

The author's defcent.—His grandfather's going into the Pruffian fervice.—John Bruce's marriage and defendants, and the author's birth, &c.—His entering into the Pruffian fervice.—Lines on the battle of Ramillies.—A remarkable ftory of the author's landlady.—His firft campaign.—His fecond campaign.—Defeat of the French.—Siege of Lifle.—A remarkable accident to prince Eugene.—Captain Dubois.—A fad accident to the enemy's cavalry.—Bon mot of the duke of Marlborough.—Siege of Ghent.—Third Campaign.—Siege of Tournay.—Battle of Malplaquet.—Story of a Swifs recruit.—Siege of Mons.—Fourth campaign.—Siege of Doway.—Siege of Bethune.—A fad misfortune to fix Scotch officers.—Sieges of Aire and St. Venant.—Terrible ftory of the Jefuits at Tournay.

THE following journal was originally written in the German, my native language; but as I have lately enjoyed the leifure of a country retirement, I have, in this year 1755, tranflated it into Englifh (to me a foreign

B   tongue),

ongue), for the entertainment of my friends, and the information of my family, that they might know their connections in Germany, and the particulars of a life spent in war for a series of years in different parts of the globe. —To begin then,

The author's descent.   James Bruce and John Bruce, cousins and descendants of the family of Airth, in the county of Stirling, (a branch of the family of Clackmannan) in Scotland, formed a resolution, during the troubles of Oliver Cromwell, to leave their native country, in order to push their fortunes abroad; and, as there were some ships in the port of Leith ready to sail for the Baltic, they agreed to go together to that part of the world: but as there happened to be two of these ship-masters of the same name, by an odd mistake the cousins embarked in different vessels, the one bound to Prussia, the other to Russia, by which accident they never again saw each other.

His grandfather goes into the Prussian service.   John Bruce, my grandfather, landed at Konigsberg, in Prussia; from thence he went to Berlin, and entered into the service of the elector of Brandenburg, and by degrees was advanced to the command of a regiment, which was the highest military preferment he ever obtained, notwithstanding the elector, in other respects, shewed him many favours: amongst the rest the following was no small instance of his regard. My grandfather one day attending the elector in hunting, when his highness, in the eager pursuit of the chace, entered a large wood, and was separated from all his attendants except my grandfather, who kept up with him. Night overtaking them in the wood, they were obliged to dismount, and lead their horses, when,

           after

after groping their way for a confiderable time in the dark, they at length perceived a light at a little diftance, and upon their getting up to it, they found themfelves at the miferable hut of a poor tar-burner, who lived a great way in the wood. Being informed by the poor inhabitant that they were a long way from any town, village, or other habitation, the prince, who by this time was both tired and hungry, afked him what he had got to eat; upon which the poor man produced a loaf of coarfe black bread and a piece of cheefe, of which the eleƈtor ate very heartily, and finifhed his meal with a draught of water, declaring he had never eat any thing with fo good an appetite before. He then enquired how large that wood was, and was told that it bordered on Mecklenburg Strelitz, and that it was of very great extent. Upon this my grandfather obferved, that it was a pity fuch a large traƈt of land fhould lie ufelefs, and if his highnefs would give him a grant of it, he would undertake to build a village in the middle of it, and another upon the fpot where they then were. To this the eleƈtor agreed, and foon after confirmed his grant by an ample charter, with great privileges annexed thereto; and my grandfather, according to his engagement, built a village in the middle of the wood, which he called Brucenwold (or Bruce-Wood); and another at the tar-burner's hut, which he called Jetzkendorf, its ancient name; for a village of that name had formerly ftood there, part of the ruins being then ftill vifible. The eleƈtor flept upon fome ftraw till day-break, when he was awaked by the noife of his other attendants, who had been in fearch of him all night; and on their arrival he departed for Berlin.

My

BOOK I.

John Bruce's
marriage and
descendants,
and the au-
thor's birth.

My grandfather married at Berlin a lady of fortune, of the family of Arenfdorf, and got with her feveral eftates in land, of confiderable value. He had by her two fons and three daughters; the youngeft of his fons was my father; his eldeft daughter was married to colonel Dewitz, who was afterwards governor of Pomerania, and who got with her a landed eftate in that province called Malchin; the fecond daughter was made abbefs of a proteftant monaftery, founded for the education of young ladies, but fhe was afterwards married to lieutenant colonel Rebeur, who got Brucenwold for her fortune; and his youngeft daughter was married to major general Lattorff, who got for her fortune his moft valuable eftates of Konikendorff and Woletz : he thus difpofed of all the landed eftates he got by his wife in favour of his daughters, and gave his two fons an education only, and a fmall ftock of money. Having placed them in the electer's grand mufketteer guards, he left them to pufh their fortunes in the army, as he himfelf had done before them. His eldeft fon, Charles, was a lieutenant at the fiege of Namur, where he was killed; his youngeft fon James, my father, married Elizabeth Catherina Detring, of a confiderable family in Weftphalia, and was himfelf then a lieutenant in a Scotch regiment, commanded by the earl of Leven, in the fervice of Brandenburg, and I was born at Detring-Caftle, (the manorhoufe of that family) in the year 1692.

This regiment was ordered to Flanders, and my father carried my mother with him, and we remained there till 1698, when the regiment returned to Scotland, and whither we accompanied him. The regiment being then put in

garrifon.

garrifon at Fort William, I was left in Fife to the care of
a grand uncle, my grandfather's youngeft brother, who
pofteffed a fmall eftate near Cupar, at which place I was
put to fchool, where I continued three years, when my
father fent for me to Fort William, and I remained there
three years more.

In the year 1704, my father got leave of abfence from   1704.
the regiment, and fet out on a vifit to Germany, whither
he carried his wife and family; and after one year's ftay
with their relations, he returned to Scotland, leaving me
behind in the care of their friends, who undertook to edu-
cate and provide for me. Their firft attempt in my favour
was to get me made a page to the king of Pruffia, and
when I was going to be prefented to his majefty by the
marfhal count Witgenftein, the prince royal enquired of
him who I was; and being informed, and alfo that I was
going to be prefented to the king for a page, he afked me
feveral queftions, and told the marfhal that he himfelf would
have me for his page. We returned without my being prefented to the king; and on my telling this piece of news
to my friends, they would by no means confent; alledging,
that the prince did not ufe his pages well, which my coufin,
a fon of general Lattorff's, had experienced, who had been
page of honour to him, and was then a gentleman of the
bed-chamber to the king, for which reafon they would not
fuffer me to accept the offer.

The next thing they endeavoured was to get me into the
Royal Academy, as a cadet; but they were told that was now
impracticable, as I had refufed the prince's offer of being   1706.
his page: however, they fent me to the academy, at their

own

own charge, to learn fortification and other neceſſary branches.
My uncle Rebeur arrived at this time from Flanders ; he was

then lieutenant-colonel of the marquis de Varen's regiment,
and when he was about to return, I expreſſed a deſire to go
with him. He very kindly approved my deſign, and on the
ſuggeſtion of my friends, that it might be hurtful to me in
my education, the colonel aſſured them that it would rather be an advantage, as there were in almoſt every town
in Flanders exceeding good maſters for teaching fortification and gunnery, &c. and that I ſhould have double advantage in improving the theory by ſeeing many parts of it
in real practice : he farther offered not only to keep me with
himſelf, but that no opportunity to improve my education
ſhould be neglected. This kind offer was very ſatisfactory
to all my friends, and he performed his promiſe with a moſt
paternal care.

His entering into the Pruſſian ſervice.
I ſat out with him accordingly for the regiment, which
was then in garriſon at Maeſtricht, where we arrived in
April 1706, and I was entered in the colonel's company
to carry arms, and ſoon became a proficient in the manual
exerciſes ; after which I found my duty very eaſy, for I had
only to mount guard once in a week, the reſt of my time
being devoted to the ſtudy of fortification, &c.

This year was memorable for the defeat of the French
army under marſhal Villeroy, at Ramillies : the battle was
fought on the 12th of May, when the duke of Marlborough gained a complete victory over them : the victory was
followed by the ſurrender of many places both in Flanders
and Brabant. This year was alſo remarkable for the king of
Sweden's entering Saxony, and dethroning king Auguſtus,
where

where he raifed five millions fterling by levying contributions. Among the prifoners who were fent in here after
the battle of Ramillies, was a marquis, who was a colonel
of horfe : general Dopff, the governor of this place, not
only gave him the liberty of the town, but alfo allowed
him to go a hunting in the country ; yet, notwithftanding
this polite ufage, and his own parole, this officer thought
proper to make his efcape, but was foon fent back under a
guard by marfhal Villeroy, and was afterwards allowed the
liberty only of the town, attended by a ferjeant for his
vade mecum.

After the battle the following French verfes made their Lines on the
appearance : battle of Ra-
millies.

> C'eft à ce coup, que Villeroy, ce maréchal incomparable,
> Pour avoir bien fervi le roy, aura l'Epée de connetable
> Car pour un moindre evenement, Tallard un governmens
> Varus rends moi mes legions ? S'écrioit l'empereur augufte ;
> Tallard rends moi mes battaillions ? Dit Lous, à Titre plus jufte,
> Tallard repond—Hé grand roy, demande lès a Villeroy.

At the houfe where I lodged with the colonel, I was told A remarkable
a very remarkable ftory that happened between my land- ftory of the
author's
lady and her former hufband, who was a native of this landlady.
town ; his name was Niepels, and was a captain of dragoons in the Dutch fervice ; he courted our landlady at the
Hague, fhe was the daughter of a merchant there, and after
a folemn promife of marriage, he firft feduced, and then
left her pregnant : her father was fo incenfed at her, that he
turned her out of the houfe ; but an aunt taking compaffion
on her kept her, till fhe was brought to bed, and afterwards
fupplied her with a little money, with which, unknown to
any

any of her friends, she equipped herself in men's cloaths, bought a horse, and went and offered herself as a volunteer in captain Niepels' troop : her offer was accepted, and she continued some time in the troop; the captain used sometimes to tell his volunteer that he was very like an old mistress of his, but never had the least suspicion that he was speaking to the very person : she staid till the end of the campaign, when captain Niepels, being informed of his father's death, left the service, and went home to take possession of his estate. By this accident she seemed to lose sight of any opportunity to call the captain to an account, which was the sole motive of her adventure : however, she followed him, but laid aside the cavalier, and re-assumed the female, and arriving at Maestricht, she prevailed upon his maid-servant (for a little money) to allow her to sleep in a private room in the house for one night, as she was a stranger, and did not chuse to lodge in any public inn. Having thus broke the ground, and got admission, she had an opportunity to reconnoitre the house, particularly the captain's apartment, who was generally abroad the whole day, and came home late at night. She kept very close, till she thought every body in the house was asleep, and then proceeding with a candle in one hand, and a poniard in the other, to his bedside, she awaked him, and asked if he knew her, and upon his demanding what had brought her there, she told him, that he now must resolve to perform his engagement to her, otherwise she was determined to put him to death. The captain thought proper to refuse, and, at the same time, called to his servants; but, before any of them could arrive she struck him in the breast; and notwithstanding all the

defence

defence he could make, she gave him several other wounds in different parts of his body; the servants at length came to his assistance, and finding their master streaming with blood, they sent for a magistrate and guards to secure her. In the mean time, the lady never offered to move off, but continued upbraiding him with his treachery, although he entreated her to save herself, as he thought himself mortally wounded; at last the magistrate came with a guard to conduct her to prison, which the captain would not suffer, but begged them to send for a priest, to whom, on his arrival, he confessed how much he had injured the young woman, and desired the priest, in the presence of the magistrate, to marry them without loss of time, which accordingly he did: upon the surgeon's declaring that none of the wounds were mortal, the guard was withdrawn, and by the careful attendance of the surgeon, and the no less tender care of his now spouse, the captain soon recovered of his wounds. They lived afterwards in the greatest harmony for several years, till an ill-fated accident put an end to his life: one evening they were walking together before the Trowen-Port, and passing by an arsenal where a number of old useless arms were lying, a gentlewoman in their neighbourhood, with whom they lived in great intimacy, met them, and taking up an old rusty pistol, said jocularly to captain Niepels, that it was decreed he should die by the hands of a woman, which he actually did, for the pistol went off and shot him dead upon the spot. He left three daughters, who were now marriageable; his widow (our landlady), some time after his death, married his nephew.

C

One

BOOK I.

1705.

One night as I was on guard with our lieutenant upon Petersberg, and standing sentry with my musket in my hand, the but-end on the ground, and pulling it after me in a careless manner over the gravel, it accidentally went off, and alarmed the whole garrison : this accident obliged the lieutenant to send a serjeant to acquaint the officer at Peterfport ; and next day I was brought before the governor, where I appeared in great fear, having been told by the soldiers that I should think myself well off if I had only to run the gauntlet ; but, to my great joy, it ended in a reprimand, and being told, if a common soldier had done the like he would have been severely punished : this reproof made me more cautious in future when on duty. I was this winter made a serjeant, it being customary in the Prussian service to go through all the low degrees before they can obtain an officer's commission ; by this promotion I was advanced two steps above the ordinary rule. In

the month of April, 1707, the prince-royal of Prussia came to this place, and reviewed our regiment ; and in passing by him, and answering to my name, according to the muster-roll, he recollected me, and blamed the colonel for making a *child* first serjeant in his company ; but on the colonel's informing him that I performed my duty very well, and was assiduous in learning the military art, the prince seemed to be very well satisfied.

In May our regiment marched from Maestricht ; and joined the army at Mildert ; and on the 9th of August, we advanced to Genap, with an intention to attack the enemy ; on the 10th, at night, we passed the Deyle at Florival, and marched till morning : at day-break we arrived.

rived at Waveren, and found the enemy had retired, upon
which we returned to Genap. The French kept retiring
before us the whole campaign, fo warily, that we were
never able to bring them to an engagement, which har-
raffed our troops by continual marches and counter-
marches, without being able to effect any thing. Towards winter the army marched to Afche, where we feparated, and went into quarters. The prince of Orange was
at this time declared general of the Dutch forces, though
no more than twenty-one years of age. Our regiment
marched to Huye for winter-quarters, where the Swedifh
general, Oxenftein, was governor: this town lies on both
fides of the Meufe, and is but indifferently fortified, yet it
is ftrengthened by a caftle and three other forts, erected
upon eminences, which protect the town. I mounted
guard one day with a Dutch lieutenant, a very plain man,
who could neither read nor write, but was advanced from
a ferjeant for a pretty extraordinary exertion of perfonal
courage and gallant perfeverance: the French had befieged
and taken a town with all its fortifications, excepting one
tower, where this ferjeant was pofted with twenty men, and
which he bravely maintained againft every effort of the
enemy, till the place was retaken the following year; to
which he alfo contributed greatly from his fituation.

As I was one day out with a party, and paffing near a
monaftery, we obferved a woman running, and feveral perfons in purfuit of her; we went and met her: being informed that we belonged to the garrifon of Huye, fhe
feemed to be overjoyed, and being thus relieved a little
from her fright, fhe told us that fhe belonged to Namur,
and had engaged herfelf to a French officer without the

C 2   confent

confent of her parents, who, upon the officer's demanding her in marriage, had fhut her up in that monaftery,

from whence fhe had juft made her efcape over the garden-
wall by the help of a ladder, and that fhe intended to go
to Liege, where fhe had relations who would protect and
favour her: the event juftified the affertion, for on her
arrival there, her friends procured a paffport for her lover,
and fhe got the hufband of her own choice.

In May 1708, we marched from Huye to join the army,
and came to Anderlech on the 23d, when the Pruffians, Hanoverians, and Dutch began to form; on the 26th, we
went to Bellinghen, where we joined the Englifh and other
troops; the army confifted of 180 fquadrons, and 112 battalions. The French army, under the duke de Vendofme,
formed at St. Ghiflain, and confifted of 197 fquadrons,
and 124 battalions; the two royal princes, the dukes of
Burgundy and Berry, were with the army. At Bellinghen
we were joined by the electoral prince of Hanover, (his
prefent majefty) and prince Eugene, whofe troops from the
Mofelle were come to Maeftricht, and foon after joined us.

The French opened the campaign with taking Ghent
and Bruges by furprize; they made a fruitlefs attack on
Damme, but they took fort Plaffendahl, between Bruges
and Oftend; and on the 9th of July, they invefted Oudenarde, but on our approach they raifed the fiege, and retired over the Scheld. We purfued them clofe, and brought
them to an engagement on the 11th. It was fix o'clock in
the afternoon before our lines were formed; Prince Eugene
commanded the right, and the duke of Marlborough the
left wings. After a moft vigorous and well-conducted attack, the French were beat, and fled under cover of the

night, which faved them from being cut to pieces. Next
day 4000 of the enemy were found dead on the field of ⸺
battle; 7000 were made prifoners; befides 535 officers (generals included); 34 ftandards, 25 colours, and 5 pair
of kettle drums, but no cannon, the battle being fought
without artillery on either fide. The lofs on our fide was
2972, killed and wounded.

After this battle, the French retired behind the canal,
between Ghent and Bruges; and count Lottum, the Pruffian general, was fent with a refpectable detachment, to attack their lines at Ypres, which we took and levelled with
little or no refiftance. The army then went and invefted
Lifle, which was afterwards befieged in form by prince
Eugene, whilft the duke of Marlborough covered the fiege.
This fiege, which lafted fo long, and coft fo much blood,
was attended with various events.

A pretty remarkable occurrence happened to prince Eugene in the time of it. His highnefs received a letter from
fome unknown hand, and upon opening it, he found it
contained a greafy paper, which he immediately and
fortunately let fall upon the ground; his aid de camp
took it up and fmelled at it, and was directly feized
with a giddinefs, fo much, that they were obliged to give
him an antidote: this paper was then tied about a dog's
neck for an experiment, and he died within twenty-four
hours, notwithftanding a counter-poifon was given him.
The officers about the prince exprefling their concern at the
accident, he replied, without the leaft emotion, " You
" need not wonder at it, gentlemen; I have received feve-
" ral letters of this fort before now."

The

The duke of Burgundy being defirous to know in what condition the garrifon was, one captain Dubois undertook to get into the town, and having got undifcovered to the outworks of the place, he ftripped himfelf, and having hid his clothes, fwam over feven canals and ditches, and got fafe into the town, and returning the fame way brought the duke a letter from marfhal Boufſeur, which he carried in his mouth, fo enveloped that it was preferved quite dry.

Sad accident to the enemy's cavalry. In the night of the 28th of September, we were alarmed with a loud crack, and in half an hour another, and at midnight there was fuch a thunder-clap that the earth was fhaken under us: this fo alarmed the whole army, that we lay under arms till day-light, when we were informed that 1200 of the enemy's cavalry, having each fifty pounds of powder in bags behind them, were endeavouring to get into the town, but being difcovered and fired upon, they fpurred haftily forwards, by which means fome of the bags got untied, and the powder pouring to the ground, catched the fire which flew from the horfe's feet, ſtriking on the caufeway, and communicating with the powder in the bags, the whole blew up; about fixty of the men perifhed on entering the lines, and an hundred near the gate; it was a fhocking fight next day, to fee the road ſtrewed with half burnt heads, limbs, and carcafes of men and horfes; the reft of the corps threw away their powder and made off, but it was believed about three hundred got into the town.

Some few days afterwards, fifty peafants were taken endeavouring to convey powder into the town in their wheelbarrows: as they had the liberty to fell milk to the army, they brought it in barrels, two on a barrow; and on this

9   occa-

BOOK I.

1708.

occafion, one of the barrels on every barrow proved to be powder; and being all convicted, they were every one hung up.

About this time, Auguftus, king of Poland, and feveral other princes, came here to be eye-witneffes of this famous fiege. The enemy, in endeavouring to obftruct our convoys from Oftend, brought on themfelves their defeat at Weynendahl. They had ftrongly fortified themfelves by a triple entrenchment round their camp at Oudenarde, where they had retired, beyond the Schelde, which greatly impeded our communication with that quarter, and the duke of Bavaria, at the fame time, befieging Bruffels, reduced us to the neceffity of living for fome time on turnips and onions. To relieve ourfelves from this diftrefs, and open the communication with our provifions, a fufficient body was detached from the army, and by a forced march in the night, croffed the Schelde, and attacked their lines next day, when they gave us much lefs trouble than we expected, for they fled with the utmoft precipitation, leaving us their whole camp, baggage, and all; in the purfuit, our cavalry took a number of prifoners; here we got a very happy relief of provifions of all forts in great plenty, after fo flender a diet. We next marched to the relief of Bruffels, but before we arrived the duke had abandoned the fiege, leaving behind him fifteen pieces of heavy cannon, and two mortars; having thus happily fucceeded in our enterprize, we returned to the fiege of Lifle.

Upon our breaking ground on the glacis, or covered way, I was with the pioneers; the engineer who marked out the ground being killed, and our men quite expofed to the

BOOK I.   the enemy's fire, I took upon me to finish what he had be-
1708.   gun, and very foon got ourfelves under cover; for which
fervice the general of the trenches for that night, recommended me to our commander in chief, general count Lottum, who wrote to the king in my favour, and in the
winter I got an enfign's commiffion *; but I was generally
employed as an engineer.   The town furrendered the 23d
of October, and as we were then quartered in the barracks,
we were better able to profecute the fiege of the citadel,
which ftill held out, and was carried on by fap, under
the direction of general Cochorn, in very cold weather and
hard froft : this fervice lafted to the 9th of December,
when the citadel alfo furrendered; on the 10th, marfhal
Bouffleur marched out with his garrifon, and was conducted to Doway.

Surrender of   During the fiege, after we had made a lodgement upon
Lifle.   the fecond counterfcarp, a Dutch captain, who was pofted
there, fled from his poft, on the approach of the enemy,
without making the leaft refiftance; his ferjeant, reflecting
on the difhonourable retreat, endeavoured to perfuade him
to return and recover it, but in vain; the ferjeant then addreffed himfelf to the men, telling them if they would follow him, he would endeavour to regain the poft they had
deferted in fo cowardly a manner; the men immediately

---

* The commiffion was fent to his uncle col. Rebeur, who concealed
it from Mr. Bruce on account of his youth, being only in his fixteenth
year, till fome time next campaign; coming to the knowlege of it, he
walked to the door of his uncle's tent, and fticking his halbert in the
ground with fome refentment, cried out, " There ftands the ferjeant !"
and walking a few fteps from it, he called out, " Here ftands the officer !"
and then received his commiffion.

agreed,

agreed, rallied, and attacked the enemy with fuch bravery,
that the poft was very foon regained. Upon a reprefen-
tation of this action, the officer was degraded for cowardice, and the ferjeant rewarded as he deferved. A foldier without courage is like a dead corpfe; forrow hangs
on the countenances of its late beft friends till it is buried out of their fight.

A bon mot of the duke of Marlborough was at this
time much talked of in the camp; when the king of Poland was going for Saxony, and the duke had taken his
leave of him, wifhing him a good journey, his majefty alfo
wifhed his grace a good voyage to England; upon which
the duke anfwered him in French, "Que le tems étant
fort froid, il ne vouloit pas pafler la mer fans Gand;"
that is, the weather being very cold, he would not pafs the
fea without gloves; the word *gand*, in French, being the
name of the city of *Ghent*, as well as the term for *gloves*;
and his grace was as good as his word.

Our army, notwithftanding the rigour of the feafon,
marched immediately for Ghent, and we invefted it on the
17th of the fame month. The duke of Marlborough
commanded the fiege, and prince Eugene covered. The
garrifon confifted of 30 battalions and 19 fquadrons; but
the water in their moats being all hard frozen over, and
apprehending a furprize, they thought proper to furrender
the 31ft of December. The garrifon marched out the 2d
of January, 1709, and was conducted to Tournay; the
duke of Argyle immediately took poffeffion of the town
and citadel. The enemy foon after evacuated Bruges, Red-
fort, Plaffendahl, and Leffinghen, which finifhed this me-

D morable

morable campaign, and our army went into quarters : our
regiment marched to Bruſſels, where we wintered : the
French made propoſals this winter for a general peace, but
they did not ſucceed.

In the beginning of June we marched to join the army,
which was formed the 21ſt, between Courtray and Menin,
110,000 ſtrong ; from thence we paſſed the Lower Deyle,
and encamped on the plains of Liſle. The French army,
which conſiſted of 130,000, encamped on the plains of
Lens, where they entrenched themſelves ſo ſtrongly, that it
was thought imprudent on our part to attempt to force
them, and it was then reſolved to beſiege Tournay ; the
enemy had ſo little ſuſpicion of ſuch an attempt, that they
had withdrawn a part of the garriſon to ſtrengthen their
army. The town was accordingly inveſted on the 27th,
under the command of the duke of Marlborough, and the
lines of circumvallation were begun the 30th ; count Lottum commanded the attack on the citadel, where I was
employed for the firſt time as engineer ; the other two attacks, againſt the city, were commanded by generals Schul-
lemburg and Fagel, and the prince of Naſſau, at this time,
took the two forts, St. Amand and Mortagne, which were
very neceſſary in covering the ſiege. The 6th of July,
the lines of circumvallation were finiſhed, and on the 7th
at night, the trenches were opened : on the 13th, our batteries began to play upon the town. In ſhort, the town
ſurrendered the 28th, and the garriſon to the number of
4000, retired into the citadel ; and two captains, four lieutenants, and 150 men, deſerted and came into our camp,
and 800 of their wounded were conveyed to Doway. In
                                                    this

this fiege we had 3,210 men killed and wounded ; the earl of Albemarle was appointed governor in the town.

On the 1ft of Auguft, they began to fire upon us from the citadel, which was immediately returned from our batteries, and on the 3d, one of our fhells fell into a powder-magazine of their's, which blew up : a ceffation of hoftilities on both fides was foon after agreed to, on condition of furrendering on the 5th of September, if they were not then relieved by the French army. During the truce, a number of deferters from our army, being then in the citadel, got leave to attempt the making of their efcape, but being informed againft by one of their number, they were all caught and hanged.

The conditions of the truce being made known to the French king, he would not agree to the propofition of furrender, which being communicated to the befiegers, hoftilities were recommenced. The enemy fprung many mines, and our counter-mining occafioned many fkirmifhes under-ground ; on the 26th, they fprung a mine, which blew up 400 of our men, and killed Mr. Du May, our chief engineer ; after this they fprung feveral others, which did us confiderable mifchief, efpecially one which left an opening fixty paces long and twenty foot deep, and which bade fair to have blown up a whole Hanoverian regiment, had it not been very opportunely difcovered, fo that we loft only one private centinel killed by it. On the 30th, we cannonaded and bombarded them fo warmly, that they beat a parley on the 31ft in the morning : they now ftipulated for conditions, but no other terms could be received than furrendering prifoners of war, which they were not, even yet,

difpofed

difpofed to agree to, fo that hoftilities were renewed, and upon our redoubled efforts, with every warlike engine, they at laft were obliged to furrender on our own terms, and march out on the 5th of September with 3500 men, befides their fick and wounded.

Before Tournay an exprefs arrived from prince Menzikoff to the duke of Marlborough, informing his grace that the czar's army had obtained a complete victory over the king of Sweden at Pultowa, on the 8th of July laft.

The battle of Malplaquet.   Our next operation was directed againft Mons: the elector of Bavaria, who refided there, hearing thereof, retired to Namur. Marfhal Bouffleur was now fent by the French king to affift marfhal Villars, with orders rather to hazard a battle than fuffer Mons to fall in the general career of our arms. On the 8th, prince Eugene joined us with his army, when we were very much fatigued with marching night and day in rainy weather, and through bad roads. On the 9th, we obferved the enemy moving towards Blarignies, in order to poffefs themfelves of the woods and hedges of Taniers and Malplaquet; upon which we moved forward in order of battle; but as the Englifh were foraging, they could not join us that day, and the two armies began cannonading each other, which continued till night, and was renewed next morning, when we did not choofe to engage, as we expected to be joined by twenty-three battalions from Tournay. This day I very narrowly efcaped, being fhot by one of our own foldiers, who being out of his rank I ordered him to it, and as he took no notice of the orders, I ftruck him acrofs the fhoulders and pufhing him into it, he ftepped back and cocked his piece which he

directly

directly prefented to my breaft ; I inftantly parried the muz-
zle downwards, and the bullet went into the ground between my feet ; the fellow immediately flung down his
mufket and run for it, but was purfued by the adjutant on
horfeback, and being a ftout fellow, he took the adjutant
by the foot, threw him out of the faddle, and was juft going to mount, when the major came up with and fecured
him. But to return ; the enemy by our delay, got time to
cut down the wood, and entrench themfelves ; in the evening we converfed with the French officers, and entertained
each other with fuch fare as we had, in a very friendly manner ; this we were the more induced to, from a perfuafion
on both fides, that a ceffation of arms was to take place
previous to a peace, but we were undeceived by midnight,
when every man had orders to repair to his poft, and prepare to engage the enemy early next morning.

On the 11th, at two in the morning, we attended at
prayers, and then prepared by forming in the order of battle ; about eight we advanced and attacked their entrenchments, which we carried, driving the enemy with great diforder and confufion in their trenches, out of which we beat
them, with numbers flain on both fides: the regiment our's
was engaged with, happened to be that with whofe officers
we had been fo focial the night before, and in it was a lieutenant, who had a brother a lieutenant in our's, and who
was with us, a French refugee ; the lieutenant in the French
regiment, furrendered himfelf a prifoner to his brother, and
was affectionately received under his protection ; but unfortunately, at the very inftant, a foldier of our's ran him
through the body, and killed him in his brother's arms :
the

the fellow alledged in excuse for himself, that he did it to protect his officer, not knowing the other; yet he had seen the brothers the evening before conversing together as such. Fatal mistakes occur too frequently in the fury and rage of contending foes, met on purpose to conquer or die, nor is it possible to brand this poor fellow with any foul design on this occasion :—but to my story. The French retiring over a hedge, we pursued them close, and finding them reinforced, we were obliged to retire in our turn, and making our way back through the hedge, we lost our colonel and several of our men; but being supported by our line of reserve, we were enabled to force the enemy a second time from the hedge, and to drive them to their second entrenchment, from which we also dislodged them, and pursued them to their third, where I found myself shot through the leg, and was obliged to be carried out of the field, and arriving at a little cot, I there found the corpse of my colonel, and got my wound dressed. After a very close engagement of six hours, the enemy gave way, and left us masters of a dear bought field, which cost us not less than 20,300 men. The particulars of this famous battle of Malplaquet, having been so well described by better pens, I shall say no more of it, only that the enemy lost, by their own confession, 540 officers killed, 1068 wounded, 301 taken prisoners; and 15000 men killed, wounded, and taken. We had two generals killed, counts Lottum and Fettace.

After this action, it was currently reported that marshal Villars was for hazarding another battle to prevent our taking Mons, but was opposed in it by marshal Bouffleur; and that the king of France had sent the duke of Berwick to deter-

determine upon the different opinions of thefe two able generals, upon the fpot. His grace came, and viewing the
ground with their late entrenchments, expreffed his furprize
at their extraordinary ftrength, declaring, as they had been
beaten out of that poft, they muft be very rafh indeed to
venture an engagement on the open field.

While the furgeon was attending the wound which confined me, he told me a diverting ftory of a young Swifs
recruit, who, when his regimentals were making, had procured a round iron plate bordered with fmall holes, which
he defired the taylor to faften on the infide of his coat, above
his left breaft, to prevent his being fhot through the heart :
the taylor being a humourous fellow, faftened it in the feat
of his breeches, and the clothes being fcarce on his back
when he was ordered to march into the field, having no opportunity to get this aukward miftake rectified, before he
found himfelf engaged in battle, and being obliged to fly
before the enemy, and in endeavouring to get over a thorn
hedge in his way, he unfortunately ftuck faft till he was
overtaken by a foe, who, on his coming up, gave him a
pufh in the breech with his bayonet, (with no friendly defign), but it luckily hit on the iron-plate, and pufhed the
young foldier clear out of the hedge ; this favourable circumftance made the Swifs honeftly confefs, that the taylor
had more fenfe than himfelf, and knew better where his
heart lay.—But to nobler deeds.

Our eminent leaders well knowing their advantage by a
reputation for habitually beating the enemy, immediately
invefted Mons, and the trenches were opened on the 25th,
under the command of the prince of Naffau; and, notwith-

4   ftanding

ftanding the continual heavy rains, the fiege was brifkly
pufhed on till the 20th of October, when this town alfo
furrendered, and the garrifon marched out 8000 men, befides 1000 that were left behind, and afterwards enlifted
in our army.

The victory at Malplaquet, and the taking of Tournay
and Mons, finifhing this campaign, our army feparated,
and went into quarters for the winter. Our regiment went
to Maeftricht; and not being yet recovered of my wound,
I was obliged to travel in a waggon with eight wounded
foldiers, under the care of a ferjeant, to Bruffels; in the
evening of the 20th, we arrived at Notre Dame de Hall,
half-way between Mons and Bruffels, where one of our
wheels broke, and the waggoner hearing that there was a
party of French in the town, thought proper to fet off with
his horfes; the French having got notice of us, came, and
after enquiring for the horfes, and finding they were gone,
fat out in purfuit of them: happily for me, I had formerly been fome time in this place, and was pretty well
known to the people, who conveyed me to a place of fafety,
which, for once, faved me from being ftripped; the party
returning, ftript the eight wounded foldiers, and carried
the ferjeant a prifoner to Namur: the ferjeant, on his arrival there, was examined by the governor, whom he informed that he had been on duty, conducting thefe wounded
men to the hofpital at Bruffels, and that the French party
had ftripped them naked, and plundered them of a month's
pay. The governor feverely reprimanded the officer, telling
him, he ought rather to have affifted the poor defencelefs
wounded men, than to have ufed them in the manner he

6   had

BOOK I.

1709.

had done; and ordered him to reftore both the cloaths and
money to the ferjeant, and fent the ferjeant, under his own
pafs, to Maeftricht: A piece of generous humanity feldom
met with in an enemy. Being ftill ill of my wound, I
determined to remain at Hall, although it was an open
place, and vifited almoft every day by parties of the French :
here I was attended by an able furgeon, who having none
but myfelf under his care, had the more time to obferve
the various effects of his treatment of the wound, which
could not have been the cafe had I proceeded to Bruffels,
where every place was full of the wounded of our army.
While I continued here, I met with great kindnefs from the
clergy of the place ; but I ftaid no longer than I was able
to walk with crutches, when I obtained a French pafs, and
moved to Maeftricht, where I found a lieutenant's commiffion waiting for me.

Early in the month of April 1710, we left our winter-
quarters, and on the 15th, arrived near Tournay, the place
of our general rendezvous ; and on the 20th, the army
being formed, was ordered to march at five o'clock in the
afternoon, and marched all night in two columns. Our
motion was fo fudden, fo fecret, and fo regularly conducted, that we entered the French lines next morning,
without the fmalleft refiftance : fo little did they apprehend
this morning vifit, that they were out foraging. Our appearance fpread fuch an alarm amongft their troops near
Lens, that they made a very hafty retreat, and we encamped in their room upon the plains of Lens.

On the 22d, early in the morning, we laid our bridges
over the Scarp, and the whole army paffed the fame night,

1710.
Fourth cam-
paign.

E and

and next morning we invefted Doway; on the 25th, we began our lines of circumvallation, and were joined by the prince of Anhalt Deffau, who fucceeded count Lottum in the command of the Pruffian troops, and now commanded one of the attacks againft the town, and the prince of Naffau the other; on the 29th, our lines were finifhed, when our cavalry had provided a great number of fafcines and gabions for the fiege; on the 1ft of May, our troops took poffeffion of the caftle of Pignonville, and on the 3d, Chateaux-Loway, where 340 men furrendered themfelves prifoners; the 4th, our trenches were opened at both attacks, and our men were covered without any lofs, as they were not perceived at their work from the town; the 9th, at ten at night, the enemy made a vigorous fally at the prince of Naffau's attack, which put the workmen in great diforder, and levelled fome parts of the parallel, but they were at laft repulfed with confiderable lofs, and purfued to the very counterfcarp; the action was fo very hot that we loft 300 men killed, or wounded, in it, and, perhaps, the enemy were not better off: the parallel was repaired the fame night, and next morning, at day-break, a battery of eight guns, and four mortars, began to play with great fury, from prince Anhalt's attack, upon a fconce in the morafs, which had greatly annoyed us by flanking our approaches: it was now foon difmounted. They made a fally the fame night on our fide, but were repulfed with confiderable lofs. Our heavy artillery arrived on the 10th, and on the 11th, a battery was completed on each attack, each mounting twenty-four guns and eight mortars; the 12th, our approaches were advanced to the firft ditch; the 14th, our

6   batteries

batteries being completed, and mounted with forty-eight guns, and thirty-two mortars and howitzers, we began to play on the enemy's outworks, but chiefly from the prince of Anhalt's fide, as the ground in the other was fo boggy, that they could not approach there with fuch regularity. The enemy made a fally on the 17th, but were fo warmly received, that they retired in great confufion, leaving above 100 prifoners behind them; on the 21ft, they made another, in which a great many fell on both fides. Our army was now ftrongly entrenched in their lines to prevent the enemy from harraffing us in the fiege, as they outnumbered us by 10,000 men, and we had reafon, from their continual motions, from the 26th to the 30th, to believe that they meant to attack us, and oblige us to raife the fiege; but on the 30th, they encamped within gun-fhot of our entrenchments, which flackened our progrefs in the fiege, as every regiment that could poffibly be fpared was taken off to ftrengthen the army. The enemy continued four days in this pofition without offering to difturb us, when marfhal Villars thought proper to retire to a league diftant from us; upon which the befieging regiments returned to their pofts, and we now again pufhed on the fiege with all poffible vigour. The enemy made frequent fallies, and fprung feveral mines, which, however, did not prevent us from making ourfelves mafters of the counterfcarp on the 5th of June; and on the 17th, we ftormed and took a ravelin, and after filling the moat with fafcines, we laid our bridges to the main breach of the town: on the night of the 22d, the trenches were opened at Fort-Scarp, which was a regular pentagon; and on the

25th,

25th, at two o'clock in the afternoon, the enemy beat the
chamade, and furrendered both town and fort on the 26th.

The befieged had upwards of 3,000 men killed, and our
lofs was 8,000 killed and wounded. On the 29th, the marquis d' Albergotti marched out at the head of his garrifon,
confifting of 4,527 effective men : general Hompefh was
made governor of the town, and brigadier des Roques,
the chief engineer, was made commandant of Fort-
Scarp.

Siege of Be-
thune.
After a few days relaxation from fuch hard duty, we
marched with an intention to befiege Arras, which the
enemy perceiving, entered their new lines, and thereby prevented us ; and then the fiege of Bethune became the object, and was invefted on the 15th of July ; the trenches
were opened the 23d for two attacks, the one by general
Schuylenburg, the other by general Fagel. The French
army made a feint as if they meant to relieve the town,
but finding us ready prepared to receive them, they were
fatisfied with fhowing themfelves, and withdrew to their lines.
The fiege advanced brifkly ; on the 29th, they made a
fally at Fagel's attack, where they almoft deftroyed a regiment of Pruffian guards, who had unluckily fired upon
them all at once, and having no fire in referve, the enemy
poured in upon them with great deftruction : our regiment
marched quickly up to their affiftance, and faved them
from being entirely cut off. There happened, the fame
A fad mif-
fortune to
fix Scotch
officers.
day, a fad misfortune to fix officers of a Scotch regiment,
who were fitting in a row on the banquet, and had their
legs all fhot off by a cannon-ball, except one, who faved
one of his by having it on the banquet ; and he was the

3   only

only one who furvived the rough amputation, the reft died
of their wounds: this ill-fated ball came from one of our
own guns at Schuylenburg's attack, directed at a baftion,
but unhappily miffing that object, the ball flanked our own
trenches. The town threw a great number of bombs at
our batteries, but falling fhort, they dropped, for the moft
part, into our approaches, which kept us who were employed there in perpetual motion to fhun them. One day
I happened to ftep into a demolifhed cellar, on a neceffary
occafion, when I had fcarce well got there, till the centry
called out, " Gare la bombe," and down it came into the
cellar, and I made the beft of my way out of it, which I
had fcarce cleared till it burft, and threw down a great
quantity of ftones and rubbifh about me, but I efcaped un-
hurt. The garrifon beat the chamade on the 28th of Auguft, and on the 31ft, M. de Vauban marched out at the
head of 1,700 men remaining of the garrifon, having loft
near 2000. It coft us 3,665 men, killed and wounded:
major general Keppel was appointed governor.

The fieges of Aire and St. Venant came next in our route;
we marched on the 2d, and they were both invefted on the
5th of September. The prince of Anhalt commanded the
fiege of Aire, and the prince of Naffau that of St. Venant.
About this time the enemy intercepted a convoy of our's
coming up the river Lys in boats with warlike ftores and
provifions, which they took and deftroyed, killed and
wounded a great number of the efcort, and took 800 prifoners: this, however, did not retard the fieges a moment,
for St. Venant furrendered on the 30th, and Mr. Bruyn, the
engineer, was appointed governor; we loft 940 men, killed

and

and wounded at this fiege. The French governor was afterwards committed to the Baftile for his bad behaviour.

At Aire the trenches were opened the 12th of September
for two attacks; on the 21ft, the befieged made a fally, in
which they were repulfed with the lofs of 40 men; the
23d, we took a redoubt with little oppofition : at this time
marfhal Villars refigned the command of the French army
to marfhal Harcourt, who was fent by the king for that
purpofe. The 8th of October we took another redoubt,
fword in hand, and at night made ourfelves mafters of the
covert-way : after much labour and fatigue to us, the enemy
beat a parley on the 3d of November, and on the 12th,
general Goefbriant, the governor, marched out at the head
of 3,628 men, befides 1,500 wounded left in the town; our
lofs on this occafion was 7,000 men, killed and wounded;
count Naffau Woudenburg was appointed governor of this
town, and our whole army marched to the plains of Lifle,
where they feparated on the 15th of November, and went
into winter-quarters; and thus ended this campaign, and
the laft I ferved in this country.

Perhaps no age or country, not even excepting thofe
fields ftill famous for the celebrated victories of Julius Cæfar,
can parallel the rapid fuccefs of the combined arms in thefe
wars; they were continually conquering armies of fuperior
numbers of well-difciplined troops, abundantly fupplied with
every warlike weapon and engine of deftruction, and commanded by generals of renowned martial knowledge and
experience, and ftill beating them from plain to plain : neither could they find a refuge in their ftrong walled cities
and towns, well fortified with every additional ftrength of

out-

out-works; thefe fell by numbers in each campaign, and
the conquering heroes fhine illuftrious in every page of
martial ftory, grateful to the eye and ear of youthful ar-
dour, and pleafing to the wifh of military ambition. But
we fhall not find them deferving fuch admiration in the
lines of civil life, where humanity conftrains us to commiferate the childlefs parent and the helplefs orphan, the fe-
vered brother, and the widowed dame's bewailed lofs of many
dear connections; and friends lamenting friends, whofe lives
were facrificed to raife the ftructure of the hero's fame, built
on the havock of the defolating fword; unfheathed on this
occafion by the boundlefs ambition of that afpiring prince,
whom nothing could pleafe fhort of univerfal monarchy,
Lewis the Fourteenth, but was at length obliged to fit down
with Gallic fovereignty.

Tournay, of which the earl of Albemarle was now go- Terrible ftory
vernor, became our quarters for this winter. An affair of the Jefuits
happened here a little while before, in the Jefuits college, at Tournay.
which amazed the whole town. A fhoemaker, near the
college, having a handfome wife, one of the fanctified fathers made frequent vifits to befpeak fhoes and flippers for
himfelf and others of the fraternity; at length, giving an
order, he defired the fair dame, when they were done, to
bring them home to the cloifter, and receive the payment
for them, and fhe accordingly carried them; fhe was admitted into the houfe, but never returned, which much
alarmed the poor hufband and his neighbours, who were
naturally led to enquire after her at the college, when they
were told, that fhe had received the money and went away
again: as the veracity of thefe fathers was held facred, no
body

body durſt preſume any farther enquiry at the college, and the woman could not be found. Some few days after, a boy in the night-time getting into a garden, next to that of the Jeſuits, to ſteal fruit, ſaw from the top of a tree (being moonlight) theſe very holy fathers buſy in burying a corpſe in the garden. The boy, knowing that the woman could not be found, told his father what he had ſeen; the father, who lived in the neighbourhood of the ſhoemaker, immediately acquainted him of it, and they both, with the boy, went to the governor, who, upon their information, ſent for the magiſtrates, and they proceeded altogether to the Jeſuits college; upon going into the garden, the boy directed to the ſpot where he had ſeen the corpſe buried: upon digging there they found the body of the poor woman with her throat cut, and all her clothes torn in pieces. The fathers declared their ignorance and innocence of the whole matter, charging the foul deed upon two of their ſociety who had diſappeared. This was all the redreſs the poor man could get for the loſs of his wife, notwithſtanding the boy declared there were eight of them at burying the body. The ſhoemaker, his neighbour, and his ſon, thought it prudent to retire to Holland, where they turned Proteſtants, to avoid the mercileſs vengeance of theſe ſacred fathers. This ſtory was told me by ſeveral officers, who were at that time in garriſon here.

BOOK

B O O K II.

He goes into the Ruſſian ſervice, a captain.—Overtakes general Bruce at Pruſs-Holland.—A curious ſtory of a man at Elbing.—They arrive at Jaweroff, where the Czar is privately married.—General Bruce's rank and honours.—Account of the Ruſſian army.—Their numbers and cloathing.—Expedition againſt the Turks—Council of war at the Neiſter.—— Prince Cantamire joins them without any troops.—A ſwarm of locuſts.— The Turks appear —The Ruſſians form on the river Pruth.—Engage the Turks three days.—The czarina ſaves the whole army and prince Cantamire.—The king of Sweden upbraids the grand vizier.—The Ruſſians return.—Colonel Pitt's lady and daughter carried off by the Tartars— The grand ſeignior approves the treaty.—Captain Bruce ſent expreſs to Conſtantinople.—Deſcription of that city.—Its moſques.—Accommodations for ſtrangers.—Strength.—The ſeraglio.—Scutari, a fine View.— The port and harbour.—Suburbs.—Arſenal.—Air and climate.—The Turks contraſted.—Domeſtic Accommodations.—Internal government of the country.—Religion.—Worſhip.—The plague.—Their games.—Diet. —Reſt.—Exerciſe of their youth—Dreſs of their ladies.—Ointment of Pilo.—Their predominant intereſt.—Matrimonial privilege.—Concubine marriage.—Policy of their religion.—Severities on the amorous ſtranger. —Their laws for debt.—In criminal caſes.—Their puniſhments.—The channel of the captain's information.—New difficulties to the Treaty at the Pruth.—Change of miniſtry.—A freſh treaty.—Freſh interruption to the peace.—Againſt which the czar remonſtrates.—Miniſtry again changed.—The Ruſſian ambaſſador, &c. ſent to the Seven Towers.— Mighty preparations for war, which end againſt the king of Sweden at Bender.—Reflexions.

THIS winter I received an invitation from general Bruce *, of the ordnance, at Moſcow, to enter into the ſervice of the czar, if I ſhould wiſh, or think it ad-

BOOK II.

1710.
He goes into the Ruſſian ſervice captain.

* This general Bruce was grandſon to James, who left Scotland with my grandfather.

F

viſeable

vifeable to quit that of Pruffia ; and acquainted me that he was then at Elbing, in Pruffia; where he would be for fome time, fo that if I accepted his offer, I might reach him before he left that place. Pleafing as the idea was to my-felf, I could form no refolution in the matter before I had confulted my relations at Berlin, whofe friendfhip I had al-ready experienced, and it was by their unanimous confent and advice, that I determined to accept of his invitation, and having obtained leave to quit the Pruffian fervice, with the rank of captain, I prepared for my departure, and left Tournay on the 25th of March, 1711. I took the route of Oudenard, Ghent, and Safs, and came to Rotterdam the 30th ; from thence I proceeded by Delft and the Hague, and got to Amfterdam the 1ft of April, and took fhipping in a Dutch veffel for Koningfberg. We paffed the Texel on the 13th, and entering the Sound on the 2d of May, we anchored at Pillaw the 7th, after above a month's paffage : this is a harbour and fort belonging to the king of Pruffia. I directly waited on the governor, who told me, he had a letter from general Bruce, defiring him, when I came there, to forward me to Elbing ; but the governor, thinking the general would not fo foon leave that place, intreated me to ftay with him a day or two, to give him the particulars of the laft campaign. After dinner, an officer came in, who told the governor, that he was informed by a gentleman juft come from Elbing, that the general was to leave it that fame day : this fixed my immediate departure, and tak-ing a boat for the oppofite fhore, I got on horfeback, and arrived at Elbing in the evening, where I found the general had fat off in the afternoon, having received

an

an exprefs from the czar to join him with the utmoft
expedition.

Major-general Balck, the governor of Elbing, told me, general Bruce had defired him, on my arrival there, to forward me immediately after him; fo I took horfe directly, in a very dark night, and overtook him next morn- *Overtakes ge-* ing, the 9th of May, at Prufs-Holland, juft as he was *neral Bruce at Prufs-Hol-* preparing to proceed on his journey. He received me very *land.* kindly, and feeing me much fatigued, defired me now to travel in his own fleeping waggon, where, indeed, I flept all day long, having neither refted, nor tafted victuals, from my dining with the governor of Pillaw. This machine is in every refpect a chariot, only the bottom is extended fufficient to fuffer one to lie at full length on a bed; and I found afterwards every officer, in the Ruffian army, provides himfelf with one of them, which is very neceffary on their long marches through ill-accommodated countries. General Bruce had engaged feveral officers of our artillery into the Ruffian fervice, two of them for engineers.

On our journey, the general entertained me with a ftory which happened during his ftay at Elbing, where he faved an old man from being burnt: this old man had an only fon, who was a druggift in town, to whom he had given all he had in the world, upon condition that he fhould maintain his father while he lived: the fon had behaved pretty well to him, but his wife treated the old man in fuch a cruel manner, that he was obliged to leave the houfe and board himfelf, for which the fon, at the inftigation of his wife, refufed to pay, and the people with whom he

F 2 lived,

lived, threatened to throw him into prifon : this unduti-
ful treatment fo affected the old man that he turned quite
frantic, and in his madnefs wrote an obligation with his
own blood to furrender himfelf, foul and body, to the devil, if he, in exchange, would give him a certain fum of
money : this was the effay on the part of the old man toward the agreement, and to found the devil's fentiments
on the fubject, he carried this paper to the croffing of two
roads, apprehending that the moft likely place to meet him,
and there he made a hole and depofited the obligation :
returning feveral times to the fpot, to fee if the devil had
accepted his bill, and finding no money, he grew quite out
of humour with the devil, and exclaimed bitterly againft
him ; fome labourers at work hard by, obferving his repeated vifits to that fpot, went to it when he was gone, and
dug up the paper, which they carried to the magiftrates :
the old man was taken up, tried, and fentenced to be burnt.
The general being informed of the whole ftory, interefted
himfelf for the old man, and convinced both the magiftrates
and judges, that his prefent diftreffed fituation, and dread
of future want, had driven the poor old man delirious,
and that not he, but his unnatural fon, was the object of
punifhment : the experiment was eafy, and the truth would
foon difcover itfelf : the old man was fet at liberty, the fon
bound to pay his board quarterly, and the effect foon juftified the meafure by his father's return to his reafon and
judgment.

They come
to the czar at
Jaweroff,
where he is
privately
married.

On the 17th, we arrived at Warfaw, and at Jaweroff
on the 29th, where we found the czar and czarina, and there
they were privately married, at which ceremony the general

ral was prefent, and upon this occafion he was made mafter-
general of the ordnance, in the room of the prince of ——————
Melita, who died a prifoner in Sweden.   General Bruce
was at this time knight of four orders, viz. St. Andrew,
the White Eagle, the Black Eagle, and the Elephant ; and
here I received my commiffion as captain in the artillery,
and engineer.   I went from hence to Lemberg to get myfelf equipped with the uniforms of my new corps, and was
recommended to a merchant there of the name of Gordon,
who fhewed me a great deal of civility.   When I returned to Jaweroff the army broke up, and we went in his majefty's retinue to Soroka, upon the river Neifter, where we
joined the Ruffian army.   This place is fix hundred miles
fouth from Elbing.

The Ruffian army is commanded by a field marfhal, and
in his abfence by the general of the ordnance, who has under him a lieutenant general and major-general : the regiment of artillery confifts of 2,400 bombardiers, gunners,
miners, and matroffes ; befides every battalion of the army
is attended by one field-piece, a three-pounder.   The army
is reckoned by divifions, each confifting of nine regiments,
one of which is grenadiers ; each divifion is commanded
by a general, a lieutenant-general, a major-general, and
a brigadier.   A regiment confifts of two battalions, or eight
companies, and is commanded by a colonel, a lieutenant-
colonel, and two majors ; and a company confifts of 150
private, commanded by one captain, two lieutenants, one
enfign, two ferjeants, one fub-enfign ; and has befides, one
captain at arms, one quarter-mafter, one clerk, a furgeon-
barber, two drums, one timberman, five denzigs (or offi-

cers

cers fervants), and fourteen waggoners; making in all
183: each company has their own feparate colours, there
being four to every battalion.   The generals have no regiments, nor the field officers, companies; nor have the
captains, the paying, clothing, arming, and recruiting
of their companies: this is performed by a commiffary, or
paymafter ; the neceffary recruits are demanded from and
provided by the governors of the different provinces.   A
regiment takes its name from the town or province where
they were firft raifed, which name they always retain, excepting the regiments of grenadiers, which bear the name
of the commanding general of the divifion ; the companies
of a regiment are commonly diftinguifhed by numbers, from
the ift to the 8th ; they always charge in battle four men
deep, the two foremoft ranks kneeling.   The czar's own
divifion, at this time, confifted of four regiments, each of
which have a company of grenadiers, which no other regiment has ; the firft of thefe regiments was that called
Prebrafinfky, of four battalions ; the fecond that of Sa-
menoffky, of three battalions ; the third that of Inger-
manlandfky, three battalions ; and the fourth, that of
Aftrachanfky, of two battalions ; in all thirteen battalions,
including the four companies of grenadiers ; each company
of this divifion has a captain-lieutenant additional: there
were likewife in his majefty's divifion two other grenadier
companies, who were bombardiers, gunners, and miners.
Each battalion of the army has at leaft one officer that is
an engineer.

The forces of Ruffia, including garrifons, confift of
200,000 foot, and 100,000 cavalry; befides Coffack and
Kalmuck

Kalmuck Tartars, who can, upon occasion, bring 150,000 men into the field. All the army wear white cockades; the horse are clad in blue, faced with scarlet; the foot in green, faced with scarlet; and the artillery in scarlet, with blue facings.

The army, which we joined at Soroka, consisted of five divisions, of 6,000 men each, commanded by count Zeremetof, field-marshal; the first was the czar's own division, the second general Weyde's, the third prince Repnin's, the fourth general Hallard's, and the fifth general Rentzel's; in all 30,000 foot, attended by a very numerous train of artillery, and intended for an expedition against the Turks. We were to have been joined by 30,000 dragoons, who had been detached to destroy a magazine erected by the Turks upon the Neister, a little above Bender, which service they performed, and beat the Turks there, but were prevented from joining us, as we did not wait their return: besides these, there were 50,000 Kalmuck Tartars, and 20,000 Cossacks in full march to have joined us, and with these reinforcements we should have been 130,000 strong.

His majesty being now resolved to march upon that ex- Expedition pedition, without waiting the junction of the rest of his against the Turks. forces, issued a general order for all the women, who attended the army to be sent away: the czarina, however, insisted on attending his majesty in the expedition, which was granted, and the generals petitioned her to obtain the same liberty for their wives, that they might attend her majesty, which was also granted; and the rest of the officers wives, conceiving themselves equally entitled to the indulgence,

dulgence, all went, notwithstanding the order.   This cir-
cumstance, although it considerably augmented the train

of our baggage, proved in the end a very fortunate one.

Our present sudden march seems to have been occasioned
by the secret engagements of Brancoven, prince of Moldavia, who undertook not only to join us with his whole
forces, but to provide us plentifully with provisions and
forage, both which were soon out of his power ; for the
grand seignor coming at the knowledge of this intended
revolt, divested him of his principality, and gave it to
Cantamire, prince of Wallachia, with orders to him to seize
Brancoven, and send him to Constantinople ; and with
orders at the same time to throw a bridge over the Danube,
to facilitate the passage of the Turkish army to oppose us ;
but the Turk was disappointed as well as we ; for some
of their principal men using Cantamire extremely ill, he
protracted the building of the bridge instead of hastening
it ; and in the mean time dispatched an officer to the czar,
praying him to join him with all expedition with 30,000
men, which number he thought would be sufficient, with
his own troops, to prevent the Turks from passing the
Danube.   The czar having just been disappointed, if not
deceived, by Brancoven (for he afterwards made a merit of
it to the Turk), could place no confidence in the sincerity
of Cantamire, nor was it sufficiently understood, till it was
too late to prevent their passing that river.

Council of
war at the
Neister.

On the 14th of June, our army passed the Neister, when
his majesty called a council of war, which was held in general Bruce's tent, when prince Cantamire's letter was read ;
the czar then mentioned his intention to march forward,

4   without

without waiting the junction of the reft of the troops; all
the generals expreffed their approbation of the meafure,
except general Hallard, who faid nothing. The czar obferving his filence, ordered him to declare his mind, and
give him his opinion freely: the general replied, that as
the council were fo unaninous he never would have made
any objection, had not his majefty infifted on his declaring
his fentiments; he then frankly told the czar, he was
very much furprifed that the king of Sweden's misfortune
did not ferve as a fufficient warning; for that prince had
been mifled by the advice of the traytor Mazeppe: he could
not help thinking our prefent flate was a fimilar one; " The
" prince of Moldavia has already difappointed us, and for
" any fecurity we have, the prince of Wallachia may do the
" fame; for although he fhould mean well himfelf, yet he
" may want the power to ferve us; for it is to be feared his
" troops, who have long been ufed to the Turkifh govern-
" ment, will not enter into his fentiments."----And this
proved to be exactly the cafe.

The march, however, was refolved on, and we fat out
the fame night to avoid the intenfe heat of the day, and continued to march for three nights through a barren defart
heath, without a drop of water all the way, which was feverely felt both by man and beaft. On the 18th, we arrived
at the river Pruth, where we loft a number of our baggage-
horfes by their drinking too plentifully of the water; we
paffed the river on the 19th, near Jaffey, the capial and
refidence of the prince of Moldavia. At this place, prince
Cantamire joined us in perfon with very few attendants, both
the Walachian and Moldavian troops having left him for

G. fear

fear of the Turks.   We continued our march down the Pruth till the 21ſt, when we met a prodigious ſwarm of

locuſts, which, at their riſing, overſhadowed the whole army like a cloud; they had not only deſtroyed the graſs of the fields, but alſo the tender bark and leaves of the trees : here again we loſt a number of our carriage-cattle for want of forage; it was very remarkable that the locuſts never left our army, and we no ſooner pitched our tents than they came down and covered the whole camp; we tried by firing can-non and ſmall arms, and burning trains of powder on the ground to chaſe them away, but all in vain; they attend-

ed us on our march along the river till the 27th, when we diſcovered the Turkiſh army croſſing the Pruth.   Upon this, general Janus was detached with a body of troops, and twelve pieces of cannon, to diſpute their paſſage; but he was too late, for half their army had paſſed before he could get up to them, ſo that he found it prudent to retreat to the army.   It was very ſurpriſing, that we had not the leaſt intelligence of ſo numerous an army, which conſiſted of no leſs than 200,000 men, till they were within ſight of us.

Our army drew up in order of battle, at ſome diſtance from the river, in hopes to bring them to an engagement; but they kept out of the reach of our cannon, and extend-ing their numerous army, endeavoured to ſurround us, and cut us off from the river.   We remained under arms till night, and being convinced of their intention, we made a very diſorderly retreat to ſecure the river, our diviſions be-ing all ſeparated from each other in the dark, and as we were now greatly deficient in horſes, we burnt a number of

our

our baggage waggons, that they should not fall into the
enemy's hands; and it was surprising, that from the number of fires that were blazing in the night, the enemy did
not perceive our confusion, which afforded them a fine opportunity to have destroyed our whole army, and they
might easily have done it with a small part of theirs; but
happily for us they seemed to pay greater attention to
their own safety than our destruction, for they happened
to be very busy entrenching themselves, by which means
we escaped their notice. At day-break, our scattered troops
were again put in order, and our army formed into a hollow square, the river serving for the fourth side, which
enabled us to give our square a larger extent; and our
waggons were formed into an inclosure within, for the protection of the ladies.

On the other side of the river, and opposite to us, the
Crim Tartars were placed, where the king of Sweden had
pitched his tent to discover the motions of our army. The
Tartars annoyed us much in watering, but bringing a few
pieces of cannon to play upon them, they were soon obliged
to keep at a distance. Our army was surrounded by a che-
veaux de frize, which was the only protection we had.

The Turkish army surrounded us on all sides, with a de- Engage the
sign to starve us into a surrender, and this they certainly Turks three
would have done in a short time, had they not been too days.
eager in attacking us, which they did three days and three
nights together; but fortunately for us, they attacked only
one side of our square at a time, which enabled us to relieve our wearied troops, from time to time, as they became
harrassed with fatigue, and it also enabled us to use our

G 2   large

large train of artillery, which did great execution among them, and luckily they had none to annoy us with, as theirs was not yet arrived.

The czarina faves the whole army and prince Cantamire.

On the fourth day, the czar, being informed that our ammunition was all spent to three charges of cannon and small-arms, ordered all the officers in the army, with a number of select men, to mount on horseback and attend his person; his intention was to force his way through the Turkish army in the night, and to go through Tranfil-vania into Hungary: but the czarina coming to the know-ledge of this dangerous refolution, and forefeeing the ha-zard that would attend the czar, and the lofs and difgrace that would fall upon his arms and army, very luckily hit upon a better expedient, which faved us all from de-ftruction. She collected all the money, plate, and jewels which were in the army, for which fhe gave her own re-ceipt and obligation to pay the refpective owners, and with this valuable prefent fhe had the addrefs to prevail on the grand vizier to conclude a peace, and the tranfaction was immediately finifhed in the name of the field-marfhal, without the czar's knowledge who was juft going to fet out on his very dangerous expedition, which her majefty ftopped by telling him, that the grand vizier had agreed to conclude a peace on reasonable terms. This piece of confummate female difcretion was followed by a moft punc-tual difcharge of her obligations for the plate, &c. on her return home. The principal conditions of the peace, on our part, were to deliver up to the Turks, Azoph, Tai-ganrog, and Caminiek, and that our troops fhould evacuate Poland; for the performance of which, the vice-chancellor

Schafirof,

Schafirof, and major-general count Zeremetof, were delivered as hoftages. They infifted alfo, that prince Cantamire of Moldavia fhould be delivered up to them; but
were told, that the prince had left our camp; which, indeed, was believed by moft of ourfelves; for the treaty
was no fooner thought on, than the czarina fhut him up
in her own coach, which was known only to the fervant
who carried him his victuals. The czar ever afterwards
entertained a great regard for prince Cantamire, and gave
him feveral landed eftates both in Ruffia and the Ukraine,
befides fettling a penfion of 20,000 rubles a year upon
him.

The king of Sweden hearing of this peace, went with
the cham of Tartary who was at that time ftrongly interefted in his favour, to the grand vizier, to know why he
had concluded a peace fo haftily, when he had it in his power
to have made the czar and his whole army prifoners. The
vizier informed him, that as the fultan had vefted him with
full powers for war or peace, he could not refufe them peace,
feeing they defired it upon terms honourable to the grand
feignor, and by which he had gained more than could have
been expected. The king anfwered, that if he had carried
the czar a prifoner to Conftantinople, they could then have
obliged him to grant what terms they pleafed; and told the
vizier, if he would now give him 20,000 of his beft troops,
he would yet recover the opportunity that had been neglected, and was on the point of being loft for ever. The grand
vizier replied, " God preferve us from breaking a treaty of
" peace without any reafon, as I have already accepted the
" hoftages for the performance of it." Poniatoffky, a Polifh

general

BOOK II. general in Staniflaus's intereft, being prefent, and feeing the
king now filent, anfwered, " There is ftill a remedy
1711. " without breaking the treaty, which is to put the king at
" the head of 20 or 30,000 of your beft troops, whereby
" he may ftop the czar, and oblige him to a more honour-
" able peace before he proceeds any farther :" The vizier
then faid, " This feems to me at leaft an indirect vio-
" lation of the treaty, in which it is provided, that the king
" may return into his own dominions, through the czar's
" territories, with a ftrong convoy of Turks, after which,
" if he pleafes, he may make peace with the czar." The
king looked full at the grand vizier, and laughed in his
face, without making any anfwer ; but in retiring, he turned fo fhort on his heel, that he tore the vizier's robe with his
fpur, and mounting his horfe, he went off highly difpleafed :
he then concerted meafures with the cham to attack us
with his Tartars on our march, of which the vifier being
informed, reinforced us with 30,000 fpahis, the beft cavalry in the Turkifh fervice, to conduct us to the Neifter :
the vizier fent us alfo feveral waggon-loads of provifions as
a prefent to our army.

The Ruffians Matters being thus accommodated, we decamped on the
return under 2d of July, in good order, with drums beating and colours
the efcort of
a bafha. flying : our artillery and baggage marched between us and
the river, and our chevaux de frize were carried, each by
two men, between us and the Turks, to be in readinefs in
cafe the Tartars had perfevered in their plan to attack us :
Colonel Pitt's we marched this day in view of the Turkifh army.   At
lady and
daughter car- our fetting out, colonel Pitt had the misfortune to lofe both
ried off by his wife and daughter, beautiful women, by the breaking
the Tartars.
of

of one of their coach-wheels; by this accident, they were left fo far in the rear, that the Tartars feized and carried them off. The colonel addrefled himfelf to the grand vizier, who ordered a ftrict enquiry to be made, but to no pur-pofe. The colonel being afterwards informed that they were both carried to Conftantinople, and prefented to the grand feignor, obtained a pafs, and went there in fearch of them, and getting acquainted with a Jew doctor, who was phyfician to the feraglio, the doctor told him there had been two fuch ladies as he defcribed, lately prefented to the fultan; but that when any of the fex were once taken into the feraglio, they were never fuffered to come out again. The colonel, neverthelefs, tried every ex-pedient he could devife to recover his wife, if he could not get both, till becoming outrageous by repeated difappoint-ment, and very clamourous, they fhut him up in a dun-geon, and it was with much difficulty he got releafed by the interceffion of fome of the ambaffadors at the court; and was afterwards told by the Jew doctor, that they both died of the plague: with which information he was obliged to content himfelf and return home.

The grand feignor receiving the news of the peace, and the advantages he had thereby acquired, ordered public rejoicings for three days, and teftified his approbation of the vizier's conduct, not only in the reception he gave him, but by complimentary letters and magnificent prefents. For want of horfes our march was fo flow, that it was the 11th of July before we reached Stepanowa, when we croffed the Pruth, and on the 14th arrived at the Neifter, after a fhort, but very dangerous campaign. Next day we croffed this

The grand feignor approves the treaty.

river

river and reached the camp where we found our dragoons, Coffacks, and Tartars, who were now rejoiced at
our fafe return, having heard very difmal accounts of us.
The baffa, who efcorted us here, faid when he faw thefe
troops, that if they had joined us, we fhould have been an
over-match for the Turkifh army.   Our army now feparated and took different routes: the czar fet out for Germany, taking general Bruce with him, but not before he
had wrote frefh inftructions for baron Schafirof, and difpatched them by exprefs for Conftantinople, of which I was
the bearer; fo that I returned with the baffa who had conducted us to this place, and who had now only 2000 troops,
the reft having left us on the difappearing of the Tartars.
The fultan, upon the reprefentations of the king of Sweden,
had, in the mean time, twice broke this peace, and renewed it again with the fame eafe; this was apprehended,
and occafioned the inftructions I now carried.

Captain Bruce fent exprefs to Conftantinople.

On our way to Adrianople, I received many civilities
from the baffa, and we arrived there the 2d of Auguft,
where we found baron Schafirof and count Zeremetof;
and who foon after fat out with us for Conftantinople;
where we arrived the 25th, being met at fome diftance
from the city by count Tolftoi, our ambaffador, who had
been confined in the Seven Towers ever fince the declaration
of the war, but was now releafed.

A defcription of that city.

This city is fituated on a point, or tongue of land, that
jets out into the fea, it is of a triangular form, and fourteen miles in circumference; the houfes are generally built
of wood, and the ftreets fo narrow, that in moft of them,
two loaded horfes cannot go a-breaft; and the houfes project

fo

fo much at the upper parts, that in many places one may with eafe ftep out of the window of one houfe into the window of another on the oppofite fide of the ftreet: this capital error in building the city does not feem to have proceeded from want of room, for it abounds in gardens and large fquares and courts; and it is owing to this circumftance that a fire is always attended with fuch devaftation, for it burns with irrefiftible fury till fome garden or fquare puts a ftop to its progrefs. The moft regular part of this city is the Befeftin, inclofed with walls and gates, where the merchants have their fhops, which are ranged and difpofed in fuch excellent order, that a buyer may difpatch his bufinefs in a quarter of an hour; every trade has its own feparate department in the place; the gates are fhut every night at ten o'clock. In another part of the city is the Hippodrome, an oblong fquare of four hundred paces by two hundred, where they exercife on horfeback: towards the end, oppofite to the feraglio, are two obelifks; the firft confifts of one ftone feventy feet high, and ftands on a fquare pedeftal of marble, adorned with feveral hieroglyphical figures in relievo; the other is a fpiral pyramid built of free ftone, without any ornament or infcription; near thefe ftands the ferpentine column, a brazen pillar of confiderable height; it is compofed of three ferpents wreathed and twifted together, with their tails on the ground, and ending at top with three gaping heads and forked tongues, expreffive of hiffing. At fome diftance from this are two other columns, in a large court appointed for the exercife of the bow and arrow, where the archers very frequently hit a mark not bigger than a fhilling, at the diftance of

H   an

an hundred paces. The Meidan, or parade, is a very large
spacious square, and is the place of general refort of all
ranks.

Among the principal mofques, or churches, in this city, the
firft is that of St. Sophia, formerly a Chriftian church; it is
an hundred and twenty paces long and eighty broad; on each
fide is a portico, fupported by thirty columns, each fixteen feet
high, ornamented with very fine cornices; it is covered with
a dome, or round roof, enriched with grand Mofaic work,
and finely gilded; the pavement is of marble, and covered
over with matting. The tomb of Conftantine the Great is
ftill preferved, and which the Turks hold in great veneration, although they fuffer neither image or picture in their
mofques; this being the only ancient building which now
remains here of that kind; for all the reft were built by the
fultans, or fultaneffes, whofe names they bear: they are
built after the fame model, differing only in fize, with a number of fountains, and variety of painting, fo that a defcription of one will convey a juft idea of all the reft. The next
is the mofque of the fultanefs Valide, ftanding in the middle of
a large fquare court, and is environed with arched canopies,
in the form of porticos, under which are many fountains,
with cocks for the people to wafh themfelves at before they
enter the mofque; it has but one gate, which is furrounded
with a portico of confiderable height, paved with white
and black marble, and fupported by fixty-four columns of
red marble, eight of which are porphyry, and placed near
the entry; the plafond is adorned with painting and figures
after the Turkifh manner; the portico is covered with little domes, furrounding a large one in the middle, and all
covered

covered with lead ; at the four corners of the building are
four very high turrets, ending in a globe, or crefcent, from
which their priefts call the people to prayers, having no bells
for that purpofe.

The city is rendered very commodious with houfes, called
Hans, or caravanferais, for the entertainment and accommodation of foreign merchants ; the Hans confift of four
fides of building, inclofing a large fquare court, with a fountain in the middle ; the walls are very ftrong, and the windows well fecured with bars for the fafety of the property
lodged there, the roofs confift of little domes, covered with
lead, like thofe of the mofques : the Hans contain only two
ftories, divided into rooms which have not the leaft communication with each other ; the lower ftory is divided into
warehoufes for goods, and the upper ftory into lodging-
apartments for the merchants, who muft provide every
thing for their accommodation, for they find nothing when
they come in but the bare walls. The caravanferais are a
poorer fort of inns, and built in the fame manner as the
Hans, which ferve the poorer fort of ftrangers, and fervants
of the caravans, and have ftabling for their camels. Befides thefe, there are no other public houfes of entertainment.

The city is furrounded by a high and thick wall, with
battlements, after the oriental manner, and towers at fome
diftance from each other, defended by a lined but fhallow
ditch, and on the land-fide thefe works are double ; thofe,
with the Seven Towers, are all the ftrength of Conftantinople. The feraglio is built on the point of the land jet-
ting into the fea ; it occupies a fpace of four miles in cir-

cumference, the greateſt part of which is laid out in gardens ; the whole ſtructure is irregular, for it is indeed only
a medley of confuſed building, ornamented with a number
of thoſe little gilded ſpires and globes without beauty or order ; the principal entry is near St. Sophia, and reſembles
the gate of an old paltry town, without architecture or ornament ; through this gate we entered into a large court,
where, on the right, are the apartments for the ſick, and
on the left are magazines of arms for a thouſand men ; from
this court we paſſed into another, bordered with two large
porticos ; on our right hand are the kitchens, and ſtables
for an hundred horſe on the left; but we were permitted
to go no farther. The ſeraglio, with its gardens, &c. is,
ſurrounded with a very high wall of grey ſtone, with a
parapet at the top, and battlements like thoſe of the city,
and which incloſes the old and new ſeraglios : in the old
one, the reigning ſultan ſhuts up the wives of his predeceſ-
for, who, at their entrance, look back on the pleaſures of
this life as gone for ever; the new ſeraglio is contiguous
to his own palace. The great officers of ſtate are but meanly
lodged, moſt of their houſes are incloſed in a kind of park,
containing a garden, and a large court, having ſtables on
one ſide, and kitchens on the other. The many gilded
globes and ſpires, reſembling ſteeples, which appear in all
parts of the city, contribute very much to its grand appearance, eſpecially at a diſtance.

Scutari, a
fine view.

Oppoſite to the ſeraglio, on the ſide of Aſia, and diſtant
about a mile and a half, acroſs the water, lies Scutari : it
is a large town, adorned with a royal moſque and a palace,
or pleaſure-houſe, of the grand ſeignior's. The brow of a

hill,

hill, near Scutari, prefents one of the grandeft and moft
beautiful profpects, perhaps, the world affords : here you
have before you, in one view, the cities of Conftantinople,
Galata, and Pera, the fmall feas of the Bofphorus and Pro-
pontis, with the adjacent countries on the fhores of each.

 The port and harbour have their peculiar beauties ; the The port and
harbour is three miles long, and one broad, clean and deep harbour.
throughout, and fo fteep to the fhore, that the largeft veffels come fo clofe you may ftep on board or a fhore without a boat; at the entrance of the port ftands Leander's
tower, a high fquare building; there is a fountain on the
rock, and fome pieces of cannon, which might defend the
city on that fide in cafe of neceffity. On the oppofite fide Suburbs.
of the port are four confiderable towns, but which are rather confidered as a part of the fuburbs of the city, as their
diftance from it, over the port, is fo fmall, that a perfon
may eafily be heard on the other fide ; they are named Pacha,
Galata, Pera, and Tophana, and are eight miles in circumference. Pera is the place where the foreign ambaffadors,
and all the Franks refide, for they are not permitted to live
in the city; Galata is, properly fpeaking, a city of itfelf,
handfomely built, being furrounded by walls, and has large
fuburbs, is exceedingly populous, and moftly inhabited by
Franks and Jews, and is a place of great trade. Franks is
the general denomination of all ftrangers that are Chriftians.
At the end of the port ftands the grand arfenal, which co- Arfenal.
vers a confiderable fpace of ground, and contains arms for
60,000 men, where alfo the gallies are laid up in an hundred and twenty arches.

            The

1711.
Air and cli-
mate.

The air is extremely pure, and so wholesome, that the inhabitants are never subject to any epidemical disease but the plague, which visits them every year, and then makes a dreadful havock amongst them. It is imagined they would live till they dropt into the grave through mere old age, if their days were not cut off by this pestilential malady; they are so little acquainted with any other mortal distemper, that when they are told the plague is hardly known in Britain, they naturally ask, " What then do the " people die of ?" The climate, being in 41 deg. 30 min. north, is so temperate, that the winters are never cold, and the summer's heat is greatly allayed by the cooling breezes from the seas.

The Turks
contrasted.

The Turks seem to contrast us in almost their whole manner: with us it has always been deemed honourable to be espoused to one woman, they marry several wives; we reckon our cloaths the most commodious for being short, they wear theirs down to their heels; we esteem long hair and a smooth face ornaments to the countenance, they shave their heads and let their beards grow; we write in a strait line from left to right, they in a crooked one from right to left: they crouch down to make water like the women.

Domestic ac-
commoda-
tions.

They have no houshold furniture, such as beds, tables, chairs, looking-glasses, or pictures; the bare walls, with a plafond, or ceiling, and a sopha, are all the riches or ornaments in their rooms; the rich, indeed, paint their ceilings and walls in the Moresco taste, and their sophas are two feet high, and reach from the one end of the room to the other, under the windows, and are ten feet broad,

covered

covered with Turkey or Perfian tapeftry ; befides thefe,
there are matts laid along the other fides of the room, five
or fix feet broad, covered with cloth or velvet, and over
thefe are laid large cufhions, ftuffed with hair or wool ;
thefe cufhions, in the houfes of the grandees, are curioufly
embroidered, or covered with a rich cloth of gold. Loiter-
ing in floth and idlenefs, crofs-legged like fo many taylors,
the Turk waftes almoft his whole time, lolling on thefe
cufhions, or fophas, fmoking tobacco, and drinking coffee or fherbet, without either diverfion or amufement, but
playing with fhells, or at trick-track, or the goofe.

  Their provinces, cities, and towns, are governed by Internal go-
baffas, fub-baffas, waiwodes, cadis, (or judges), and col- the country.
lectors. The baffa is invefted with the fupreme executive
authority, and is accountable for the revenues of his government to the grand fignior ; but to fecure a free tole-
ration to be as arbitrary a tyrant in his province as his mafter is in his empire, he farms his oppreffions at an annual
tribute to the fultan, of money and flaves, exclufive of the
ordinary duties, cuftoms, and impofts of the province : the
fultan thus gratified, and a wide door opened to the rapa-
cious avarice of the imperious baffa, he exercifes all manner of cruel oppreffions, when there is any thing to be got
by it, in his whole dominions, without regard to quality or
condition, widow or orphan, it is all the fame. The in-
creafing treafure of fome of thefe baffas enables them to
maintain a ftanding army of their own, whereby they become formidable to the grand feignior himfelf, who then is
obliged to wink at their crimes rather than run the hazard
of punifhing them ; for the baffa can rely on his forces

while

while he is able to pay them; so that between the despotic
tyrant and his grim lieutenant, it is no very desirable privilege
to be a Turkish subject. The waiwode is a city magistrate:
the collector is a receiver of the customs, and has great authority to take cognizance of all fraudulent practices in the
pecuniary revenues, and in all his decisions he is both judge
and jury; and his sentence is always regulated by the profit
it yields. The cadi is a judge of the law.

Religion.   The Turkish religion acknowleges four prophets;
Enoch, Moses, Jesus Christ, and Mahomet; they believe
that Judas, who intended to betray his master to the Jews,
was by them crucified in his stead, and that Christ was
translated into heaven; they upbraid the Christians with
folly and impiety, for believing that he, whom they adore
as God, was put to such a shameful death, and the very
sight of a crucifix fills them with anger and rage. They
believe that Christ will come to judge the world, but that
he will first reign a thousand years upon the earth, and
marry, and beget children; but they will not acknowlege
a Trinity of persons in the Godhead, alledging, that such
an opinion would absolutely destroy the unity of that sovereign Being, without which he could not be God. They
say that Christ was succeeded by Mahomet, after whom
there shall come no other prophet. They believe that there
is an infinite number of angels, some good, others bad;
some white, others black: they imagine, that every man
has two angels who constantly attend him, the one writes
down all his good, the other all his bad actions. They
are of opinion, that the souls of the wicked enter not into
hell till the day of judgment, but remain with their bodies

in the grave, where they are tormented by the black angels till the laſt day, when they will be ſent to hell, and ſuffer moſt cruel puniſhments for a certain period, according to the enormity of the crimes they have committed in this life, at the expiration of which they will be releaſed and admitted into paradiſe, where they will enjoy the ſame happineſs that is appointed for good men; for, ſay they, it is inconſiſtent with Divine goodneſs to puniſh a being eternally for the offences of ſo ſhort a life. They pray five Worſhip. times a day; at day-break, noon, three o'clock, ſix o'clock, and an hour after the cloſe of the evening: on Friday, being their ſabbath, they aſſemble for public worſhip, when the Iman, or prieſt, ſays prayers, and delivers a kind of ſermon, or exhortation, to his hearers, but none of their women are ſuffered to appear at their public devotions. They keep Lent, which laſts thirty days, and they are obliged to faſt every day from morning till night during all that time, being permitted neither to eat, drink, or ſmoak tobacco: lent ends with the moon, and every body is ſo impatient to ſee the new deliverer that is to releaſe them from their loathed abſtinence, that they run to the tops of houſes, and even of mountains to ſee its riſe; and as ſoon as it peeps in the horizon, they ſalute it with ſeveral reverential bows; their caſtles alſo proclaim the welcome news by repeated diſcharges of their great guns: the three ſucceeding days are ſpent in mirth and jollity. They are allowed at no time to eat hog's fleſh, or drink wine. They are ſo entirely abſorbed in their faith of predeſtination, that they uſe no precautions in the time of the plague; and are offended at the Chriſtians for taking care of their health on

I   ſuch

such occasions, by shunning the houses where the infec-
tion is, asserting they ought not to forsake dying or dead
men.

The plague, which sweeps away such vast numbers of the inhabitants, seems in some degree necef-
sary to the preservation of the country, as they are increased
one fifth part of their number yearly; which is easily accounted for, when it is considered that every man is allowed to marry four wives and keep several concubines;
and there are besides, fifty thousand slaves brought into
Turkey every year; so that the country would soon be
overstocked with inhabitants, and the people in danger of
starving, if their numbers were not curtailed by this malady: yet, notwithstanding the terrible havoc made by the
pestilence, the land is still full of people.

Genius.   Their manners and customs, as I observed before, are
opposite to ours in almost every respect: they are so far
from studying to improve their understanding, that they in
a manner glory in their ignorance; and their ambition is so
small that they never attempt any thing that has not some
sordid interested view for its object; living for the most part
a recluse and lazy life, scarce ever looking beyond the sphere
of their own families; and provided their wives are handsome, their horses well curried, and their servants submif-
sive and respectful, they have not the smallest curiosity about
the affairs of the rest of the world. Contented with their
lot they sit whole days on a sopha, without any other occupation than drinking coffee, smoaking, or caressing their
wives; so their whole life is a continual revolution of eating, drinking, and sleeping, intermixt with some dull re-
creations.

creations. Yet they cannot be accufed of luxury in cat-
ing, for a fowl boiled with rice, coriander-feed, and fugar, ———————
is the beft difh that is ferved up, (which they call pilaw) ;
that, with a difh of fifh, &c. and a defart of fweetmeats,
makes their meal. When the hour of dinner comes,
a fervant brings an octangular table of walnut-tree, inlaid
with ivory, not above a foot and a half diameter, which
he places on the fopha, and having laid the cloth, ferves
up the difhes one after another; another fervant fpreads
a napkin on his mafter's knees, and ftands behind him to
carve and help him to what he choofes, for it is beneath
the grandeur of a Turk to do any thing for himfelf. They
never drink at meals, though they are in no hurry in difpatching them, but as foon as the table is removed, a fervant brings a cup of fherbet, and then the coffee and tobacco, with which his mafter beguiles the reft of the day :
their veffels are all earthen or porcelain. At night, a
mat, fheets, and coverlet, are brought, and they fleep in Reft;
the fame place where they ate, drank, fmoaked, played,
and loitered all the day. This is their conftant courfe
of life, after they ceafe to be youths ; for from the age Exercife of
of fifteen to twenty they learn the ufe of arms, the art of their youth.
riding, the bow, throwing the dart, and other exercifes of
that nature ; and, indeed, they are excellent horfemen,
notwithftanding their high faddles and fhort ftirrups, for
they rule their horfes with great dexterity without whip
or fpur, inftead of which they ufe a batoon, three feet
long, holding it by the middle, and ftriking with the
ends as they find it neceffary to direct the horfe's motion. Their horfes are very fwift, and ftretch them-

felves fo far, in running, that their bellies feem to touch
the ground.   The Turks throw the dart fo admirably
well on horfeback, that they hit the mark at full
fpeed, very feldom miffing their aim; and what is more
furprifing, they will throw their batoon as far before them
as they can, and following at full fpeed, catch it on the
ground as the horfe paffes, without giving him the leaft
check.

Drefs.

The men's drefs confifts in long and wide breeches,
reaching to their ancles, with leathern ftockings faftened to
the lower part of them, and is called a chackfir, and fhort
boots of red leather: a fhirt of very fine cotton cloth, made
exactly like a woman's fmock, only wider, efpecially at the
fleeves, which are open: over this they wear a cafetan, which
is a kind of long caffock, with narrow fleeves buttoned at the
' wrift; the fummer cafetan is made of white cotton cloth,
and in winter of filk ftuff quilted with cotton, and are girt
about the waift with a filken fcarf, in which they faften their
poniard, the handle of which is made of filver or ivory, enriched with jewels: they never appear with a fabre but
when they go into the country.   The upper garment is a
cloth gown, which they call a veft; in fummer it is lined
with taffety, and in winter with coftly furs, thefe with the
turban complete the drefs of the man.

Drefs of the
ladies.

The habit of the women is not much different, and
that chiefly confifts in being a great deal richer. They wear
a cafetan of gold brocade, faftened before with large pearls,
or a fmall knot of diamonds; it covers their fhoulders entirely, but is cut fo low before at the top, that their breaft
would remain naked if it was not covered with their fmock,

and

and a little waiftcoat they wear over it ; this waiftcoat fits
very clofe to the body and keeps up the breafts : above
the cafetan, they wear a leathern girdle, covered with
plates and ftuds of gold and filver, fet with precious ftones
of beautiful luftre. Their fmock is always of the fineft
flowered filk, and hangs over their chackfir, which, in
fummer is made of the fame filk as moft agreeable in the ex-
ceflive heat. Their upper veft is either of fine cloth or velvet, embroidered, or of rich cloth of gold. Their head drefs
is very elegant and becoming ; the talpo is a large high
velvet cap, fomewhat refembling a clofe crown, is made to
fit neat round the head, and widens upwards ; it is adorned with the richeft embroidery of gold, filver, and pearls,
and is fo high, that it would fall back on the fhoulders,
were it not artificially fupported above the head, where they
plait and fold it with much art : it is alfo enriched with
long ftrings of pearls curioufly interwoven and ftrewed with
diamonds, rubies, and all forts of jewels ; it is faftened to
the head, with a frontlet two fingers broad, and fo rich that
it may compare with a diadem ; round the frontlet are little
gold chains, with a diamond hanging at the end of one,
an emerald at another, &c. which dangle upon the forehead and on both fides of the face. Their hair is braided in
a long trefs, four fingers broad, hanging down an incredible length, on fome even to the heel ; they wear a little
curl on each fide of the forehead, which hangs in a ringlet
down the fide of the face, and thefe curls ingrofs much of
their attention ; they dye them black, as they do alfo their
eye-brows, which are extremely regular, for they fhape them
with a razor ; the women, in general, paint, and are,
not-

notwithſtanding, moſt charming creatures. They ſeem to be made for love, their actions, geſtures, diſcourſe, and looks, are all amorous, and admirably fitted to kindle that ſoft paſſion : ſince they have nothing elſe to do they make it their only buſineſs to pleaſe. Beſides their elegance and beauty, their extreme neatneſs is none of their leaſt conſiderable charms ; they bathe twice a week to keep themſelves clean ; and then, by a peculiar art, they crack all

Ointment of pilaw.

the joints in every limb ; and to deſtroy all excreſcent hairs they anoint the ſkin with pilaw, which makes the hairs fall off, and gives an additional whiteneſs and ſoftneſs to the ſkin.

Their predominant intereſt in marriages, &c.

The Turks, who are commonly governed by their intereſt in their marriages, are obliged to court by proxy, and to be ſatisfied with a character inſtead of an interview, which he is only indulged with for the firſt time when they

Matrimonial privileges.

marry ; but there are ſo many other conveniences allowed them, that they have not the leaſt reaſon to complain, for they are permitted to marry four lawful wives ; and thoſe who deſire a greater variety may marry twenty concubines if they pleaſe, for this alſo is a ſort of marriage, not to mention the pretty ſlaves whom they buy and ſell. Thoſe who are weary of their wives may turn them away when they pleaſe, paying their dowry. It is a pity we have not ſuch a faſhion, for if we had, we ſhould ſee many a fatal knot untied.

Concubine marriages.

The concubine-marriage is ſtill more commodious than the other ; the man takes the woman he fancies before the cadi, and tells him that he is willing to keep her after ſuch a rate, and when he has no farther

occa-

occafion for her, he will give her fuch a certain fum of money.

This is the ufual refuge of ftrangers, for if they are caught in making free with their females, they run a rifque of coming under the talons of the fub-baffa for a heavy fine, which if they cannot pay, they are pretty fure of meeting with the baftinado: and as for the poor kind finner, fhe is immediately mounted on an afs, with her face toward the tail which fhe holds in her hand, and in that pofition fhe is carried through the town, and then fold for a flave; this feverity makes moft ftrangers conform to the cuftom of concubinage, or purchafing a flave, to keep clear of the baffa; though the women are far from being cruel, yet by the feverity of the baffa, and the fufpicious vigilance of the cautious hufband, it is almoft impoffible for a gallant to thrive in this place.

The Turks have no written laws but what are con- tained in the Koran; all civil affairs are judged by the cadi, according to evidence upon oath, without any regard to writings; and the higheft bidder is fure of the decifion in his favour; but he that lofes, if it be for debt, muft pay it immediately or go to prifon; and if it fo happens that his effects are infufficient to fatisfy the demand, the poor debtor muft receive a baftinadoe on the fole of his foot for every piafter of fuch deficiency, unlefs the fum exceeds five hundred; for they do not punifh with a greater number of baftinadoes as the ftouteft man would not be able to endure it without the manifeft danger of lofing his life; and after this his creditor may take or fell him for a flave.

5

Judg-

Judgment, in criminal matters, belongs to the baſſa, who proceeds in the fame manner; for money atones for the moſt barbarous crime, and without it juſtice degenerates into cruelty; ſo that the ſtake and the gibbet is only the portion of the poor villain : nor can there be a ſtronger proof of a man's poverty, than his being executed for robbery or murder.   There is, indeed, a proviſion ſeemingly favourable to murderers, for if the perpetrator is lucky enough to get out of the way before he is diſcovered, the baſſa and waiwode can charge the blood on the people before whoſe door the murder was committed, if it happens in a town or village, and levy upon them forty thouſand aſpers, (the ſtated price), ſo that there is ſeldom much diligence uſed to apprehend the criminal himſelf; nor are theſe tribunals leſs favourable to the robbers who infeſt the country.

The moſt uſual puniſhments in Turkey for capital offences are beheading, drowning, hanging, ſtrangling, burning, impaling, and the ſtrappadoe; the two laſt are the moſt cruel, and are appointed only for Turks who renounce the Mahometan faith, or renegadoes who return to the Chriſtian religion : robbers and murderers are hanged; women are drowned; perſons convicted of rebellion or ſedition are beheaded; and burning falls to the lot of Chriſtians and Jews who blaſpheme againſt Mahomet or the Koran, or lie with a Turkiſh woman.

The channel
of the cap-
tain's infor-
mation.

The baſſa, under whoſe eſcort I came from the river Neiſter to Conſtantinople, ſhewed me much civility on the way, and treated me with great kindneſs after our arrival : it was owing to my acquaintance with him that I obtained

moſt

moft of thefe accounts of their government, laws, cuftoms, and manner of living. At our firft arrival we lived very com- fortably here, but that was foon interrupted by the reftlefs intrigues of the king of Sweden, the cham of Tartary, and the French ambaffador. By an article of the treaty at the river Pruth, the grand vizier engaged, that the Swedifh king fhould leave the Turkifh dominions; but the king appearing in no forwardnefs to depart, we ftill held Azof beyond the time ftipulated for our furrendering it, and this produced a fecond declaration of war, which was the more readily entered into, as the vizier, who had negotiated with us had been difmiffed, and was fucceeded by another, en- tirely in the Swedifh intereft; but the fultan being informed, that this minifter had been won over to that intereft by largeffes, difmiffed him; and, by the mediation of fir Robert Sutton and count Colyar, the Britifh and Dutch minifters at this court, a peace was again concluded on the 16th of April, 1712, and the grand feignor acquainted the king of Sweden with it by letter, defiring him to think of returning into his own dominions.

This peace was of no long continuance, for the Swedes foon interrupted it in Poland, where the ftaroft Gruzinfki, who had been in Turky with the king of Sweden, made an irruption with a body of 4,000 Wallachians, Coffacks, &c. and penetrated into Great Poland, where he furprifed and carried off a whole regiment of Ruffians, who were free from all fufpicion of an enemy: another party got beyond Pofnania, where they took a magazine and 300 Ruffians. General Baur, coming at the knowlege of what had happened, pofted to Pofnania, and haftily collected a body of

K   4,000

4,000 Ruſſians, with whom he ſurpriſed and attacked Gru-zinſki, who ſo little expected it, and was ſo much off his guard, that he did not diſpute the matter a moment, but left his camp as it ſtood. General Baur purſued him ſo cloſe, night and day, that he came up with him at Kruterſchien, where Gruzinſki, not chooſing to riſque an engagement, and taking his officers with him, abandoned his troops, and re-turned into Sileſia ; the whole body of the troops ſurren-dered priſoners of war.

Againſt which the czar remon-ſtrates.

The czar now remonſtrated againſt this violation of the treaty by the Turks ; and the king of Sweden, although he was the aggreſſor, exclaimed loudly againſt the Ruſſians, who had purſued ſome of the Coſſacks into the grand ſeig-nor's territories : and the ſultan ſuffering himſelf to be im-poſed on by the cham of Tartary, the French ambaſſador (M. Deſaleurs) and the Swediſh miniſtry, once more broke the peace, on pretence that there were ſtill ſome Ruſſian troops remaining in Poland. The ſultan, however, to ſa-tisfy himſelf, diſpatched an aga into Poland, to know if any of our troops were in that kingdom ; and this aga having alſo taſted the ſweets of Swediſh influence, made his report accordingly ; while the grand vizier, falling under the im-

Miniſtry a-gain chang-ed, and the Ruſſian am-baſſador, &c. ſent to the Seven Tow-ers.

putation of being influenced by the czar, got himſelf diſ-miſſed, and Solyman Baſſa was made vizier ; the reſult of all which was another declaration of war, and an order for the Ruſſian ambaſſador, hoſtages, and all the officers in their retinue, to take up their abode in the Seven Towers.

Mighty pre-parations for war.

This ſudden declaration of war was accompanied with orders to all the baſſas to raiſe troops ; and the ſultan, with

his

his whole court, removed to Adrianople. King Auguftus,
and the republic of Poland, had prepared a folemn embaffy
to the fultan, which was now on its way, at the head
of which was the palatine of Maffovia, with a fplendid
retinue of three hundred perfons; but the fultan, who
acknowledged Staniflaus as king of Poland, prevented
the arrival of this embaffy, by feizing them on the road
and imprifoning them. King Auguftus, however, had
addrefs enough to bring the cham of Tartary over to
his intereft; and Ali Coumourgi, the grand feignior's
reigning favourite, coming into meafures with the czar,
found means to perfuade his mafter that the aga, who had
been fent into Poland, had made a falfe report refpecting
the Ruffian troops there. Solyman the vizier, and the mufti,
being minions of the favourite, although they had both
advifed the war, now finding it no longer agreeable to him,
came as eafily into his defigns; and, notwithftanding all thefe
mighty preparations, they foon prevailed on their inconfift-
ent mafter to liften to propofals for an accommodation,
which was now again fet on foot. The negotiation was
foon fettled, as the chancellor Schaferof and count Zeremetof had full powers, and engaged for the czar that his
troops fhould, bona fide, evacuate Poland; and the grand
feignior engaged to oblige the king of Sweden to depart
the Turkifh dominions. Upon matters being brought
thus far towards a conclufion, I was difpatched for Peterfburg, where I arrived the 13th of October; but before I
got there, our troops had evacuated Poland. This peace,
for twenty-five years, was afterwards ratified by the czar;
and on the king of Sweden's refufing to comply with the

K 2   grand

grand feignior's requifition to depart the Turkifh dominions,'
the cham and baffa had orders to force him to it ; and that
brought on the famous action of Bender, the particulars
of which are fo univerfally known, that I think it needlefs to repeat them.

BOOK III.

Marriage of the czarowitz.—The czar's celebration of his old wedding.—General Bahr's discovery of himself to his friends and brother officers.—The empress Catherine's descent and rise.—Prince Menzikof's rise; and the czar's narrow escape from poison.—Expedition against the Swedes.—Description of the city of Moscow.—An ambassador from Persia; a great fire in Moscow. A young physician burnt by the clergy, who are therefore deprived of the power of life and death, and holidays and convents abridged.—Manners of the gentry.—Description of the women.—Entertainments of the common people.—Marriage.—The princess Natalia's humorous fancy in the marriage of the dwarfs.—Three women punished for drowning their husbands.—The punishment of the knout.—The czar's birth and marriage.—A virtuous young lady.—Muscovite robberies and murders.—The czar's danger by them.—Remarkable murder of Swedish officers by Jews.—Suppression of the robbers.—Seat of empire changed from Moscow to Petersburg.—A description of the czarowitz's person and manners.—Russian restrictions of consanguinity in marriage.—Ridiculous custom in burying.—Their images.—Their baths.—Manner of travelling.—Religious fasts.

THE czar had been in Germany to concert measures with his allies, and then went to Carlsbad, to drink the waters for his health, from which he found benefit; and from thence he returned, by the way of Dresden, to Targau, where he met with his son, the czarowitz, on the point of his marriage with the princess of Wolfenbuttel, sister to the empress of Charles the Sixth: the czarowitz was in the twenty-second year of his age, and the princess in her eighteenth. Here the queen of Poland made great preparations for celebrating the nuptials, and the ceremony was performed by a priest of the Greek church, with no great.

great pomp, on the 25th of October 1711, the day after
the czar's arrival; the czarowitz was led to the altar by the
czar, and the princefs by duke Anthony of Wolfenbuttel,
her grandfather; the queen of Poland, and her court, the
duke of Wolfenbuttel, father to the bride, and the duchefs,
her mother, were prefent. There was a magnificent entertainment at the queen of Poland's; and if the czar would
have fuffered the old duke to put himfelf to that expence,
he intended the fplendor of his grand-daughter's nuptials to
have been beyond example; but inftead of fplendor in the
introduction, it were to be wifhed there could have been
greater happinefs in the fequel of this matrimonial engagement, which here indeed could fcarce well be expected,
as inclination, on his part, had no fhare in the union. The
czarowitz was entirely given up to low, fenfual pleafures
and mean vicious company, and had no defire at all to marry,
nor had any other view at prefent than an endeavour to fhun
the danger he was in of forfeiting his fucceffion to the
crown: and the princefs, whofe amiable perfon and engaging accomplifhments deferved a better fate, entirely miffed
her road to happinefs.

The czar's
celebration
of his old
wedding.

A few days after the marriage, the young couple took
the route for Wolfenbuttel, and the czar that of Silefia,
for Peterfburg, where the czar's marriage with the czarina
was publicly folemnized the 20th of February, 1712, in
the following manner. M. Kyking, one of the lords of
the admiralty, and Jaguzinfki, adjutant-general, were fent
to invite the company *to his majefty's old wedding*, which
were the terms they were ordered to ufe. The czar was married in his admiral's uniform, which occafioned the naval

officers

officers to bear a principal share in the solemnities of the day; Vice-admiral Kruys, and the rear-admiral of the gallies, were the bridegroom's fathers; the emprefs-dowager and the vice-admiral's lady, were the bride-mothers; the bride-maids were two of the emprefs Catherine's own daughters; but as these princeffes were too young to bear the fatigue, the czar's two nieces, daughters to czar John, his majefty's elder brother, performed as proxies: after the ceremony, all the company met at the czar's palace, according to invitation, in a moft magnificent proceffion. Prince Menzikòff carried the marfhal's ftaff, and vice-admiral Kruys was in the fledge, with the czar on his right hand; the whole entertainment was very fplendid; the evening concluded with a ball and fire-works, and the city was illuminated the whole night, which finifhed the old wedding.

Prince Menzikoff was foon after fent into Pomerania, to take the command of the Ruffian army, confifting of 36,000 men, and was then joined by the Danes and Saxons: his majefty foon followed, and taking Berlin in his way, had a conference with the king of Pruffia; from thence, by Hamburgh, he went into Holftein, where he took Frederickftadt, jointly with the king of Denmark: Taking leave of the Danifh monarch he went to Schonhaufen, where he had another interview with his Pruffian majefty. The troops left in Holftein, affifted the Danes in reducing Toningen, and making general Steinboch and his army prifoners of war; and thofe in Pomerania took Stettin, and blockaded Stralfund. Prince Menzikoff at that time levied, by contribution, from the city of Hamburgh.

8

burgh 250,000 crowns; from Lubeck 100,000, and from Dantzig 150,000.

1772.
General
Baur's difco-
very of him-
felf to his
friends and
brother offi-
cers.

At the time our troops were in Holftein, general Baur, who commanded the cavalry, and was himfelf a foldier of fortune, his family or country being a fecret to every body, took an opportunity to difcover himfelf, which furprifed and pleafed thofe who were about him. Being encamped near Hufum, in Holftein, he invited all his field-officers, and fome others to dine with him, and fent his adjutant to bring a miller and his wife, who lived in the neighbour-hood, to the entertainment. The poor couple came very much afraid of the Mufcovite general, and were quite con-fufed when they appeared before him, which he perceiving, bad them make themfelves quite eafy, for he only meant to fhew them kindnefs, and had fent for them to dine with him that day, and talked with them familiarly about the country: the dinner being fet, he placed the miller and his wife next to himfelf, one on each hand, at the head of the table, and paid great attention to them, inviting them to make free and eat hearty. In the courfe of the entertainment, he afked the miller a great many queftions about his family and his relations : the miller told him, that he was the eldeft fon of his father, who had been alfo a miller at the fame mill he then poffefled ; that he had two brothers, tradefmen ; and one fifter, married to a tradefman ; that his own family confifted of one fon and three daughters. The general afked him, if he never had any other brother than thofe he had mentioned : he replied, he had once an-other, but he was dead many years ago, for they had never heard of him fince he enlifted and went away with foldiers

diers when he was but very young, and he muſt certainly
have been killed in the wars. The general obſerving the
company much ſurprized at his behaviour to theſe people,
thinking he did it by way of diverſion, ſaid to them,
" Gentlemen, you have always been very curious to know
" who and whence I am; I now inform you, this is the
" place of my nativity, and you have now heard from this
" my eldeſt brother, what my family is."——And then turning towards the miller and his wife, he embraced them very
affectionately, telling them, he was their ſuppoſed dead brother; and, to confirm them, he related every thing that had
happened in the family before he left it. The general invited them all to dine with him next day at the miller's,
where a plentiful entertainment was provided, and told
them that was the houſe where he was born. General Baur
then made a generous proviſion for all his relations, and
ſent the miller's only ſon to Berlin for his education, who
turned out an accompliſhed young man.

As general Baur was the perſon by whoſe means the
empreſs Catherine arrived afterwards to ſo great a height
of grandeur, this leads me to relate her ſtory, as I heard
it told by thoſe who knew her from her infancy.

She was born at Runghen, a ſmall village in Livonia, of
very poor parents, who were only boors, or vaſſals; her
father and mother dying, left her very young in great want;
the pariſh-clerk, out of compaſſion, took her home to his
houſe, where ſhe learnt to read. Dr. Glack, miniſter of
Marienburgh, ſeeing her there, enquired of the clerk who
ſhe was; and being informed ſhe was a poor orphan he
had taken into his houſe out of charity, what from a

with

wish to relieve the poor clerk from a burthen he 'was not well able to support, and a liking to the little orphan, the doctor took her home to his house, notwithstanding he had a numerous family of his own. Here her company and opportunities for improvement were better, and her deportment such, that she became equally esteemed by the doctor, his wife, and children ; her steady, diligent, and careful attention to all their domestic concerns, ingratiated her so much with the doctor and his wife, that they made no distinction between her and their own children.   She ever after showed her acknowledgment with the utmost gratitude, in richly providing for all those who could lay claim to any alliance to the doctor's family ; nor did she forget her first benefactor the clerk of Rughen.   In this happy situation she grew up to woman, when a Livonian serjeant, in the Swedish service, fell passionately in love with her ; she likewise liking him, agreed to marry him, provided it could be done with the doctor's consent, who, upon enquiry, into the man's character, finding it unexceptionable, readily gave it. The marriage-day was appointed, and indeed, came, when a sudden order came to the serjeant that very morning, to march directly with a detachment for Riga, who was thereby disappointed from ever enjoying his lovely bride. Soon after this, general Baur, at the head of an army, came before the town and took it, in the year 1702, when all the inhabitants were made prisoners, and amongst the rest this lovely bride. In the promiscuous croud, overwhelmed with grief, and bathed in tears at her unhappy fate, the general observing her, saw a *je ne sçai quoi* in her whole appearance, which attracted him so much,

that

that he afked her feveral queftions about her fituation; to which fhe made anfwers with more fenfe than is ufual in perfons of her rank; he defired her not to be afraid, for he would take care of her, and gave immediate orders for her fafety and reception into his houfe, of which he gave her the whole charge, with authority over all his fervants, by whom fhe was very much beloved from her manner of ufing them; the general afterwards often faid, his houfe was never fo well managed as when fhe was with him.

Prince Menzikoff, who was his patron, feeing her one day at the general's, obferved fomething very extraordinary in her air and manner, and enquiring who fhe was, and on what footing fhe ferved him, the general told him what has been already related, and with due encomiums on the merits of her conduct in his houfe: the prince faid, fuch a perfon would be of great confequence to him, for he was then very ill ferved in that refpect; to which the general replied, he was under too many obligations to his highnefs to have it in his power to refufe him any thing he had a mind to, and immediately calling for Catherine, told her, that was prince Menzikoff, and that he had oceafion for a fervant like herfelf, and that the prince had it much more in his power to be a friend to her than he had, adding, that he had too great a regard for her to prevent her receiving fuch a piece of honour and good fortune. She anfwered only by a profound courtefy, which fhewed, if not her confent, that it was not then in her power to refufe the offer that was made: in fhort, the prince took her home the fame day, and fhe lived with him till the year 1704, when the czar, one day dining with the prince, happened to fee

L 2   her,

her, and fpoke to her; fhe made a yet ftronger impreffion on that monarch, who would likewife have her to be
his fervant ; from whence fhe rofe to be emprefs of Ruffia.

Prince Men-
zikoff's rife,
and the czar's
narrow ef-
cape from
poifon.

As prince Menzikof was alfo a perfon raifed from a very
low degree, I was told the following circumftances of his
rife. He was born of gentle, but very poor parents ; and
they dying, left him very young without any education,
infomuch that he could neither read nor write, nor ever
did he to the day of his death : his poverty obliged him
to feek fervice in Mofcow, where he was taken into the
houfe of a paftry-cook ; who employed him in crying
minced-pies about the ftreets; and having a good voice,
he alfo fung ballads: whereby he was fo generally known
that he had accefs into all the gentlemen's houfes. The
czar, by invitation, was to dine one day at a boyar's,
or lord's houfe, and Menzikoff happening to be in the
kitchen that day, obferved the boyar giving directions
to his cook about a difh of meat he faid the czar was
fond of, and took notice that the boyar himfelf put fome
kind of powder in it, by way of fpice ; taking particular
notice of what meat that difh was compofed, he took
himfelf away to fing his ballads, and kept fauntering in
the ftreet till the czar arrived, when exalting his voice, his
majefty took notice of it, fent for him, and afked him if he
would fell his bafket with the pies : the boy replied, he
had power only to fell the pies, as for the bafket he muft
firft afk his mafter's leave, but as every thing belonged to
his majefty, he needed only lay his commands upon him.
This reply pleafed the czar fo much, that he ordered Alexander to ftay and attend him, which he obeyed with great
joy.

joy. Menzikoff waited behind the czar's chair at dinner, and feeing the before mentioned difh ferved up and placed before him, in a whifper begged his majefty not to eat thereof ; the czar went into another room with the boy, and afked his reafon for what he had whifpered to him, when he informed his majefty what he had obferved in the kitchen, and the boyar's putting in the powder himfelf, without the cook's perceiving him, made him fufpect that difh in particular; he therefore thought it his duty to put his majefty upon his guard. The czar returned to table without the leaft difcompofure in his countenance, and with his ufual chearfulnefs ; the boyar recommended this difh to him, faying, it was very good ; the czar ordered the boyar to fit down by him, for it is a cuftom in Mofcow for the mafter of the houfe to wait at table when he entertains his friends, and putting fome of it on a plate, defired him to eat and fhew him a good example. The boyar, with the utmoft confufion, replied, that it did not become the fervant to eat with his mafter ; whereupon the plate was fet down to a dog, who foon difpatched its contents, which, in a very fhort time, threw him into convulfions, and foon deprived him of life : the dog being opened, the effect of the poifon was clearly difcovered, and the boyar was immediately fecured, but was found next morning dead in his bed, which prevented all farther difcovery.

Menzikoff's remarkable introduction foon gained him credit and confidence with his royal mafter, which from being one of the meaneft and pooreft, raifed him to be one of the richeft fubjects in the Ruffian empire ; he was not only dignified with the title of a prince in Ruffia, but alfo declared a prince of the Roman empire. He was tall, well-

4.   fhaped,

shaped, very handsome in his perfon, and of great pene-
tration : he acted as vice-czar at the imperial court, the
czar himself appearing at all public meetings as a private perfon, attended by two fervants at moft, and, inftead of pleafing himfelf with the pomp of grandeur, his
delight was the improvement of his empire, which he vifited every where in perfon.

The czar, in his return from Germany, came to Riga,
where he met the czarina, who had been delivered of a
princefs, and foon after fet out for Peterfburg, where he
got three hundred veffels in readinefs, and embarked the
beginning of May 1713, with 12,000 men, and landed at
Helfingfoo, in Finland ; returning immediately to Peterfburg, he embarked 6000 more, and went back himfelf with
great expedition, and landed them at the fame place. He
gave prince Galitzin the command of the army, confifting
of 20,000 foot, 4000 horfe, and a large train of artillery,
to act by land, and he himfelf put to fea with twenty men
of war in queft of the enemy's fleet, but found them fo
advantageoufly fheltered, that he did not think proper to
attack them, but returned and joined the army at Shrendo;
from thence he marched to Abo and befieged it, and the
place furrendered the 8th of September : then leaving orders
with his generals to follow and drive the Swedes out of Finland, he returned to Peterfburgh, where he launched feveral men of war and gallies.

This city being then in its infancy, many thoufand workmen were employed in building, and lodgings were very
fcarce. I had the good fortune to be accommodated in
lieutenant-general Bruce's houfe, who was commandant of
Peterfburgh, and brother to the mafter-general of the ordnance ;

nance; but the mafter-general being left in Germany, fent
me orders to go to Mofcow, and ftay in his houfe with his
lady, till he fhould arrive; for which place I fet out the
beginning of this year, and coming in view of it, in a clear
fun-fhine day, I never faw fo glorious a fight as this city
prefented at a diftance with the vaft numbers of gilded
domes and fteeples: but my expectations were greatly difappointed when I entered it, finding only ill-built wooden
houfes, and timber-ftreets interfperfed with churches, and
brick-houfes, with large courts and gardens, the habitations of the grandees and people of fortune; and coming
to general Bruce's houfe, I met with a very kind reception
from his lady, who treated me with the affection of a mother: they had then no child.

Mofcow is divided into four parts; the firft is called the
Middle, or Red-Town, which is furrounded by a ftrong
brick wall; part of it is taken up by the caftle, called Kremelin, being two miles in circumference, and inclofed by
three ftrong walls, each higher than the other, with a deep
ditch on the outfide, planted with a great number of cannon; and the two rivers, Mofcow and Neglina, flow by
two fides of this divifion of the city. The caftle is fo extenfive, that it contains the czar's palace and dwellings for
his courtiers, the archbifhop's palace, with many others;
and two cloifters, one for monks, the other for nuns; befides fifty churches, all built fquare, each with five domes,
the larger one in the middle, and the four leffer ones on
each corner, and are all covered with copper gilt: in the
middle of the caftle ftands a very high fteeple, called Ivan
Welika, or Great John, in which is a bell that weighs
336,000 lb.; it is 19 feet high, 23 in diameter, 64 in circumference,

cumference, and two in thickneſs, and was founded in czar Boris-Goodanof's time, and requires twenty-four men on each ſide of the clapper, to draw it from one ſide to the other; the bell itſelf is moveable, but is never rung except on ſome great occaſion. The other part of this diviſion, without the caſtle, is moſtly inhabited by the grandees: here alſo ſtands the grand market, which is a very large ſquare, divided into ſtreets, where the merchants and tradeſmen have ſhops for the ſale of goods; and as every kind of merchandize, or manufacture, is claſſed by itſelf, in its own department in the market, makes it very convenient for the buyer, who may ſuit himſelf with very little trouble. All the ſhops are locked at ſun-ſet, and the four gates of entrance into the ſquare, are ſhut by the officer of the guard, who places centries all round it, and is accountable for the property in the place: the ſhops are opened at day-break. This is the only place allowed for the ſale of goods, and is much the ſame with the befeſtin at Conſtantinople.

The ſecond part, or diviſion, is called Zaargorod, and is ſurrounded by a ſtrong wall with battlements, after the Oriental manner, and towers at proper diſtances; this is alſo called Bela-Stena, or White-Wall; the river Neglina runs through it; here are the czar's ſtables, a foundery for cannon and bells, the arſenal, prince Menzikoff's palace, general Bruce's houſe, and many other gentlemen's houſes of rank.

The third diviſion is called Skorodom, or the Houſe-Market, which the word imports, *ſkoro* ſignifying *haſte*, and *dom*, a *houſe*. Here one may buy a wooden houſe of any dimenſions, have it carried to the place where it is to

ſtand,

ftand, fet up, and ready to dwell in, the third day after the purchafe; this part is furrounded with mud-walls fupported with planks; the river Jagufa runs through it.

The fourth divifion is called Strelitza Slaboda, where the military are generally quartered, and is furrounded by an entrenchment; it ftands on the other fide of the river Mofcow, with a fine bridge built over it by prince Galitzin, favourite of the princefs Sophia, his majefty's eldeft fifter, who gave him fo much trouble in the reign of czar John.

It is generally computed that there are in this city fifteen hundred churches, chapels, and cloyfters; this furprifing number is accounted for by every grandee's having a chapel and prieft of his own. Mofcow lies in 55 deg. 36 min. north latitude, and is in circumference fixteen Englifh miles. A great number of foreigners live in the city, as Greeks, Armenians, Perfians, Turks, and Tartars, and are allowed the public exercife of their religious worfhip. At a fmall diftance from the city, ftands a large fuburb called Inoi-femfka Slaboda, or Foreign Town, where the Englifh, Dutch, and Germans live; there are four Proteftant and one Roman Catholic church in it; but none of them are allowed to have fteeples or ufe bells. It is pleafantly fituated on the river Neglina, on the banks of which are a number of pleafure-houfes with fine gardens; the famous general le Fort, built a magnificent palace here; the people live very agreeably among themfelves, without interfering with the natives except upon bufinefs. As the country abounds with great plenty of every neceffary of life, people live at a very cheap rate, and regale themfelves with balls and

M   enter-

entertainments, which they can furnifh at a very fmall expence.   In the fummer-time they carry tents, and pitch
them in the neighbouring woods, where they make merry
with dancing on the green till night.   The czar, when
in Mofcow, ufed always to make one in their parties
of pleafure and entertainments, and paid them frequent
vifits.

An ambaffa-
dor from Per-
fia : a great
fire in Mof-
cow.   An ambaffador from Perfia came here with a very great
retinue, and remained waiting the czar's arrival; the prefents he brought were ten Perfian horfes, a very large elephant, a lion, a tyger, an oftrich, and feveral kinds of
parrots, and other birds; befides a great quantity of Perfian filks and tapeftry, and other rarities. Soon after there
happened a great and dreadful fire, which confumed the
greateft part of the city, efpecially the wooden houfes; the
fire broke out in a maiden monaftery without the town, and
a ftrong weft wind blew the fire upon the city, which fet it
all on a blaze : the only method they ufe to ftop the progrefs of a fire is, by pulling down houfes at a diftance
before it, as it is impoffible to ufe fire-engines; the ftreets
being all of timber, burn at the fame time with the houfes.
On this occafion, a poor fuperftitious man feeing the fire advancing to confume his all, took a picture of St. Nicholas,
and holding it between him and the fire, prayed fervently
for that faint's protection, but in vain, for the flames foon
feized his houfe, for which he became fo enraged at the
faint that he threw him into the fire, faying, fince he
would not fave him, he might now fave himfelf : this
coming to the ears of the clergy, the poor man was
fentenced to be burnt alive. All the brick buildings, fuch

I   as

as churches, and other religious houses, noblemen, and
gentlemen's houses, escaped this conflagration, only the
roofs of the latter were burnt without being otherwise damaged, for all the houses of three or four stories high are
arched to the top, and their street-doors and window-
shutters are of iron.

After the fire, the city was very soon rebuilt from the
Skorodom before mentioned, as every body could fit the
dimensions of his premises with a house; and it was truly
surprising to see with what dispatch the timber was conveyed
to the place appointed, and with what dexterity the timber-
men rear it. In two days the house was under roof, when
the purchaser gave directions where the doors and windows
should be, the parts being cut out they put in the frames,
which are all ready prepared.

An instance of the superstition of the people, and power   A young
of the clergy, happened some time before this fire. A physician
young man, whom the czar had sent to Leyden for his edu- clergy.
cation, having finished his studies in physic, returned a gra-
duated physician, and at a merry-meeting with his friends,
they questioned him concerning his religion: he being
then in his cups, told them, he was as much of the Greek
church as ever, but that he had lost all his faith in saint's
pictures, and to prove what he said, he took one down
from the wall, and threw it in the fire; whereupon he
was immediately seized, and put into the hands of the
clergy, who very soon sentenced him to the flames, and
burnt him in a most cruel manner; laying the fire at
some distance from him to keep him the longer in torment. The czar, being informed of the cruelty of the

clergy,

clergy, as he had formerly aboliſhed the dignity of patriarch, took this opportunity to deprive them of the
1713.
Who are
therefore de-
prived of the
power of life
and death. power of life and death, and made a law that all the
clergy ſhould apply themſelves to ſtudy, allowing them
five years for that end ; after which they were to undergo
an examination, and thoſe who were found capable to
perform their functions were to be promoted, the others
to be diſcarded.   And as three fourth parts of the year
were holidays in commemoration of ſome ſaint or other,
whereby the people were for the moſt part idle, he made
a law that no holiday ſhould be kept but in commemoration
of our Saviour, the Virgin Mary, the twelve Apoſtles, and
St. Andrew, and St. Nicolas, the tutelar ſaints of Ruſſia.
And as there were in the empire many thouſand convents
full of lazy monks, who lived in idleneſs, he reſtricted
the number of theſe houſes to fifty, each houſe to contain
no more than fifty monks, each monk to be above forty
years of age ; the reſt of them to be appropriated to hoſ-
pitals for ſuch of the army and navy as were become unfit
for ſervice, and other indigent perſons not able to maintain themſelves ; and their revenues for their ſupport : and
the monks, who had been bred to no handicraft, and were
fit for ſervice, to be employed in the army.

The people of rank and faſhion in Moſcow having
laid aſide the old cuſtoms and manners of their fathers,
now live very gay, dreſs in the French faſhion, and converſe
with more freedom than formerly ; and as the fair ſex are
allowed all manner of freedom in company, they live in a
perpetual round of pleaſure and diverſion, ſpending moſt
part of their time in balls and entertainments, inviting each
other

other by turns to their houses; and as they were left lonely
by their hufbands, who are for the moft part employed
abroad, the ladies took Swedifh officers who had been
taken prifoners at Pultowa into their families; fome as
ftewarts, others as governors to their children, and fome
to teach them mufic and dancing.   So that all their balls
were made up with Swedifh gentlemen, and other foreigners, of whom they were very fond.

The Ruffian women are of a middling ftature, generally Defcription of the wo-men.
well proportioned, and might pafs for handfome in any part
of Europe; their features far from defpicable, were it
not for that prepofterous cuftom of painting their faces,
which they lay on fo abundantly, that it may truly be faid
they ufe it as a veil to hide their beauty.

As for the fecond rank of the people, they ftill retain Entertainments of the common peo-ple.
much of their old manner of living; at their entertainments
none but the men appear; the mafter of the houfe waits
on his guefts till the defert of fweatmeats comes on the
table after dinner, when he takes his feat amongft them,
and does all he can to encourage them to drink, for it
would be a great reflexion upon them if any of the company fhould get out of the houfe without being drunk.
When the guefts offer to go away, the miftrefs of the
houfe makes her appearance, at a call, and barely enters
the room, when turning round to the corner where the
family-faints are placed, crofling herfelf, makes a very low
bow, and then pays her refpects by a bow to the company,
without coming a ftep farther, but remains ftanding, clad
in a loofe gown lined with fur, and a fable cap on her
head, and her face covered over with paint and patches;
but

but her whole body is unconfined, wearing neither stays, waistcoat, or petticoat, or even garters to her stockings, and she wears very high heeled slippers : in this situation, the landlord introduces all his guests to salute his spouse, one after another, and a servant is ready behind her with a salver and four glasses filled with brandy, wine, mead, and beer, which every body is obliged to drink to the good health of the lady ; after which she retires without so much as opening her mouth ; after that other females of the family are introduced in the same manner, and thus they end their entertainments very drunk.

Marriage.　　In Russia they commonly marry very young ; the parents make the match without consulting the inclinations of their children, who do not so much as see one another till they are introduced in their bed-chamber : this was also customary among the first rank, till the czar put a stop to it by allowing young people to pay their addresses in person, without imposing a match upon either against their inclinations, whereby many fatal marriages were prevented ; but the old custom still prevails among the inferior ranks. When the maiden becomes marriageable, the parents send for a broker, or match-maker (commonly an old woman), and give her instructions to look out a proper husband for their daughter ; delivering her, at the same time, an inventory of what they propose to give with the damsel, as money, jewels, plate, houshold-goods, and her clothes, even to her shifts ; likewise, the number of boors, or vassals, who are commonly valued at ten rubles each per annum. With this list, the broker goes from one bachelor to another, whom she deems a suitable match for the young lady, enquiring of
them

them if they have an inclination to marry, fhe can recommend them to a pretty young lady with a handfome fortune ; fhewing them at the fame time the conditions. If
the inventory pleafes the young man, he figns his name to
it ; and, after fhe has got feveral fubfcribers, fhe returns
the paper to thofe who employed her ; then the parents of
the girl make enquiry into the characters and circumftances
of the fubfcribers ; and having pitched on three or four of
the moft eligible, they are invited by the father to an entertainment, where there is a meeting of friends, upon which
occafion the glafs goes brifkly about : the mother, daughter,
and other female relations, take their ftations in the houfe,
fo as to fee the company without being feen by them ; enquiring of the girl which of them fhe would choofe for a
hufband, and when the point is fettled, as to their choice,
the company, after a hearty drink, is difmiffed, none knowing who is to be the happy man. The next day fome of
the girls relations are fent to confer with thofe of the intended bridegroom. If the match is accepted, two or three
women, deputed by the intended bridegroom, are permitted
to examine the perfon of his intended fpoufe, before whom
fhe appears ftark naked, to fhew if there be any perfonal
defect ; after this the friends fettle the marriage, the intended couple not being allowed to fee one another till they
they meet in the bed-chamber.

The princefs Natalia, only fifter to the czar, by the The princefs
fame mother, ordered preparations to be made for a grand morous fan-
wedding for two of her dwarfs, who were to be married ; cy in the mar-
on which occafion feveral fmall coaches were made, and little dwarfs.
Shetland horfes provided to draw them ; and all the dwarfs

in

in the kingdom were fummoned to celebrate the nuptials, to the number of ninety-three ; they went in a grand proceffion through all the ftreets of Mofcow ; before them went a large open waggon drawn by fix horfes, with kettle-drums, trumpets, French horns, and hautboys ; then followed the marfhal and his attendants, two and two, on horfe-back ; then the bridegroom and bride, in a coach and fix, attended by their bride man and maid, who fat before them in the coach ; they were followed by fifteen fmall coaches, each drawn by fix Shetland horfes, and each containing four dwarfs.   It was fomewhat furprifing to fee fuch a number of little creatures in one company together ; efpecially as they were furnifhed with an equipage conformable to their ftature ; two troops of dragoons attended the proceffion to keep off the mob, and many perfons of fafhion were invited to the wedding, who attended in their coaches to the church, where the fmall couple were married ; from thence the proceffion returned in order to the princefs's palace, where a grand entertainment was prepared for the company ; two long tables were covered, on each fide of a long hall, where the company of dwarfs dined together ; the princefs, with her two nieces, princefs Anne and Elizabeth, the czar's daughters, were at the trouble themfelves to fee them all feated and well attended, before they fat down to their own table. At night the princeffes, attended by the nobility, conducted the married couple to bed in grand ftate : after that ceremony, the dwarf-company had a large room allotted them to make merry among themfelves ; the entertainment concluded with a ball, which lafted till day-light. The company which attended the princeffes on this

occa-

occasion were so numerous, that they filled several rooms.

Some little time after this I saw three women buried alive for drowning their husbands: they had, it seems, crossed the Mosco in a boat, all three together in search of their husbands, whom they found all drunk in a public house, and endeavouring to persuade them to go home, were severely beaten by them; however, by the assistance of some other people, they got them at last into the boat where they fell asleep; the wives to be revenged on their husbands for beating them, when the boat had reached the middle of the river, threw them one after another into the river, and after they had drowned them, they came a-shore very unconcerned. The matter immediately came to light; they were seized, tried, condemned, and ordered to be put alive into the ground up to their necks, there to remain till they died; two of them lived ten, and the other eleven days; they spoke the first three days, complaining of great pain, but not after that; they had certainly got some sustenance in the night time, or they could not have existed so long; the oldest of them was not twenty years of age.

If a man kills his wife, or slave, under correction (as they term it), he is only whipt with the knout; which is thus performed: a lusty fellow takes him upon his back, and another ties his feet with a cord, which comes through between the legs of the person who carries him. In this posture he is held so fast that he cannot stir, and being stript to the middle, the executioner with the knout, which is a strap of dried elk-skin, untanned, fastened to a stick, which

N

he

he applies to the back fo dexteroufly, that every lafh brings
the blood, or leaves a wale as thick as one's finger: this is.
called the moderate; but when the fentence orders it to be
more fevere, then the executioner, advancing three or four
fteps, till he is within reach of the offender, gives the firft
ftroke in the middle of the back, retreating at every ftroke,
and is fo expert that he never hits twice in the fame place;
each ftroke brings the flefh with it. Where the punifhment
is ordered with the utmoft feverity, he ftrikes the flanks, and
often cuts into the bowels, which few furvive. It is a general
remark that lean people turn fat after the knout; and
that it is an infallible cure for thofe who are hide-bound.

Befides this, they have another way of chaftifing, called
the batoags, which is ufed in families for the correction of
children and flaves, and alfo in the army. The perfon to
undergo this, after pulling off his clothes to his drawers,
is laid flat on his belly on the ground; one fits acrofs his
head and neck, another upon his feet, each furnifhed with
a good fwitch, with which they foundly tickle his back.

The czar's birth and marriage.   During my refidence in Mofcow, I was told the following particulars of the czar. He was born in the year 1672,
and was married in 1690, at the age of eighteen, to Otto-
kefla Lupochin, a boyar's daughter, by whom he had prince
Alexis: fome time after he turned her away, and fhut her
up in a monaftery, on fufpicion of difloyalty to his bed.
It was faid, that in one of her jealous fits, fhe charged
prince Menzikoff with carrying the czar to drabs of his
former acquaintance, who had been his cuftomers for
cakes; upbraiding him with his firft occupation, and that
Menzikoff ever after bore an irreconcilable enmity to
                                                        both

both her and her fon. After the divorce, one mifs Mons, a
very beautiful young lady, born at Mofcow, of foreign parents, was much in favour with the czar ; but when he was
abroad, Mr. Keyferling, then refiding at Mofcow as envoy
from the king of Pruffia, paid his addreffes to, and married her. When the czar returned, he was fo much offended
at Keyferling, that he ordered him to leave Mofcow, which
occafioned his immediate recall by the king his mafter, who
fent another in his room. It was believed, if his public
character had not protected him, he would have feverely
felt his majefty's difpleafure.

The czar was fome time after fmitten with the charms of
another beautiful young lady, the daughter of a foreign
merchant in this city: he firft faw her in her father's houfe,
where he dined one day ; he was fo much taken with her appearance, that he offered her any terms fhe pleafed, if fhe
would live with him ; which this virtuous young woman
modeftly refufed, but dreading the effects of his authority,
fhe put on a refolution, and left Mofcow in the night, without communicating her defign even to her parents. Having
provided a little money for her fupport, fhe travelled on foot
feveral miles into the country, till fhe arrived at a fmall village
where her nurfe lived with her hufband and their daughter,
the young lady's fofter-fifter, to whom fhe difcovered her
intention of concealing herfelf in the wood near that village: and, to prevent any difcovery, fhe fet out the fame
night, accompanied by the hufband and daughter. The
hufband, being a timber-man by trade, and well acquainted
with the wood, conducted her to a little dry fpot in the
middle of a morafs, and there he built a hut for her habi-

N 2   tation.

tation. She had depofited her money with her nurfe to procure little neceffaries for her fupport, which were faithfully

conveyed to her at night by the nurfe or her daughter,
by one of whom fhe was conftantly attended in the night-
time.

The next day after her flight, the czar called at her father's to fee her, and finding the parents in anxious concern
for their daughter, and himfelf difappointed, fancied it a
plan of their own concerting. He became angry, and began
to threaten them with the effects of his difpleafure, if fhe was
not produced : nothing was left to the parents but the
moft folemn proteftations with tears of real forrow running
down their cheeks, to convince him of their innocence and
ignorance what was become of her, affuring him of their
fears that fome fatal difafter muft have befallen her, as nothing belonging to her was miffing, except what fhe had on
at the time. The czar, fatisfied of their fincerity, ordered
great fearch to be made for her, with the offer of a confiderable reward to the perfon who fhould difcover what
was become of her, but to no purpofe : the parents and relations, apprehending fhe was no more, went into mourning for her.

Above a year after this fhe was difcovered by an accident. A colonel who had come from the army to fee his
friends, going a hunting into that wood, and following his
game through the morafs, he came to the hut, and looking into it faw a pretty young woman in a mean drefs. After enquiring of her who fhe was, and how fhe came to
live in fo folitary a place, he found out at laft that fhe
was the lady whofe difappearance had made fo great a
noife:

noife : in the utmoft confufion, and with the moft fervent intreaties, fhe prayed him on her knees that he would not betray her; to which he replied, that he thought her danger was now paft, as the czar was then otherways engaged, and that fhe might with fafety difcover herfelf, at leaft to her parents, with whom he would confult how matters fhould be managed. The lady agreed to his propofal, and he fat out immediately and overjoyed her parents with the happy difcovery : the iffue of their deliberations was to confult Madam Catherine (as fhe was then called) in what manner the affair fhould be opened to the czar. The colonel went alfo upon this bufinefs, and was advifed by madam to come next morning, and fhe would introduce him to his majefty, when he might make the difcovery and claim the promifed reward. He went according to appointment, and being introduced, told the accident by which he had difcovered the lady, and reprefented the miferable fituation in which he found her, and what fhe muft have fuffered by being fo long fhut up in fuch a difmal place, from the delicacy of her fex. The czar fhewed a great deal of concern that he fhould have been the caufe of all her fufferings, declaring, that he would endeavour to make her amends. Here Madam Catherine fuggefted, that fhe thought the beft amends his majefty could make was to give her a handfome fortune and the colonel for a hufband, who had the beft right, having caught her in purfuit of his game. The czar, agreeing perfectly with Madam Catherine's fentiments, ordered one of his favourites to go with the colonel, and bring the young lady home; where fhe arrived, to the inexpreffible joy of her family and relations, who had all been in mourn-

ing

ing for her. The marriage was under the direction, and at the expence of the czar, who himfelf gave the bride to the bridegroom ; faying, that he prefented him with one of the moft virtuous of women ; and accompanied his declaration with very valuable prefents, befides fettling on her and her heirs, three thoufand rubles a year. This lady lived highly efteemed by the czar, and every one who knew her. Befides the concurring reports of other people, I had this her ftory from her own mouth.

Murders are fo frequent in Mofcow, that few nights pafs without fome people being found dead in the ftreets in the morning. The robbers go in ftrong parties, and kill before they rob : this they do with fo little fear, that they often perform it before the perfons own door ; and the terror of thefe ruffians is fo great, that none of the neighbours dare affift the unhappy victim for fear of being butchered themfelves, or at leaft having their houfes burnt. This obliges people who have occafion to be in the ftreets in the night, to go in companies together, or have a fufficient guard of fervants on horfeback to attend them. The weapon ufed by thofe villains is called *a dubien*, which is a long ftick with a round knob at one end, and made heavy with iron, with which they knock a man down dead at one ftroke ; and if any of them happens to be taken, a good fum of money from the gang they belong to, gets them off : it is even affirmed, that gangs of them were protected by fome of the nobility, who partake of the booty; which affertion I believe not ill grounded.

The highways are alfo much infefted by thofe *Rafocnicks*, as they are called, which makes it very dangerous travelling

in

Mufcovite robberies and murders.

in any part of Ruffia ; for they have their fpies in the
towns, who inform them when any body is to fet out on
a journey, how they are to be attended, and according to
this information, they prepare themfelves for an attack, and
way-lay them in fome wood through which they are to pafs.

A gentleman of the name of Knipercron, whofe father
had been refident from Sweden before the war, told me,
how the czar himfelf had been attacked in his younger
days: his majefty frequented their houfe very often, and
always fhewed a great regard for their family.. One even--
ing the czar intending them a vifit, being only attended.
by two fervants, the one riding before and the other ftanding behind the fledge, up comes a fledge with eight Rafbonicks in it, and were juft going to faften his fledge to.
theirs with a grapling-iron, which they commonly make ufe.
of on thefe occafions ; but the czar being then young, ftout,.
and vigorous, got up, and feized one of the robbers by.
the hair of his head, and pulled him out of their fledge ;
and, keeping his hold, drove out of their reach, dragging.
the fellow along with him till he reached the refident's.
houfe, which was not far, and entered to their great furprize.
all in a fweat, ftill holding the fellow by the hair. He ordered.
the gates to be immediately fhut, that none of the fervants.
might go out till he had examined the robber.   When the.
fellow understood that it was the czar they had attacked, he
fhook and trembled, faying if they had known who he
was they would not have meddled with him, and then begged,
he might be put to death, without being put to the torture.
To this his majefty confented, on condition he difcovered the
reft of his gang ;. but this the fellow would not do, without.
a promife of his life and a reward, which was alfo granted
him,

him, and he went with a detachment of foldiers to the rendezvous of his companions, and coming to the houfe he called to them to open the door. On hearing his voice, they directly opened it, and in rufhed the foldiers, and feized not only his feven accomplices, but thirteen others of the fame gang, who were foon after all executed, except the informer.

At another time the czar was attacked on his way from Mofcow to Novogorod, when he was attended by four fervants only. Going from Twer, he was ftopt by a ftrong party of Rafbonicks, on which he immediately jumped out of his fledge, with a fword drawn in one hand, and a cocked piftol in the other, and told them he was the czar, afking them what they wanted? They replied, they were poor fellows reduced to great want, and as he was their lord and mafter, he was the propereft perfon to relieve them: he told them he had no money about him; to which they anfwered, if he had, they would take none from him, but defired that he would give them a written order to the governor of Novogorod for what fum he pleafed to beftow upon them, begging that it might be fuch as would relieve them from their ftraits. The czar then afked them, if one thoufand rubles would be fufficient; and on their faying it would, he wrote an order for that fum payable at fight, and for which they directly difpatched one of their number, who very foon returned with the money: they then obliged the czar to return to Twer, and to pledge his royal word not to profecute, or ever enquire after them, promifing to amend their lives and become good fubjects for the future. Inftead of proceeding to Novogorod, the czar returned back to Mofcow.

I cannot

I cannot omit mentioning what happened in my own
time to two of the Swediſh officers who had been made
prifoners at the battle of Pultowa. They were miſſing :
great ſearch was made and much enquiry, but nothing
could be heard of them, from which it was concluded they
had been murdered : ſome little time after four others difappeared, but were not miſſed, till one of them, a captain
Horn, returned ſhot through the ſhoulder with a piſtol-ball ;
who privately addreſſed himſelf to a lieutenant of our artillery, who had been his former acquaintance in the Swediſh
ſervice, to whom he told the misfortune that had happened
to him and his comrades. The lieutenant immediately informed major-general Gunter, of the artillery, what had
happened to the Swediſh officers, and that the villains informed againſt were then at a houſe in that part of
the town where the artillery men were quartered ; the general directly ordered them to be ſecured, being four in
number. The ſtory in ſhort was this :—A Jew who had
embraced the Chriſtian religion, of the Greek church, and
who was an engraver by trade, counterfeited paſſports
under the chancellor's ſeal, and agreed with the two firſt for
a ſum of money to carry them into Poland, from whence
they might ſafely paſs into their own country. In the paſſ-
port they were deſcribed as two officers going to the army,
and each of them with one ſervant ; they arrived at the
borders of Poland without the leaſt interruption or ſuſpi-
picion, and having paſſed by Smolenſko, the Jew deſired
them to write to their companions in Moſcow, and inform
them with how much ſafety they had made their eſcape ;
which they did, recommending the Jew as the fitteſt per-

O

ſon

fon they could employ, if any of them intended to get
away as they had done. After he had got thefe letters of
recommendation, the Jew offered to conduct them a day's
journey farther, which they accepted of, and the officers
riding together through a wood, congratulating each other
on their happy efcape, the Jew and his companion riding
behind them as fervants, took out each a piftol, and aimed
fo well, that they fhot both the officers dead, and having plundered them, returned to Mofcow, where they entrapped captain Horn, and three others, into the fame fnare, by fhewing the letters from thofe who had already made their efcape,
and fetting out with a paffport for four officers, and as
many fervants : they alfo arrived on the frontiers of Poland,
and riding late at night, the fervants fired, and each killed his
mafter, except captain Horn, who being fhot through the
fhoulder, fell from his horfe, and they thinking him to be
dead as well as the reft, went in purfuit of the horfes which
had taken fright at the report of the piftols, and ran away:
in the mean time, captain Horn recovering himfelf, made
the beft of his way into the wood, where he concealed himfelf; the villains returning, miffed, and fearched for him,
but it being then dark they could not find him, and having
plundered the other three, they returned for Mofcow, giving themfelves little concern about captain Horn, as they
concluded he durft not return there to inform againft them.
The captain, however, to prevent thofe villains from doing
more mifchief, and to get them punifhed, determined to
return ; and difcovering himfelf to a nobleman's fteward near
Smolenfko, who happening at that time to be fending fome
carriages with provifions to his mafter at Mofcow, the captain

tain took the opportunity and went with them, and on his arrival made the difcovery as has been related. The four villains being fecured, were examined, and confeffed what I have mentioned, but pretended they had done a meritorious action, by deftroying his majefty's enemies, who were endeavouring to make their efcape from prifon. Horn's prefervation was a happy circumftance, for they might have done much mifchief if they had not been detected, as they had now alfo recommendations from the four laft unfortunate gentlemen. The villains were tried, condemned, and all broke alive on the wheel.

The czar being informed of thefe frequent murders and robberies, whereby he was continually lofing many of his moft ufeful fubjects, fent the moft exprefs and pofitive orders to Knez Romadanoffki, whom he had appointed vice-czar in his abfence, to put an effectual ftop to thefe diforders at his peril. The vice-czar immediately iffued his orders to all houfe-keepers and publicans to give in the names of thofe who belonged to their families, and to be anfwerable for every one who lodged under their roof, and on pain of death, to fecure all thofe who could not give a fatisfactory account of themfelves, and difcover all fufpected perfons. The end of every ftreet was barricadoed, and had a guard, and none were fuffered to appear in the ftreets at night without a pafs from the vice-czar : parties of dragoons were ftationed on all the public roads, and the people in the country were made anfwerable and liable for thofe who lodged under their roofs in the fame manner as the inhabitants in the cities. Great numbers were taken, who were executed in a very extraordinary manner, being hung up by one of

their

BOOK III. their ribs on an iron hook, in which torment they lived
——————— eight or nine days : I faw them hung up by dozens in one

1713. day. Thefe executions had fo much the defired effect, that
one might travel through Ruffia, by day or night, with as
much fafety as in any part of the world.

1714. On the firft of January, 1714, general Bruce arrived in
Seat of em- Mofcow, to remove and conduct his family to Peterfburgh,
pire changed
from Mofcow when a thoufand of the beft and moft fubftantial families
to Peterfburg.
in Mofcow had received orders to prepare for the fame purpofe, in order to people that new city, propofed for the feat
of empire. The emprefs, dowager of czar Feodor, (fifter to
admiral Apraxin), with her court ; the emprefs, dowager of
czar John, with her three daughters ; namely, the princefs
Anne, dowager of Courland (afterwards emprefs of Ruffia) ;
the princefs Catherine, afterwards duchefs of Mecklenburg ;
and the princefs Profcovia, (who died unmarried) ; the princefs Natalia, the czar's only fifter by the mother, and his two
daughters the princeffes Anne and Elizabeth ; with all the
families of rank and quality, fet out this fpring for Peterfburg,
with all the foreign merchants, as no more merchandize was
to be allowed to come to Mofcow by the way of Archangel ;
fo that this metropolis, once the pleafanteft and moft agreeable
city in all Ruffia, became quite deferted, none remaining in
it but the vulgar ; which was a great mortification to all
ranks of people, being obliged to leave a place of fuch plenty
for one where every thing was both fcarce and dear.

Defcription The czarowitz arrived in Mofcow this winter, where I faw
of the czaro-
witz's perfon him for the firft time. He kept a mean Finlandifh girl for
and manners. his miftrefs. I went often with the general to wait on him,
and he came frequently to the general's houfe, commonly

6   attended

attended by very mean and low perfons. He was very
flovenly in his drefs; his perfon was tall, well made, of a
brown complexion, black hair and eyes, of a ftern countenance, and ftrong voice. He frequently did me the honour
to talk with me in German, being fully mafter of that language: he was adored by the populace, but little refpected
by the fuperior ranks, for whom he never fhewed the leaft
regard; he was always furrounded by a number of debauch-
ed ignorant priefts, and other mean perfons of bad character, in whofe company he always reflected on his father's
conduct for abolifhing the ancient cuftoms of the country,
declaring, that as foon as he came to fucceed, he fhould
foon reftore Ruffia to its former ftate; and threatening to
deftroy, without referve, all his father's favourites. This
he did fo often, and with fo little referve, that it could not
mifs reaching the emperor's ears; and it was generally
thought he now laid the foundation of that ruin he afterwards met with. The czarowitz remained in Mofcow till
the emperor arrived at Peterfburgh; who finding that his
fon had left his confort in a melancholy fituation, he ordered
the prince without delay to return to his family.

The Ruffians may not marry any one that is related to
them within the fourth generation; thofe of an equal degree
of confanguinity call each other brother and fifter, with the
diftinction of firft, fecond, and fo on, to the fourth degree;
and thofe of a higher or lower degree, are called uncles,
nephews, &c. with the fame diftinction. At their chriften-
ings they commonly have three or four godfathers, with an
equal number of godmothers, who, after that ceremony,
reckon themfelves fo nearly related that they can no more
marry

Ruffian re-
ftrictions of
confangui-
nity in mar-
riage.

marry each other than if they were children of the same
parents.

Ridiculous
cuftom in bu-
rying.

     They have a very ridiculous cuftom at their funerals. Juft
before the coffin is fhut up, the father-confeffor of the deceafed, puts a teftimonial, or pafs, for the other world, in
writing, between the fingers of the corpfe, in thefe words :
" ——We N. N. do certify by thefe prefents, that the bearer
" hereof hath always behaved himfelf and lived among us
" as became a good Chriftian, profeffing the Greek reli-
" gion ; and although he may have committed fome
" fins, he hath confeffed the fame, whereupon he hath re-
" ceived abfolution, and taken the communion for the re-
" miffion of his fins.   That he hath honoured God and his
" faints ; that he hath not neglected his prayers, and hath
" fafted on the hours and days appointed by the church ;
" that he hath always behaved himfelf towards me, who am
" his confeffor, in fuch a manner that I have no reafon
" to complain of him, or to deny him the abfolution of
" his fins.   In witnefs whereof we have given him thefe
" teftimonials, to the end that St. Peter, upon fight of
" them, may not deny him the opening of the gate to
" eternal blifs."

Their images.

     Refpecting their images, they fuffer none that are carved
or graven, either in their churches or houfes, but fuch only
as are painted on wood, in oil colours, by thofe of their
own religion. They never will own to have bought their
faints, but go to the god-market, and, having chofen a
figure they like, depofit the money for the exchange of it ;
if the faint-maker thinks it not fufficient, he fhoves it
back, and the other party is obliged to add more to it, till

                                                  he

he is fatisfied. The walls of their churches are every where full of them : over the porch of their churches, in the market-place, and over the gates of their cities, you are fure to meet with the picture of fome faint or other ; fo that go which way you will, you fee numbers of people croffing themfelves with a moft profound inclination of the head, repeating the *Gofpodi Pomilui,* or, God have mercy upon me. Thefe images they confider fo abfolutely necef-fary, that without them they could not perform their de-votion : they are the chief ornament of their houfes, and whoever enters, firft pays his refpects to the faint, and then to thofe of the family. A Ruffian once coming to me with a meffage, looked round about the room for an image, and feeing none, afked me, Where is thy God ?—— I anfwered, in heaven : upon which he immediately went away without delivering his meffage. I told the general this circumftance, and he directly ordered a faint's picture to be hung up in my room, to prevent giving any farther of-fence of that kind.

All Ruffians, of what degree or condition foever, fleep after dinner ; fo that about noon, the fhops are fhut up, and there is no more fpeaking with any body than if it was at midnight. They bathe frequently : people of quality have their own private ones, and bathe twice a week at leaft ; but the public bathing-places are all built near the fides of the rivers. Their ftoves are clofe places with furnaces, which they heat exceedingly, and for the better raifing of vapour, frequently throw cold water on the ftove : there are benches all round, at fome diftance one above an-other, differing in the degrees of heat, fo that every one

Their baths.

choofes

chooses the temperature that best suits him : upon one of those benches they lay themselves down at full length, quite naked, and having sweated as long as they think proper, they are well washed with warm water, and well rubbed with handfulls of herbs ; after which they take a dram of aqua vitæ, and go their ways. But what is most admirable is, when they find the heat too intense, both men and wo-men will run out of the stove, naked as they are, plunge into the river, and swim about for some time ; if it is in the winter, they will roll in the snow. These public baths are so carelessly built, that it is an easy matter to see the people in the next room through the aperture of the boards which divide them, which, to the women who frequent them, is of no great consequence, as they are not nicely de-licate in being seen naked ; both sexes going out and com-ing in at the same door naked, when they want to cool themselves. These baths are the universal remedies of the Muscovites, whether for cleanliness or health ; and thus ac-customed from their infancy to the extremes of heat and cold, they become both stout and hardy, and in general long-lived, little subject to any distemper : thus they live for the most part without physicians, and many of them without diseases. They begin their day at sun-rising, and end at sun-setting, so that their night begins as soon as the sun is down, and ends when it rises.

Manner of travelling. The manner of travelling in Russia is extremely commo-dious, especially in winter, when their sledges glide away on the surface of the ice or snow, in a flat country, with incredible dispatch, and so very little labour to the horses, that they can easily perform fifty or sixty miles a day. Their

sledges

sledges are made of the bark of the linden-tree, fitted to the size of a man, lined with some thick felt, and when a man is laid along in them, he is wrapped up and quite covered in good furs. The driver for the most part runs by the sledge to keep himself warm, or sits at the feet of the person who travels; the sledges being built very low, should they happen to overturn, there is little danger in the fall. In this mode of travelling, the time is mostly spent in sleeping, the easy, almost imperceptible, motion favouring their repose. When they happen to pass through deserts, or great forests, where they are obliged to remain all night in the open air, they kindle a great fire, round which they range their sledges, so that being well closed on all sides, and well covered up with their furs, they rest more commodiously than in a country cottage, where men and beasts being lodged together in one room, greatly disturb a man's rest. The greatest inconvenience in travelling those parts is the want of inns on the road, which obliges the travellers to carry provisions along with them, and other necessaries they may stand in need of; but those who travel singly commonly go post, when they pay the whole expence of the journey at setting out, and have no more occasion to put their hand in their pocket till they come to the end of it, which is very convenient. The post-boy receives a written order, which he delivers to the next who succeeds him, and so on to the end; and they go day and night, having fresh horses every ten miles, so that the traveller may sleep all the way in his sledge, if he chooses. They commonly travel an hundred and fifty miles in twenty-

P   four

four hours. I have often travelled three stages without
waking.

In the summer they travel either by water, on the rivers,
with which this country abounds ; or by land on horseback,
by coach, or sleeping-waggon ; the roads in Russia being
very broad, beautiful, and easy for travelling. For passing
the rivers they have a kind of floating-bridges made of large
fir-trees, fastened together, which can support a great weight.
But the violent heat of the summer, and the prodigious
quantities of muskitoes and flies, are very troublesome, and
greatly interrupt the pleasure a stranger would otherwise
have in passing through this country from the beauty and
variety of its forests, rivers, and lakes.

No religion in the world could well be conceived to im-
pose a more severe mortification on its professors than the
Russian ; for, if it were not sufficient to have enjoined the
keeping of two constant fast days in the week, as Wednes-
day and Friday, and the eves before holidays, when they
are obliged to abstain so strictly from all kind of flesh, that
they must not taste butter, eggs, or milk, they have four
Lents every year ; the longest of them is seven weeks, the
first of which is called *Butter Week,* and that being their
carnival, they have liberty for all manner of food except
fish. In this week their extravagancies exceed almost all
belief ; and as if this time was allotted for the purpose of
preparing to fast the other six, they employ it in the most
extravagant excess in drinking brandy and melted butter,
which they pour down their throats in such amazing quantities, that one would imagine the least spark of fire would

set

.fet their bodies in a flame; nay, they are very often ob- BOOK III.
liged to quench this inflammation with milk to prevent
their dying on the fpot, which frequently happens. Woe Religious
to the ftranger that meets thefe drunkards at night, unlefs faſts.
he is well guarded, their infolencies being fo great that a
number of perfons are murdered every night ; not to reckon
thofe who being overcharged with liquor, and wanting attendants to carry them home, fall down upon the fnow
and fo are frozen to death.   During this week, it is very
common in a morning, although a fhocking fight, to fee ten
or a dozen dead bodies carried upright in a fledge, frozen to
death ; yet thefe are the daily objects one meets in a morning,
in the ftreets of Mofcow. All the atonement they make for
thefe enormities, when the week is over, is by frequenting the
baths, to wafh away the impurities contracted in their exceffive debauches : they live temperately during the reft of
the Lent, and fome of the more rigid will not even tafte
fifh all that time, but live upon honey, herbs, and pulfe,
and drink only quas, or water.

They celebrate the feaft of Eafter with great ceremony
and rejoicing ; as well in remembrance of the refurrection
of our Saviour, as that it puts an end to the mortification
they endured during Lent.   They now rejoice fifteen days,
feafting together on all manner of good cheer ; and to make
a full amends for their fufferings in Lent, the public houfes
are now continually crouded by all forts of people, women
as well as men, ecclefiaftics and laics; and the ftreets almoft not to be paffed for the multitudes of drunkards at
night.   For thefe fifteen days they have eggs ready dyed
all manner of colours, which they fend or give in prefents

P 2   to

to each other ; and when they meet in this time, they falute with thefe words, *Chriftos wos Chreft* ;—that is, Chrift
is rifen :—to which the other having anfwered, *Woiftin wos
Chreft*,—that is, He is certainly rifen,—they kifs one another ; he that falutes firft is obliged to prefent the other
with an egg ; nobody, of whatever condition or fex, daring
to refufe the egg or kifs : the people of quality have them
covered with gold or filver leaf, or very curioufly painted
both outfide and in.

Moft of their religious feftivals are folemnifed with pro-
ceffions, among which that of Palm Sunday, reprefenting
our Saviour's public entry into Jerufalem, is performed with
great folemnity. Before the patriarchal dignity was laid
afide, the patriarch ufed to ride in the proceffion, mounted
on an afs, the czar leading him by the bridle, from the
caftle to the church called Jerufalem, without the caftle-
gate ; and the patriarch, in acknowledgment of the honour
conferred on him by his majefty in leading his afs, prefented him with a purfe of one hundred rubles.

BOOK

BOOK IV.

*City of Novogorod.—The Sterlit fish.—Marshal Zeremetof's military mis-
takes.—The readiest method to get out of the Russian service.—The city
of Petersburgh.—The czar's usual table.—His entertainments.—His present of boats to different ranks, and its good design.—An ambassador from
Usbeck Tartary.—A naval excursion for his entertainment.—Cronstadt and
Cronelet.—Oranianbaum, Petershoff, and Catharinhoff.—The grand
dutchess born, and the prince's behaviour on the occasion. His disrespect
to the czar.—Naval expedition, in which the czar was rear-admiral.—
His gallant action with Ehrenshield.—He takes Aland.—His triumphal
entry at Petersburg.—Promoted to be vice-admiral.—He compliments Ehrenshield's bravery.—His speech to the senate.—His resentment of the
czarowitz's disrespect.—He institutes frequent social assemblies and a royal
academy.—Court-martial on admiral Kruys.—The order of St. Catherine.—Confusions in the revenue, and the consequent distress.—Many delinquents punished.—Fiscals appointed.—The czar's public entertainments.
—Mr. Slitter's perpetuum mobile.—The old Finlander.—Hard frost at
Petersburgh.—Experiments on bears.—Method of killing them.*

ON the first day of March general Bruce set out from
Moscow, with his family, on his way to Petersburgh;
we past by the town of Twer, over the river Wolga, and
arrived at the city of Novogorod the 10th; it is situated in
a very fair spacious plain upon the Wologda, a river
different from the Wolga. The Wologda derives its source
from the lake Ilmen, about three miles above this city,
from whence it falls into lake Ladoga, and emerging from
thence in the river Neva, near the fortress of Noteburgh,
at last by the gulph of Finland, empties itself into the
Baltic sea. This river is of great advantage to Novogorod,
not only by the plenty of all sorts of most excellent fish

BOOK IV

1714.
City of No-
vogorod.

with

with which it ſtores their market, at a very moderate price, but by being navigable to its very ſource. The ſurrounding country is very fertile, abounding in wheat, flax, hemp, honey, and wax. Ruſſia leather is one of its principal commodities, being ſuppoſed to be dreſſed here to greater perfection than in any other part of Muſcovy ; Novogorod is reputed one of the chief cities in the empire for trade. In former ages, this city was deemed one of the moſt potent in Europe, and was ſo famous that it became proverbial in thoſe parts, *Who can oppoſe God and the great city of Novogorod.* But the czar Ivan Waſilowitz, the great tyrant of Moſcow, having plundered it, laid moſt part of the city in aſhes, and removed all the conſiderable citizens to Niſni, or Lower, Novogorod. The great extent of the ruins of the ancient walls, and the number of ſteeples ſtill remaining, are ſufficient evidence of its former glory, and that its preſent condition bears no proportion to what it was before its deſtruction, being now only ſurrounded by a wooden wall, and the houſes built of the ſame materials. A caſtle ſtands on the other ſide of the river, oppoſite to the city, and joined to it by a bridge ; this caſtle is ſurrounded by a ſtrong ſtone wall, and is the reſidence both ·of the governor and metropolitan. In this city, and oppoſite the caſtle, is a monaſtery dedicated to St. Anthony, of whom they relate moſt ſurpriſing miracles : amongſt the reſt, they ſhew a great mill-ſtone lying againſt the wall of .the convent, upon which they ſay St. Anthony performed his voyage from Rome to this place ; that he came down the Tiber into the Mediterranean, through the ſtreights, over all the ſeas in his way to the Baltick, on this ſtone, and

going

going up the Wologda, at laft fixed his refidence at Novo-gorod; after he came afhore, he agreed with fome fifher-men for the firft draught of their net, which proved to be a large cheft containing the faint's canonical robes, his books, and money; with the money he built this monaftery, where he ended his days, and his body ftill remains uncorrup'ed. Upon my afking the monk, who gave me this information, in what fhip the faint arrived upon this mill-ftone, and how they got up the falls in the lake of Lagoda, he fell into a paffion, and told me I was an unbeliever and no Chriftian, and fo went away without fhewing me the un-corrupted body of his faint.

There are at prefent in this city one hundred and forty-four religious houfes, befides a great number of churches and chapels. Peterfburgh is fupplied from hence with all forts of provifions and neceffaries, conveyed in flat-bottomed veffels, many of which are loft in the falls, or rapids, of the lake Ladoga, by ftriking on the rocks, which lie hid under water, with fuch violence, from the rapidity of the ftream, that they are beat to pieces. The czar, to prevent fuch re-quent loffes, ordered a canal to be cut in a ftrait line from the river Wologda to the river Neva, and 30,000 men are employed every fummer at this work, and an equal number of foldiers and peafants. This canal is near one hundred miles in length, and eighty feet broad; the banks on each fide, raifed by the earth dug out of the canal, are fixty feet broad, and make a road on both fides; the country is plain and level all the way with a fmall northern declination, but full of woods and marfhes. When this work is complet-ed, it will be of unfpeakable advantage to the country, as

the

the communication of Novogorod with Peterſburgh will be both ſhort and ſafe; it will alſo be a great convenience for thoſe who travel that way by land in the ſummer, as they are now obliged to go a great way about to ſhun theſe fens and marſhes. The czar alſo intends, when this is finiſhed, to make a communication between the Wolga and the Wologda, which, in faſt, will be a navigable conveyance from the Caſpian ſea to the Baltic, and conſequently to any port in Europe.

The ſterlit-ſiſh.

Some time ago, ſome veſſels going for Peterſburgh, with live fiſh, called ſterlit, in paſſing the falls of Ladoga, were beat to pieces, by which accident the fiſh regained their liberty, and ſome of them were afterwards taken at Cronſlot, and one catched at Stockholm, which were conſidered very great curioſities, as none of them had ever been ſeen in thoſe ſeas before. They are about eighteen inches long, of a ſhape peculiar to themſelves; their head like that of a pike, but longer, and inſtead of ſcales, they have a ſort of ſhells on their back, not unlike the turtle-ſhell, but have no bones at all in them; and when dreſſed they are the moſt delicious fiſh in the world, being very fat and pleaſant to the taſte; their common price at Peterſburgh is a ducat a-piece. Brigadier le Fort, who was then a priſoner at Stockholm, and ſeeing this fiſh in the market, bought it, and invited prince Dolgorouky and general Weyde, alſo priſoners, to dine with him, and when the fiſh came on the table, they were both much ſurpriſed, knowing it was a native only of the Caſpian, or the Wolga. I never heard if they propagated their ſpecies in theſe ſeas.

General

General Bruce being governor of this province, it detained
him a few days to infpect the affairs relating to his government; and while he ftaid, was entertained by the principal
people of the city: one day, dining with the deputy-governor, the difcourfe turned upon fome miftakes made by
field-marfhal Zeremetof, when the czar firft began to new
model his army after the German difcipline. For the en-
couragement of foreign officers to come into the army, he
had given orders to the marfhal that, if they came well recommended, they fhould be promoted one ftep above the
rank they held in the fervice they had left; at that time
there happened to come a brigadier from the Auftrian fervice, well recommended by the emperor, and defired his
preferment as a major-general, agreeable to the czar's inftructions; the marfhal conceiving that to be a ftep too much,
told the gentleman he ought to be fatisfied with being firft
made a lieutenant-general; and the officer fubmitting to gratify the marfhal, his commiffion was fent to the czar to be
confirmed, and the marfhal claimed a merit in having fatif-
fied the foreigner fo eafily: the czar was much diverted with
the marfhal's miftake, yet he confirmed the commiffion, but
cautioned the marfhal not to make fuch miftakes in future.
Notwithftanding this caution, a little time produced another
miftake; a German captain *des armes*, which is below the
poft of a ferjeant, and whofe bufinefs it is to take care of the
arms belonging to the company, folicited to be employed in
the army; the marfhal, by his German interpreter, afked what
poft he laft ferved in, and was anfwered, Captain *des armes*;
the word *arm*, in the German language, fignifying *poor*;

Q the

the interpreter reported, that he had been *a poor captain* ;
if that be the cafe, faid the marfhal, I'll make him a rich

captain ; and made out a captain's commiffion for him ;
but the czar, inftead of confirming it, made him only enfign, which made the poor captain very happy.

The readieft method to get out of the Ruffi.. u fer-vice.   In thofe times it was much eafier getting into the fervice
than out of it, as was evident in the cafe of major-gene-
ral Gordon, who wanted very much to quit the fervice, and
folicited his difcharge by every application in his power, but
all in vain ; and being in Poland on a feparate command,
aiter the battle of Pultowa, he took that opportunity to fend
to Mofcow for his wife and daughters, and on their arrival
in Poland, he carried them to Dantzig, where he took
fhipping and failed for Scotland.   A fimilar cafe happened,
in my time, to a colonel of dragoons, who, after a long fer-
vitude, folicited, and obtained his difcharge from the fervice
with little difficulty, but found it out of his power to obtain a pafs to get out of the country, being always put off
from time to time with fair promifes, with which they
amufed him fo long, that he was at length obliged to draw
bills on his friends in Germany for money to fubfift on.
The Ruffian policy is, that money faved by the government's fervants, fhould remain in the country, and having
obferved this officer, while in Poland with his regiment,
making confiderable remittances to his friends in Germany,
took care when they had granted his difcharge to detain his
perfon, with a view to bring fome of the money back again.
The colonel finding he was like to ruin himfelf, without hopes
of getting out of the country, applied to fome of the foreign generals for their council, who advifed him immedi-
diately

diately to petition to be employed again in the fervice; which he did, and foon found himfelf once more at the head of a regiment of dragoons; the regiment being ordered into Poland, he there made the beft ufe of his time till he thought himfelf fufficiently reimburfed, then went into Germany, from whence he wrote to prince Menzikoff, excufing him-felf for leaving the fervice in fuch a manner, but he had no alternative, for he was not permitted to do it in a more ho-nourable way; advifing the prince not to detain foreigners in the fervice againft their will, for fuch meafures would only prevent men of abilities and merit from entering at all into their fervice. But all this did not mend the matter; and it would be too tedious to enter into a detail of the dif-ficulties ftrangers have to encounter in endeavouring to get out of this country. We fat out from Novogorod the 25th, and arrived at Peterfburg the 1ft of April. The diftance from Mofcow to Peterfburgh is 541 Englifh miles, or 812 Ruffian werfts.

The nobility, and people of fafhion and fortune, who had removed with their families from Mofcow, found here a fad reverfe in their fituation. Inftead of their fpacious pa-laces and lofty houfes in that city, and their country houfes and villas in its vicinity, where they had every thing in plenty, they found provifions very fcarce and moft conveniences wanting. As this place was agreeable both to the defigns and humour of the czar, he paid little regard to the com-plaints of thofe who confidered their own eafe and luxury more than the advantage of their country. The merchant and fhopkeepers found their account in this new city, where every thing bore an exceffive price.

The city of Peterfburgh.

Q 2

This

This city was now in its infancy, it being yet but barely
ten years fince its firft foundation was laid. When the czar had
made himfelf mafter of Noteburgh and New Schantz, he
went down to the mouth of the river Neva, where it falls into
the Baltic by feveral ftreams forming fo many iflands ; the
fituation pleafed him fo much, that he refolved upon building this city. He found only four fifhermen's huts, to which
he added a houfe for himfelf on an ifland in the.north fide
of the river, and called it Peterfburgh. This houfe was
only a fhelter from the weather and to reft in ; it is a low
hall built of wood, inclofed with a wooden gallery, and
the year 1704, in figures, carved over the door ; but in memory of this great undertaking, it has been preferved ever
fince. Lieutenant-general Robert Bruce, commandant of
the city, has the charge and ufe of this original hall, and
has built a very good houfe adjoining to it for himfelf, which
was one of the firft that made a fhow in this place. The firft
thing that was undertaken was the building two forts ; one
here, and another at Cronflot, to protect the place from infult from the Swedes by fea ; it being naturally guarded
againft any attempt on the land-fide, as the country round
it is almoft one general morafs.

Every body now beheld with furprize and admiration
fuch advances toward a city, in fo fhort a time, as many
thoufand houfes were already built.   In that part called Peterfburgh, ftands a large fquare brick building, with a fpacious court within, for merchants and tradefmen, where
they have their fhops below and ftore-rooms above, and are
fhut up every night, being under the fame regulations with
the grand market-place at Mofcow ; and the merchants all
refide

refide in this part of the town. Here is alfo a large long brick building, which contains the fenate-houfe, all the fupreme courts of the kingdom, chancery-court, court of juftice, the boards of admiralty and ordnance, the war-office, &c. &c. The prefident of every court, or board, is a fenator. The feat of trade, the courts of juftice, all the pub-lick offices, and the grand council of the empire, being combined in fuch a fmall fpace, makes it extremely conve-nient for the difpatch of bufinefs. On another ifland, to the north of this, are the habitations of Afiatic merchants, viz. Armenians, Perfians, Turks, Tartars, Chinefe, and Indians; but no Jew is now allowed to trade, or indeed, live in the Ruffian empire. Oppofite to the fenate-houfe, on a fmall ifland, ftands the fort by itfelf, and being in the center, commands the whole city; the fort is a hexagon, ftrength-ened by ravelines; the ramparts are all cafemated, bomb-proof: it contains houfes and barracks for the officers and foldiers belonging to the garrifon, a large arfenal, ftore-houfes, and magazines; a fine large church, with a very high fteeple, furnifhed with a fet of mufical bells, which play every day from eleven to twelve at noon; in this church is a large vault intended for the fepulchre of the imperial family; the works, and all the interior buildings are of brick, and the only communication with the fort is, by draw-bridges, oppofite the fenate-houfe. Below the fort, on the fame fide of the river, is Wafilio Oftrof (or Ifland), where prince Menzikoff has built a very grand palace, and a number of fine brick houfes for the accommodation of thofe belonging to his court: this ifland is large, and well laid out in gardens and parks, and here the grandeur of the

Imperial

Imperial court is difplayed, and all foreign ambaffadors
and minifters have their audiences; on which occafion, the
czar appears always as a private gentleman; as indeed, he
does every where, attended only by one page and one footman who carries his mathematical inftruments and draughts,
for he is an excellent draughtfman, and underftands all the
branches of the mathematics, and is well verfed in fortification, architecture, fhip-building, and the conftruction
of all kinds of engines. As he is a prince that has a
knowledge of every thing, he is not eafily impofed on by
others. Oppofite Wafilio-Oftrof on the fouth-fide of
the river, is the admiralty and dock-yard for building
fhips and gallies. This ifland being formerly low and
marfhy, was interfected by feveral canals, and the ground
raifed and made commodious for the purpofe it is applied
to; it is inclofed by the river, and like the reft of the
place, has its natural defence from the moraffy confines of
the river. The people employed in fhip-building are all
quartered here, as alfo the officers and failors belonging to
the fleet.

Above the admiralty, ftands the Inoifemfka Slaboda, or
Foreign Town, where all European foreigners live, and
have feveral Proteftant and one Roman Catholic, meet-
ing-houfes: here ftands admiral Apraxin's fine palace.
This ifland was alfo low and marfhy, but was drained and
raifed by digging feveral canals through it. The czar has
both his winter and fummer-palace on this ifland; the former is next the river, and the latter at the eaft, or upper-
end of the ifland, where his yatchs and pleafure-boats are
ranged clofe up before the door; here are exceeding fine
gardens

gardens and a large park, inclofed by a large and deep canal; the gardens are full of water-works, Italian ftatues,
covered walks and arbors. A fine avenue of large trees,
which ftand by the fide of the river, were dug out of the
ground in the winter, with large quantities of frozen earth
fticking to their roots, and brought in that condition and
planted here, and flourifhed to the furprize of all who faw
them. In the park was built a houfe which contains all
forts of mathematical inftruments; alfo the famous globe of
Gothorp, contrived by Tycho Brahe, in which twelve people
can fit round a table and obferve the celeftial conftellations
as it turns on its axis. In the garden was a long gallery,
or hall, where the czar attended every day from eleven to
twelve o'clock at noon, when every body had free accefs, and
he then received petitions from all ranks of his fubjects;
after that hour none were permitted to addrefs him except
upon affairs of confequence. He dined commonly at twelve The czar's
o'clock, and only with his own family; one difh only was uſual table.
ferved up at a time, and to have it hot he dined in a room,
contiguous to the kitchen, from whence the difh is received
through a window from the cook; at one o'clock he lays
down and fleeps an hour; he fpent the afternoon and evening in fome diverfions or other till ten o'clock, when he
went to bed, and got up again at four in the morning,
fummer and winter.

In the holidays, he invented all manner of diverfions, His enter-
and frequently entertained company in his long hall in the tainments,
garden, which being furrounded by water, the guefts come
in their boats, which, as the company difembark, are all
fecured under a guard in the harbour, that no body may

.S give

give him the flip before the company depart altogether, which feldom happened before next morning. Coaches, or

other wheel-carriages, are of little ufe in this city, where the whole is furrounded either with rivers or canals, which having no bridges, every body is obliged to go by water.

His prefent of boats to different ranks, and its good de-fign.

To accommodate this inconveniency, the czar prefented every one of the firft quality with a yacht; a buyer, which is a failing-boat with a large cabin in the middle of her after the Dutch fafhion; a barge of ten or twelve oars, and a wherry of four or two: thofe of the fecond rank, a buyer and a wherry; and to thofe of a lower degree, a wherry only; obliging every one to keep their veffels in repair, and when worn out, to rebuild them at their own expence; this was alfo a political prefent, for one day in the week was appointed for muftering thofe veffels, for failing or rowing, as his majefty's fancy directed, and the proper fig-nal was made by the fort. If they rowed it was on the broad river, in their fmaller veffels, when they made a de-lightful appearance, and the pleafure much heightened by the bands of mufic: moft of the firft quality had bands of their own. If the fignal was made for failing to Cronftadt, then all the yachts and buyers went in three fquadrons: in this expedition, they were taught all the different ma-nœuvres of a fleet of men of war, by fignals, as making or fhortening fail, tacking, forming the line of battle, coming to an anchor, &c. &c. by which the young nobility and gentry became acquainted with the nature of the fervice, and many hands were taught the manual duties of feamen, and fitted for the navy. Eaft from the fummer palace, on a dry rifing ground, ftands the grand arfenal, and foundery

for

for cannon, mortars, &c. and a fine houfe built by the mafter-general; and here alfo refide all the officers, &c. of the ordnance; thofe alfo of the blood-royal live here on account of its fine fituation and air, as it is not fubject to inundations as the other parts; the czarowitz and his confort have their court here; the princefs Natalia his majefty's fifter, the two Imperial dowagers of the czar's Feodor and John, befides a number of noble families; and at the caft end of this place ftands the monaftery of Alexander Newfki, where an archbifhop refides. The great ftir there was at this time in all parts of the city is paft defcription, nothing was to be feen or heard all day long but tradefmen and labourers at work in building fhips and galleys, or houfes either of brick or timber, digging canals and paving ftreets. The river was continually full of large veffels bringing all forts of materials, as bricks, tiles, and ftone for the ftreets. Large floats of timber came daily down the river for building fhips and houfes. Every body being employed in one fhape or other, there was not an idle perfon to be feen.

On the 17th of May an ambaffador arrived here from the cham of the Ufbeck Tartars, who had an audience of the czar the next day. His commiffion confifted of thefe three articles; firft, that the cham rejoiced at his majefty's fuccefs in war, and the increafe of his power, and recommended himfelf to his favour and protection; fecondly, he defired the czar to enjoin his vaffal, the cham of the Calmuck Tartars, to keep good neighbourhood and peace with him, for he feemed inclinable to join with the Tartars, fubject to China, and to ftir up others of his neighbours againft

R   him;

him: for which the cham of Ufbeck offered in acknow-
ledgement, to keep 50,000 foldiers always ready for the
czar's fervice, to march at his command. Thirdly, as a
farther teftimony of the cham's friendfhip, he offered a paffage through his dominions for the annual caravans to China,
and to enter into a treaty of commerce with Ruffia, by
which an incredible advantage was to accrue to his majefty,
as the caravans were then obliged to make their journey to
Peking with great inconvenience, and took a whole year to
travel the whole extent of Siberia, where there was no beaten
road, whereas they might go thither through his mafter's
dominions on a good road in four months. The ambaffador
then laid many filks, and other Chinefe and Perfian goods,
together with curious furs, at the czar's feet, as a prefent
from his mafter; telling him, that he had left fome Perfian
horfes and beafts behind him at Mofcow, and expreffed his
concern that a fine leopard and an ape had died on the road.

A naval ex-
curfion for
his entertain-
ment.
    On this occafion the fignal was made for the yachts and
boyars to attend his majefty to Cronflot; I went with the
mafter-general in his yacht, and arrived at Cronflot in the
evening, where we flept on board at an anchor. The czar
had defired the Tartarian ambaffador to follow him next
day with the great chancellor, count Golofkin, on board a
fnow, and they fet off about noon with feven fenators on
board; the weather was fultry, and they failed with a gentle breeze, till being got about two leagues from Peterfburgh,
by the unfkilfulnefs of the Ruffian captain they got among
the flats, and the veffel got a-ground on a fand and ftuck
faft: the failors wrought till feven in the evening before
they got her off; and about nine, fo violent a ftorm arofe

as

as had not been known in thofe parts for feveral years; about twelve all their boats were beat to pieces, their beft anchor gone, and with it all their hopes, looking for nothing but death. The ambaffador having never been on fuch a fea before, turned pale, and at length wrapping himfelf up in a filk quilt made his prieft fit down on his knees before him, and read fomething out of a book of the prophet Ali, being of the Perfian religion. Towards morning the ftorm began to abate, the veffel was happily towed out of the flats, and as foon as it came to an anchor, his majefty went on board, and congratulated him on his fafe arrival, continuing with him in the cabin above two hours. The ambaffador ordered feveral kinds of fruit of his country to be ferved up, and called for his muficians, vocal and inftrumental, to entertain the emperor. The czar afked the ambaffador feveral queftions relating to his country, efpecially concerning the river Darien, which runs through it, and falls into the Cafpian fea. There is a great deal of gold found in the bed of this river, wafhed down from the mountains, where there are rich gold mines. The czar brought the ambaffador on fhore, and fhewed him his fleet and harbours, at which he was not a little furprifed, as it was the firft of the kind he had ever feen.

We were detained here three days, and I took the opportunity to furvey the ifland of Retufary, which was new to me, and where the czar had begun to build a new town called Cronftadt: the houfes are all built of brick, and large; the lower ftories are calculated for fhops and warehoufes, for the convenience of foreign merchants to trade or fettle here, as they did not approve the method obferved in the grand

Cronftadt and Cronflot,

R 2   market-

market-places of Mofcow and Peterfburgh, in having their
fhops in one part of the town, and living themfelves in another; here the ftreets are broad, and have a canal in the
middle, that goods may be conveyed or removed, at the
eafy charge of water-carriage. There are two fine harbours,
the one for the royal navy, and the other for merchant-men,
the piers being all mounted with cannon. Within gun-
fhot of the harbour, and a mile from Ingria, ftands the
caftle of Cronflot, founded on a fand-bank in the fea: the
foundation was laid in winter upon the ice, with ftrong
wooden caffoons filled with ftone, upon which the fuper-
ftructure was afterwards built of wood filled up with earth;
this caftle is round with three galleries about it, one above
another, and well furnifhed with cannon, and thus the entrance up to Peterfburgh is fufficiently guarded againft every
attempt of an enemy by fea: befides, there is no getting up
againft the ftrong currents without a favourable wind, and
even then it requires a fkilful pilot to bring them through
the fhoals and fand-banks, which yearly alter their fituation.

A fleet of thirty fhips of the line, befides frigates and
yachts, now lay here ready for fea; and the troops which
were encamped in the neighbourhood, were ready to embark on board eighty gallies, and one hundred fcampavies,
or half-gallies: the czar ordered the fhips and gallies out to
fea, where they formed the line, and gave a general falute
with all their guns, which ftruck the Tartarian ambaffador
with furprize and amazement, having never feen the like
before; this done, the fhips came to an anchor again and
the gallies on fhore.

His

His majefty then went to Oranianbaum, a country-houfe
of prince Menzikof's, oppofite to Cronflot, on the fide of
Ingria, where a grand entertainment was prepared by the
prince's directions; from thence he went to Peterfhoff, a
country palace of his own, and thence to Catherinehoff, a
palace of the czarina's, at both which the company were
entertained with royal magnificence.   The emperor now returned to Cronflot to go to fea with the fleet, and the emprefs, with the reft of the company, returned to Peterfburgh.
From Oranianbaum to Peterfburgh the country rifes gently
from the fhore, and abounds with the feats of the grandees,
about half a mile diftant from each other, which affords
a beautiful profpect from the fea.

On the 29th of June, the governor of Wybourg, in Finland, took Nyflot, the capital fortrefs of the province of
Savolaxia, and made the garrifon prifoners of war.

The Imperial princefs, confort to the czarowitz, was
brought to bed of a daughter on the 23d of July, who was
baptized by the name of Natalia, and had the title of grand
duchefs given her.   The czarowitz, at that time, on a pretended indifpofition, had withdrawn himfelf to Carlsbad,
with his Finlandifh miftrefs, but merely to be out of the
way at the delivery of his amiable, but unhappy wife: in
this difagreeable fituation, fhe had only the princefs of Eaft
Friefland, a relation of her own, to comfort her.   The
czar, fenfible of her diftrefs, treated her with the higheft
efteem, allowed her a fplendid court, and fpared no coft to
aggrandize it, and appointed frequent balls and affemblies
at her houfe on purpofe to divert her, and fhe had every
mark of refpect and regard fhewn her by the czarina; indeed,

deed, she had greatly endeared herself to them both by the gentleness of her dispositions, and the sweetness of her temper and manner, but the brutal conduct of her husband embittered all. When the czarowitz returned from Carlsbad, which was in consequence of the emperor's express orders, he not only shewed the utmost disregard to the princess, but maltreated those of her court in such a manner, that they were all going to leave her, which ill usage threw her into a deep melancholy; his father's frequent remonstrances on the subject seemed only to make bad worse, for he accused her of carrying complaints of him to the czar, and told her plainly, if it was not for the fear of his father's anger, he would turn her whole court out of doors, and oblige her to live after the old Ruffian custom. Although they lived in the same house, they were such strangers to each other, that they were never seen to eat or converse together, except when he came to upbraid her with her numerous houshold. This was not the only mortification this amiable princess underwent; none of the grandees paid their court to her, except when ordered by his majesty, out of fear of disobliging the prince, so that the foreign ministers were the only persons that could venture to pay her any respect.

All this bad usage of so good a princess was the more surprising, when it is considered she was his own free choice. The czar had sent him to travel for his improvement, and recommended to him the choice of a princess abroad for his wife; and seeing, in the course of his travels, the princess of Wolfenbuttel, sister to the empress of Germany, he made his addresses to her, and wrote to the czar for his consent,

which

which was readily granted. His majesty arriving soon after
at Torgau, concluded that unhappy marriage.

It was very remarkable, that the prince never appeared at His difrespect
any of the public meetings, when his majesty was attended to the czar.
by all persons of quality and rank, such as birth-days, celebrating of victories, launching of ships, &c. General Bruce,
who lived next door to the prince, had orders always to give
the prince notice the day before, of such public days or
meetings, and I had the honour to carry and deliver the
message; but his highness, to avoid appearing in public,
either took physic, or let blood, always making his excuse,
that he could not attend for want of health; when, at the
same time, it was notoriously known that he got drunk in
very bad company, when he used constantly to condemn all
his father's actions.

Immediately on his majesty's return to Cronflot, he put Naval expe-
out to sea with the fleet, on an information that the Swedish dition, in
which the
fleet, under admiral Watrang, had sailed with an intention czar was
rear-admiral.
to block him up in the harbour; and that their rear admiral, Ehrenshield, had seized on the port of Twerwin, in Finland, where he had sunk several of our ships, and taken about
two hundred prisoners; by which acquisition, they hoped
to be able to repulse any descent on the island of Aland.
Our fleet was commanded by admiral Apraxin, vice-admiral
Kruys, and, as rear-admiral, the czar himself; and sailed
directly in quest of the enemy. The czar was sent to watch
their motions; he soon reported their station, and that their
vice-admiral, Lilie, was detached with several men of war
and bomb-vessels, steering towards Revel; he desired the
admiral to advance with the fleet, and on rejoining them,

it

BOOK IV. it was determined to difpatch vice-admiral Kruys in queſt of
the Swediſh vice-admiral, and to ſend twenty gallies under
the command of general Weyde, and commodore Iſmaie-
witz, to paſs within the enemy's fleet as near the ſhore as
they could go. The gallies performed this ſervice under favour
of a calm ; the enemy endeavoured to prevent them, and
fired many guns at them, but the draught of their large
ſhips did not ſuffer them to come near enough to do any
execution ; on which fifteen more gallies were ſent under
brigadier le Fort.   The Swediſh admiral hereupon made a
ſignal for his vice-admiral to return, which he did, without a ſingle effort made by admiral Kruys to intercept him,
notwithſtanding his ſuperiority ; for this he was directly put
under arreſt, and afterwards tried by a court-martial at Pe-
terſburg.

His gallant action with Ehrenſhield.   The next day our fleet paſſed cloſe by the enemy, and
ſuſtained all their fire, with the loſs only of one galley, which
had the misfortune to run aground, and they blocked up
admiral Ehrenſhield, who refuſing to ſurrender to the czar's
ſummons, by his adjutant-general Jaguzinſki, was vigorouſly
attacked at three in the afternoon by the czar's own diviſion,
now vice-admiral. The action was gallantly fought on both
ſides for two hours, when, notwithſtanding their ſuperiority
in number of guns, the Swedes were boarded and taken,
and Ehrenſhield, having received ſeven wounds in the engagement, delivered himſelf up to our vice-admiral, by
whom he was politely received, and by whoſe expreſs orders
he was moſt carefully attended in the cure of his wounds,
none of which were mortal : the czar had ever afterwards a
very great regard for him.

The

The Swedes left in this engagement one frigate of twenty-four guns, fix large gallies of fourteen guns each, and three demi-gallies of four each, all taken; they loft alfo in this action nine hundred thirty-fix foldiers and failors, of whom five hundred feventy-feven were alive, and made prifoners of war. The lofs on our part was, one colonel, two captains, four lieutenants, one adjutant, one hundred and three foldiers, and eighteen feamen, killed; one brigadier, feven captains, feven lieutenants, one enfign, three hundred and nine foldiers, and fixteen feamen wounded; amounting in the whole to one hundred and twenty-four killed, and three hundred and forty-one wounded. The Swedifh veffels and prifoners were fent to Revel.

After the victory, the fleet failed to the ifland of Aland, where the czar landed 16,000 men, and took the fort and other pofts, intending to tranfport his troops, encamped at Abo, to this place, diftant only twelve leagues from the coaft of Sweden, with a defign to make a defcent at Stockholm; which obliged the Swedes to recall their fleet, under Watrang, to guard their coafts: but it was now too late in the feafon to begin an enterprize of that importance; fo his majefty returned by Revel to Cronflot, where he ftopped a few days, and from thence to Catherinehoff, the 18th of September, where he found the czarina delivered of another princefs, to whom he gave the name of Anne. *He takes Aland.*

On the 20th of September, part of our fleet, with the Swedifh veffels and prifoners being arrived, the czar made a triumphal entry at Peterfburgh, and approaching the admiralty and fort, he was faluted from one hundred and fifty guns. They came up the river in the following order: *His triumphal entry at Peterfburg.*

S 1. Three

1. Three Ruffian gallies.

2. The three Swedifh demi-gallies.

3. The fix Swedifh gallies.

4. The Swedifh frigates, all with the Swedifh colours hanging down.

5. The czar in his galley as rear-admiral.

6. All the reft of our gallies.

When the gallies came oppofite the triumphal arch, which was erected in front of the fenate-houfe and oppofite the fort, they faluted with all their guns, which was returned with the like difcharge from the cannon of the fort and admiralty ; then all the men came a-fhore, and began a proceffion in the following order.

1. A company of the guards, with major-general Galitzin at their head.

2. The cannon that were taken laft winter by prince Galitzin from major-general Arenfelt, near Wafa.

3. Sixty-three colours and ftandards taken in that action.

4. Two hundred Swedifh fubaltern officers, foldiers and feamen.

5. Two companies of the guards.

6. The Swedifh fea-officers.

7. The flag of the Swedifh rear-admiral.

8. The Swedifh rear-admiral Ehrenfhield.

9. The czar, as rear-admiral, followed by the remainder of the regiment of guards.

As foon as his majefty came under the triumphal arch, the grandees, fenators, and foreign minifters, repaired thither to congratulate him on his victory ; but the czarowitz neither appeared in perfon, nor by proxy. The governor of Mofcow, in the name of the empire, complimented his

majefty

majefty on his bravery, and thanked him for his great and
eminent fervices.   The triumphal arch was magnificently
adorned with feveral emblematical reprefentations; and
amongft the reft, the Ruffian eagle feizing an elephant,
alluding to the Swedifh frigate called the Elephant, with this
infcription, *Aquila non capit Mufcas.*

The proceffion proceeded in the fame order to the fort,
where the vice-czar, Romadanoffky, feated on a throne,
and furrounded by the fenate, caufed rear-admiral Peter to
be called before the affembly, and received from his hands
a relation, in writing, of the victory obtained ; which being read, they took it into confideration, and propofed feveral queftions to the rear-admiral ; after which, they unanimoufly declared him vice-admiral of Ruffia, in recompence of his faithful fervices done to his native country ;
which being proclaimed in the affembly, the whole houfe
refounded with, " Health to the vice-admiral !" The czar
having returned them thanks, went on board his floop, where
he hoifted his vice-admiral's flag, having received many
compliments on that occafion.

His majefty, attended by numbers of the nobility and
officers, went to prince Menzikof's palace, where a grand
entertainment was provided ; after dinner, he fhewed particular marks of his attention to rear-admiral Ehrenfhield ;
and, addreffing the company, he faid—" Gentlemen, Here
" you fee a brave and a faithful fervant of his mafter, who
" has made himfelf worthy of the higheft rewards at his
" hands, and who fhall always have my favour while he is
" with me, although he has killed me many a brave man :"
" I forgive you," faid he, turning to the Swede with a fmile,

S 2   " and

" and you may ever depend on my good-will."—Ehrenſhield,
having thanked the czar, anſwered,—" However honour-
" ably I may have acted with regard to my maſter, I did
" but my duty; I ſought death, but did not meet it ; and
" it is no ſmall comfort to me, in my misfortune, to be a
" priſoner of your majeſty's, and to be uſed ſo favourably,
" and with ſo much diſtinction, by ſo great a ſea-officer,
" and now worthily vice-admiral." Mr. Ehrenſhield affirmed, that the Ruſſians had fought like lions, and that nothing but his own experience could have convinced him,
that the czar had made ſo good ſoldiers of his ſubjects ; ſuch
is the effect of ſtrict diſcipline, time, and prudence. The
troops were diſciplined in ſuch a manner, and were brought
to ſuch a degree of reputation, eſpecially the infantry, that
there were no troops in the world they would yield to.

The czar, on this occaſion, addreſſed the following diſcourſe to his ſenators :

His ſpeech
to the ſenate.
    " Brethren, who is the man among you, who, twenty
" years ago, could have conceived the idea of being em-
" ployed with me in ſhip-building here on the Baltic, and
" to ſettle in thoſe countries conquered by our fatigues and
" bravery ? Of living to ſee ſo many brave and victorious
" ſoldiers and ſeamen ſprung from Ruſſian blood ? And to
" ſee our ſons coming home accompliſhed men from foreign
" countries ? Hiſtorians place the ancient ſeat of all ſci-
" ences in Greece ; from whence being expelled by the fa-
" tality of the times, they ſpread into Italy, and afterwards
" diſperſed themſelves all over Europe; but by the per-
" verſeneſs of our anceſtors, they were hindered from pene-
" trating any farther than into Poland ; the Poles, as well

" the Germans, formerly groped in the fame darknefs in
" which wo have hitherto lived, but the indefatigable care
" of their governors at length opened their eyes, and they
" made themfelves mafters of thofe arts, fciences, and fo-
" cial improvements, which formerly Greece boafted of. It
" is now our turn, if you will ferioufly fecond my defigns,
" and add to your obedience voluntary knowledge.   I can
" compare this tranfmigration of the fciences to nothing
" better than the circulation of the blood in the human
" body ; and my mind almoft prognofticates that they will,
" fome time or other, quit their abode in Britain, France,
" and Germany, and come and fettle, for fome centuries,
" among us ; and afterwards, perhaps, return to their ori-
" ginal home in Greece.   In the mean time, I earneftly re-
" commend to your practice the Latin faying, *Ora et la-*
" *bora* (pray and work) ; and in that cafe be perfuaded you
" may happen, even in your own life-times, to put other
" civilized nations to the blufh, and raife the glory of the
" Ruffian name to the higheft pitch."   The fenators heard
this harangue of their monarch with a moft refpectful filence ; and anfwered, that they were all difpofed to obey
his orders and follow his example.   Whether they were fincere in their declaration is another queftion.

The next day a grand entertainment was given at the
vice-czar's, Romadamoffky, where a battalion of the guards,
and a company of grenadiers were ordered to attend. Having
marched through the whole town, they were drawn up before
the vice-czar's palace, and went through their exercife. The
czarowitz being yet only a ferjeant of grenadiers, marched
all the way on the right, with his halbert on his fhoulder,

His refent-
ment of the
czarowitz's
difrefpect.

4.   and

and paffing his own palaçe, the princefs, his confort, looking out with her friend the princefs of Eaft Friezland, and
feeing him march in fo *grand* a manner, fainted away and
was carried to bed. When the exercife was over the officers were all invited to the entertainment, but the men
remained under arms, and the czarowitz ftood upon his
poft till the battalion marched off again.

This mortification was put upon the czarowitz for his
neglect of duty, in not meeting his father at his triumphal
entry, nor wifhing him joy on his fafe arrival : it is certain,
a victory by fea gave him greater joy than any other victory
whatever; fo that a neglect of this kind was worfe taken than
any thing elfe that could have happened. However, when his
majefty heard of the princefs's illnefs, and what had been the
occafion of it, he went to fee her, and told her, that fhe ought
not to be furprifed at the prince's being a ferjeant, for he himfelf had gone through all the loweft degrees both of the land
and fea-fervice, till he had rifen by his merit to be a general in
the army, and now vice-admiral of the navy; and notwithftanding the prince had not attended to his duty as he ought
to have done, yet he had recommended him to the vice-
czar, and procured him an enfign's commiffion in the
guards, and that he was now come to give her joy on her
hufband's preferment. This kind condefcenfion in the czar,
in a great meafure, reftored the princefs's drooping fpirits.

The rejoicings on this occafion continued a confiderable
time, for the grandees gave entertainments in their turns;
but, notwithftanding his majefty's refentment againft the
prince for his former neglect of duty, he never appeared
at any of thofe public meetings, although he had regular

notice

notice sent to him by general Bruce, who sent me several times to inform him of his majesty's displeasure at his non-appearance; but the old excuse—want of health—served on every occasion.

As the czar had the welfare and aggrandizing of his nation very much at heart, he neglected no opportunity to accomplish his subjects. He at this time made a regulation for holding assemblies : he appointed two every week to be held at the houses of the grandees alternately; one room being allotted for conversation, one for cards, and one for dancing; to meet at eight o'clock and end at eleven; the master of the house to provide a side-board of liquors, which should not be presented until called for, and to find cards and music : free admission to be given to all of the rank of gentlemen, foreigners as well as natives, with their wives and daughters. This new regulation extremely pleased the ladies, as it freed them from the severe restraint they laboured under, not being permitted to appear in public company; but by this means they both learned to converse and dress.

He institutes frequent social assemblies.

His majesty also instituted an academy this winter for the education of young gentleman; and was at much pains to provide able masters from abroad for teaching the several sciences. He likewise gave orders to the admiralty to get ready, against the ensuing spring, fifty ships of the line, with a great number of gallies and other vessels, to enable him to make a descent on Sweden next year, and to keep his forces employed, as he had been obliged to withdraw his troops from Germany by the king of Denmark's taking Holstein, and the king of Prussia Pomerania under sequestration;

And a royal academy.

tion; which much displeased the czar, as he wanted, by all means, to have a footing in Germany, and to be admitted a member of that empire; but the emperor, and the rest of the princes of the Germanic body, jealous of his growing power, took this method to get his troops out of their country. The king of Sweden, attended only by colonel During, and two servants, and travelling three hundred German miles in sixteen days, arrived at Stralsund the 22d of November, and directly commenced hostilities against the Prussians, which defeated the whole scheme of the Germanic body, by his not agreeing to the sequestration, brought a new enemy on himself, and afforded a decent pretext for the czar to re-enter Pomerania with his army.

Court martial on admiral Kruys. A court-martial was now appointed to enquire into the conduct of vice-admiral Kruys, for not attacking the Swedish squadron agreeable to his orders; and he was found guilty, and sentenced to be shot for cowardice and neglect of duty. He complained of the severity of his sentence, alledging that no other nation, conversant in naval affairs, would have passed such a sentence for his conduct on that occasion; which being represented to the czar, he transmitted copies of the trial to all the neighbouring maritime powers, especially Holland which was the admiral's native country, for their opinion concerning the sentence; and they all agreed that it was just, and would have been inflicted on any officer, in their respective services, who had been guilty of the like behaviour. This declaration of the maritime powers being shewn to the admiral, he prayed for mercy, which the czar granted with respect to his life, but banished him to Olonetz for the remainder of his days; and having set

out,

out, and travelled one day's journey toward the place of his BOOK IV.
exile, his majesty recalled him, then gave him a free pardon, and appointed him one of the commissioners of the
admiralty, but was never employed at sea again, in which
office he ended his days with credit.

The czar, this year, instituted the order of St. Catharine, The order of
in honour of the czarina, to perpetuate the memory of that St. Cathe-
love and fidelity which she manifested towards him in his
distressed situation, reduced and surrounded by the Turks on
the banks of the Pruth. The ensign of the order is a medal, enriched with precious stones, and adorned with the
image of St. Catherine, with this motto, *For Love and Fidelity :* the medal is pendant to a broad white ribbon, wore
over the right shoulder. The empress had the liberty of
bestowing it on such of her own sex as she thought proper,
and appeared in it herself for the first time at the festival of
St. Andrew this year ; the czarina first conferred the order
on her two daughters, the princess Anne, afterwards married to the duke of Holstein, and the princess Elizabeth, afterwards empress of Russia ; and some time after she be-
stowed it on the emperor's three nieces, the daughters of
czar John, viz. Anne, duchess dowager of Courland, Catherine, duchess of Mecklenburg, and the princess Paskovia ;
and also on the princess Menzikof.

His czarish majesty having, with infinite pains and assi- Confusions in
duity, been searching into the causes of the disorders that the revenue,
had crept into the administration of his affairs ; and, at frequent dif-
length discovered from whence it proceeded that his army trels.
and fleet had been so ill paid and suffered so much, that
many thousand workmen had miserably perished for want of

BOOK IV. fubfiftence (it was computed that upwards of one hundred
thoufand men loft their lives at Peterfburgh) his trade decayed, and his revenues in confufion, took a firm refolution
to remedy thefe evils; and in the beginning of 1715, eftablifhed a grand inquifition under the direction of general
Knex Dolgoruky, to examine certain lords and others, who,
it was faid, had defrauded his majefty of feveral millions.

1715.

Many delin-
quents pu-
nifhed.

Moft of the great men in Ruffia were affected by this
enquiry, and were obliged to give an account of their conduct. The great admiral Apraxin, prince Menzikof, and
Bruce, mafter of the ordnance, alledged for their excufe
their abfence in foreign parts, or in the field on duty, fo
conftantly, that fo far from being able to difcover, or prevent
the ill practices of their officers, they were ignorant of what
was done at that time in their own houfes, which was admitted for their excufe : but their unfaithful officers fuffered
feverely for their infidelity, as did all others who could not
juftify themfelves. Korfakof, vice-governor of Peterfburgh,
Kekin, the prefident ; and Sinawin, the firft commiffioner
of the admiralty; with an incredible number of other officers of the fecond and third rank, were called to an account; Korfakof publicly fuffered the knout ; Apouchin
and Wolchonfky, both fenators, fuffered the fame, and
had red-hot irons drawn over their tongues ; fome of inferior degree were chaftifed with the batoags, and were fent
into Siberia and other remote places, and all their eftates
confifcated. Several delinquents were put to the torture to
make them confefs the truth, as by their law no man can be
condemned, if the matter is ever fo clearly proved againft
him, unlefs he confeffes the fact.

The

The fevereft torture they have is the ftrapado, which is
thus inflicted ; they hang up the malefactor with his hands
tied behind him, with a large beam faftened to his feet,
upon which the executioner every now and then gets up to
expedite the diflocation of his joints, which gives exquifite
torment; a fire is lighted under his feet, the fmoke and
heat of which both ftifles and burns him. If they want
to improve upon this torture they fhave his head, and when
he is hung up as before, they prepare cold water to drop,
from a confiderable fall, on the crown of his head; which
is the moft exquifite torment that can be invented.

This inquifition, which had filled Peterfburgh with fuch
confternation, being ended, things were put on a much
better footing to prevent in future fuch frauds in commif-
faries, and lighten the burthen on the fhoulders of the people; an entire new fet of officers were appointed, called
fifcals, or informers. The fifcal-general was always to at- Fifcals
tend his majefty ; a head, or over-fifcal, was appointed in
the army, navy, and one in every government ; and ordinary
ones were appointed in every regiment, fhip, or garrifon,
and every court in the nation ; whofe bufinefs it was to report every thing they obferved wrong in the fervice or admi-
niftration to the head fifcals, and they to the fifcal-general,
who laid their informations before the czar.

This new fet of men were more feared than the czar
himfelf; fome of them being very litigious, and bringing
people often into trouble without a caufe, whereof we had
afterwards too many inftances, which the czar perceiving
put a ftop to, by inflicting the punifhment on them they intended for others, if they could not prove their informations:

this

this obliged them to behave with more moderation afterwards.
Neverthelefs, thofe againft whom an information was given,
underwent very great hardfhips, being, the moment they
were arrefted, deprived of their falary or pay, to which they
can lay no claim till they have cleared themfelves of the
alledged crime and are reinftated in their office or commiffion ; and if they acquit themfelves ever fo honourably,
they feldom or ever receive their arrears. In cafe of a furlough, none in the fervice were allowed pay till they entered again upon duty. If an officer, a native Ruffian,
was broke by a court-martial for negleft of duty, he was
commonly fentenced to carry arms as a private foldier, and
never arrived at his former rank except his merit raifed him,
and then he loft his feniority. It is to be obferved, that
if this were not the cafe with the Ruffians, the greateft part
of them would endeavour to be reduced to get free from
the army. The diftinftion made between their pay and that
of foreigners, creates no fmall difcontent among them and
very juftly. Officers of equal rank, and in the fame regiment, have three different pays; for inftance, a captain,
who is a foreigner, has eighteen rubles * a month; a captain, of foreign parents, born in Ruffia, has fifteen rubles;
and a native Ruffian has only twelve rubles; and fo through
every rank in the fervice in proportion : this makes them
look on all foreigners with an evil eye.

The czar's
public enter-
tainments.
The czar now gave frequent balls and entertainments at
his own winter and fummer palaces, and not at prince Menzikoff's as formerly ; but finding this inconvenient, ordered
a large houfe to be built mid-way between them, for a

* The value of a ruble is about 4s. fterling. They have befides, forage,
quarters, &c.

general

general Poft-Office, with fpacious rooms above ftairs for
public balls and entertainments; but on grand feftivals,
and extraordinary occafions, the entertainments were given
at the fenate-houfe; between which and the fort was a fpacious open place where they played off the fire-works.
Upon thefe public meetings, a great many tables were covered for all degrees of perfons; one for the czar and the
grandees; one for the clergy, one for the officers of the
army, one for thofe of the navy; one for the merchants,
fhip-builders, foreign fkippers, &c. all in different rooms;
the czarina, and the ladies, had their rooms above ftairs;
all thefe tables were ferved with cold meat, and fweet meats,
wet and dry, interfperfed with fome difhes of hot meat:
thefe entertainments commonly ended with very hard drinking. After dinner, the czar went from one room and table
to another, converfing with every fet according to their different profeffions or employments; efpecially with the mafters of foreign trading veffels, inquiring very particularly
into the feveral branches of their trade. At thefe times, I
have feen the Dutch fkippers treat him with much familiarity, calling him by no other name but *Skipper Peter*,
with which the czar was highly delighted. In the mean time,
he made good ufe of the information he got from them, always marking it down in his pocket-book.

The emperor having engaged one Mr. Slitter, a famous
architect, with a number of good tradefmen in his fervice,
he was lodged in the fummer-palace to be near the czar.
This gentleman had, at this time, a multiplicity of bufinefs
on his hands in building palaces, houfes, academies, manufactories, printing-houfes, &c. and as he had but few hands
for

Mr. Slitter's
perpetuum
mobile.

for drawing his plans, I offered him my affiftance in that way, provided he would inftruct me in the rules of architecture, which he gladly accepted of, and I attended him every day. The czar was frequently with him, and feeing my drawings, was fo much pleafed with them, that I was afterwards much employed in drawing his plans, both of civil and military architecture.

Mr. Slitter was of a weak fickly conftitution, and being much fatigued with continual bufinefs, he fickened and died, when he had been but one year at Peterfburg; he had fpent much time in endeavouring to contrive a perpetuum mobile, the intenfe ftudy of which had much impaired his health, and before he died he had brought it the length of being put in motion; the model of his machine was a circular brafs frame, eighteen inches deep, and two yards diameter, with hollow plates of the fame metal, four inches in length placed round on the infide, into which a cannon ball was put; the plates being moved by fprings, forced the ball in a perpetual round; each of the plates directing feveral wheels which occafioned many different motions; but the fprings and wheels frequently breaking, it took up much time in repairing them. Mr. Slitter always locked himfelf up when he was at work upon it, and nobody was fuffered to enter the room except the czar, who was frequently fhut up with him. After his death, his foreman was employed about it, but he alfo foon after fickened and died, and the machine was locked up; and I never could learn whether any perfon afterwards attempted to bring it to perfection. During my attendance on the architect, I only had twice an opportunity of feeing it.

At

At this time Knez Golitzin, general of our army in Fin-land, fent an old man to Peterfburgh, aged one hundred and twenty years; of a healthy conftitution, had all his fenfes entire, and walked ftrait. The czar took much plea-fure in converfing with him, and offered to keep him at court, where he might end his days in eafe; but the old man begged his majefty to permit him to return to his native place, faying, he had been ufed to hard labour and fpare diet, and if he fhould now alter his way of living, it would very foon cut him off: if he were allowed to live in his former way, he hoped God would add fome few years more to his days; upon which confideration, the czar, having given him a prefent, fent him home again; I heard fix years after this that he was ftill alive.

There was fo fevere a froft here this winter, that numbers of people loft their nofes, ears, fingers, and toes by it; it was very common with people in paffing each other to call out to take care of their nofes, for thofe bit by the froft are not fenfible of it themfelves, when it is eafily perceived by others, on feeing the parts affected white with the froft; the only cure is to rub the part with fnow, till they recover their feeling; it is dangerous in that condition to enter into a ftove, or warm room, as it is commonly attended with the lofs of the part affected. The river Neve was covered with ice the latter end of September, and was paffable in twenty-four hours, occafioned by large fhoals of ice coming down from lake Ladoga; they were cemented by the froft, and as the ftrong current forces one piece above another, it becomes very thick, and fo rugged a furface, that people were em-

5

ployed

ployed in cutting smooth paths every where across the rivers,

from one part of the city to another; it was the first of May before the river broke up again, when the people were warned by the firing of a gun to get off the ice; then it broke very suddenly with a great noise, and in two or three hours time there was no more ice to be seen; some part of it floats down into the sea, but the much greater part sinks to the bottom. Notwithstanding this precaution, great numbers are drowned here every spring, the break is so sudden.

Experiment on the bear.

Having been often told, that the bears are buried all winter under the snow, and have nothing to live on but sucking their paws; as this appeared to me incredible, I procured a cub, and brought him up till he grew very large: I fixed a mast in the ground, with a wheel on the top of it, and put a ring round the mast, with a chain about the bear's neck, placing a large box at the foot of the mast for him to lay in. He used to climb up the mast, and sit upon the wheel, where he played many tricks which were very diverting; I fed him with bread and oats, but never gave him flesh: sometimes he broke his chain, and found his way to some shops where they sold honey, in the neighbourhood of my quarters, where he used to fill his belly with honey, as they did not dare to prevent him for fear. Upon the falling of the snow, in the beginning of winter, he took to his box, where he remained a month without once offering to stir out, nor had any thing to eat, but sucked his paws; I laid bread at the door of his hut, but he would not come out to eat it, yet he ate it when thrown in to him. Toward the

the fpring, a young hog happening to ftroll too near his cell, he got hold of it and pulled it in; but all we could do, we could not fave it from him, and after he had once drawn blood and tafted flefh, he grew fo fierce that he became unmanageable, attacking every body that came near him, fo that I was obliged to kill him; his fkin ferved me for a cover to my faddle. It is remarkable, that when he was beaten, he would put his nofe between his fore-paws, from an inftinctive knowledge of his natural weaknefs, for the leaft ftroke on the nofe kills them.

The Ruffians kill many thoufands of them every winter for their fkins, and only eat their paws, which is efteemed a delicious repaft; they never fhoot them for fear of fpoiling the fkin, but as the bears commonly build their hut at the root of a tree, they mark the tree, and when they are buried in the fnow, the fteam of their breath afcending, makes a hole up through the fnow, by which their den is difcovered; the country people go in a body upon fketzers, to prevent their finking down in the fnow, furround the place, and making a noife, frighten him out of his hut, and as he cannot make his way through the loofe fnow, they are commonly killed by a ftroke on the nofe.

U   BOOK

B O O K   V.

BOOK V.
_____

1715.

Descent on
Sweden.

AS to the operations of this year's campaign, field-marshal count Zeremetof was sent, in the month of March, with 12,000 men, to strengthen the army of the allies in Pomerania, who were to reduce Weismar, the only place the king of Sweden had now left in Germany.

The czar, as soon as the river and sea were clear from the ice, embarked his troops on board the gallies, and went with them to Cronslot, where he joined his fleet, consisting of fifty ships of the line ; he sailed from thence to Revel, where he continued to the end of June, and then sailed to Gothland, and stationed the fleet so as to prevent the Swedes from sending any reinforcements from Stockholm into Pomerania. In the mean time, a body of cavalry were detached

tached from the army in Finland, round the Bothnic gulf, to penetrate the northern provinces of Sweden, which threw that kingdom into great confternation.   About the middle of September, the czar failed from Gothland to the coaft of Sundermania, and landed 15,000 men at Jevel, within a few leagues of the Swedifh army, and having laid wafte all the country round them, he re-embarked with a great booty and failed to Revel, and from thence to Peterfburgh, where he arrived the beginning of October.

On the 22d of that month, the Imperial princefs, confort to the czarowitz, was delivered of a fon, who was baptifed by the name of Peter, and had the title of grand duke conferred on him to the great joy of the czar, but that was foon interrupted by the death of the princefs who brought him into the world, which happened on the ninth day from her delivery, in the twenty-firft year of her age, having been married four years and fix days, to a hufband utterly unworthy of fo virtuous and every way deferving a princefs.   When fhe was convinced of her end approaching, fhe defired to fee the czar, and when he came, fhe took her leave of him in the moft moving language and affecting manner, recommending her two children to his care, and her fervants to his protection ; and having embraced her children, and bedewed them with the tears of maternal affection, fhe delivered them to the czarowitz, who carried them to his own apartments, but never once returned, or made the leaft enquiry after their mother and his amiable confort; indeed, he had never, from the day of their marriage to that of her death, nor on the prefent moving tender fcene, fhewed the fmalleft conjugal regard or concern for

Birth of the emperor's grandfon, Peter, and death of the princefs his mother.

U 2   her,

BOOK V. her, fo that fhe may be faid to have been truly unhappy.

1715. When her phyficians would have perfuaded her to take fome medicine, fhe faid with emotion, " Do not torment " me any more, but let me die in quiet, for I will live no " longer." She expired on the firft of November, and her corpfe, by her own defire, was interred, without being embalmed, in the great church of the fortrefs on the feventh, with all the funeral pomp and honours due to her birth.

Birth of Peter Petrowitz the emperor's fon.

On the day after the princefs's interment, the emprefs was brought to bed of a prince, to the unfpeakable joy of the czar; the rejoicings on that occafion lafted eight days, and he was alfo baptifed by the name of Peter. The folemnities on this occafion were attended with moft extraordinary pomp; as fplendid entertainments, balls, and fireworks : at one of the entertainments, three curious pies were ferved up ; upon opening the firft at the table of the grandees, out ftepped a naked female dwarf, having nothing on but a head-drefs ; fhe made a fpeech to the company, and then the pie was carried away ; at the table of the ladies, a male dwarf was ferved up in the fame manner ; out of the third, at the table of the gentlemen, fprung a covey of twelve partridges, with fuch a fluttering noife, as greatly furprifed the company ; in the evening a noble firework was played off, in honour of the new-born Peter, with feveral curious devices, and on the top of all was this infcription, in large characters :

HOPE WITH PATIENCE.

A carnival. Thefe rejoicings were followed by a kind of carnival ; the czar having united the patriarchal dignity, and the great

revenues

revenues belonging to it to the crown, and to render the
character of the patriarch ridiculous in the eyes of the people, he appointed Sotof, his jefter, now in the eighty-
fourth year of his age, mock-patriarch, who on this occafion was married to a buxom widow of thirty-four, and
the nuptials of this extraordinary couple were celebrated in
mafquerade by about four hundred perfons of both fexes,
every four perfons having their proper drefs and peculiar
mufical inftruments ; the perfons appointed to invite the
company were four of the greateft ftammerers in the kingdom ; the four running footmen were the moft unwieldy
gouty, fat men, that could be found ; the bride-men, ftewards, and waiters were very old men ; and the prieft that
joined them in marriage was upwards of one hundred years
old. The proceffion, which began at the czar's palace,
and croffed the river upon the ice, proceeded to the great
church near the fenate-houfe, was in the following order :
firft, a fledge, with the four footmen ; fecondly, another
with the ftammerers, the bride-men, ftewards, and waiters;
then followed Knez Romadanoffki, the farcical czar, who
reprefented king David in his drefs, but inftead of a harp,
had a lyre, covered with a bear-fkin, to play upon ; and
he being the chief character in the fhow, his fledge was
made in imitation of a throne, and he had king David's
crown upon his head, and four bears, one at each corner,
tied to his fledge, by way of footmen, and one behind ftanding and holding the fledge with his two paws; the bears
being all the while pricked with goads, which made them
roar in a frightful manner ; then the bridegroom and bride,
on an elevated fledge made on purpofe, furrounded with
cupids

cupids holding each a large horn in his hand; on the fore-
part of the fledge was placed by way of coachman, a ram
with very large horns; and behind, was a he-goat by way
of lacquey; behind them followed a number of other fledges,
drawn by different kinds of animals, four to each, as rams,
goats, deer, bulls, bears, dogs, wolves, fwine, and affes;
then came a number of fledges, drawn by fix horfes each,
with the company; the fledges were made long, with a
bench in the middle, ftuffed with hair and covered with
cloth; twenty perfons in one fledge, fitting behind each
other, as on horfeback. The proceffion no fooner began to
move, than all the bells of the city began to ring, and all
the drums of the fort, toward which they were advancing,
began to beat upon the ramparts; the different animals were
forced to make a noife; all the company playing upon, or
rattling their different inftruments, and altogether made fuch
a terrible confufed noife, that it is paft defcription. The
czar, with his three companions, prince Menzikof, and the
counts Apraxin and Bruce, were clad like Friefland boors;
each with a drum. From church the proceffion returned to
the palace, where all the company were entertained till twelve
at night, when the fame proceffion went by the light of
flambeaux to the bride's houfe, to fee the young married
couple fairly bedded..

This carnival lafted ten days, the company going every
day from one houfe to another, at each of which were tables
fpread with all forts of cold meat, and with fuch abundance
of ftrong liquors every where, that there fcarce was a fober
perfon to be found during that time in Peterfburgh. On
the tenth day, the czar gave a grand entertainment at the
                                                          fenate-

fenate-houfe, on the clofe of which, every one of the guefts was prefented with a large glafs with a cover, called the Double-Eagle, containing a large bottle of wine, which every body was obliged to drink; to avoid this I made my efcape, pretending to the officer upon guard, that I was fent on a meffage from the czar, which he believing, let me pafs, and I went to the houfe of a Mr. Kelderman, who had formerly been one of the czar's tutors, and was ftill in great favour with him; Mr. Kelderman followed me very foon, but not before he had drank his double-eagle, and coming into his own houfe, he complained that he was fick with drinking, and fitting down by the table, laid his head on it, and appeared as if fallen afleep; it being a common cuftom with him, his wife and daughters took no notice of it, till after fome time they obferved him neither to move or breathe, and coming clofe up to him found he was ftiff and dead, which threw the family into great confufion. Knowing the efteem in which he ftood with the czar, I went and informed him of the fudden death of Mr. Kelderman. His majefty's concern at the event, brought him immediately to the houfe, where he condoled with the widow for the lofs of her hufband, and ordered an honourable burial for the deceafed at his own expence, and provided an annuity for her life. Thus ended that noify carnival, but it was fome time before the members could fully recover their fenfes.

On the 14th of January, 1716, in the fifty-firft year of her age, died Martha Apraxin, czarina dowager, the widow of czar Feodor, his majefty's eldeft brother; fhe was fifter to the great admiral Apraxin; fhe had only lived

four

four weeks in the matrimonial ſtate; her funeral was by torch-light, and the pomp thereof ſuited to her exalted rank; the corpſe was depoſited in the church of the fortreſs, where already lay one prince, two princeſſes, the czar's children, and the imperial princeſs.

The czar's attention to improve his capital and country.

The czar was all this time indefatigable in the improvements of his country, not only in building ſhips, forts, and houſes, but he provided his new academy with able maſters, to teach all the branches of learning neceſſary for the education of young gentlemen; he alſo erected printinghouſes, well ſupplied with able tranſlators of all languages, who tranſlated all the moſt valuable books then in Europe into the Ruſſian language, his agents abroad buying up the moſt valuable books, and whole libraries at auctions; and it was truly ſurpriſing, to ſee ſuch a grand collection already in Peterſburgh. Here was alſo an elegant chamber of rarities, containing every thing that was curious in all the different parts of the world, and likewiſe a fine collection of coins, medals, &c. &c. over which preſided, as keeper, Mr. Shumacker, a very ingenious and learned man, who had formerly been ſecretary to Dr. Erſkine, his majeſty's chief phyſician. The famous globe of Gothorp, mentioned before in the obſervatory, was a preſent from the king of Denmark, and brought to Peterſburgh at a vaſt expence. The king of Pruſſia preſented the czar with an amber cabinet, reckoned one of the greateſt curioſities in Europe of its kind; there was a curious collection of wild beaſts, birds, &c. one of the largeſt elephants in all Aſia, with all his warlike accoutrements, attended by ſeveral Indians; rein-deer, with their ſledges, and Laplander attendants; the

Vene-

Venetian gondolas, with their gondoliers, &c. &c. all which
shews, that the czar intended, in the courfe of time, to make
Ruffia worthy the obfervation of every traveller.

At Mofcow he erected large manufactories for woollen
and linen cloth, as alfo glafs-works for making window-glafs
and looking-glafs, under the direction of Englifhmen.   The
Ruffians had formerly only ufed ifinglafs for their windows
and coaches ; for at the building of Peterfburgh, they were
obliged to take all their glafs from England.   Although
they fhipped yearly great quantities of hemp to all parts of
Europe, yet they were obliged to bring their fail-cloth and
cordage, manufactured abroad, from their own hemp. To
remedy this evil, the czar erected manufactories for fail-
cloth, and rope-walks at Mofcow, Novogrod, and Peterfburgh ; and that nothing might be wanting for the improvement of his country, fkilful miners were got from
Hungary and Saxony, who difcovered metals of all forts,
gold, filver, copper, lead, and iron ; which laft article they
were obliged formerly to purchafe from Sweden, but they
now fupply other countries with it.

It was furprifing to fee fo many great things undertaken
and put in execution by one fingle perfon, without the affiftance and help of any one ; his own great genius and indefatigable application to things, prefiding over all, and feeing
every thing with his own eyes, without trufting to the reports
of others ; fo that never monarch was lefs impofed on than
himfelf. It is to be obferved, that the natives, from the higheft to
the loweft, if they difcover any thing of value in their grounds,
let it be of what quality it will, keep it a fecret, left their
flaves fhould be employed to work it ; fo all difcoveries of ,

            that

that kind are owing to foreigners : by this means many valuable things remain undiscovered, which otherwise might redound to the riches of this nation.

In the month of February, colonel Swarts arrived here from Casan ; he had been sent thither with a German regiment of twelve hundred men, composed of the Swedish prisoners, and now brought intelligence that he had fallen in with a body of six thousand Cuban Tartars, who had made an irruption into the kingdom of Casan, and were returning home with about eight thousand Russian captives whom they were carrying into slavery ; that he had not only relieved the captives, but defeated the Cubans, and made a great number of them prisoners, among whom was the chan's son, whom he caused to be hanged up immediately, with several of his companions in robbery : for this service the czar made him a present of an estate of an hundred boors.

His military rewards and punishments.

It was an invariable maxim with the czar to reward merit wherever he found it : after a victory by sea or land, every officer was presented with a gold chain and medal, of a value proportioned to his rank, and every soldier a silver one, or a month's pay in lieu of it ; and the officer who had distinguished himself out of the common way had the first promotion : on the other hand, the soldier or officer who had misbehaved, was punished with great severity. The czar took no notice of people on account of their high birth and family, but promoted merit in every station, even in the meanest plebeian, saying, that high birth was only chance, and if not accompanied with merit ought not to be regarded. History scarce affords an example where

so

so many people of low birth have been raised to such digni-ties as in czar Peter's reign, or where so many of the higheft birth and fortune have been levelled to the loweft ranks in life.

On the 6th of February, their majefties fet out for Dantzig, accompanied by the princefs Catherine, fecond daughter of czar Ivan, (or John) and niece to his majefty, and arrived the 29th. On the 19th of April, the princefs was married to Charles Leopold, duke of Mecklenburgh.

I was ordered this winter to difcipline thirty grenadiers, intended for a prefent to the king of Pruffia; they were collected from different parts of the czar's dominions, and were from fix feet fix, to fix feet nine inches high, without fhoes; they were taught the Pruffian exercife, armed in their manner, and clad in their uniform and caps: amongft the number, there was one Indian, who had attended the elephant, one Turk, two Perfians, and three Tartars, and it might probably be faid with propriety, that no prince in the world had a guard compofed of fo many different nations as the king of Pruffia, confidering the prefents of men fent him from all parts of Europe.

Thirty tall grenadiers for the king of Pruffia.

By orders from prince Menzikoff, I fet out on the 25th of March from Peterfburgh, to conduct the thirty grenadiers to Berlin; and as the roads were ftill good for travelling on the fnow, we were furnifhed with horfes and fledges to Riga: we arrived at Narva the 30th, and at Riga the 12th of April, where I refted three days to refrefh the men. Here we faw twelve men broke alive upon the wheel; their crime was as follows:

A man who kept a tavern, or inn, without one of the gates of the city, and had alfo a windmill on his ground,

A horrid murder at Riga.

X 2   —   having

having detected one of his men-fervants in feveral frauds,
turned him away, and retained his wages for fome little
indemnification ; the fellow, at his going away, threatened
his mafter he would make him repent detaining his wages ;
whereupon he went and affociated himfelf with eleven more
as bad as himfelf.   Soon after this they went to the houfe
in the middle of the night, and meeting one of the maid-
fervants going for water, they murdered her, and put her
body under the ice ; they then entered the houfe and fta-
bles, and murdered three other women, and five men-fervants ; at laft, they entered the landlord's apartments, and
murdered his wife and three of his children before his face ;
the fourth, a boy of five years old, had hid himfelf in the
confufion, below a bed unperceived ; they then forced the
landlord to open all his chefts and drawers, and carried away
what was portable and valuable out of the houfe ; they then
tied the landlord neck and heel to the foot of a large table,
at which they fat down and regaled themfelves with the
beft things the houfe afforded : here they concluded putting
hay and ftraw in all the apartments, and then fet the houfe
on fire, that the villain of a landlord, as they called him,
might be burnt alive, and which would alfo confume the
murdered bodies, and prevent any poffibility of difcovery ;
and to make all fure, they brought the fervant maid's body
from under the ice, and laid it down by her living mafter :
after this well-laid plot, they fet the houfe on fire, and fled
with their booty.   The little boy, who was hid under the
bed, was forced from thence by the fmoke, and the father
perceiving the child called to him, and defired him to take
a knife out of his pocket, and cut the cord from off his
hands,

hands, which the child did: the father being thus cleared, BOOK V.
took his little fon in his arms, and made his way through
the flames, and immediately retired into the covered way of   1716.
the town, for fear of being difcovered by any of the villains
who might be ftill lurking near the place.   The houfe and
outhoufes being all in flames, the governor ordered the gates
to be opened, and fent out a party of men to try to fave
what they could from the fire; but before they could get
to the place all was burnt to the ground; fo that the plot
of thofe villains was fo well laid, that if it had not been
owing to the miraculous prefervation of the child and his
father, it might have remained a fecret to this day. The
landlord difcovering himfelf to the officer that was at the
head of the detachment, intreated that he might be privately carried to the governor, to whom he difcovered the
whole of this dreadful fcene, and who gave orders to fecure
and examine all perfons who fhould enter the town that
morning; by which caution the villains, apprehending
themfelves fecure from every poffibility of difcovery, as all
evidence had perifhed in the fire, were, on their entering
the town, every one taken.

The 16th of April I fet out from Riga, and went by Mit-
tau and Polangen, and arrived at Memel the 24th, having
travelled all the way in waggons; from hence I went by
water to Staken, paffing the haff, or bay of Courland,
which is fifteen German miles, and from thence to Konigf-
berg, where I arrived on the 26th; where I was kindly received, and great care was taken of the men, as they were to
be of the king's guards. It being rumoured about the town
that thefe men were of feveral different nations, it brought

I   great

great crouds of people to fee them. We remained here in free quarters to the 2d of May, when I fet off for Elbing, and arrived at Dantzig the 5th, when I found the city fo crouded, that I could not get my men quartered there, and was obliged to march forward to Clofter of Oliva. There were at this time refiding in Dantzig, the czar and czarina, king Auguftus of Poland, and the duke and duchefs of Mecklenburg, with all their numerous retinues; the czar was at prefent gone to Pillau to review forty-five of his gallies, that were arrived there from Peterfburgh, with eight thoufand men on board; I waited, therefore, upon the czarina, who ordered me to ftay at Oliva till his majefty's return, which happened on the 9th; and he came next day with the duke of Mecklenburgh to Oliva, where he reviewed the grenadiers, making them go through their exercife, and was very well pleafed with their performance: his majefty then ordered me to proceed to Berlin, by flow marches, for fear of fatiguing the men.

His contributions on Dantzig.

The Dantzigers did not feem much pleafed either with the czar, or the king of Poland at this time; who had obliged the city not only to renounce all commerce with the Swedes, but to equip four fhips of war to cruife againft them; and alfo to pay the czar one hundred thoufand rixdollars. His majefty fetting out from thence, the 10th, for Mecklenburgh, with all his retinue, was faluted by one hundred and fifty pieces of cannon, to convince him they were in no want of artillery. I fat out with my men the next day, and got to Stolpe the 15th, where I underftood that the czar and the king of Pruffia had held a private conference three days before; in which they had agreed, as I afterwards

wards learnt, not to fuffer the king of Sweden to make any
attempt on the dominions of the Dane; nor to affift the
Danes in any attempt againft the Swedes, who were already
fufficiently reduced; having loft all their foreign provinces,
and had now nothing left but Sweden itfelf.

I cannot here omit mentioning the czar's defigns relative
to the town and fort of Weifmar, which lay very convenient for the duke of Mecklenburgh, being near to Schwerin and Roftock. The czar had promifed the duke to take
that place from the Swedes, and put him in poffeffion of it;
for this purpofe he affembled an army of twenty-fix thoufand
men to befiege it; but the troops of Denmark, Pruffia, and
Hanover, having got poffeffion of it, put each two battalions
of their troops in garrifon, without admitting any of the
Ruffian troops, which entirely fruftrated that defign, to the
no fmall difappointment of the czar. This tranfaction of
the allies he could never digeft, but refented it upon every
occafion, as will be afterwards feen in the intended defcent on Schonen, and other tranfactions. The czar had
it always much at heart to get footing in Germany: firft,
he offered to affift the emperor with twenty-five thoufand
men, at his own expence, againft France, if he fhould be
admitted a member of the Roman empire; but in this he was
difappointed; fecondly, by the marriage of his niece with the
duke of Mecklenburgh, and promifing him Weifmar; intending thereby to get a fafe harbour for his fhipping in thofe parts.
It was afterwards propofed to the duke to exchange Mecklenburgh for an equivalent, which muft have been either
Courland or Livonia. But the princes of the empire having
grown very jealous of the czar's exorbitant power, fruftrated
him in all his views of getting any footing in the empire.
Even

Even the regent of France interefted himfelf fo far as to get the czar's promife to withdraw his forces out of Germany.

On the 16th of May, I fet out from Stolpe, and arrived at Berlin the 27th, with all the men, in good health and high fpirits. I was conducted, by an officer upon guard, to the houfe of field-marfhal count Wartenfleben, to whom I delivered a letter from prince Menzikoff ; the field-marfhal immediately ordered the men into quarters of refrefhment, till the king fhould return from Potfdam, which he did in two days after ; and when his majefty reviewed the men, he declared they were the beft fhaped, and handfomeft men of their fizes, he had ever feen ; and was very much pleafed with them. When I had delivered up my charge, I retired ; and the next day the field-marfhal prefented me with a purfe of two hundred ducats: the diftance between Peterfburgh and Berlin is 1210 Ruffian werfts, or 807 Englifh miles.

As many of my relations refided in and about Berlin, from whom I had now been abfent ten years, I paffed three months very agreeably among them : they endeavoured to perfuade me to leave the Ruffian, and return to the Pruffian fervice, from an opinion that it might eafily be obtained at prefent, as I had juft brought his majefty the moft defireable prefent he could receive ; and my friends confulted field-marfhal Wartenfleben and general Gerodorf about it, who were both of opinion, that it might be eafily accomplifhed at prefent, if I could obtain my difcharge from the Ruffian fervice. While my relations were ufing all their intereft to get this change brought about, an exprefs was brought me from field-marfhal count Zeremetof, with orders to join him immediately at Rof- tock, in Mecklenburg, and to attend him as aid-de-camp to

Denmark,

Denmark, as he had none at that time that could fpeak the language. Upon which I fet out immediately from Berlin, and I arrived at Roftock the 24th of Auguft; the marfhal fet out next day for Warnemunde, where we found our troops embarking.

His majefty the czar had held a long conference with the king of Denmark at Ham and Horn, near Hamburgh, which lafted from the 28th of May to the 4th of June; in which a defcent upon Schonen was agreed upon and concerted. On the 5th of June, the czar fet out for Pyrmont, to drink the waters; and returned the 30th to Schwerin, the refidence of the duke of Mecklenburgh. The 4th of July, he went to Roftock and Warnemunde, where the forty-five gallies were arrived from Dantzig, with eight thoufand troops on board, with which he then fet fail for Denmark, and was met at Proveftein by his Danifh majefty, who went on board the czar's galley, and they arrived together at Copenhagen the 17th.

Conference with the king of Denmark, and arrival at Copenhagen.

On the 28th of Auguft, marfhal Zeremetoff fet fail from Warnemunde with ten thoufand men, and arrived at Copenhagen the 29th. The marfhal going afhore to the houfe fitted up for him in the city, the cuftom-houfe officers came on board to fearch his baggage, but were prevented by the officer then upon guard; upon which they ftopped the fhip from entering the harbour, and I was fent to the cuftom-houfe to know why the fhip, with the marfhal's baggage, was hindered from entering into the harbour? There they told me it was to fearch for merchandize; I replied, it was not cuftomary for Ruffian generals to turn merchants, and affured them there was no merchandize at all on board the

Y   fhip;

fhip; and that the marfhal would certainly refent fuch in-jurious treatment: upon this an order was fent to bring the fhip into the harbour, and upon landing the baggage, the cuftom-houfe officers had a watchful eye on every thing that was brought on fhore. The next day, a gentleman was fent from court to the marfhal, to apologife for the inde-cent behaviour of the cuftom-houfe, and to affure him the officers concerned in that rudenefs were all fined and turned out of their places.

The combined fleets.

At this time admiral Norris, and rear admiral Graves, lay before Copenhagen with an Englifh and Dutch fqua-dron, to whom the czar now propofed to join the Ruffian and Danifh fleets, and drive the Swedes into port; which was agreed to, and the czar to command the combined fleet, with admiral Norris to command the van, the czar the centre, and the Danifh vice-admiral the rear divifions; and admiral Graves was to convoy the trade of both na-tions to their refpective harbours. The czar accordingly hoifted his imperial flag, and weighed with the fleet; but paffing by Bornholm, they were informed that the Swedifh fleet were gone to Carlfcroon; upon this the combined fleet feparated; the czar went to Stralfund, embarked his troops that were quartered there, and carried them to Co-penhagen.

The Danes alarmed.

By this augmentation, our army confifted of 24,000 men, all encamped very near the capital, which roufed the jealoufy and alarmed the fears of the Danes fo much, that they drew their forces together from all parts of Zealand to Copenhagen; great part of which were encamped upon the ramparts all round it, and they placed a ftrong guard at every gate,

gate, with ſtrict orders not to ſuffer above one hundred Ruſſians to enter the city at once to get water, as there was none elſewhere to be got. This water was brought from the king's park, a conſiderable diſtance, into the city through pipes : but one hundred men being found inſufficient to carry water for ſuch an army, they permitted fifty more to enter at a time, one party being ready to enter as ſoon as the other came out ; but as they were often hindered from ſupplying themſelves by the Daniſh ſoldiers, who thought themſelves entitled to be firſt ſerved, this occaſioned great diſorders ; at laſt, it came to blows, and ſeveral were killed and wounded on both ſides : the Ruſſians finding the guard too partial to their own people, ſeized, diſarmed, and drove them off. After they arrived at the camp, they began to dig for water every where, and happening upon one of the pipes that conveyed the water into the city, they cut it, by which they were afterwards very well ſupplied : but being ill ſupplied with fire-wood for dreſſing their victuals, they began to cut down the trees in the park, and had cut down a great number before a ſtop could be put to it by their officers ; ſeveral of the ring-leaders were ſeverely puniſhed for it.

The Danes had agreed to ſerve us with proviſions only for the 16,000 men the czar ſtipulated to bring to their aſſiſtance, and now refuſed ſubſiſtence for the 8000 brought from Stralſund, alledging they came without their conſent or knowledge : ſo that from henceforth there was nothing but jealouſy and miſtruſt on both ſides, which, however, did not interrupt the court diverſions of balls, aſſemblies, and maſquerades. During the three months the czar was

Refuſe ſubſiſtence to th troops.

BOOK V. at Copenhagen, he attentively vifited their colleges and academies, and faw every thing that was curious in the place;

1716. he went alfo almoft every day out in a boat, founding and
furveying the coafts both of Denmark and Sweden fo exactly,
that the leaft bank of fand did not efcape his obfervation;
and he laid down the whole in a chart. One day when
he was coafting Schonen, to difcover a proper landing-place,
on his return he met with a frefh contrary gale of wind,
which prevented his reaching Copenhagen with day-light;
the czarina fent to the governor to defire the gate might be
left open till the czar's arrival, which he promifed to do;
and upon my being fent by the marfhal to fee if this was
complied with, I found it fhut; and was told by the officer of the guard that the keys were fent to the king. I reported this to the marfhal, who went himfelf to the governor, who, after fome frivolous apology, that the keys had
been fent by miftake to the king, told him, now that his
majefty was at reft, he durft not difturb him.   It was one
o'clock in the morning before the czar could make the land,
and not being able to make the harbour, or get the boat
near the fhore, he jumped out up to the neck in water,
waded afhore, and walked in his wet clothes all the way
up to the gates, which finding fhut, he returned to the
fuburbs, went into the lodging of an officer of his own
guards, where he fhifted himfelf with the officer's linen and
clothes, and refted the remaining part of the night : in the
morning he dreffed in the officer's regimentals, and although
they were much too fhort for him, yet he walked up the
city in them, where he was met by the czarina, the marfhal, and feveral others.   Many were the apologies for the

miftakes

BOOK V.

1716.

miftakes and blunders committed, and both the governor and colonel of the guard were put under arreft; but the czar laughed at it, and interceded for them, faying, they had only done their duty; and they were accordingly re-leafed.

A few days after this the two crowned heads met, and held a council of war, attended only by their prime minifters and field-marfhals, thereby to keep the meafures they were to take a profound fecret: it was refolved at this meeting to make a defcent on Schonen without lofs of time. Not-withftanding the method taken to keep this intended expe-dition a fecret, it was immediately known all over the city, infomuch, that I heard every ftep that was to be taken from a Danifh officer in a public coffee-houfe. When I informed the marfhal thereof, he was very much furprifed; and the czar, with the prime minifter, coming at the time to dine with him, he repeated what I had heard in the town, where-with the czar feemed very much diffatisfied.

A conference with the king of Denmark, with its con-fequences.

The troops, however, were all in motion getting ready to embark, and a demand was made for one month's pro-vifion for the army; to which we were told, there was no occafion for any, as there had been a plentiful harveft at Schonen, where we would meet with every thing we ftood in need of; and befides, as there was an open communi-cation with Copenhagen, we could be fupplied from thence as we had occafion. The czar not relifhing this, told the king it was now too late in the year to attempt fuch an en-terprize, as nothing was provided beforehand, and therefore it ought to be laid afide till next fpring; but if his majefty was refolved to venture on the defcent this feafon, the czar,

agree-

agreeable to the treaty made at Stralfund, would affift him with the fifteen battalions therein ftipulated. The king then defired the affiftance of thirteen more battalions, which the czar refufed, faying, that he had occafion for his troops elfewhere. To this the king returned, that fince matters ftood thus, he defired none of his troops, and wifhed that they might all fpeedily be withdrawn from his dominions, that the tranfports which coft him 40,000 rixdollars a month might be difcharged: accordingly, all our troops embarked on the 19th of September, and we lay near a month wind-bound before Copenhagen, and became fo diftreffed for fire-wood, which was not to be procured at any price, that the czar ordered ten of his gallies to be cut up for that pur-pofe, and diftributed among the fleet.

The ftory of lieutenant-general Bohn.

While we were at Copenhagen, a circumftance happened to a lieutenant-general of our fervice, whofe name was Bohn, which I cannot omit mentioning. He was born on the ifland of Bornholm, where his father had been a minif-ter; his mother was left a very poor widow, and now hear-ing that her fon was at Copenhagen, a general in the Ruf-fian fervice, fhe came to fee him, and calling at his lodgings, was told by his fervants that he was not at home: fhe de-fired the fervants to tell their mafter that fhe was his mo-ther, and was come from Bornholm on purpofe to fee him, and would call again next morning. Upon this informa-tion, the general flew into a great paffion, faying, his mo-ther had been dead many years ago, and that this muft be fome needy perfon or other, or perhaps, out of her mind; and ordered his aid-de-camp, if fhe called again, to give her ten ducats, and fend her away, that he might not be

9   farther

farther troubled with her. The mother calling next morning, the aid-de-camp did as he was directed, and offered
her the ten ducats as his master's charity; she threw them
with disdain upon the ground, and said, with tears in her
eyes, she did not come to beg charity, but to see her son;
and since he could both deny and despise his mother, she
would return from whence she came, and trouble him no
more. This made so great a noise all over the town, that
it came to the czarina's ears: she sent for the woman, who
soon satisfied the empress that she was the general's mother;
he was sent for, and received a reprimand for his unnatural
behaviour, and was ordered to settle two hundred rubles a
year on his mother for her life, which was complied with;
and he was, in the mean time, twitted with general Baur's
generous behaviour to his poor relations, who was not
ashamed of them, though of a lower degree than his. This
reprimand put the general into great confusion, and he was
afterwards very much disregarded.

We weighed from Copenhagen early in the morning of
the 12th of October, with a fresh breeze at North, and arrived the next day at Warnemunde, in Mecklenburgh; the
whole army disembarked the same day and encamped.
Two days after our departure from Copenhagen, the czar
had a grand entertainment from the Danish monarch, and
having taken leave of that court, sat out next day, with
the empress, in his way to Hamburgh, and having passed the
Belt, and taken a view of Toningen and Frederickstadt,
proceeded for Lubeck and Schwerin.

Field-marshal count Zeremetof was now ordered to march
with 12,000 men through Pomerania into Poland; and
12,000

Oppressive
scheme of the
duke of
Mecklen-
burgh.

BOOK V. 12,000 men were quartered in Mecklenburgh, under the
command of general Weyde, at the duke's own defire, as
1716. a means to diftrefs and humble the nobility of his country,
who were at law with him at the Imperial court to fupport their rights.   When the marfhal was fent into Poland,
with part of the army, I was ordered, on account of the
language, to remain with general Weyde as his aid-de-
camp, at his own requeft : we were quartered at Guftrow,
and the army upon the eftates of the nobility, by an order
from the duke himfelf, who laid them under moft oppreffive contributions, which utterly ruined them : they had recourfe to the Imperial court, and the diet of the empire, for
redrefs of their grievances, who did all they could to perfuade the czar to withdraw his troops out of Germany;
but the czar was now gone from Schwerin to Havel-
berg, where he had a private interview, for two days together, with the king of Pruffia, and then went to Ham-
burg, and from thence to Amfterdam, where he arrived the
6th of December, and waited for the arrival of the emprefs,
who, when fhe was preparing to fet out from Wefel, was
1717. delivered of a prince, the 2d of January, 1717; but the child
died the day it was born, fo that it was the 10th of February
before fhe arrived at Amfterdam; and their majefties went
to the Hague the 9th of March, where they continued till
the 4th of April.

A report was fpread that the circular troops of the empire were forming an army upon Grander Heyde, near Hamburgh, with an intention to diflodge our troops in Mecklenburgh; upon which our army took the field, and encamped at Gadebufh, under the command of lieutenant-

8   general

general Lacy, major-general Slippenbach, and bregadier-general Le Fort; general Weyde was then indifpofed at Guftrow, and fent me to Grander Heyde to learn what number of troops were encamped there; when I came I could neither fee nor hear of any troops being affembled at that place: I then proceeded to our refident in Hamburgh, to obtain intelligence, but inftead of hearing of any circular troops forming againft us, it was currently reported there, that the Ruffian army were going to make an irruption into the electorate of Hanover; which falfe report fo much alarmed the Hanoverians, that many of the people of property moved off their effects, to fecure them in Hamburgh, and other places of fafety: all this being occafioned by our forming a camp at Gadebufh, fo that we were alarmed on both fides without the fmalleft foundation. Upon my return to Guftrow, and reporting what had paft, I was immediately difpatched to our camp, with orders for our army to break up and return to their quarters. This falfe alarm being over foon fettled people's minds again; but the poor fubjects of Mecklenburgh, were daily more and more haraffed by our troops, at the defpotic commands of their unrelenting prince, which occafioned many petitions from the ladies of the nobility and gentry, to the duchefs, to commiferate their deplorable fituation, and intercede for their relief. She really pitied their miferable condition, but could not prevail with the duke to fhew them the fmalleft favour; on which fhe determined to fend an exprefs to the czar, to plead in behalf of the diftreffed people, and to lay before him feveral grievances of her own: but as fhe could fend none of her own domeftics without the duke's knowlege, fhe therefore fent

· Z   Mr.

Mr. Beſtuzof, then gentleman of her bed-chamber (after-terwards great chancellor of Ruſſia), to general Weyde, de-firing the general to fend an expreſs, in his own name, to the czar: upon this the general fent me with Mr. Beſtuzof to Schwerin, to receive the duchefs's commands, and to get into the duchefs's apartment unknown to the duke, who was of a very fufpicious temper. We went by a back door through the garden, and on entering the houfe, he was the firſt perfon we met, which put us into fome .confufion ; we made him a low bow, and paſt without his fpeaking a word, or taking any notice of us ; but inſtead of going directly to the duchefs as we had propofed, Mr. Beſtuzof conducted me to his own apartments, where I remained till it was dark, when I was introduced to the duchefs who gave me my in-ſtructions, with which I returned the fame night to Guf-trow. The general having by this time prepared his dif-patches, I fet out next day on my way to Holland, and ar-rived at Amſterdam the 8th of May ; but the czar being gone from thence to Paris, I waited upon the czarina, who or-dered me to follow his majeſty ; and having received her packet, I fet out the next day and got to Paris the 13th, fix days after his majeſty's arrival. The reception and honours paid the czar at Paris are fo well known, that it would be tedious to repeat them ; I fhall only therefore juſt mention that it was now the duke of Orleans (regent of France) ob-tained a promife from him to withdraw his troops from the German dominions.

Having received his majeſty's difpatches for Amſterdam, on the 3d of June, I fet out and arrived there the 9th ; and receiving her majeſty's commands, I fet out thence the

3　　　　　　　　　　next

next day and got to Schwerin the 16th, where I delivered both their majesty's difpatches into the duchefs's own hands. The contents of what I brought were fo very acceptable, that I met with a very gracious reception, and had a handfome prefent made me ; and, to prevent difcovery, I left Schwerin privately in the night time, and fet off for Guftrow. The czar's difpatch to general Weyde, brought him orders to levy no more contributions on the inhabitants of that country.

The duke was fo much diffatisfied with this new order, that he employed his own troops to exact contributions from them, with greater rigour than ever, which reduced his nobility to the neceffity of felling their plate and jewels, and at laft their equipages and furniture, and became fo entirely ruined, that they were obliged to fly their country; and their boors for the moft part, went into the Pruffian territories, where they offered themfelves, with their wives and children, for vaffals or flaves. At the defire of fome of my friends, I engaged a number of thefe poor families for their behoof, and that with the confent of their late owners who told me that they had no farther ufe for them, being reduced to fo low a ftate that they were left without the means to cultivate and fow their lands for want of cattle and feed ; fo that their mifery and calamity were paft defcription, which made the princes of the empire intereft themfelves earneftly in their behalf, in an application to the czar to withdraw his troops from thence, which was foon after complied with, and the affair at laft ended in the utter ruin of the duke himfelf, for his country was put under

The diftrefs of his people.

Z 2

fequef-

sequeſtration, and he was obliged to live ſeveral years an
exile at Dantzig.

. When we ſet out on our expedition to Denmark, the
czarowits had his fathers's expreſs orders to attend him;
he rather choſe to abſent himſelf than obey, and abſconded
without the knowlege of any body : meſſengers were ſent
all over Europe in queſt of him, and he was at length difcovered at Naples, by captain Romantzof of the guards. The
captain acquainted count Tolſtoi, our ambaſſador at Vienna,
with the diſcovery, and the count went to him at Naples,
and perſuaded and prevailed with him to return to Moſcow,
and ſubmit himſelf to his father's clemency, aſſuring him
that no prince in Europe would riſque the czar's reſentment
by protecting him.

The captain
refuſed leave
to quit the
Ruſſian ſer-
vice. My friends at Berlin had by this time procured me a
company in general Gerodorf's regiment of the Pruſſian army,
if I could procure my diſcharge from the Ruſſian ſervice;
and as I had a company in their artillery under general
Bruce, and was aid-de-camp to general Weyde, I applied
to them both, and to prince Menzikof for my diſcharge,
but could by no means obtain it ; ſo I was obliged to continue in the Muſcovite ſervice, very much againſt my inclination, nor could I think of quitting it without my difcharge, knowing I could not be admitted into the Pruſſian.
ſervice without it.

The latter end of June, we received orders from the czar
to march out of Mecklenburgh, after nine months free
quarters, leaving four battalions there for the duke's ſervice,
at his deſire ; and we began to march the firſt of July. By
thoſe

thofe and 4000 of his own troops, he thought to prevent the circular troops from entering his territories. Our army were no fooner gone, than he got intelligence that a body of Hanoverians were on their march to enter into his territories, upon which he ordered general Schwerin, with his own and the Ruffian troops, to fecure the pafs which was at a mill-dam, by which the Hanoverians were to enter; there the Duke's forces entrenched themfelves with feveral pieces of cannon. The Hanoverians advancing, endeavoured to force their way, and a very bloody rencontre enfued, in which a number were killed and wounded on both fides, and the Hanoverians obliged to retire : but upon a complaint being made to the czar, that his troops had been the aggreffors, he ordered them to leave Mecklenburgh and join our army; the duke's troops foon followed and were retained in the czar's fervice, and the duke himfelf retired to Dantzig.

On the 13th of July, our army affembled at new Brandenburg, and we marched through Stettin and Landfberg, to Polifh Schwerin, where we arrived the 25th ; and as we were now in the dominions of Poland, we refted till the 7th of Auguft, and then marched by Friedland to Tuchol the 1ft of September, where we were to remain till farther orders.

The czar left Paris the 21th of July, and travelled by the way of Soiffons, Charleville, Namur, Huy, and Liege, taking a minute view of all the fortifications in his way, but more particularly at Namur, where the governor fhewed his majefty a moft refpectful attention during his ftay ; he arrived at Spa the 28th, where he ftopt to drink the waters, and went the 2d of Auguft for Amfterdam, in which city the

The czar's return from Paris.

the czarina had impatiently waited his return.　After a month's ftay at Amfterdam, in which time he had feveral private conferences with baron Gortz, minifter to the duke of Holftein, at Loo, (a palace belonging to the prince of Orange), the czar fet out the 2d of September on his way to Berlin, and arrived there the 19th; and the czarina in three days after, being met at fome diftance from the city by the queen of Pruffia, and the margravine of Branden-burgh, who conducted her into Berlin; where the duke and duchefs of Mecklenburgh came to pay them a vifit.

The return of his army to Peterfburgh.

Their majefties continued here but three days, and then took the route for Dantzig, where they arrived the 15th of September, and where general Weyde waited on the czar to receive his commands.　His majefty fet out on his jour-ney for Peterfburgh, and we returned to Tuchol the firft of October.　Mr. Gruzinfky, a commiffary appointed by the king of Poland, attended us through Poland, till we arrived in the Ruffian territories.　We began our march on the 2d of October, by Warfaw, Wilda, (the capital of Li-thuania), Riga, and Narva, paffing many rivers in our way, fuch as the Viftula, or Weixel twice, twice over the Weper; and over the Zaas, Memel, Wilda, Swenta, Dwina, and Narva; as we were in no hurry, refting in good quarters, four days in every week, and plentifully fupplied with pro-vifions, we fpent feven months moft agreeably on this march, and arrived at Peterfburgh the 19th of February; the di-ftance from Guftrow, our head quarters in Mecklenburgh, to Peterfburgh, is 1,959 Ruffian werfts, or 1,306 Englifh miles.　The Polifh commiffary, Gruzinfky, was handfomely rewarded, by the czar, for providing fo plentifully for the troops.

The czar having arrived at Peterſburgh on the 21ſt of Oĉtober, after an abſence of ſixteen months, a multiplicity of affairs of great importance waited his return. Great charges were exhibited againſt thoſe who had been entruſted with the reins of government in his abſence : in order to examine into the accuſation againſt the parties concerned he attended the ſenate every morning at four o'clock ; but finding it would require much time to judge thoſe who were accuſed, he erected an extraordinary court of juſtice, to enquire into theſe matters. Wolchonſky, the governor of Archangel, and many others being capitally convicted, ſuffered death ; many more were knouted and ſent into baniſhment.

Various attempts had been made by the czar's orders and directions, with ſhips from Archangel, to diſcover a north paſſage to the Eaſt Indies ; but that was found impracticable, by reaſon of the many large ſhoals of ice, like iſlands, floating upon thoſe ſeas. Before the czar ſet out for Germany, he ſent a gentleman who underſtood the mathematics, as his envoy, with preſents to ſeveral of the northern Tartar princes, to diſcover if there was a continuation of the ſea to China, by the north of Tartary. This gentleman being returned, reported that he met a very friendly reception, and great civility from many of the Tartarian princes, who eſcorted him for his ſafety from one to another, till he came within the 70th degree of north latitude, to a province called Iakuti, on the river Lena, which empties itſelf into the Frozen Sea at 80 degrees, near an iſland called Tazata, the prince of that country would neither accept his preſents, nor ſuffer him to proceed down the river;

but:

but threatened if he did not return from whence he came,
he would give orders to cut him and his men to pieces; this

put an end to his farther progrefs and difcoveries, and he
was obl'ged to return. He made a very accurate map of the
feveral Tartar kingdoms through which he paffed, with a
particular defcription of the countries and the inhabitants,
much more than was before known of thofe wild parts;
which map, &c. he prefented to the czar. Hé reported,
that they were all vagabond Tartars, living in tents, and
fnifting their refidence from place to place for pafturage,
as all their riches confifted in herds of cattle; but he obferved a fort of houfes, or huts, on the fides of rivers, and
fome corn, and in thefe fituations their chams generally
refided. But while the northern Tartars remain fo favage,
it will be impoffible to make a full difcovery of thofe parts.

The fatal ex-   About this time his majefty received a very difagreeable
pedition of
prince Becke- account of the iffue of an attempt that was made on the
witz.   eaft fide of the Cafpian fea, towards Ufbeck Tartary. The
czar having been informed, that great quantities of gold
fand came down the river Daria, he fent prince Alexander
Beckewitz, at the head of 3000 men, to land at the mouth
of that river, and build a fort there; and then to proceed
farther up the country to difcover the mines from which this
gold fand came; the prince accordingly built a fort without
the fmalleft oppofition, although the Ufbeck Tartars were
upon the very fpot; but, inftead of hindering, they gave
him every affiftance in their power, providing the troops
with all kinds of provifions, and maintained a moft friendly
intercourfe with each other. The fort being finifhed, the
prince wanted to proceed up the river to difcover the mines,
which

which the Tartars obferving, told him, if he propofed to
follow the courfe of the river, he would find it unfurmount-
able, by its many turnings and windings; and if he wanted
only to come to the mines, there was a much nearer way
by land, which they could march in three days, and that
they were ready to conduct them. The prince, trufting
to their feeming friendfhip, and having no reafon to fear
their inconfiderable number, left a captain with 200 men
to garrifon the fort and fecure the fhips; fet out through a
defert with his Tartarian guides, and having marched feven
days, inftead of three, they were in the utmoft diftrefs for
water; and, at length, after abundance of fatigue, they arrived at the mines, but found there, before them, the cham
of Ufbeck with 50,000 of his Tartars, who now, with every
appearance of friendfhip, offered prince Beckewitz all the
affiftance in his power; affuring him, fince he underftood
that the prince was to erect a fort there, he would give orders to his people to provide materials for the building; and
offered to canton the army in the kibbits, or tents, with
his own men, as they had fuffered fo much on their march
through the defert for want of water, and might now
be diftreffed for provifions, with which he alfo offered to
fupply them till they could be otherways provided: the cham
all the while entertaining the prince, and all his officers,
with fo much feeming friendly familiarity, that they thought
themfelves extremely happy. When the prince propofed
cantoning the men among the Tartars, all his officers to a
man protefted againft it, alledging, the Tartars ought not
to be trufted; for fo long as they kept themfelves together
in a body, they had nothing to fear from the Tartars, not-

A a   withftanding

withſtanding their numbers ; but as ſoon as they ſeparated themſelves, they would run the riſque of being every one maſſacred.

The Tartar cham obſerving that they were not inclined to truſt him, ſaid to the prince and his officers, that they had no reaſon to miſtruſt his kindneſs, as it entirely proceeded from his regard to the czar, their maſter, whom he knew to be engaged in great wars in Europe, which could not be carried on without gold ; and for that reaſon, he freely gave them liberty to take as much of it as they pleaſed ; for his own part, he neither valued gold nor ſilver, as it was of no uſe in their country, for they lived without that, or even bread, conſequently had no uſe for either ; their whole riches conſiſting in herds of cattle, which, with their tents, they could remove at pleaſure ; and, conſequently, could not fear having either caſtles, towns, or villages, rifled or taken from them ; for they lived here one day, and elſewhere the next. As to his offer to quarter their men amongſt his people, it was made with a kind intention, and to provide for them till the arrival of their own ſtores from their ſhips, which could not be long, as he had ſent a party of his men with camels to haſten them forward.

The general, at length, by theſe inſinuations, againſt the advice of all his officers, was prevailed upon to quarter his army amongſt the Tartars ; while this was doing, the cham was entertaining the prince, and his principal officers, in his own tent, till late in the night, when, in the height of their merriment, a Tartar entered and told the cham, his orders were executed ; on which the cham put on a ſtern countenance, ordered all the officers to be diſarmed

and

and bound, which was inflantly done; he then told the
prince that all his troops were maffacred, and that fince he
had prefumed to enter into his territories, and taken poffeffion without his leave, he, and his officers were to be put
to death: the officers were that inflant difpatched before
his face, and prince Beckewitz was ordered to kneel down
on a piece of red cloth, fpread on the ground for that purpofe, to meet his fate; but the prince began to upbraid the
cham with his treachery, and affured him, that the czar
would refent it in the moft ample manner; he was immediately cut on the legs with their fcymetars till he fell, and
then they inhumanly cut him in pieces. At the fame time,
the party that had been fent to the fort for provifions, furprifed and maffacred the whole garrifon that was left there,
and then deftroyed the fort and burnt the fhips, leaving not
the leaft appearance that any thing of that kind had ever
been there.

This difafter occafioned various conjecture and fpeculation
all over Ruffia, as not the leaft accounts had been received either of the men or fhips, till at laft it was concluded they muft
have all perifhed in the Cafpian fea. The whole of this affair
was difcovered to the czar by an officer, a German by birth,
who had been taken prifoner at the battle of Pultowa, in the
Swedifh fervice, and went on this expedition as a captain and
aid-de-camp to the general, and was an eye-witnefs to the whole
tranfaction, from firft to laft; he was preferved in the general
maffacre by his hoft, in order to fell him; but as he had not
been ufed to hard work, he was often fold from one mafter
to another, till at laft he fell into the hands of an Armenian
merchant, who had a correfpondence with other Armenians

at Aftrachan : he difcovered himfelf to this merchant, who, on having fecurity for the money he coft, gave him his liberty ; by which means we got this information, otherwife it might have remained a fecret for ever.

Prince Alexander Beckewitz was the only fon of prince Archilla, of Iveria and Mongrelia, who fell in difgrace with the Perfian fovereign for refufing to refign his wife to him (mother to this prince), a moft beautiful woman ; this obliged the prince to fly his country, and put himfelf under the protection of the czar. He dying foon after, left his only fon, prince Alexander, all the immenfe treafure he had brought with him. This prince married a princefs of the houfe of Galitzin, the greateft beauty in all Ruffia ; this lady, intending to go to her hufband, was unfortunately drowned in the Wolga, on her way to Aftrachan.

A new regulation at Peterfburgh, and a filk manufactory at Mofcow.

The czar, finding the abufes in the management of his revenue arofe chiefly from the confufed method of his courts, he now modelled them on a new plan, formed on his own obfervations at Paris. The firft was the fenate ; the fecond for foreign affairs ; the third for finance ; the fourth for juftice ; the fifth for revifion ; the fixth for war ; the feventh for marine ; the eighth for commerce ; the ninth for receipts and expenditure ; and the tenth for arts, fciences, mines, buildings, &c. At the fame time, he erected a filk manufactory at Mofcow, having engaged a number of filkweavers at Paris, and being fufficiently fupplied with raw filk from the province of Gilan, on the fouth coaft of the Cafpian fea, which is efteemed the beft in Perfia, and is brought acrofs that fea to Aftrachan, from thence up the rivers Wolga and Ocka to Mofcow.

BOOK

BOOK VI.

Return of the czarowitz to Moscow, and his exclusion from the succession.—
His accomplices.—The princess Mary concerned in it.—The trial of the
czarowitz at Petersburgh.— His death and character.—The Swedish field-
marshal Rheinshield's return home.—Negotiation at Aland, for peace
with Sweden, renewed.—King of Sweden's death.—The death of baron
Gortz.—The fiscal's information against the grandees for misdemeanours,
and their trial.—Prince Gagaren's unaccountable behaviour.—More of
the czarowitz's confederates.—Death of prince Peter Petrowitz.—Prince
Peter Alexowitz made a serjeant, taught his exercise, and made ensign.
—Negotiations for peace renewed, but fruitless.—The czar resolves to
command it.—Memorable descent on Sweden.—The British fleet came too
late.—The czar disgusted with Britain.—The Jesuits banished. –The
czar seized with a fit at Revel.—General Weyde's illness, and the czar's
concern for him.—Affairs of Sweden.—Marshal Weyde's death.—Ill
treatment of his family.—His funeral.—The czar reproves Menzikof.—
Captain Bruce's ineffectual attempt to quit the Russian service.—The new
king of Sweden notifies his accession.—A second invasion.— The Swedes
attack our fleet with loss.—The czar receives the duke of Holstein into
his protection.— court martial on lieutenant colonel Graves.—A curious
law-suit between two brothers at Revel.—Fresh preparations against
Sweden.—Proposals on their part for a cessation of hostilities, rejected.—
A third descent on Sweden, which obliged them to sign the preliminaries,
and conclude the peace.—The fleet and army in a storm, and a child re-
markably preserved.– The fleet arrive at Petersburgh.—The czar ho-
noured by his senate with the title of Peter the Great, &c.—A wise re-
formation in the business of the law.—The captain again refused leave to
quit.—Triumphal entry into Moscow.—A proclamation and oath regard-
ing the succession.

HIS majesty set out for Moscow on the 3d of February, having received intelligence that count Tol-
stoi was on his way thither from Naples, with the czarowitz;
where they arrived the 11th.   A grand council was held at

6.   Moscow.

Mofcow on this occafion, confifting of the great men of
the empire; the czar being determined to exert, in a moft
folemn manner, his juftice on the prince for his difobedi-
ence.   The council being met, the czarowitz was brought
into the hall as a prifoner before them: at his entering he
prefented a writing to his majefty, containing a confeffion of
his crime. The czar demanded of him what was his defire:
the prince implored his mercy and begged he would fave
his life; his majefty granted his requeft, on condition he
made a full difcovery of all his accomplices, and renounce
all his claim and title to the fucceffion, under his hand; upon
this the prince figned an inftrument fetting forth that, finding himfelf not qualified for government, he difclaimed all
right of fucceffion to the crown; and afterwards confirmed it
upon oath, acknowleging his brother Peter, lawful heir to the
crown.   This being done, all the minifters and great men
prefent, took the oaths, excluding prince Alexis from the
crown, and acknowleging prince Peter to be the undoubted
fucceffor to it, engaging to ftand by him with their lives,
againft all that fhould dare oppofe him; and that they never
would, under any pretence whatever, adhere to prince Alexis,
or affift him in the recovery of the faid fucceffion. The fame
oath was afterwards adminiftered to the army and navy at
home and abroad, and to every fubject of the Ruffian empire.   Neverthelefs the prince was ftill kept under confinement, and nobody admitted to him, except count Tolftoi,
and fuch others as were appointed by the czar.

This being over, the prince's accomplices were fecured;
in which number were his mother, formerly czarina, now
abbefs of the monaftery of Sufdale, and her gallant, the boyar
Glebof,

Glebof, who not only had lived a lewd life with the mother, but was a principal agent in the conspiracy, between her and her son, the czarowitz ; the letters they had written to each other were published, and were both treasonable and scandalous. Next the boyar Abraham Lupochin, brother to the late czarina, and uncle to the prince ; Alexander Kikin, first commissioner of the admiralty, formerly a very great favourite with the czar ; the bishop of Roftof, and Pustinoi the late czarina's confeffor and treasurer, were all tried and sentenced. Glebof was impaled alive, and the other four were broke alive on the wheel. A high square wall was built before the Castle gate for that purpose : the impaled corpse of Glebof was placed in the middle, and the heads of the other four, were each on a long pole, set up at the corners. Several others suffered death at the fame time, among whom fifty priests and monks, late compa-nions to the czarowitz, who had led him into all manner of debauchery, were all beheaded on one block, which was a tree provided for the purpose of holding them all at once.

BOOK VI.

1717.

In this conspiracy, the princess Mary, half-fister to the czar, was also concerned ; she was afterwards confined in a monaftery near to lake Ladoga ; and the late czarina Otta-kefa Lupochin, was confined in the fortrefs of Slutelburgh, upon an ifland in that lake. All the czarowitz's domestics, and his mistress Euphrofina, were taken up ; as was also prince Wafilia Dolgoruky, lieutenant-general and colonel of the guards, knight of the order of the elephant, and director-general for enquiring into the mifmanagements of the czar's revenues ; in which post he had behaved with the utmost infolence to prince Menzikof, admiral Apraxin,

The princefs Mary con-cerned in it.

and

and several others. He was banished to Cafan for life : the Siberian czarowitz, and the fenators Woinof, Worof, and John Kikin, brother to Alexander Kikin, were alfo banifhed ; but the fenators count Peter Apraxin, brother to the admiral, and count Samarin were acquitted. One of the czar's pages and feveral nuns fuffered fevere corporal punifhment, and were, with moft of the czarowitz's domeftics, fent into banifhment ; but Euphrofina making it appear that it was by her perfuafion the prince returned, and that after her firft lying in, having conformed with the Ruffian faith, fhe was actually married to the prince, when they were on their journey, by a Grecian prieft, who was feized at Leipzig and brought prifoner to Mofcow ; fhe was not only fet at liberty, but had feveral of the czarowitz's jewels reftored to her, and a handfome fortune appointed for her fupport, out of the treafury. She could never be prevailed upon to marry : fhe was but of mean extraction and a captive of Finland.

When this grand inquifition at Mofcow was finifhed, his majefty fet out from thence, and arrived at Peterfburgh the 4th of April, and the czarowitz, arriving two days after, was confined in the fortrefs. The czar was no fooner come to Peterfburgh than he went to the dock, and ordered the men of war that were ready, to be launched, and to get his fleet equipped with all expedition, to endeavour to prevent Britain and Holland from compelling the king of Sweden to a feparate peace with the former.

About the latter end of May the firft conference was held at Aland, whither it was transferred from Abo at the defire of baron Gortz, as it was much nearer Stockholm, and therefore more convenient for the difpatch of bufinefs. The
pleni-

plenipotentiaries from the czar, at this congrefs, were count
Bruce, grand-mafter of the ordnance, and baron Ofterman,
a privy-counfellor; and from the king of Sweden, baron
Goitz and count Gullenburg. None of the foreign minifters
were admitted to thefe conferences but baron Mardefelt,
envoy from the king of Pruflia.

From the numerous executions and punifhments after The czaro-
witz's trial at
Peterfburg.
the inquifition at Mofcow, every body believed that bufinefs
at an end; but from the frefh difcoveries made every day, it
appeared, the prince had not been genuine in his confeffion
of all his confederates in the confpiracy; and the accomplices appearing fo numerous, and the plot fo deep laid,
the czar found it abfolutely neceffary to bring the prince
to a formal trial. For this purpofe he fummoned all the
nobility and clergy, the principal officers of the army and
navy, the governors of provinces, and many others of different ranks and degrees, to attend at the fenate-houfe, to
examine and try the faid prince. The trial was begun the
25th of June (the particulars of which have been fo fully
related by others, that I thought a repetition of it needlefs),
and continued to the 6th of July, when this fupreme court,
with unanimous confent, paffed fentence of death upon the
prince, but left the manner of it to his majefty's determination : the prince was brought before the court, his fentence
was read to him, and he was re-conveyed to his prifon in
the fortrefs.

On the next day, his majefty, attended by all the fenators His death
and charac-
ter.
and bifhops, with feveral others of high rank, went to the
fort, and entered the apartments where the czarowitz was
kept prifoner. Some little time thereafter marfhal Weyde
B b came

came out, and ordered me to go to Mr. Bear's the druggift,
whofe fhop was hard by, and tell him to make the potion
ftrong which he had befpoke, as the prince was then very
ill: when I delivered this meffage to Mr. Bear, he turned
quite pale, and fell a fhaking and trembling, and appeared
in the utmoft confufion, which furprifed me fo much, that
I afked him what was the matter with him, but he was unable to return me any anfwer; in the mean time the marfhal himfelf came in, much in the fame condition with the
druggift, faying, he ought to have been more expeditious,
as the prince was very ill of an apopleɛtic fit; upon this
the druggift delivered him a filver cup with a cover, which
the marfhal himfelf carried into the prince's apartments,
ftaggering all the way as he went, like one drunk.   About
half an hour after, the czar with all his attendants withdrew with very difmal countenances, and when they went,
the marfhal ordered me to attend at the prince's apartment,
and in cafe of any alteration, to inform him immediately
thereof: there were at that time two phyficians and two
furgeons in waiting, with whom, and the officer on guard,
I dined on what had been dreffed for the prince's dinner.
The phyficians were called in immediately after to attend
the prince, who was ftruggling out of one convulfion into
another, and, after great agonies, expired at five o'clock in
the afternoon.   I went directly to inform the marfhal, and
he went that moment to acquaint his majefty, who ordered
the corpfe to be imbowelled; after which it was laid in a
coffin, covered with black velvet, and a pall of rich gold tif-
fue fpread over it; it was then carried out of the fort, to
the church of the Holy Trinity, where the corpfe lay in
ftate

ftate till the 11th in the evening, when it was carried back to the fort, and depofited in the royal burying-vault, next the coffin of the princefs his late confort; on which occafion, the czar and czarina, and the chief of the nobility, followed in proceffion. Various were the reports that were fpread concerning his death: it was given out publicly, that on hearing his fentence of death pronounced, the dread thereof threw him into an apopleétic fit, of which he died; very few believed he died a natural death, but it was dangerous for people to fpeak as they thought. The minifters of the emperor, and the ftates of Holland, were forbid the court for fpeaking their minds too freely on this occafion, and upon complaint againft them were both recalled.

Thus died prince Alexis, undoubted heir to that great monarchy; little regretted by people of rank, as he always fhunned their acquaintance and company. It was faid, the czar had taken uncommon pains in the education of this prince, but all in vain; indolent and flovenly by nature, he kept the loweft of company, with whom he indulged himfelf in all manner of vice and debauchery. His father, to put a ftop to this, fent him abroad to fee foreign courts, thinking thereby to reclaim him, but all to no purpofe; on which he ordered him to attend him in all his expeditions, thereby to have a watchful eye over him himfelf; but the prince evaded this, by continually pretending to be fick, which might probably be the cafe, as he was moft part of his time drunk: The czar, at laft, thought to reclaim him by marrying him to fome foreign princefs; what effect that had has been already mentioned. After the death of his amiable princefs, his majefty ordered him to attend him in his expedition to

B b 2

Ger-

Germany; and being on his journey, under pretence of go-ing to join'him in Mecklenburg, he fled privately, and fought the protection of his brother-in-law, the emperor of Ger-many, whom he endeavoured to engage in a war against his father.

It was made appear on his trial, that he threatened when-ever he came to the throne, to overturn 'all his father had done, declaring, that he then would be revenged on prince Menzikof, and his fister-in-law, by impaling them alive, as also the great chancellor count Golofkin, and his fon, for perfuading him to marry the princefs Wolfenbuttel; that he would fend all his father's favourites into banifhment, and expel all foreigners out of the country; that he would re-leafe his mother out of confinement, and put dame Cathe-rine, and her children, in her place; after this, he would form his court of people who had the ancient manners and cuftoms of Ruffia moft at heart, for he hated all innova-tions.   Nothing could have touched the czar more fenfibly than threatening to overthrow all he had been doing for fo many years for the welfare and glory of his country, with fo much danger, toil, and labour, without ever fparing his own perfon; which made him fay, with great emotion, that he would rather give his dominions to a worthy ftranger, than be fucceeded by fo worthlefs a fon: at the time of this expreffion, he had no other fon but the czarowitz, which fhewed plainly, he had the good of his country more at heart than the fucceffion in his own family.

The Swedifh field-marfhal Reinfhield's return home.   Count Reinfhield, the Swedifh field-marfhal, who had been a prifoner at Cafan fince the battle of Pultowa, arrived at Peterfburgh with twenty officers, to be exchanged for the

two

two Ruffian generals, knez Trubetzkoi and count Gollowin,
who had both been prifoners at Stockholm fince the battle
of Narva.   Count Reinfhield was very gracioufly received
by the czar, who recommended him to the particular care
of field-marfhal Weyde ; he was daily invited by one grandee
or other, where the czar always made one of the party ; and
on thefe occafions converfed very familiarly with the count,
telling him, one day, that he defired nothing fo much as
to be perfonally acquainted with his brother king Charles,
which he hoped would foon happen by concluding a lafting
peace to both their fatisfactions ; and that he hoped to have
a perfonal interview with him, where matters might be concerted between themfelves without many witneffes.   Count
Reinfhield being detained much longer than he expected,
was afraid that the king, his mafter, would not confent to
the exchange, which made him fo uneafy, that he complained
thereof to our marfhal ; who affured him, that if the king
of Sweden fhould refufe the exchange, he fhould not be detained, for the czar would let him go on his parole ; but,
in a few days after, I was fent at midnight with the agreeable news that he was to fail in the morning for Stockholm,
as a yacht lay ready to take him and his officers on board.
When I came the marfhal was afleep, but I communicated
the good news to his officers, who received it with fo much
joy, that, by their noife, they awaked the count ; and, on
his enquiring what the matter was, I ftepped up to his bed-
fide and delivered my meffage, which fo agreeably furprifed
him, that he got up and embraced me, faying, If ever I
went to Sweden he would make me a fuitable return for the
good news I brought him, as he had nothing then to reward

ward me with, according to his wish. I staid with him till day-light, and then went on board the yacht with him. About eleven o'clock the czar, attended by marshal Weyde, came on board to take his leave of the count, and prefented him with a sword from his own side, which was enriched with diamonds, wishing him a good voyage to Stockholm.

Negotiation at Aland for peace with Sweden renewed.

Baron Gortz being returned from the king of Sweden with his final resolution, the conference at Aland, between our ministers and those of Sweden, were continued. The czar set out from Cronflot with his fleet, in the month of August, for Revel, and from thence he went to Abo to be near the place of conference; where it was agreed, that the czar should give up Finland, and part of Carelia, to the king of Sweden; and he should have in lieu thereof Wyburgh, part of Carelia, all Ingria, Efthonia, and Livonia; and the czar was besides to affist the Swedes to recover Swedish Pomerania, and Bremen and Verden; and to reinstate the duke of Holftein in his dukedom, as also to persuade the duke of Mecklenburgh to resign his dukedom to Sweden for ever; for which he was to have an equivalent elfewhere (supposed to be Courland); and to replace Staniflaus on the throne of Poland, according to the agreement made with king Augustus at Alt Ranstadt; and if Great Britain interfered in retaking Bremen and Verden, that they would, with their joint fleets and forces, make a descent on Britain with the pretender, and place him on the throne.

Upon this, it was agreed, that baron Gortz should once more return to the king of Sweden with these proposals: for which purpose he set off the end of September, in full expectation of prevailing with the king to come into them.

In

In the mean time, nothing was done to difturb the king of Sweden in his expedition againft Norway, as the czar returned with his fleet to Cronflot, and arrived at Peterfburgh the 15th of September, where he found the czarina delivered of a princefs, whom he named Natalia. His majefty ordered the fleet to be laid up at Cronflot, fo that every body confidered the peace with Sweden at no great diftance : thefe hopes, however, were foon blafted by the death of the king of Sweden, which happened in the night between the 29th and 30th of November, being fhot through the head before Frederickfhal in Norway, and it was generally believed to have been done by one of his own people. Field marfhal Reinfhield being then in the trenches, and going to wait on the king, found him kneeling on the banquet, with his head on the parapet inclining to one fide ; the marfhal thinking he was afleep, endeavoured to waken him, but found him cold and dead.

King of Sweden's death.

Baron Gortz was arrefted in his way to Frederickfhal to wait on the king, and foon after beheaded, and his corpfe buried under the gallows ; feveral perfons in the confidence of Gortz, were arrefted, and an officer was difpatched to Aland to feize on fecretary Stamble and all his papers, by whom we were apprifed of the king of Sweden's death, and that his fifter, the princefs Ulrica, had been proclaimed queen. Secretary Stamble went to Peterfburgh, where he remained under the czar's protection, and afterwards engaged himfelf in the Ruffian fervice. This fudden change overturned all advances towards peace, which then, to all appearance, only waited for figning.

The death of baron Gortz.

The

BOOK VI.
The fiscal's information against the grandees for misdemeanors, and their trial.

The fiscal-general, on the czar's return, gave information against several great men in the administration, for oppressing the subjects and defrauding his majesty of considerable sums of money. The czar directly established a tribunal to enquire into those matters ; and appointed marshal Weyde president of this court, saying, he was the only man he had never found faulty in any one thing, and joined with him as assistants, the lieutenant-generals Butterlin and Slippenbach, major-generals Galitzen and Jagusinsky, and the brigadier generals Wolkof and Mamonof. This tribunal was to examine into the mismanagement of such persons as the fiscal-general should lay before them, and to pronounce sentence on those who should be found guilty, as the nature of their crime deserved, without respect of persons. The first that was cited before this court was prince Menzikoff, who pleaded guilty to the charge laid against him, and having submitted to the sentence of the court, delivered up his sword, and went to his own house to remain in confinement till his majesty's pleasure was known ; the next were the great admiral Apraxin, and his brother, a senator and governor of Astracan, and director-general of the salt-works : being all three found guilty, they received sentence to be dismissed from their employments, and their estates to be confiscated to his majesty's use, and themselves to be sent into banishment : they were accordingly degraded, and their trials published in print. Prince Dolgoruky, paymaster-general, was next called upon, but he pleaded his own cause so well, that he was acquitted. Several others were tried and found guilty, and when every body expected their sentence would have been put in execution, the czar, in remembrance of

their

their former merits and faithful fervices, reſtored them again
to his favour, after their paying great fums into the treaſury.

Prince Gagarin, governor of Siberia, was next impeached
by the fiſcal-general, on a charge for having, by parties of
Tartars, he kept for that purpoſe, way-laid and robbed his
majeſty's caravan coming from China, whereby feveral
men of the detachment fent by the faid prince to protect that caravan, had been killed, fo that the crime was
not only for plundering his majeſty's caravan, but of de-
ſtroying the lives of fo many of his innocent fubjects; by
which unlawful and wicked means, he had accumulated immenfe riches. The proofs againſt him were fo clear, that
the court fent him priſoner to the fortreſs till his majeſty's
farther pleaſure fhould be known : upon his commitment,
the czar himſelf went to the fort, and examining, told him
if he would make a fair confeſſion to him how far he was
guilty of the crimes laid to his charge, upon the faith of
his royal word, he would pardon him; upon this, the
prince freely confeſſed his being guilty of the whole charge
laid againſt him, and figned this confeſſion in writing. The
fenate was ordered to meet next day; prince Gagarin's confeſſion was produced, and read before the fenate; and then
his majeſty told them, that he had fully pardoned the prince
on his making the faid confeſſion; and that he had convened
them on purpoſe to fhew them that he inclined more to lenity than feverity, by which he hoped to reform thofe who
had been hitherto remifs in their duty. Prince Gargarin being then brought from the fort into the fenate, his confeffion in writing, and figned by himſelf, was publicly
read before him; and being afked if he now acknow-

ledged

BOOK VI.
1718.
Prince Gaga-
rin's unac-
countable be-
haviour.

ledged the fame before the fenate, he faid that he was innocent of the crime laid to his charge ; but the czar had
frightened him fo much, that he forced him to write and
fign that confeffion againft his will. This declaration confounded the czar fo much, that he remained fome time filent,
and the whole fenators looked amazed : at laft the czar faid,
that although the prince laid fo notorious a falfhood to his
charge, and prefumed fo much on his own innocence, he
fhould neverthelefs have fair play for his life ; and then ordered the witneffes againft him to be produced : at the head
of whom appeared his own fecretary, who proved undeni-
able facts againft him.   The prince, not knowing till then
that his fecretary was an informer againft him, was fo much
confounded, that he fell down on his knees, and faid, he
had been a hardened finner, and deferved no mercy.

This unaccountable behaviour in prince Gagarin, after
being fully pardoned, greatly furprifed every body ; fome
thought him mad, others that he was afhamed to confefs to
the whole world fo publicly, that he had been guilty of
fuch atrocious crimes, who had always paffed for a pious
and godly man.   He was charitable to a great degree, and
the prifoners in Siberia loft a very good friend in him ; efpecially the Swedifh officers, who could not enough extol
his liberality to them.   On his arrival at Peterfburgh, he
was very profufe with his prefents, efpecially to the czarina,
to whom he gave fome not only curious, but valuable ; and
it was owing to that lady's powerful interceffion, that he
was pardoned at all : but after fuch bare-faced infult to
majefty itfelf, in full fenate, no body durft prefume to fay
one word in his behalf.   The czar being exafperated to the

5   higheft

highest degree against prince Gagarin, ordered a gallows, BOOK VI.
in imitation of Haman's, fifty cubits high, to be erected ─────
before the fenate houfe, on which he was hanged in pre- 1713.
fence of all the fenators, to moft of whom he was either related or allied. His fentence was to hang till he dropt in
pieces from the gallows ; but to entice fomebody to cut him
down fooner, the prince put two bags with money, in each
fide pocket of his breeches : this was prevented by placing
a ftrong guard every night, to watch the corpfe, fo that he
actually hung till the money, with part of his limbs, fell
down ; the money was fhared among the foldiers, and the
gallows, with the remainder of the corpfe, was at laft removed.

At this time there were feveral more of the late czarowitz's More of the
domeftics, put to death ; as Puftinoi, his confeffor ; Affona- czarowitz's
fief, his mafter of the horfe; Woinof, his fteward of the confederates.
houfhold ; Dubroffky, a gentleman of his bedchamber, and
four others of his fervants : the firft four were beheaded,
and afterwards twifted on wheels; the reft were knouted.

On the 15th of January, 1719, Mr. Jefferies, the Britifh re- 1719.
fident at the court of Sweden, arrived at Peterfburgh from
Stockholm ; but inftead of bringing any propofals of accommodation, as was expected, he faid he came to demand thofe of
the Ruffian court. In the beginning of February, baron Ofterman was fent from Aland to Peterfburgh, for frefh inftructions, and the conferences went on in the mean time, between
the counts Bruce and Gullenburgh ; but in the month of April,
baron Ofterman was fent to Sweden, to declare, that unlefs
they accepted in two months time, of the conditions formerly agreed on; they muft expect a vifit from forty thou-

C 2   fand

fand plenipotentiaries, who would force them to it, fword in
hand.

1719.
Death of
prince Peter
Petrowitz.

Prince Peter Petrowitz, his majefty's only furviving fon,
died on the 6th of May, in the fourth year of his age, to the
great grief of his father: his corpfe lay fome time in ftate,
and was carried, with great funeral pomp, to the church in
the fortrefs, where it was depofited in the royal burying
vault.

Prince Peter
Alexowitz
made fer-
jeant, taught
his exercife,
and made en-
fign.

After this, the great-duke, Peter Alexowitz, fon of the
late czarowitz, grandfon to his majefty, was taken from
under the care of his governefs (who had educated his mother), and was made a ferjeant in the guards, and mafters were
appointed to inftruct him in all manner of fciences. I was
ordered to attend him two hours in every day, to teach
him the military exercife, gunnery, and fortification : a corporal with twenty-four men and a drum, mounted as his
daily guard ; the duke exercifed thofe men every morning
himfelf, with his halbert in his hand, and took great delight in it ; after the excercife, he always fired three brafs
cannon, of one pound fhot, which were placed before his
door for his diverfion.   The czar came frequently to fee
him perform his exercifes, and was vaftly pleafed with his
fprightlinefs and attention ; and feeing fome draughts and
models of fortification laying on the table, he afked the
young prince the ufe and advantage of each particular work,
to which he gave his anfwers fo readily, and with fo much
judgement, confidering his years, that his grandfather was
fo well pleafed, that he embraced him moft heartily, and
made him a prefent of his picture richly fet with diamonds,
and gave him an enfign's commiffion in the firft regiment of

guards ;

guards: and finding he had a genius far above his age, he
ordered feveral artifts, as fhip builders, architects, &c. to
wait upon him, and fhew him their draughts, and explain
them to him.   It was very remarkable that he would not
amufe himfelf with any kind of children's play, for when
his fifter, the great-duchefs, propofed to amufe him with
play, he told her that it became one of her fex better than
him, for he ought to employ his time in improving himfelf
as became a prince.   This fort of behaviour made him be
admired by every body, and filled their minds with great expectations from him, as he was then the apparent heir to the
crown of Ruffia.

The queen of Sweden at laft named baron Lilienfted, to
fupply the place of the late baron Gortz, at the congrefs of for peace renewed, but
Aland; where he arrived in the month of June : but the death fruitlefs.
of the king of Sweden, whofe ambition had given great umbrage to all his neighbours, had now wholly changed the
difpofitions of the princes of Europe towards that kingdom. The king of Great Britain fent lord Carteret, his ambaffador, to Sweden, to conclude a treaty and an alliance
with that crown ; by which it was agreed that Bremen and
Verden fhould remain with the king of Great Britain, for a
million of crowns, and in cafe the war with Ruffia continued, Great Britain fhould pay Sweden three hundred thoufand
crowns a year, and act with her forces againft the czar. A
fhort time after this the Swedes made peace with the king of
Pruffia, on terms fomewhat fimilar, for ceding to his majefty Stetin, and its diftricts ; and at the fame time the king,
of Poland had concluded a treaty with the emperor and his
Britannic majefty.

The.

1719.
The czar re-
folves to com-
mand it.

The czar, now finding himfelf forfaken by all his allies, was refolved to make a defcent on Sweden, thereby to force them to a peace, ordered all his gallies and fhips of war to be got ready, and embarked on board his fleet 40,000 men, under the command of Apraxin, his great admiral; with orders to wafte and deftroy the coafts of Sweden. The ad-

miral held a council of war at the ifland of Capel, and fhaped his courfe for the Dalder Ifles, where he took feveral pri-foners of note; he then went and ruined the chief copper-mines, and burnt the woods, and feveral noblemen's houfes thereabouts; from thence he went to South Telle, where he landed fifty coffacks on horfeback, who advanced within a league of Stockholm, defeated an out-guard, and brought off a major and eight men prifoners. The 19th of July, the fleet arrived at Landfort, having taken on their paffage two fhips laden with corn, bound to Stockholm; the gal-lies, in the mean while, were divided into three fquadrons, one landed between north and fouth Talle, another on the coaft of Geefle, and the third at Nikoping; feveral detach-ments of dragoons and Coffacks were landed at Sandmar, who burnt and deftroyed all the country near to Stockholm. Our fleet, at the fame time, arrived at the mouth of the river of Stockholm, where they took five barks laden with provifions; from thence they proceeded to the northward, where a number of towns and villages were deftroyed, efpe-cially thofe near which the moft confiderable iron-mines of the kingdom lay; the deftruction of which was an irre-parable lofs to Sweden. In fhort, the landing the Ruffian troops in fo many different places of that kingdom, made it impoffible for the Swedifh army to prevent it: no fooner had

had they deftroyed one place of the country, than they immediately removed to another. According to the report of
the damages fuftained by thefe defcents on the coafts of Sweden, they confifted in the deftruction of eight towns, eleven palaces, one hundred and thirty noblemen and gentlemen's houfes, one thoufand three hundred and fixty-one villages, forty-three mills, twenty-fix magazines, two copper-
mines, fourteen iron-mines, befides all their corn and cattle; and all the inhabitants they met with, old and young,
of both fexes, were taken and carried off in tranfports over
to Finland, to the amount of fixty thoufand and upwards,
where they were detained till the conclufion of the peace.
The Swedes, relying too much on the promifed fuccours from
their allies, would not come into the meafures that had been
agreed on between the czar and their late fovereign; the
czar, therefore, now infifted on keeping all Carelia and
Keckfholm, over and above what he formerly demanded of
Sweden: but thefe propofitions were rejected with fcorn,
the congrefs of Aland broke up, and the minifters retired.

The Englifh fleet, under admiral Norris, came before The Britifh
Stockholm the 21ft of Auguft, eight days after our fleet late.
were retired into their different harbours. Soon after Mr.
Berkeley arrived at Aland, with letters from lord Carteret
and admiral fir John Norris, for his majefty, defiring a pafs
from count Bruce to Peterfburgh; but the count being informed of the contents, refufed to fend the letters to the
czar, nor would he give Mr. Berkeley a paffport to Peterfburg, but fent him back with an anfwer to lord Carteret,
wherein he told him, that he found the contents of the letters they had fent to his majefty fo fingular, and fo little
con-

BOOK VI. consistent with the ties of alliance and friendship, that still subsisted between his czarish majesty and his Britannic majesty, that he could not prevail on himself to do what was desired of him, until he first received orders from the czar, his master; besides, he was persuaded, his Britannic majesty would not fail to acquaint the czar with his thoughts or pretensions on a matter of so great importance, either by letter to himself, or by his minister at Peterburgh; and therefore there was no occasion to use such extraordinary ways and means. Upon this answer, the sieurs Jefferies and Weber, the British and Hanoverian ministers, received orders to leave the court of Petersburgh, as did all British subjects to quit the Russian service; on which the czar caused all the English merchants in his dominions to be put under arrest, threatening, if the British nation made war upon him, he would confiscate all their effects, which amounted to above fifty millions of rubles.

1719.

The czar disgusted with Britain.

The Jesuits banished.

At this time the Jesuits, those pests of society, who had got footing in Russia, through the recommendation of the emperor, were now banished for intermedling too much with state-affairs, and ordered to quit the Russian dominions within four days after having notice given them;. as the world was sufficiently apprised of their dangerous machinations, in troubling the political affairs of every country they are received into. The padres were now in great hurry and confusion, being obliged to set out immediately, leaving their rich chapel to the Capuchins, who were the only order of the Romish profession that were suffered to remain in Russia; and they were tolerated for the sake of the Roman Catholics, who were numerous in the Russian army.

It

It came out on the late trial of prince Menzikof, that Mr.
Wefaloffky, his late fecretary, had been principally concerned with the two Solowiofs, the prince's agents, in carrying
on an illicit trade to the great detriment of the nation; the
two Solowiofs fuffered for their crime, and as Wefaloffky
was then envoy at the Britifh court, he had orders to return
home, and Mr. Beftuzof was appointed to fucceed him at
that court: but as Wefaloffki dreaded, not without reafon,
to be brought to an account for malpractices, thought proper, inftead of returning, to write a letter to the emperor,
in which he acknowledged his guilt, and that, to avoid his
majefty's juft refentment, he had changed his name, and was
refolved to return no more to Ruffia, but to fpend the remainder of his days in fome remote and free part of the
globe where he fhould never be heard of more. It was,
however, generally believed, that he married and fettled in
England, and was afterwards naturalized there. Mr. Beftuzof had not long fucceeded him, before he difobliged the
court of London by a memorial, wherein he reflected on
the miniftry, for which he was ordered to depart the kingdom.

When his majefty went to furvey the fortifications of Re- The czar
vel, in the month of September, I had orders to attend him: feized with a fit at Revel.
he propofed to make that one of the ftrongeft places in Eu-
rope, and alfo for the equipment of his fleet. One day
when he was furveying the fortifications, and giving orders
about the additional works he thought neceffary to be made,
he was feized with a violent fit of the colic, which threatened
his life, but the vigour of his conftitution got the better
of it. He foon after returned to Peterfburgh, where he made

D d great

great preparations for the enfuing campaign : by his orders I remained fix weeks after he was gone, to draw the plans, and give the neceffary directions for erecting the out-works. Notwithftanding the perpetual hurry of bufinefs his majefty was continually employed in, he did not neglect to folace himfelf every evening, when the fatigues of the day were over, with fome diverfion or other, efpecially affemblies, which were held every evening at the houfes of people of rank, who held them by turns, at which meetings he converfed very familiarly with all ranks and degrees of people, which made thofe affemblies very much frequented.

General Weyde's ill- nefs, and the czar's con- cern for him.

At my return to Peterfburgh marfhal Weyde was juft ar- rived from Olonitz, where he had been drinking the mineral waters for his health, which, inftead of being of fervice, had made him a great deal worfe. His majefty interefted himfelf fo much in the marfhal's recovery, that he went in perfon every day to fee him, and gave ftrict charge to the phyficians never to leave him, but to ufe their utmoft fkill for his prefervation; declaring, that if he died, he fhould lofe the beft general and the moft faithful fervant he had in his whole empire; and now by much care and attention, the general recovered his health pretty well again.

The czar had made marfhal Weyde a prefent fome years ago of an eftate in Livonia, of the value of twelve thoufand rubles a year, by charter to him and his heirs whatfoever : he had only two daughters, the eldeft was married to major- general Le Fort, nephew to the grand Le Fort, the czar's peculiar favourite; and fhe, dying foon after, left only one daughter. The youngeft, and then only daughter, being afked in marriage by Mr. Weber, the Hanoverian minifter,

was

was refufed, on account of his belonging to a foreign court; befides, his majefty did not approve of the match. Then Mr. Romanzof, adjutant-general to the czar, made his addreffes, but that was not agreeable to the lady herfelf, as he was a Ruffian and of a different religion. The marfhal, apprehending the czar would infift on that marriage, betrothed her, againft her inclination, to lieutenant-general Bohn, a man fhe could neither love nor efteem, being of an age more like a father than a hufband; the grief thereof threw the young lady into a lingering indifpofition.

The czar being now informed, that the queen of Sweden had refigned the crown to her confort, the hereditary prince of Heffe Caffel, and that the regent of France had paid Sweden fix hundred thoufand crowns of arrears, with affurance, that the fubfidies fhould be regularly paid in future; befides one million of crowns they got from Britain for Bremen and Verden, and the ftipulated fubfidy of three hundred thoufand, while the war lafted with Ruffia; all this made the Swedes take frefh courage, and they gave the czar to underftand he was not to expect peace, unlefs he gave up all the provinces he had conquered from them fince the commencement of the war. On the other hand, the czar finding his enemy thus largely fupplied with money, fupported by an Englifh fleet, favoured by the kings of Pruffia and Denmark, and on the point of concluding a peace with Poland, while he himfelf was deferted by every ally, fent a numerous army into Finland, and endeavoured to make himfelf mafter of the Bothnick gulf by a large fleet.

Early in the fpring 1720, admiral Norris arrived in the Sound with a Britifh fquadron; and failing from thence, he

D d 2   joined

BOOK VI. joined the Swedish fleet before Stockholm ; and the 5th of
March, the palatine of Maſſovia arrived at Peterſburgh as
ambaſſador from Poland, inviting the czar to enter into a
peace with Sweden, jointly with Poland ; but the czar had
already formed his reſolutions to force Sweden to a ſeparate
peace, and to convince the world, notwithſtanding the powerful aſſiſtance afforded his enemy, while he ſtood by himſelf
alone, he had it ſtill in his power to command his own terms
with the Swedes.

Marſhal
Weyde's
death.

Marſhal Weyde now loſt his only daughter, who died the
day ſhe was to have been married to general Bohn, of a
broken heart, at being obliged to marry ſo much againſt
her inclination : her affections had been engaged to Mr.
Weber, the Hanoverian miniſter. Her father took the loſs
of his only child ſo much to heart, that he ſickened again,
and died the 4th of June, very much regretted by both
their majeſties, and by all ranks of people ; but more eſpecially by the army, who adored him, notwithſtanding his
ſtrict diſcipline, for he had the art of making them obey
his orders with pleaſure, by his affability in checking thoſe
in private who tranſgreſſed againſt his orders : ſo that court-
martials and puniſhments were rare during his command
of the army. Notwithſtanding this lenity, the Ruſſian
army was never under better diſcipline, or in finer order.
The marſhal was born at Moſcow, of German parents ;
had made ſeveral campaigns in his youth in Hungary, under prince Eugene, and was employed by him as one of his
aid de camps, under whom he always confeſſed to have
learned the military art. He was made a priſoner of war in
the year 1700, at Narva, and detained at Stockholm till the
year

year 1710, when he was ranfomed, and was appointed
field-marfhal, when count Zaremetof died after his march
through Poland.

The marfhal no fooner expired than lieutenant general
Romantzof came to the houfe in his majefty's name, and
fealed up every thing in the prefence of general Le Fort
and me, and then took an inventory of all the plate and furniture in the houfe, to the great furprize of the general,
who was father to the marfhal's grand daughter, the only
undoubted heirefs to his great fortune. Upon this general
Le Fort defired to know, fince all the money, to the amount
of fixty thoufand ducats, was fealed up, how his father-in-
law was to be buried, as he had no cafh to defray the charges.
Romantzof then told him, that his majefty intended the
marfhal's corpfe fhould have a fplendid funeral, and that no
coft fhould be fpared, and then one of the chefts was opened,
and ten thoufand rubles taken out, which were delivered to
me, with orders to lay it out as I fhould be directed by general Le Fort, and when that was expended. I might call
for more ; keeping an exact account of every thing that
was laid out, which I was to deliver in with the proper re-
receipts and vouchers, after the funeral ceremony was over.

This mal-treatment of Mr. Le Fort proceeded from a
refentment in Romantzof, as he apprehended it was owing
to Mr. Le Fort, that he did not fucceed in his addreffes to
the marfhal's daughter; and to mortify him ftill more effectually, he begged and obtained the marfhal's eftate of the
czar, who refufed him nothing, as he was then a rifing fa-
vorite ; and to fatiate his revenge, lord Nerefkin, a near relation of the czar's, being juft arrived from his travels, and
wanting

wanting a houſe, Mr. Romantzof adviſed him to purchaſe the late marſhal's, with all the furniture and plate, which was done by appraiſement, on an order from court; but no part of this eſtimated price was ever paid, and the heireſs, then a child, had only the few jewels her grand-father left, and twelve thouſand rubles for her portion: the remainder was generally believed to have been applied to Mr. Romantzof's own uſe. In this general plunder I ſuffered alſo; the marſhal by his will, had left me two hundred ducats, his beſt ſuit of cloaths, and his beſt horſe with the furniture; I received the money and cloaths, but the fine horſe and furniture were brought to the czar's ſtable, and for which I was promiſed three hundred ducats, but never got any thing. This was chiefly owing to Mrs. Le Fort, the general's ſecond wife, to whom he was married in Germany: as ſhe had been very ſevere on Mr. Romantzof's conduct, he reſented it in part againſt me, as ſhe was my near relation, although I was otherwiſe very much in his favour.

As this was the firſt inſtance of foreigners being uſed in ſo arbitrary and unjuſt a manner, it occaſioned much ſpeculation amongſt all ranks of people, eſpecially as it happened to a man of ſo great perſonal merit, and general eſteem, beſides to one who was nephew and heir to the grand Le Fort, and ſon-in-law to marſhal Weyde, both great favourites of the czar; ſo that after this none could think themſelves ſecure in their poſſeſſions. This unjuſt action gave me ſuch an idea of Ruſſia, that nothing after could induce me to ſettle amongſt them, notwithſtanding all their proffered advancements and advantages.

The

The marſhal's corpſe being embowelled and embalmed, lay in ſtate twelve days, in a coffin under a canopy, dreſſed in a white embroidered ſuit of cloaths, in boots, with a full-bottomed wig, and the order of ſaint Andrew about his neck. Several ladies and gentlemen watched the corpſe every night, which is the cuſtom of the country. As there was nobody in the houſe belonging to the marſhal, but his domeſtics, I ſuperintended the whole. The laſt night being at ſupper with the company who were to watch, I took a fancy to frighten them, by removing the corpſe into another room, and laying myſelf down in its place ; accordingly, when the company were entered the room, and ſeated ſome time, I began to ſtir under the cover that was laid over me, on which the company took to their heels, and ran out of the houſe, nor did they return to aſk what was the matter, but ſpread a moſt dreadful report of the viſion they had ſeen. Next morning crouds came to enquire into the wonder of that night, but went away no wiſer than they came : the re-report reached the czar's ears, who ordered my attendance, and demanded of me what the affair was. Without the leaſt heſitation, I told how it had happened, before the czarina and the two princeſſes, which diverted them very much, but her majeſty thought proper to give me a very ſevere reprimand.

The 16th of June, being appointed for the interment, it was attended with great pomp, and the proceſſion was conducted in the following manner.

1. A battalion of the guards, the officers in black ſcarfs, and the drums covered with black.

2. A harbinger on horſeback, in a mourning cloak.

3. A mar—

3. A marſhal with a ſtalf, covered with black and white crape.

4. A pair of kettle-drums, covered and carried by two men in black.

5. Four trumpets, four hautboys, and two baſſoons, in pairs.

6. A white ſtandard, with the deceaſed's coat of arms.

7. A gentleman on horſeback, in complete armour, with a ſword in his hand.

8. A black ſtandard.

9. A horſe in mourning, led by two men in black.

10. A maſter of the ceremonies.

11. A war-horſe with complete furniture, led by two officers in their regimentals.

12. A helmet.

13. A cuiraſs.

14. A pair of gilt ſpurs.

15. A maiſhal's truncheon.

16. A ſword.

17. The order of ſaint Andrew ; all theſe carried ſeparately on velvet cuſhions, by officers.

18. Two officers with their ſwords pointed to the ground, followed by twenty-four halbardiers, in pairs.

19. The corpſe of the marſhal drawn by ſix horſes, capariſoned with black cloth, each led by a groom in black, attended by three gentlemen on each ſide ; the canopy was ſupported by eight lieutenant-colonels, and eight colonels held up the taſſels of the canopy ; the corners of the pall were ſupported by four brigadiers.

20. A marſhal.

21. Miſs

21. Mifs Le Fort, grand-child to the deceafed.

22. A colonel's lady (his niece.)

23. General Le Fort's lady; both thefe ladies led by two gentlemen each.

24. A great number of ladies in pairs.

25. His majefty, attended by all the grandees and foreign minifters.

26. The officers of the army and navy.

27. The proteftant minifters, merchants, and burghers.

28. Another battalion of the guards; which clofed the proceffion.

In this order, they went to the monaftery of Alexander Newfky, at three miles diftance; minute guns were fired from the fort, all the while till the corpfe was interred, and was concluded by three vollies from the two battalions of guards. His majefty, with the reft of the company, returned to the houfe of the deceafed, where a grand entertainment was prepared for them. Every one of the company was prefented with a mourning ring, of the value of two ducats, with the dates of the marfhal's birth and death engraven thereon; near feven hundred of thefe rings were given among the company.

At this meeting, a debate happened between prince Menzikof and prince Galitzin, abufing each other in a very unbecoming manner. The czar being in the next room, overheard them, and fent for Menzikof, and gave him a moft fevere rebuke, telling him he ought not to forgot himfelf, but confider he was only of yefterday, whereas prince Galitzin was of the ancient family of the Jagellons, princes of Lithuania, afterwards kings of Poland; and ordered him to

E e   afk

BOOK VI. afk pardon of Galitzin before the whole company, which
———— he was obliged to do. The two princes lived ever after in
1720. enmity, but the family of Galitzin were too powerful to fear
the refentment of Menzikof.

Captain
Bruce's inef-
fectual at-
tempt to quit
the Ruffian
fervice.

The day after the funeral, Knez Repnin was declared
field marfhal, and fending for me, afked if I chofe to be his
aid-de-camp. I told him I had already ferved under two
field marfhals in that ftation, and as I had been fo long in
that employ, I hoped he would excufe me : he took my refufal fo much amifs, that he threatened to make me repent it.
As I was now heartily tired of the Ruffian fervice, I thought
this a favourable opportunity to afk my difcharge, which I
did next day, by prefenting a memorial to the czar himfelf :
his majefty afked me why I wifhed to leave his fervice ? I
anfwered, that fince marfhal Repnin had threatened me, for
refufing to ferve him as aid-de-camp, it would be unfafe for
me to remain any longer in the army. The czar replied, that
I was not to be under the command of the marfhal, and had
nothing to apprehend from him. I could not then prefume to infift farther on my difcharge, for fear of fharing
the fate of captain Dean, of the fleet, who was fent into
banifhment, for laying down his commiffion, upon a proclamation by king George the Firft, forbidding all Britifh
fubjects to ferve in Ruffia; a copy of which proclamation was
given captain Dean, by Mr. Jefferies, the Britifh minifter.
The captain was releafed fome time after, and returning to
England, was fent conful to Oftend.

The czar having appointed me to be a captain in his own
divifion, I got my company in the regiment of Aftrachan,
which was then at Revel, to which place I received orders

to

to repair directly, there to infpect and forward the additional works of the fortification, planned by his majefty laft year. On my arrival, the 24th of July, I found the works well advanced fince I had left it. I was now billetted on the houfe of a merchant in town, who led me to a houfe of pleafure he had at the farther end of his garden, which confifted of a cellar, a room for fervants, and two rooms over them, handfomely furnifhed. The landlord feeing me feemingly much pleafed with my lodging, faid he was afraid I fhould be difturbed with fome noife in the night-time, and named an officer of my acquaintance, then in town, who had been obliged to leave his houfe on that account: I afked him what noife could difturb me in a place fo remote from other houfes? He faid it was haunted by a ghoft: I told him if that was the cafe, I could, upon occafion, act a ghoft myfelf, and as two of the fame profeffion feldom agreed under the fame roof, it fhould be my bufinefs to diflodge the other: at the fame time I ordered my fervants, before the landlord and his people, to load their pieces with ball, that in cafe of any difturbance, they might be ready to go and fire on thofe who made it. Thofe orders prevented any difturbance all the time I lodged there, and others were not afraid to lodge in that haunted houfe after I left it.

About this time the new king of Sweden fent an adjutant-general to Peterfburgh, to notify to the czar, his acceffion to the throne, by the confent of the queen, his fpoufe, and the ftates of the kingdom; and as he had a particular efteem for the czar, he wifhed for nothing more earneftly than to conclude a firm and lafting peace with him; to which hewas ready to contribute every thing in his power.

The

BOOK VI. The czar anfwered, that he heartily gave the king of Sweden.
joy on his acceffion to the throne, and thanked him for his
notification of it to him; that he was moft willing to conclude a lafting peace with Sweden, if his Swedifh majefty
would alfo come to a firm refolution on that point.   This
gentleman was detained for fome time at Peterfburgh, that
he might be an eye-witnefs of the preparations that were
going forward for next campaign, and was fhewn all the
fhips, gallies, and troops; and, after many civilities, was difpatched to Stockholm, with the czar's anfwer to the king
of Sweden's letter.

The czar, to return the compliment he had received from
the king of Sweden, fent adjutant-general Romanzof to
Stockholm, to felicitate the hereditary prince of Heffe Caffel
on his acceffion to the throne, and affure him how true an
efteem he always had for his perfon; that he earneftly wifhed
to find in him, the fame inclination to peace that he had
himfelf.   This envoy was received with as much fplendor
at Stockholm, as that of his Swedifh majefty had been at
Peterfburgh; was carried wherever the court went, and was
always one in every court-party of pleafure; and after fome
ftay there, he returned to Peterfburgh, highly pleafed with
the honours he had received at the Swedifh court.

A fecond in-   In the mean time, our forces in Finland were not inactive;
vafion.
prince Galitzin advancing as far as Aland with his gallies,
to attempt an invafion on Sweden as foon as the froft broke;
and before the arrival of the Britifh fquadron under fir John
Norris, but was prevented by the ice: however, it drew the
attention of the Swedes to that fide, and favoured the execution of another defign.   The prince had ordered brigadier

8   Von

Von Mengden to embark 5000 men at Wafa, and proceed directly to Uma, in Lapland, which he did; took feveral officers and foldiers prifoners, and burnt the town, in which were feveral magazines; and then penetrating into the country on both fides, burnt and deftroyed two gentlemen's feats, forty-one villages, containing above one thoufand houfes, feventeen mills, one hundred and thirteen magazines, and other buildings; which done, they returned to Wafa loaded with booty, and without fuffering the fmalleft lofs. BOOK VI. 1720.

On the 7th of Auguft, the Swedifh vice-admiral attacked our fleet under Ameland, commanded by prince Galitzin; but they met with fuch a warm reception as made them fheer off, with the lofs of four frigates and two gallies, one hundred and fifty pieces of cannon, and four hundred prifoners taken, befides two hundred men killed, and three hundred wounded: the prifoners, &c. were afterwards carried in triumph into Peterfburgh, at which ceremony both the czar and czarina were prefent, which was conducted with great pomp, becaufe no victories were fo much prized by the czar as thofe he gained at fea. *The Swedes attack our fleet with lofs.*

The feafon of the year at length obliged admiral Norris to leave the Baltic, where it may be faid he had done much, by fuffering the Ruffians to do little. The czar not doubting but the Britifh fquadron would return next year, and feeing, from the conduct of the Swedes, that they muft be conftrained to fue for the peace they had rejected when offered to them, began early to prepare for a decifive campaign, by augmenting his navy, to put himfelf in a condition to face both the Britifh and Swedifh fleets.

Mr.

1720.
The czar re-
ceives the
duke of Hol-
stein into
his protection.

Mr. Stamke, minister of the duke of Holstein, had been at Petersburgh, since he left Aland on the king of Sweden's death; and had done every thing that lay in his power to obtain the friendship and protection of the czar for that prince, his master, who waited at Breslaw in Silesia, to know the success of this negotiation. The duke of Holstein, being son of the late king of Sweden's eldest sister, claimed a right to the crown preferable to that of the princess Ulrica, who was the younger sister, but now considered himself farther removed from it, by the resignation the queen had made of her right to her husband, the prince of Hesse. The czar, commiserating the unfortunate circumstances of the duke, whom the late king of Sweden designed for his successor, determined to afford him his protection, and for the first proof of it sent him a hundred thousand crowns, with an invitation to come from Breslaw to Riga.

Court-martial
on lieutenant-
colonel
Graves.

The over-fiscal having laid an information this winter against lieutenant-colonel Graves, of the artillery, an Englishman, for embezzling his majesty's stores, and selling them to foreign ship-masters, I sat on the court-martial. In the course of the trial we found the accusation to be entirely false, and proceeded from malice, because he refused the fiscal some stores he wanted, who had suborned two gunners as witnesses against the colonel, but who were both found guilty of perjury, and sent to prison. The fiscal being ill-pleased with our proceedings, complained to the fiscal-general of our partiality; and he laid the matter before the czar, who ordered the court-martial, the accused, and evidence, to repair to Petersburgh, where the affair was brought before

a board

a board of general officers ; and the litigioufnefs and villany of the fifcal appeared fo evident, that he and his two wit-effnes were knouted and banifhed to Siberia. We had our travelling expences paid, and returned to Revel; but, not-withftanding colonel Graves was honourably acquitted, he could never recover the fix months pay for the time he was under arreft on his trial, which is fufficient evidence of the hardfhip officers labour under in this fervice : the plea they ufed was, that he had done no duty in that time. The co-lonel was fo much difgufted with this treatment, that he left the fervice without taking leave.

At my return to Revel, a comical law-fuit was commenced between my landlord and his brother, both merchants in the town; the cafe was thus :——The two brothers had always lived at great variance with each other ; my landlord, who was very rich, was determined, in cafe he fhould die, his brother fhould not fucceed him ; he had been married fe-veral years to a very handfome woman, without having any children by her ; the blame whereof he attributed more to himfelf than to his wife ; and being refolved that his wife, at any rate, fhould have a child, to deprive his brother from being his heir, he took a lieutenant into his houfe as a lodger, a handfome young fellow, to whom he gave all manner of opportunities to converfe with his wife, having before-hand concerted the matter with her, by which means fhe foon proved to be with child : fhe then made the gentleman a prefent of a purfe with a hundred ducats, defiring him, at the fame time, to feck out another lodging, as her hufband was grown jealous and began to fufpect her, which made it abfolutely neceffary for him to remove, promifing, that

if

if he ever ftood in need of her affiftance, he might depend upon her. The gentleman finding her very pofitive, notwithftanding all his remonftrances, was, at laft, obliged to comply, flattering himfelf to find frequent opportunities to converfe with her; but in this he found himfelf miftaken, for fhe fhunned all occafion of ever being alone with him. This exafperated him fo much, that one evening, when he knew her hufband to be from home, he forced his way into her bed-chamber, and defired to know why fhe fhunned his company. She very frankly told him, that fhe had cohabited with him, not from luft, but with an intention to have a child by him to inherit her hufband's eftate; and as fhe was now with child, fhe hoped he would not envy its being heir to a good eftate; and defired, therefore, he would not be an inftrument in defaming her and ruining his own child; defiring him to give over any thoughts of enjoying her any more, fhe being fully determined againft it. After this fpeech fhe gave him a diamond ring, and a purfe with fifty ducats and retired, locking herfelf up in another room: upon this he went away in a great paffion, and in a fit of ill-humour, divulged the whole intrigue to fome of his companions, who foon fpread it over the town, by which means his brother got notice of it, and commenced the law-fuit; but the hufband acknowledging the child to be his, the fuit was dropt in courfe.

Frefh preparations againft Sweden.

As the Swedes ftill perfevered in refufing peace on the terms that had been agreed upon by the late king, the czar was now determined to compel them; and for this purpofe augmented prince Galitzin's army in Finland with five battalions and two grenadier companies, from his own divifion,

and

and two other regiments from Revel; we all embarked on board the gallies early in the morning of the 9th of May, 1721, and arrived in the evening at Elfingfoo, in Finland, being fifty Englifh miles over.

The Swedifh monarch had fent Mr. Dahlman, his adju- tant-general, to the czar, with propofals for a fufpenfion of hoftilities for one year, and, in the mean time, to fettle affairs towards a lafting peace; but as the czar had made great preparations for the enfuing campaign, he would by no means confent thereto. He confented, however, to the mediation of France, which Mr. Campredon, the French minifter at the court of Sweden, had, in fome fort, before propofed. Upon this declaration, Mr. Campredon, at the defire of the Swedifh court, fet out for Peterfburgh, to know what were the propofitions of the czar, and found his ma-jefty in the fame mind he was before the congrefs of Aland, notwithftanding the many advantages he had gained fince that time. Mr. Campredon returned to Stockholm, and Newftadt, in Finland, was appointed for the congrefs, where the plenipotentiaries met.

In the month of April, the duke of Holftein arrived at Riga, where the Ruffian court then refided, and was moft gracioufly received by the czar and czarina; and, at this meeting, the foundation was laid of a nearer alliance with that prince. Our operations in Finland were pufhed with great vigour: we were no fooner arrived at Elfingfoo, than fent, under lieutenant-general Lacy, to make a defcent on the coafts of Sweden; 5000 men, and 370 Coffacs, with their horfes, embarked on board of fifty gallies, were under fail the 27th of May, and landed next day near Gevel, on

the

on the Swedish coast, and marched along the coast to Sun-
derham, and from thence to Uma, which is above a hundred leagues. In all that way we met with so. little resist-
ance from the Swedes, having, as it seemed, lost their former bravery, that we had only eleven men killed; whereas
they had one hundred and three of their's killed, and we
took forty-seven prisoners, with one standard and four colours, two brass and five iron cannon, three trumpets, and
ten kettle-drums; we also took and burnt six of their gallies, lately built, with two merchant-ships, and twenty-five
other vessels; and burnt and destroyed a magazine of arms
and ammunition; ruined a manufactory of muskets, and
two iron forges; burnt and destroyed thirteen mills, four
towns, five hundred and nine hamlets, ninety-eight parishes,
and three hundred and thirty-four barns, &c. &c.

which ob-
liges them to
sign the preli-
minaries, and
conclude the
peace.

This destructive expedition alarmed the Swedes to such a
degree, that their plenipotentiaries at Newstadt had orders
to sign the preliminaries directly; upon which we received
orders to reimbark with our detachment, and return to
Finland, and we arrived at the Junfer Sheerin, the 9th of
September, where the peace was proclaimed. On the 14th,
we went and joined the grand army, under the command of
prince Galitzin, at Elfingfoo, where the peace was celebrated
with every demonstration of joy, every one now being in
hopes of enjoying some ease and rest after this long destructive war, which had lasted twenty years; but we found our-
selves mistaken, for the Swedish war was no sooner ended
than another was begun, as will be seen hereafter. On the
16th, I was ordered to demolish the fort at Elfingfoo, and
three thousand men being employed on that service, the

mate-

materials were foon thrown into the fea, which choaked up the harbour, and the fort was fo effectually rafed, that not the leaft appearance remained of a fort having been on the fpot.

On the 7th of October, the army embarked on board the gallies, to return to Peterfburgh, and general Lacy failed the fame day with the vanguard, and we followed him the next with the main body, under the command of prince Galitzin; and major-general Von Mengden brought up the rear. On the 10th, we were overtaken by a violent ftorm, in which we loft feveral gallies, and a number of our men; we faw feveral wrecks on the rocks, which were of general Lacy's detachment, and met a number of feather-beds, tables, chairs, and barrels, floating on the fea; amongft the reft, a barrel floating paffed one of the gallies, was taken up, and in it was found a child afleep, which proved to be the child of a major, who, with his lady, perifhed in the ftorm; and, as they were both foreigners, the infant was left a deftitute orphan without a relation to take care of it; but the cafe being made known to the czarina, her majefty took care of the child. We had feventeen gallies dafhed to pieces in this ftorm, and feveral hundred men drowned. We reached Sand-Ifland on the 11th, and on the 13th Black-Ifland: it was ftill blowing frefh with froft and fnow, fo that it was with difficulty our men could manage the fails, or handle the oars. On the 17th, we got to White-Ifland, making our way through the fhoals of ice, with a great deal of fnow, whereby we were fo benumbed, that we were obliged to keep ourfelves in heat by hard labour. On the 18th, we got to Beloforof, where we refitted our damaged

The fleet and army in a ftorm, and a child remarkably preferved.

gallies, and on the 20th arrived at Cronflot. We did not
ftop here, but proceeded and got into the river Neva the
next day, where the gallies were collected, and followed
each other up the river in grand parade, each faluting the
fort as they paffed, and coming oppofite to the fenate-houfe,
were ranged at an anchor, in fix lines, acrofs the river; and
on a fignal made by a rocket, we difcharged all our guns
and fmall-arms at one general volley; which was returned
by the fort and admiralty with all their cannon : this was
repeated three times, and the prodigious noife made us all
fo deaf, that we could fcarce hear for feveral days after. This
falute being ended, all the officers, above the degree of a
fubaltern, came afhore, by invitation, to the fenate-houfe,
where a grand entertainment was provided for all ranks of
people, on which occafion numerous fire-works were played
off, and the entertainment lafted till day-break, when the
officers retired on board the gallies, and brought them to
the wharfs where they were to be laid up; the men debarked,
and we were put into winter-quarters, hoping now to enjoy
our eafe for fome time after fo much fatigue and danger.

Great rejoicings were now every where difplayed throughout the empire; nothing was to be feen but treats, balls,
and mafquerades; the prifoners on both fides were fet at
liberty; a general promotion took place both in the army
and navy; our plenipotentiaries were loaded with favours;
general Bruce was made a count of the empire, and had a
prefent of ten thoufand rubles given him; Mr. Ofterman
was made a baron, and had a prefent of eight thoufand;
the fecretary got two thoufand; a general pardon was given
to all thofe whofe crimes deferved arbitrary punifhments;
                                                    and

and all who were under fentence for public debts, which
amounted to feveral millions, were difcharged.

On this important occafion, the fenate, with the grandees,
the chief clergy of the empire, and the deputies of the feveral provinces, went in a body, and thanked his majefty for
the fatherly care and unremitted attention, with which he
had applied himfelf to advance the happinefs and profperity of the empire, and prayed him that he would be pleafed
to receive the grateful acknowlegement of his faithful people, and accept, after the example of other monarchs, the
titles of *Father of his Country*, *Emperor of all the Ruffias*, and
Peter the Great: which titles being offered him by all the
ftates of the empire, he took fome time to confider of it ;
and after fome deliberation, accepted their offer, on which
the fenate repeated three times, long live *Peter the Great,
Father of his Country*, and *Emperor of all the Ruffias* ; and
the whole affembly teftified their applaufe with the found of
trumpets and kettle-drums, at the fame time the cannon were
difcharged from the ramparts of the fort and admiralty, and
that was followed by a falvo from the mufketry, of 24,000
foot, befides fome battalions of the guards that were drawn
up before the fenate houfe. His majefty then made a fpeech
to the ftates, and thanked them for their loyal addrefs ; to
which they replied by a profound reverence, and thanked his
imperial majefty for his paternal and gracious fpeech, which
was followed by a fecond falute of cannon and fmall arms,
and loud acclamations of the people ; and this falute by a
third. The fenate next went in a body and congratulated
the emprefs, and the imperial princeffes, who very gracioufly
thanked them. The emperor and emprefs then went to the
hall

1721.
The czar ho-
noured by his
fenate with
the title of
Peter the
Great.

hall of the fenate, where the duke of Holftein waited with all his retinue, and with him all the foreign minifters, who, every one congratulated their majefties on their entrance into the hall. After this ceremony, the company fet down to table, where above a thoufand perfons of both fexes were entertained; the conduits in the ftreet ran with wine; an ox was roafted whole, ftuffed with fowls, for the populace; and the evening concluded with illuminations and fire works, which ended thefe rejoicings that had now continued fifteen days, to the great fatisfaction of every body.

A wife reformation in the bufinefs of law.

The emperor having been informed how much his fubjects fuffered from law-fuits, by the avarice of thofe they employed, in delaying to end a procefs, while any money was to be got from their clients, now took the matter into confideration, and ordained that a fufficient number of lawyers and attornies fhould be employed, and that each of them fhould have a handfome yearly falary, for which they fhould officiate to all his fubjects, in every matter of law, gratis; and to prevent one perfon being preferred to another, they were obliged to infert every fuit as it was laid before them in their daily regifters, and proceed in them according to their dates of entry, without refpect of perfons; and whoever fhould be found to accept bribe or fee, or dilatory in forwarding a procefs at law, fhould be knouted and fent to Siberia into perpetual banifhment: and whatever fubject fhould conceive himfelf injured by the judge's fentence, might appeal to the emperor in perfon. This new regulation was highly acceptable to all his majefty's fubjects, but more efpecially to the lower clafs: and as they had hitherto no written laws, the emperor caufed a code to be compofed of

the

BOOK VI.

1721.

the civil law, in as plain, fhort, and eafy a method as poffible, agreeable to the method which marfhal Weyde had
formerly adopted in compiling the military law; which was
contained in a fmall pocket volume, printed in the Ruffian
and German languages, and of which every officer had one
given him for his inftruction.

I was now informed from Scotland, that a fmall eftate had
devolved to me there, by the death of my grandfather's brother, upon which I begged count Bruce to procure me leave
from the emperor, to go to Scotland, to fee my friends and
fettle my affairs in that country; but his majefty told him
he intended to take me with him upon a certain expedition,
where he would have occafion to employ me, and promifed
when that was at an end, I fhould have leave to go to Scotland.

The captain again refufed leave to quit.

The emperor intending to make a triumphal entry into
Mofcow, the metropolis of his empire, ordered his own divifion, or guards, confifting of four regiments, or twelve
battalions, and four grenadier companies, to repair to Mofcow, where we were to meet on the 26th of December, every
one being permitted to make the beft of his way to the place
of rendezvous, as fuited him; but this was now attended
with great inconvenience to the officers, having left all our
horfes and equipages at Revel, which we were obliged to fell
at a very low rate, and were now hard put to it for want
of horfes, as the prefent demand made them very fcarce,
and exceffive dear. Upon my communicating my difficulty
to count Bruce, he gave me fix of his coach-horfes, which he
intended to have fent away before him to Mofcow. By which
means I fet off by myfelf the 1ft of November, but the
froft being not hard enough to carry the weight of the horfes,

Triumphal entry into Mofcow.

I found

I found it exceeding bad travelling, and proceeded with the utmoft difficulty; the horfes legs foon became fo cut and wounded by the ice, which broke at every ftep they made, that it was the 25th before I could reach Novogorod, where I left the general's horfes to be cured of their wounds, and fet forward with hired horfes to Seragorod, where I got the 4th of December, and joined our regiment who were forming there, and we marched from thence in a body on the 15th, and arrived near Mofcow on the 26th, where we joined the reft of our divifion, and were augmented with two field regiments, making in all feventeen battalions.

On the 29th of December, his imperial majefty made his triumphal entry in Mofcow, in a very fine order; he walked on foot, drefled in his colonel's uniform, at the head of the firft regiment of guards, preceded by a company of grenadiers, and a band of martial mufic, confift-ing of a pair of kettle-drums, two trumpets, two French horns, eight hautboys and four baffoons; after the emperor walked two lieutenant-colonels, Menzikof and Butterlin, behind them four majors, Galitzin, Ufupof, Matufkin, and Romanzof; after them four captains, followed by four captain lieutenants; next followed the colours of the fixteen companies of the firft regiment of guards, in two ranks: the other regiments followed in the fame order; and the balconies, windows and ftreets through which we marched, were crouded with fpectators innumerable. Being arrived at the firft triumphal arch, erected in Twer ftreet, his majefty was received with the found of trumpets, and a general dif-charge of all the artillery in the city, and ringing of bells. When he arrived at the fecond triumphal arch, he was com-

8   plimented

plimented by the archbifhop of Novogorod, vice-prefident
of the fynod, at the head of the fecular and regular clergy,
where he was entertained fome time with vocal and inftrumental mufic, performed by young ftudents, in various foreign languages, before the duke of Holftein, the fenators,
and others of rank. His majefty then proceeded to the third
arch, erected by the directions of prince Menzikof, where
he ftopt a little to gratify the curiofity of the populace,
who gave every demonftration of their joy. His majefty
then continued his march towards the fourth arch, erected
by the magiftrates, when he was received by Knez Trubetzkoi,
prefident of the magiftracy, and by the whole body of magiftrates, accompanied by a great number of eminent merchants; from thence we proceeded to the Inoifemfka Slaboda, which is that part of the city where all the foreigners
dwell, where we were entertained with eating and drinking-
ing till very late : from whence we went to our refpective
quarters.

This triumphal entry was fucceeded by fix weeks feafting,
with balls, mafquerades, and other diverfions; amongft the
many other fhews that were exhibited on this occafion, was
a little yacht, of fine wormanfhip, and gilded all over,
mounted with twelve fmall brafs guns, with colours and
pendants flying; this veffel was fet upon a fledge and drawn
by horfes, in which the emperor and the duke of Holftein,
with others, to the number of twenty, all dreffed in feamen's
cloaths, drove for feveral days through the ftreets of Mofcow,
attended by a band of mufic, from one grandee's houfe to
another, where magnificent entertainments were prepared
for them; the guns from the yacht firing at every houfe

G g   where

where they ſtopped. All the ſtreets of the city were illuminated every night ; and this ſhew was very pleaſing to the
inhabitants, who had never ſeen any thing like a ſhip before;
people of all ranks minded nothing but their pleaſures during the whole time, till a new and ſudden affair put a ſtop
to all their merriment, which was this:

    On the 22d of February 1722, a proclamation was made
by the ſound of trumpet, requiring every natural-born ſubject of the Ruſſian empire, and all foreigners then reſiding
there, to ſwear and ſign an oath, " That they will acknow-
" lege as ſucceſſor to the empire, the perſon whom his ma-
" jeſty ſhould nominate for their ſovereign, after his death."
This order ſtruck a damp on the ſpirits of every body, when
they reflected on the undoubted title of the young prince Peter,
his majeſty's grandſon, and only remaining male heir of the
imperial family ; who was as promiſing and hopeful a young
prince, as any of his age could poſſibly be. The order however muſt be obeyed, and was complied with by many with
a reluctant heart, as the innocent prince could not help his
father's faiiings. All the officers of our diviſion were ordered
to different pariſhes, to adminiſter this oath and ſee it ſub-
ſcribed ; one of the pariſhes within the city fell to my lot,
which being very numerous, took me no leſs than five weeks
cloſe attendance, from day light in the morning till late at
night by candle ; this was to me, the moſt diſagreeable ſervice I ever performed in Ruſſia, as I was ſo well acquainted
with the excellent temper and genius of the young prince,
having had the honor to teach him the military excerciſes
and fortification, and to whoſe prejudice this oath was certainly adminiſtered.

B O O K   VII.

The reafon for the Perfian expedition.—Embark on the river Mofcow.—
Nifmi-Novogorod.—Embark on the gallies.—The Ceremifs Tartars.—
Cafan Tartars.—Manner of fifbing in the Wolga.—Kinds of fifb.—
Alabafter quarry.—Bulgarian Tartars, and the Maiden-Hill.—Kalmuck
Tartars.—Aftrachan.—Nagayan Tartars.— Short account of the Tartars
in general.—The Nagayan Tartars manner of life.—Defarts near Aftra-
chan rich with falt.—Fruits at Aftrachan.—The Banyan woman's burn-
ing herfelf at her hufband's death.—The inhabitants of India.—The
Banyans.

AFTER this point was fettled, the emperor made preparations for an expedition to take fatisfaction for
the injuries he had received from the rebel Perfians, bordering on the Cafpian fea. Mr. Wolinfky, whom his majefty had fent ambaffador to Myr Maghmut, the ufurper, was
juft returned from Perfia, with a very unfatisfactory anfwer.
The people about mount Caucafus, on the weft fide of the
Cafpian, had taken Schamachi, in the province of Shirvan, and put three hundred Ruffian merchants to the fword;
who were there on their mercantile affairs, and feized their
effects to the amount of above a million of rubles: the
Ruffian caravan from China, had been treated in the fame
manner by the Ufbeck Tartars, who were in alliance with
the ufurper; and the inhabitants of Androfika, near the
borders of Ruffia, had made frequent inroads on the Ruffian territories, and pillaged, burnt, and deftroyed, every
thing they met with, and carried off a great number of
people, of both fexes, into flavery. Mr. Wolinfky, who had
been fent to demand fatisfaction for thefe infults, returning

BOOK VII.
———
1722.
The reafons
for the Per-
fian expedi-
tion.

G g 2   with-

without being able to obtain the leaft fatisfaction, determined the emperor to feek redrefs by force of arms, and to com-

mand the expedition in perfon. While this was in agitation, there arrived three fucceffive expreffes from Chach Huffein, the dethroned monarch of Perfia, imploring his majefty's aid and affiftance againft the ufurper, on conditions too advantageous for fo wife a prince to neglect, and which haftened forward the expedition.

Embark on river Mof-cow.

When the emperor firft refolved on this expedition, he gave orders for building at Nifni Novogorod, a fufficient number of gallies and ftore-fhips to carry 30,000 of his regular troops down the river Wolga to Aftrachan; and having now fettled how the affairs of government were to be conducted in his abfence, we embarked on the river Mofcow, for our expedition into Afia, on the 26th of April. In going down the river, we had a fine view of one of the moft fertile and pleafant countries in the world. On the 3d of May, we arrived before the town of Columna, which is one hundred and eight werfts by water from Mofcow, but not half that diftance by land; it is a town of confiderable fize, environed with a ftone wall and towers, and is a bifhop's feat. Here the river Mofcow falls into the Occa, which coming from the fouth, is not only a much larger river, but has on its banks a noble country, very populous and fruitful; and the vaft number of ftately oaks on both its fhores, renders it one of the moft delightful countries in the world. The city of Wolodimer ftands between the Occa and Wolga, and is fituated in the moft fertile country in all Mofcovy; it was for a confiderable time the refidence of the great dukes, till the imperial feat was transferred to

Mof-

Mofcow, fince which it is much decayed. To this province
are annexed the two Tartarian principalities of Caffinou
and Mordwa ; the capital of the firft is Caffinogorod, fituated on the right of the river Occa, furrounded with a great
many villages and monafteries, which ftand moft pleafantly
among the woods. The chief city of the fecond is Moruma,
which ftands on the left of the Occa, which here receives
the ftream of the Clefna, which comes from Wolodimer.
Two unfortunate accidents befell us here ; a foldier loft his
leg by a cable at the letting go an anchor, and a foldier's
wife was fqueezed to death between two veffels, having
fallen down in ftepping from the one to the other.

On the 25th of May, we arrived before Nifni-Novogorod,
feven hundred and fifty werfts from Mofcow. This city is
built at the conflux of the two great rivers Occa and Wolga;
the Wolga is, at the junction of the two rivers, four thoufand
five hundred geometrical feet wide. This river hath its rife
from a lake called Wolga, in the province of Rofhovie, and
is, without doubt, the largeft river in Europe, being from
its fource to the Cafpian, into which it falls, above two
thoufand nine hundred werfts long ; but from its fource to
this city, running for above four hundred werfts through
the fouthern parts of Mofcovy, it has but an indifferent
ftream, and touches upon few places of note. This city
received its name from the famous city of Novogorod, the
inhabitants of which were, by order of the tyrant Ivan
Bafilowitz, tranfported to this place ; it is furrounded by
very ftrong ftone walls and towers, and the fuburbs are
larger than the city, being near three miles in circumference ;
it is inhabited by Tartars, Ruffians, and Dutch, moft of
                                                    them

them merchants; the Dutch have a Proteftant church
here.

All the army deftined for this expedition were affembled
here in one body, and embarked in the new gallies built
here; and as they were but fmall, fixteen of them were allotted to each regiment, which, with a great many ftore and
hofpital fhips, made a very numerous fleet.   The emperor
and emprefs arrived here the 27th, in a fine yacht, built for
them at Mofcow.   His majefty's birth-day being on the
30th, the army was drawn up in order on the fhore, and
after firing three vollies, went all again on board the gallies;
in firing the guns on board his majefty's yacht, one of them
burft, and killed a grenadier on fentry, and wounded one
of the maids of honour fo dangeroufly, that fhe died in a
few hours.   On this occafion, a grand entertainment was
prepared in the city, for their majefties and all the field officers, by Mr. Strogenof, a merchant, reputed to be a man
of the moft extenfive trade and riches, of any merchant in
all Ruffia. He fent plenty of beer and brandy on board the
gallies for the foldiers; and at the conclufion of the entertainment, the emperor created Mr. Strogenof a baron.
Their majefty's went on board the yacht the fame evening,
and fet out before us on their paffage to Aftrachan, to fee
every thing prepared that was neceffary for the expedition
over the Cafpian, but the fleet was detained fome days in
getting all things ready.
    There was here a Capuchin friar, who had been a captain
in the Swifs fervice; but having killed an officer in a duel
he turned Capuchin, and was now in his way as a miffionary
to Perfia: underftanding he was to preach, curiofity led me

to

to accompany fome officers of the Romifh perfuafion, to hear him, and his difcourfe far exceeded our expectation. After he had ended his fermon, he addreffed himfelf to his audience defiring a paffage to Aftrachan ; but, notwithftanding there were then prefent, feveral field-officers of his own perfuafion, none of them had the civility to make him the offer, at which he appeared much concerned. After all the officers were gone out, I went up and told him, if he would accept of a paffage from a heretic, he fhould be very welcome to a fhare of my cabin, which he very thankfully accepted ; and I muft acknowledge, I never travelled with a more agreeable companion, who afterwards, upon all occafions, fhewed his utmoft gratitude. When we arrived at Aftrachan, he fucceeded to one of the fraternity, who was lately dead, and fettled there, which was a happy circumftance for this friar, confidering the convulfed ftate in which Perfia then was.

On the 10th of June, our fleet fet out under the command of admiral Apraxin. We found vaft quantities of afparagus, growing wild on the banks of the river in great perfection, occafioned by the overflowing of its waters from the melting of the fnow in the fpring. On the 11th we arrived at Bafiligorod, on the right fide of the Wolga, built by the tyrant of that name, as a frontier place againft the incurfions of the Tartars, called Ceremiffes; but fince the Ruffians have extended their conquefts over the Tartars on that fide, all the way to the Cafpian fea, this place has been much neglected, and now only refembles a large village.

The Ceremiffe Tartars inhabit both fides of the Wolga, from hence to the kingdom of Cafan. They are a people

bar-

barbarous, treacherous, and cruel, living by robberies ; their food is wild-fowl, fish, and honey, with plenty of milk, which their pastures furnish them with, and they eat the flesh of their horses and cows, when they die of their own accord, for they never kill any for themselves : they have no houses, but most wretched huts. Those on the right side of the river are called Nagarin, or Mountaineers, and those inhabiting the left, are called Lugoivi, from their meadows, which supply them on both sides of the river with hay : they are all heathens, using neither circumcision nor baptism ; they give a child its name from the first person they meet that day six months after its birth ; they acknowlege an immortal God, the author all good, who ought to be adored, but ridicule the immortality of the soul ; although they believe not in a hell, yet they dread the devil as the author of all misfortunes, and therefore they pretend to appease him with sacrifices : when they offer a sacrifice to God, they kill a horse, cow, or sheep, and extend its skin on a high pole, which they implore to intercede for them with God, that he may increase the number of their cattle. They have a high veneration for the sun and moon, as the authors of the productions of the earth. They make use of no churches, priests, or books : polygamy is used among them, so as to marry two or three sisters at a time. Their women and maids are all wrapped up in a piece of white coarse cloth, and scarce any thing to be seen but their faces ; the men wear a long coat made of linen cloth, under which they wear breeches : they all shave their heads ; the young men that are unmarried, leave a tress of hair to hang down their back by way distinction. Their language is peculiar to themselves, having no resemblance to that

of other neighbouring Tartars, or with the Turkiſh or Ruſſian; although ſome of them that are converſant with the
Ruſſians have attained ſome knowlege of their tongue. Forty
werſts diſtant from Baſiligorod, is the town of Kaſmademi-
unſki, ſituated at the foot of a hill on the right ſide of the
river, the whole country thereabouts being as one continued
foreſt of elm-trees, of an extraordinary compaſs. Forty
werſts farther down the river, on the ſame ſhore, ſtands the
town of Sabakzar, the moſt pleaſant of any in thoſe parts,
from its ſituation. Twenty-five werſts lower, and having
paſt three ſmall iſlands on the left ſide of the river, we come
to the town of Kockſhage. On the ſame ſide, ſome werſts
lower down, ſtands the town of Suiatſki, built on the aſcent
of a hill; the caſtle and churches are of ſtone, the reſt of
the buildings and fortifications are of wood.

Going from this in the night, towards the river Caſanſki, Caſan Tar-
my veſſel ſprung a leak, and was very near being loſt be- tars.
fore we diſcovered it: we got aſhore with the utmoſt
difficulty, and having cleared the veſſel of water, and ſtopped
the leak in the beſt manner we could, we ſtood up the river
Caſanſki, to the city of Caſan, ſeven werſts from the Wolga,
and there I got my veſſel repaired. This city is very large,
and ſtands in a fertile plain, on the left ſide of the Wolga;
its houſes and fortifications are of wood, but the caſtle and
its works, which conſiſt of four baſtions and a good many
towers, are of ſtone; the river ſurrounding it, ſerves for a
ditch. The garriſon conſiſts of Ruſſians only, under a governor, but the city is inhabited by Tartars and Ruſſians,
who have their own governor. The kings of Caſan, in
former times, maintained very bloody wars with the Ruſſians,

and frequently laid them under contribution, bringing commonly an army of fixty thoufand men into the field; but
they were at laft fubdued by Ivan Bafilowitz, in the year
1552, and the royal family brought prifoners to Mofcow,
where their pofterity ftill remain, the chief whereof is called
the Cafanfki czarowitz to this day. It is to be obferved that
the courfe of the river Wolga, from Mofcow to Cafan, is
eaft; and from thence to the Cafpian, is fouth. The kingdom of Cafan lies on the left fide of the Wolga, and its inhabitants live all in houfes, and fubfift by agriculture: they
fupply the fouthern provinces with all forts of provifions, and
by this means they are the moft civilized of all the Tartars.
They are partly Mahommetans, but moft of thofe who inhabit cities and towns, are of the Greek church; they are
forbid, under fevere punifhment, to enter within any of the
fortifications. They are bounded on the fouth by the Tartars of Bulgaria, and on the north by thofe of Siberia.

Having got my galley repaired, I departed from Cafan on
the 17th of June, but did not overtake the fleet again till
we arrived at Aftrachan, as they made no ftop by night or
day. About fixty werfts below Cafan, the river Kama falls
into the Wolga on the left fide; and thirty werfts below
that, the river Zerdick alfo falls in; and at thirty werfts diftant
from thence, on the right fide of the river, ftands the town
of Tetus, refembling, by its diforderly buildings, rather a
great village than a town. Twenty-five werfts below that,
on the oppofite fide, the river Utka falls in, which rifes near
the city of Bulgar, the capital of the Tartarian kingdom of
that name. Some werfts lower is an ifland called Staritza,
fifteen werfts long; and not far below that, ftands the ruins

of

of a confiderable city among the Tartars, called Urenefkora, deftroyed by Tamerlane; it is moft delightfully fituated, and famous this day for the fepulchre of one of their faints, to whom they pay great devotion.

A good many werfts below this, on the right fide, are likewife to be feen the ruins of two other great cities, not far diftant from each other; pleafantly fituated near the banks of the river : the firft was called Simberfka, the fecond Arbuchim; they were likewife deftroyed by Tamerlane. Here I overtook three gallies and one ftore-fhip; they had loft three of their anchors, and had three foldiers and one gunner drowned. Being the fenior officer, I took them under my command, and this meeting made the remainder of the voyage fo much the more agreeable, as there were fome officers ladies and a band of mufic on board the ftore-fhip, paffing our time with dancing in the evenings, and with fifhing and fowling by day, both kinds being of the beft fort in great plenty; all forts of butchers meat and others kind of provifions we bought for little or nothing, and as we had good ftore of all forts of liquors on board our veffels, we paffed our time altogether in the ftore-fhip, where we were not ftraitened for room, very agreeably.

The Wolga, hereabouts, is full of fmall iflands and fandbanks, lying fcattered up and down on both fhores, which renders the paffage very difficult, and at certain feafons impracticable for veffels of great burthen, who are obliged to go for the moft part, in the months of May and June, when by reafon of the fnow melting, and rivers which fall into it being thawed, its waters fwell to fo great a height, that boats can often pafs over the fmaller iflands. This river

con-

contains prodigious ſtore of fiſh of all ſorts, and which are a valuable commodity in Muſcovy, on account of their numerous faſt days, which both Tartars and Ruſſians catch with a cord, but in a different manner. The Tartars take a long rope, to one end of which they faſten a large ſtone which ſinks it to the bottom, and to the other end they faſten ſeveral large pieces of wood, which float in the water; all along this rope, and at ſome diſtance from each other, they faſten many ſmall cords, with a hook at the end of each, baited with a certain ſmall fiſh, which the large ones are fond of; they lay ſeveral of theſe ropes acroſs the river every evening, and take them up in the morning, and ſeldom miſs a fiſh of one kind or other on every hook, ſome of them ten, twelve, or more, feet long. The Ruſſians alſo uſe a rope, and faſten a baited hook to the end of it, and have alſo their ſmall cords baited with ſmall wooden fiſh, tinned over, which being dragged behind a boat, by the reflection of the ſun reſembles the ſcales of fiſh, by which means they

Kinds of fiſh. draw up fiſh of a very great ſize, to the bait. Among the great variety of fiſh with which this river abounds, the ſturgeon is none of the leaſt conſiderable, whoſe eggs afford what the Ruſſians call Ikari, and we caviar: the beluga, or white fiſh, deſerves alſo to be mentioned; they are from five to ſix yards long, and thick in proportion; they likewiſe make caviar of the eggs, or roe of this fiſh, which is of a clear grey colour, larger and more delicious to the taſte than thoſe of the ſturgeon, but not ſo fit for exportation, as they cannot find out the method to preſerve them; the roes of the ſturgeon are black and ſmall, and after ten or twelve days preparation in ſalt, are put up in a paſte and tranſ-

ported

ported to all parts of Europe: this commodity affords a confiderable trade to Ruffia. Befides the fturgeon and beluga,
it yields alfo the ofotrin, another very large fifh, very fat
and delicious: this river alfo abounds with falmon, fterlitz,
a moft delicious fifh, and innumerable other forts too tedious to mention.

Going down the river we met feveral ftruffes, or flat-bottomed veffels, carrying from eight to nine hundred tons,
which go loaded from Aftrachan to Mofcow, with falt, fifh,
caviar, and all forts of Indian and Perfian goods ; they
feldom carry lefs than two hundred men, on account of the
laborious work they have to undergo, in going up againft
the ftream when the wind fails them, which is often the cafe ;
and where the fhore is rough, they fend their boats a head
with warp anchors to a confiderable diftance, one after another,
by which means they warp themfelves up againft the ftream
very expeditioufly; the men running with the warp-rope on
their fhoulders, relieving each other by turns : where the
banks are plain and even, the people are fet to tow her.

Near the ruined city of Arbuchim, was a ftone ten yards
long, and fix broad and deep, funk in the ground ; on the
upper fide was an infcription in the Ruffian language, fignifying, whoever lifted this ftone up fhould be rewarded for
their pains ; feveral of the inhabitants affembled and turned
it up, and found another infcription on the reverfe fide,
" Fools, what do you feek? there is nothing laid here."

From hence we came to a village called Tenefowa, where Alabafter
there was a fine alabafter quarry, of which I took three quarry.
large pieces, and put them in the ftore fhip, to fhow them
to his majefty. On the 20th of June, we arrived at Samara,

mara, on the left fide of the river, a town belonging to the
kingdom of Bulgar; the river Samar, from which it takes its
name, falls into the Wolga here, and is above three hundred
werfts from Cafan. The form of Samara is fquare, and the fortifications and buildings are all of wood, except the churches
and monafteries. The garrifon confifts of a number of regular
troops and Coffacks under a governor. The life and manners
of the Bulgarians, are much the fame with thofe of Cafan.
Not far from this place, and near the river Uffa, ftands a
remarkable hill, called Dewitza-Gora, or the Maiden-hill,
of which they relate many fabulous ftories that are not worth
repeating. It was formerly the rendezvous of a body of
Coffack robbers, who from its top, could fee a confiderable
diftance both up and down the river, and were thereby enabled to intercept and rob fuch veffels as they thought proper; but at this time it was converted into a convent of
monks. The hill is in fhape like a fugar-loaf, with an eafy
afcent winding round it to the top; and at fmall diftances
on this winding road, are cells containing one monk each;
at the top is the dwelling of their fuperior, whofe houfe,
as alfo the chapel, is built of wood, on a fpacious flat piece
of ground; from hence is one of the moft beautiful profpects I ever faw. By the fides of this winding road, from
the bottom to the top, large pine trees ftand at fuch regular
diftances, as if they had been planted on purpofe; and have
a moft pleafing effect to the eye. At a fmall diftance from
hence, rifes another hill, which reaches near forty werfts
along the river, and the vallies between are ftored with ap-
ple-trees, which yield plenty of cyder, which the Ruffians
call yablona quas. Some of thofe mountains run a long
way

way into the country. In this moſt delightful voyage, we
found great convenience from the pinnaces belonging to the
gallies, from ſix to ten oars each, which enabled us to
gratify our curioſity, without hindering our veſſels from proceeding on their voyage.

On the 27th of June we got to Saratof, ſeventeen hundred and eighty werſts by water from Moſcow; here we
caught two large ſturgeon and a beluga, or white-fiſh, ſix
yards long, and thick in proportion; theſe three fiſh were
a ſufficient meal for all the people on board the five veſſels.
The city of Saratof is ſituated on a very fair large plain,
about four werſts from the main river, on a branch of the
Wolga; it is inhabited, or rather garriſoned, by a great
number of Ruſſian ſoldiers and Coſſacks, who are put here
as a guard againſt the incurſions of the Kalmuck Tartars, inhabiting, a vaſt territory lying between the
Wolga and the river Jaick, toward the Caſpian ſea,
and poſſeſs the left ſide of the Wolga from hence near
to Aſtrachan, in all which immenſe tract there is not ſo
much as one ſingle houſe to be ſeen, as they all live in tents,
and remove from one place to another in queſt of paſturage
for their large herds of cattle, conſiſting of horſes, camels,
cows, and ſheep; they neither ſow, nor reap, nor make
hay for their cattle, ſo that they live without bread, or any
ſort of vegetable; and in the winter their cattle fare as other
wild beaſts. Their food is fleſh (eſpecially that of horſes),
fiſh, wild-fowl, and veniſon, and have a great plenty of
milk, butter, and cheeſe; but mare's milk is the moſt
eſteemed among them, and from it they make a very ſtrong
ſpirit, of which they are very fond; it is clear as water, but

I could

I could never learn how it is made. The Kalmucks are divided into an infinite number of hordes, or clans, every one
under their own particular chan, and all of thofe acknowledge the authority of one principal chan, who is called
Otchicurti-chan, or the king of kings, and who derives his
pedigree from the great Tamerlane. He is a very potent
prince, and lives in great fplendor; is formidable to all the
neighbouring Tartars, and to the Ruffians themfelves, who
are obliged to keep confiderable garrifons on the right-fide
of the river, all the way from Saratof to Aftrachan to prevent their excurfions, as the Kalmucks are in poffeffion of
the oppofite fhore, and are alfo under the neceffity of furnifhing the Negayan Tartars about Aftrachan with arms to
defend themfelves, in the fummer, againft the incurfions of
the Kalmucks, who formerly ufed to come every fummer to
ravage the country of the Nagayans about Aftrachan, but
fince they have been made fenfible of the effects of the fmall
arms and cannon now put in their hands by the Ruffians,
they content themfelves with coming once a year to the
great plains of Aftrachan for the conveniency of food for
their cattle, at a feafon when their more northern poffef-
fions are quite deftitute of it. This is commonly done
with not lefs than one hundred thoufand men, and they rarely
return without having received their accuftomed prefent of
bread, brandy, and tobacco, from the governor of Aftrachan.

There is no doubt but the Ruffians are powerful enough
to curb the infolence of thefe vagabonds, were it not for
the confideration of a benefit arifing from the traffic for their
furs and horfes, which they bring every year in great abundance to Aftrachan; and alfo for the fervice they are of to

the

the Ruffians in their wars with the Turks and Crim-Tartars, being accounted the moſt alert at pitching and removing their tents of any people in the world, which they are ac-cuſtomed to by their conſtant incurſions to ſome or other of the neighbouring countries. It is principally from this view that the Ruffians looked upon it as a piece of policy rather to allay their fierceneſs by ſome preſents, which, however, by continuance of time, they now demand as an obligation, than to engage in a war againſt a multitude of vagabonds who have ſo little to loſe ; having neither houſe nor fixed reſidence in all their dominions, but live the year round in tents covered with felts, in which, however, both for neat-neſs and conveniency, they far exceed all the neighbouring nations, even thoſe who live in fixed habitations.

The Kalmucks, as well as the other nations of Great Tartary, are Pagans. As to their perſons, they are of a low ſtature, and generally bow-legged, occaſioned by their be-ing ſo continually on horſeback, or ſitting with their legs below them ; their faces are broad and flat, with a flat noſe and little black eyes, diſtant from each other like the Chi-neſe ; they are of an olive-colour, and their faces full of wrinkles, with very little or no beard ; they ſhave their heads, leaving only a tuft of hair on the crown. The bet-ter ſort of them wear coats of ſtuff or ſilk, above which they wear a large, wide, fur coat of ſheep-ſkins, and a cap of the ſame : in the time of war, they cover their head and body with iron net-work, which they call a pantzer, the links of which are ſo cloſe, that it is proof againſt any kind of weapons except fire-arms, as a bullet will break it, and generally carries ſome broken pieces into the wound,

I i

which

which makes them ftand in great awe of fire-arms. Their
only weapons are the fcymitar, lance, and bow and arrow;
but they are coming into the ufe of fire-arms, which, in
time, will make them more formidable.   Their cattle are
large, and their fheep are of the largeft kind, having great
fat tails, weighing from twenty-fix to thirty pounds; their
ears hanging down like our dogs, and inftead of wool they
have foft curled hair, fo that their fkins are all converted
into fur coats. Their horfes are but fmall and of a bad fhape,
but fwift, hardy, and ftrong, and many of them pace naturally, and trot at an incredible rate.   They eat the flefh of
camels, cows, and fheep, but univerfally give the preference
to that of the horfe.

They are, in their own way, the happieft people on the
earth, being fatigued with no kind of labour, but diverting themfelves with fifhing and hunting; and I can conceive
nothing preferable to their way of living in the fummer:
but in winter they are obliged to crofs the river, and live
on the bare plain of Aftrachan, where their only firing is
the dried dung of the cattle, and the cattle themfelves ftarving on the fcanty produce of a barren defart. Here they remain till the fpring, when their former habitation, on the
eaft fide of the river, is overflowed for near a month to a
vaft extent by the melting of the fnow, and their country
appears one continued fea over-grown with trees: as foon
as this fubfides, they return with great joy, fwimming their
loaded camels and cattle over the river, where the interven-
ing iflands make their paffage eafieft. It is to be obferved,
that the Kalmucks, when they go upon any expedition, have
no regard either to bridges or boats; they no fooner come

to a river, than in they plunge with their horfes, and flid-
ing from their backs hold faft by the manes till they get
over, and then immediately mount again, and fo proceed.
But to return to our paffage down the river.

The 2d of July we arrived at Kamufinfki, which is a well
fortified town, fituate on the river Kamus, and has a numerous garrifon of foldiers and Coffacks. A canal was begun
here to make a communication between the rivers Wolga
and Don, or Tanais, and after being greatly advanced, was
at laft found impracticable by the vaft quantity of hard rock
lying in the way, which could only be removed by blowing
at fuch an immenfe expence of time and treafure that the
attempt was dropt. Oppofite to Kamus, a branch of the
Wolga points its courfe into the country, north-eaft, one
werft, quite contrary to the current of the great river; but
afterwards refuming its former courfe, returns to the fouth-
eaft, and continues in that direction, till it falls into the
Cafpian fea. About forty miles from this, and at a fmall
diftance from the river-fide, are to be feen the ruins of a
great city, formerly called Czarefgorod, built, as is related,
by Tamerlane: its palace and walls were all of brick, and
have ferved the city of Aftrachan with materials, thefe many
years, for building their walls, churches, and monafteries.
The 4th of July, we came before Czaritza, which is fortified with feveral baftions and towers, but all of wood, and
inhabited only by foldiers and Coffacks. All about here,
and even as far Aftrachan, the ifland of Zerpinfko excepted,
which, being twelve werfts long, fupports the cattle belonging to the garrifon, the foil is fo very barren, that it affords
no manner of corn: this defect, however, is eafily fupplied

by

by the help of the river, the fertile lands of Cafan furnifhing thofe parts, and even the city of Aftrachan, with
wheat and rye, at a very moderate price. Forty werfts below Czaritza, this great river cafts out her fecond branch,
which joins the firft, and with it falls into the fea. From
hence, on both fides the Wolga, as far as the fea, grow
vaft quantities of liquorice of a very large fize, its ftalk
being as thick as a lufty man's arm, and fometimes
above four feet high, the feeds lying in cods upon the ftalk;
yet this is inferior, both in fize and fweetnefs, to that which
grows near the river Araxis in Afia.

The 6th, we arrived before Zornayar, feated on the right
fide of the river, on a high fhore, near a vaft plain, without
trees or eminences ; the form of the place is a fquare, fortified with wooden towers and ramparts, and garrifoned with
foldiers and Coffacks, all horfemen. A few werfts below
this is a third branch of the Wolga, called Buchwoftowa,
which falls into the two preceding ; and at twenty werfts
farther down fhe fends out her fourth branch called Donitofka, which does not mingle with any of the other three,
but flows by a particular channel into the Cafpian fea. In
paffing the left fhore, we frequently vifited the Kalmucks in
their kibbits, or tents, which we always found pitched on
the moft delightful places I ever faw, their country being a
large plain, full of wood and meadows ; and we were much
diverted with the numbers of their children of both fexes,
running naked along the fhore ; and upon our throwing
bread into the water, they fwam in crouds to take it up,
there being none of them but can fwim to admiration.
About fixty werfts above Aftrachan is the fifth branch of the
Wolga,

Wolga, and is called Mitufka, which, at fome diftance from the main river, divides again into two ftreams, one of which unites with the Donitofka, and the other returns again to the Wolga. Twenty-five werfts above Aftrachan lies the ifle of Bufan, and ten werfts below that ifle is the fixth branch of the Wolga called Baltzick; and fome werfts lower, the feventh, called Kniluffe, which forms the ifle of Dolgoi, upon which ftands the city of Aftrachan: having encompaffed this ifland, it falls through feveral channels into the Cafpian fea.

On the 10th of July I arrived at the city of Aftrachan, where I joined the army again. They were all furprifed to fee me, as they had been informed by a galley, which paffed us in the night, when we were in our greateft danger, that we were all drowned. Here my agreeable companion, the Capuchin, entered into a cloyfter of his own order, as there happened to be a vacancy by the death of one of their brethren, which was very fortunate for the Capuchin, as the confufions then in Perfia made it impracticable for him to proceed thither, as he at firft propofed. I met with the utmoft gratitude and civility from him and the reft of his brethren, and when I went away, upon our expedition over the Cafpian fea, I left every thing I had no occafion for at their convent; and he fent me afterwards, by every fhip that arrived, provifions of all kinds, by which means I was better provided than any officer in the army: fo that I loft nothing by my civility to the Capuchin.

The city of Aftrachan is fituated on the confines of Europe and Afia, which are divided by the river Wolga. It ftands on the ifland of Dolgoi, which is formed by the

branches

branches on that river, as has been already mentioned, in 46 deg. 22 min. north lat. two thousand six hundred and thirty werfls from Mofcow, allowing ninety werfts to a degree. The city is of a confiderable bignefs, and at prefent inhabited almoft entirely by Ruffians; the former inhabitants of the country, being Tartars, are not permitted to live within the walls, but in the adjacent fuburbs, which are only fenced round with pallifades : the fortifications of the city are all of ftone, very high, and at a diftance make a very gallant appearance, efpecially toward the river, by the great number of ftone turrets and fteeples; but the houfes within the city being all of wood, and very low, its infide does not appear anfwerable to the reft. There is a great train of artillery in this place, no lefs than five hundred brafs cannon, with a proportionable number of mortars; the garrifon, in peaceable times, is commonly fix thoufand men, under the command of a governor and other officers. Aftrachan being fituate on a navigable boundary, between the two moft confiderable quarters of the globe, is naturally the feat of an immenfe trade; being frequented not only by the neighbouring Tartar nations, but by Perfians, Armenians, and Indians : the Indians have a particular diftrict affigned them within the walls of the city.

Nagayan Tartars.

Czar Iwan Bafilowitz, having conquered the kingdom of Cafan, in the year 1552, turned his arms againft the Nagayan Tartars, and took Aftrachan, their capital, by affault, in the year 1554; and to fecure his conqueft he furrounded the city with a ftrong wall. Czar Michael Fedrowitz, befides ftrengthening the city with fome new fortifications, built that part of it called Strelitza-Gorod, or the city of foldiers, as the military

military had their quarters affigned them there. I will now
endeavour to give a fhort defcription of this country and
its inhabitants.

It feems beyond a difpute, the Tartars were unknown to
the ancient geographers, who comprehended them under
the general-appellation of Scythians and Sarmatians ; it is
evident the Tartars confift of feveral nations, diftinct among
themfelves, in their names, language, and cuftoms.   The
Nagayans, with the Tartars of Cafan, and fome others
inhabiting between the Wolga and the Don, or Tanais, are
faid to have been Indians, who revolting from their fove-
reigns about the year 1212, emigrated and fettled themfelves
on the Palus Meotis, near the Euxine fea, and extending
their conquefts to the river Don, and from thence at laft to
the Wolga, near which they inhabit at this day.   The Nagayans are feated along the fhores of the Cafpian, from the
river Iaick, to the Wolga.   Aftrachan, their principal city,
they relate to have been built by a Tartar king, whofe name
being Aftra, gave his city the name of Aftra-chan, or king.
Before this country was conquered by the Ruffians, it was
inhabited altogether by Tartars, but now they are neither
fuffered to refide within this city, nor build a new one, nor
fortify any of their towns or villages with walls.

The Nagayans live for the moft part in round huts made
of bull-rufhes, or canes, and feldom exceed twelve or thirteen yards in circumference, with a hole at the top to let out
the fmoak ; yet the leaft of thefe huts has a falcon, or hawk,
as thofe Tartars are great mafters of this fport : they have
hawks of all forts and fizes, each bred to fly at different
kinds of game.   The Ruffians call the Nagayans, vagabonds,

as they have no settled habitations in the summer, but ram-
ble up and down. They pack up their huts in carts; their
wives, children, and goods, on camels, horses, and oxen; and
move about from one place to another, where they can find
better pasturage for their cattle. When winter approaches,
they begin to reassemble with their flocks, to pass it in several troops near Astrachan, where they are furnished with
arms to repulse any inroads from the Kalmucks, or other
Tartars from the River Iaick; and as soon as the winter is
over, they are obliged to return all their arms. They pay no
tribute to the Russian emperor, but are obliged to serve him
in his wars under their own commanders, as they are, in
time of peace, governed by their own petty princes and
judges. To secure their obedience to the emperor, he has
always some of their princes, or myrzas, hostages in the
castle of Astrachan.

Their religion is Mahometanism, of the same sect with
the Turks, except some few who have embraced the religion of the Greek church: they are used to dedicate some
of their children, like the Nazarites, to God or to some saint
or other; they are distinguished from the rest by a ring,
which the boys wear in their right ear, and the girls in their
nostril. They live upon what their cattle, hunting, and fish-
ing supply them with. They make use of fish dried in the
sun instead of bread, although they also make cakes of meal
and rice; they eat camels and horse flesh, and they hold
mares milk in great esteem: their common drink is milk
and water, yet, besides wine, hydromel (or mead), and brandy,
they find indifferent good beer in Astrachan: their cattle are
much the same with those of the Kalmucks.   The Naga-

I   yans

yans in their perfons are handfomer than the Kalmucks, ef- BOOK VII.
pecially their women ; the men wear a loofe coat of fome ——————
coarfe cloth, and over that a fort of cloak of fheep fkin, the   1722.
woolly fide outwards, with a cap of the fame on their heads;
the cap is commonly of a black colour.   Their women are
clad in white linen, with a plaited coif on their heads, both
fides of which is ornamented with a great many pieces of
filver coin, hanging down.   The climate here is very hot ;
the heat in the months of September and October much exceeds the dog-days in Britain ; notwithftanding which, the
winter, which feldom continues longer than two months, is
fo exceffive cold, that this great river is frozen up, and the
ice ftrong enough to carry horfes and fledges.

On the weft fide of the Wolga, towards the Euxine Sea, Defarts near
lies a vaft defart, above three hundred and fifty werfts in Aftrachan, rich with falt.
length, and fouthward, along the fhore of the Cafpian,
another near four hundred werfts long ; on neither of which
ftands city, town, or village, nor is there a hill or even a tree
to be feen in all this immenfe extent, only here and there a
little fpot of grafs; neither is there any water, but what the
river Kifliar or fome ftanding pools of falt water afford:
yet thefe very deferts are enriched with prodigious quantities of
falt ; for from ten to twenty werfts diftance from Aftrachan,
there are large falt veins, which being congealed by the fun,
fwims on the furface of the water of the thicknefs of a finger,
as clear and tranfparent as rock cryftal, and fmells like a vio-
let ; from hence all Ruffia is fupplied with falt.   The three
principal of thefe falts-pits, are called Mozakofski, Kain-
kowa, and Goftofski, where the falt is in fuch abundance,
that one may buy a hundred weight for two pence, on the

K k   fpot.

BOOK VII. spot. It is carried to the Wolga, and from thence tranſported to other parts.

  The Iſle of Dolgoi, or Long Iſland, about Aſtrachan, and ſome other parts of this province, abound with moſt excellent fruits, yielding neither for beauty nor flavour to any, even thoſe of Perſia or the Indies ; their apples, quinces, nuts, peaches, and melons, exceed their other kinds in goodneſs, and eſpecially the water-melon, the rhind of which is of a lively green colour, the meat carnation, and the ſeeds black, moſt pleaſant to the eye and delicious to the palate, and are ſold ſo very cheap as two for a penny, and ſo large that one is ſufficient for two men, and ſo refreſhing, that people in fevers may eat them without danger. It is not yet above one hundred years ſince the grape was ſeen in theſe parts, but the Perſians having brought ſome ſetts of the vine to this place, they were firſt planted by a monk, a German by birth, in the garden belonging to his convent, ſituated in the ſuburbs of Aſtrachan ; this ſmall ſtock has been ſince improved and encreaſed to that degree, that not only the walks and arbours of the gardens, but large vineyards are planted ; the grapes are ſo extraordinary large and plentiful, that the tables are not only liberally provided with excellent wine, both red and white, but made in ſuch quantities that our army was now ſupplied with it. Beſides this, there is to be found near Aſtrachan, and all along the Wolga, abundance of ſimples, which grow very large. The herb eſula is here about as high as a man, and the angelica root as thick as a man's arm. About thirty werſts below Aſtrachan, is one of the beſt fiſheries in the Wolga, and from

which

2

which the city is plentifully furnished with salmon, sturgeon,
beluga, osotrin, sterlit, and many other kinds of delicious
fish; and the small islands hereabouts abound with great variety of wild-fowl; and although the neighbouring countries are not fertile in corn, yet that defect is so well supplied
from the fruitful country of ·Casan, that, taken altogether,
this city may justly be reckoned one the most convenient
and pleasant in Europe. But to return where I left off.

The day after my arrival here, I waited on his imperial
majesty, and presented him with the three pieces of alabaster
I had brought with me from Tenesowa, which pleased him
so much, that he gave immediate orders to work that quarry,
which proved to be most excellent of its kind. The emperor
observed, when I had presented him with these pieces of alabaster, that no mineral of any kind whatever, had been discovered to him by any of his own subjects, but that many
had been discovered to him by foreigners: but his majesty
did not reflect upon the hardships those were put to upon
whose lands any thing of that kind was found, as they not
only lost the benefit of it, but were obliged to work the mine
by their vassals, without the least emolument to themselves;
which verifies the common saying they have in Russia, that
every thing they have belongs to God and their emperor.

I was quartered, in this city, at the house of a widow, who
had a maid servant that had been purchased as a flave from
the Tartars: this servant had stolen several things from her
mistress, which being found in her custody, she was severely
punished for the theft; for which she threatened to be revenged on her mistress, who disregarded the menace at that
time: however, she was seized, in a few days after, with

such

such a fit of madnefs, that they were obliged to bind her;
on which the girl difappeared, and in her cheft were found
a variety of herbs, roots, and powders; and upon the phyficians examining into the nature of them, they foon found out
the caufe of the woman's diforder, and applying the proper
remedy, fhe recovered her fenfes again.   A party of Tartars
brought back the flave, who, upon examination, confeffed
what fhe had done, pretending that fhe underftood witch-
craft, and could avenge herfelf on thofe who injured her:
on which fhe was firft whipt through the city, and delivered
to the Tartars to fell her at fome diftance.

The Banayan
woman's
burning her-
felf at her
hufband's
death.
　　　The Armenians have one of the fuburbs of this city allotted for their refidence, and carry on a great trade from
hence into Perfia; but the Banyans without doubt contribute moft to its flourifhing condition.   They are a fort of
Pagan Indians, whofe principal purfuit is trade, and have
their factory within the city.   One of their chief merchants
dying at this time, his widow defired leave of the emperor
to burn herfelf with his corpfe, according to the cuftom of
their country: but his majefty, unwilling to encourage fo barbarous a cuftom, refufed her requeft, and the Indian factory
were fo much diffatisfied with it, that they threatened to
withdraw from the city with their effects.   His majefty
finding no argument could prevail on the woman to alter her
refolution, at laft gave them leave to do as they thought
proper.   The corpfe being dreffed in his cloaths, was carried
to fome little diftance from the town, where a funeral pile of
dry wood was raifed, and the body laid upon it: before the
pile were hung Indian carpets, to prevent its being feen.
The wife in her beft apparel, and adorned with ear-rings,
　　　　　　　　　　　　　　　　　　　　　　　　feveral.

feveral rings on her fingers, and a pearl necklace, attended by a great number of Indians of both fexes, was led by a bramin, or prieft, to the funeral pile, which on her approach was kindled : fhe then diftributed her upper apparel and jewels among her friends and aquaintances, of whom fhe took her laft farewel with a great deal of ceremony, and the pile being in full flame, and the carpets taken down, fhe leaped into the midft of the fire ; her friends then poured quantities of oil over her, which foon fuffocated her, and reduced both corpfe to afhes, which were carefully gathered and put into an urn, to be conveyed to their relations in India.

This barbarous cuftom was firft introduced upon a political account; for polygamy, caufing abundance of heart-burning and jealoufy among the women that were rivals in their hufband's affeCtions, it often happened that fuch as thought themfelves negleCted, ufed frequently to procure their hufband's deaths ; wherefore, to make them more careful of the lives of their hufbands, it was ordered that thofe wives only, who were willing to accompany their hufbands to the other world, by being burned with his corpfe whenever he died, fhould have the reputation of being honeft and virtuous; and fuch as would not give that proof of their affeCtion, fhould be deemed infamous for ever after the death of their hufband. Notwithftanding the obligation to burn with their hufbands, impofed no other penalty on fuch as refufed than being accounted infamous for not conforming to fuch a dreadful cuftom, yet fuch was the fenfe of honour and love for reputation, among the Banyan women, that there are innumerable examples among them, of fuch as have voluntarily facrificed.

crificed their lives upon the burning pile : and what makes them undergo this with so much chearfulness, is a persuasion, that if a woman has so great an affection for her husband, as to burn herself with him after his death, she shall live with him in the other world seven times as long, and shall enjoy him with seven times as much satisfaction as she has done in this, without a rival ; so that they look upon this kind of death, as a passage through which they are to enter into the enjoyment of those pleasures, of which they had but a small share of in this world. This custom prevails only among the Banyans, and not in general over India.

India is inhabited by three distinct sorts of people; first, the Indostans, who are the ancient natives of the country, an idle and a slovenly generation ; secondly, the Moguls, who came out of Grand Tartary, a warlike people, and much addicted to arms ; these are all Mahometans ; thirdly, the Banyans, who came originally from China, and are all Pagans, and who apply themselves entirely to manufacture and trade. The Banyans are incomparably more ingenious, subtle, and civil, than any of the other Indians : there is no trade in Persia, or the Turkish dominions, which is not principally managed by them, nor any commodity throughout all the Indies which they do not deal in. The Banyans are distinguished from those who profess Mahometanism by their habit, for they do not wear their hair long, neither shave their heads, nor do their women cover their faces, as the Mahometans do. Black teeth are in so much esteem amongst them, that they call the white-teethed Europeans *bondra*, or apes. They wear no breeches, as the other Indians

do

do, but only a piece of thin filk ftuff, which is wrapped
about them, hanging down to their hams, over which they
wear their fmocks, and on them their upper garment, which
they tie with a girdle round the waift; under thefe a narrow waiftcoat, the fleeves of which reach no farther than
the elbow ; they wear fhoes of velvet, brocade, or gilt leather, faftened to their feet with ftraps, and they pull them
off when they go into any room, where the floors are generally covered with tapeftry, but when they walk abroad they
wear wooden fhoes.

Their bramins, or priefts, are diftinguifhed from the
reft only by what they wear about their heads, which is
made of linen cloth, wrapped feveral times round the head
to cover their *facred hair*, which is never cut; they have
alfo two pieces of packthread next their fkin, crofling the
breaft from the fhoulders to the waift, which they never put
off, though it were to fave their lives. They are, moreover,
in fuch reputation for fanctity, that no marriage is holy
where the bride has not been confecrated by the facred ini-
tiation of the prieft, to whom fhe is always conducted for
that purpofe ; and he rates this part of his *holy office* at an
exorbitant price, befides a ftrong folicitation to relieve the
bridegroom from his drudgery ; and thus the crafty prieft,
by impofing on the fimplicity of his flock, improves his natural talent to the beft advantage, and fatisfies at once both
his appetite and his avarice. But this is not all, for the
hufband retains fo much pious regard for his co-partner,
that if they go any journey, or upon any occafion are detained from home, he recommends his whole family, but
                                                      efpeci-

eſpecially his wife to the care of the prieſt in his abſence,
to ſupply his place till his return ; and the wife makes it
her care to cheriſh his languiſhing ſpirits with powerful re-
ſtoratives, at which the Indian women are the moſt expert
of any in the world, as they are alſo perfect miſtreſſes of
the eaſieſt methods, upon certain occaſions, of diſpatching
their huſbands to the other world. Theſe are the accounts
I received at Aſtrachan.

BOOK

BOOK VIII.

Army embark at Aſtrachan, 18th of July.—Variety of wild fowl on the little iſlands.—Terki, the capital city of Circaſſia.—Herring in the Caſ- pian.—Voyage to Buſtrow.—General Waterang's account from the pro- vince of Andreof.—Circaſſia and its inhabitants, their manners, religion, &c.—Continuation of the voyage and view of mount Caucaſus, &c.— The army land at Agrechan.—March into Aſia.—Kindneſs of the Da- geſtan Tartars.—The army paſs the river Sulack.—General Waterang joins the army.—Embarraſſed on their march, and ſevere puniſhment on the officers of the guards.—Arrive at Tarku, with a deſcription of the Dageſtan Tartars.—Interview with the ladies.—The Dageſtan ladies wait on the empreſs.—Erect a monument at Tarku, and march for Der- bent through a fine country.—Sultan Udenach's cruelty, and its conſe- quences.—Twenty deſperate Tartars.—A beautiful Tartar youth ſlain.— Undaunted reſolution of the prieſt.—Arrive at Derbent.—Deſcription of the city.—Remarkable tombs.—Alexander and Melkehatura.—Jackcalls and ſand hares.—Thirteen tranſports loſt and buried in the ſand.—Suck- ary bread.—Two expreſſes and one ambaſſador arrive at the army.—A Turkiſh ambaſſador obliges the emperor to return.—Occaſion of the trou- bles in Perſia.—The army return.—Cold nights.—Dangerous and har- raſſing march.—The new town of Swetago-Kreſt.—Fort at the river Nitzi deſtroyed, and revenged.—The army re-imbark at Agrechan.—The proviſions for the captain's galley loſt; a ſtarving voyage.—Arrive at Aſ- trachan the 15th of October.

G Eneral Waterang had been diſpatched ſome time ago, through the great deſart of Aſtrachan, with an army of 7,000 dragoons, and 10,000 Coſſacks, attended by 20,000 Kalmuck Tartars, with a very large train of camels to carry their proviſions and water; and with orders to at- tack and deſtroy the province of Andreof, to revenge the many ravaging incurſions made by them on the ſubjects of

L l Ruſſia;

Ruffia : the general was fhortly after followed by 10,000.
Coffacks and 20,000 Kalmuck Tartars more, to augment
his army, and enable him to complete the deftruction of
that province.

On the 18th of July, our army embarked on board two.
hundred and fifty gallies, attended by thirty-five ftore and
hofpital-fhips ; our infantry confifted of 33,000 of thofe
warlike veterans, who had been in every campaign during
the long war with Sweden.   We fat out from Aftrachan the
fame evening, under a general falute from all the artillery of
the city and fleet ; we dropt down with the ftream all night,
and arrived next day at the mouth of the river, which is
fixty werfts from Aftrachan, where we got fight of the Cafpian for the firft time.   We went down the wefternmoft
ftream of the Wolga, which is the only one that can carry
veffels of heavy burden ; the reft of the ftreams, which form
a prodigious number of fmall iflands, are to the eaftward,.
and fall into the Cafpian fea in thirty-two different channels.

Thefe iflands feed a vaft number of cattle in the fummer ;.
and as they are all furrounded by vaft quantities of thick.
tall reeds, the great number of wild fowl, efpecially fea-fowl,
is paft defcription ; upon firing of a gun, they rife in the
air like a cloud, when numbers of them may be killed with
great eafe ; a greater variety is not to be feen any where in.
the known world.   Befides fwans and common wild geefe,
there is a very large kind called by the Ruffians *baba,* or
crop-geefe, and by others pelicans ; their bills being a foot
and half long, and two inches broad, are forked at the
ends ; fome of thefe fowls, from the head to the feet, are
above feven feet in length ; under their bills they have a

9   fhrivelled

fhrievelled fkin hanging, refembling a bag, which when dilated, contains three gallons of liquor; this bag they make ufe of to hold the fifh that they catch, which they afterwards eat at their leifure. There is another kind called fpoon-geefe; their beaks are long and round, and at the extremity are flat like the mouth of a fpoon beaten out; this fowl, when it puts its beak in the water, makes a moft hideous noife, fomewhat like the braying of an afs: another kind, by fome called the red geefe, by others flamingos, are in great flocks on the Cafpian fhores; they walk after their leader in a very regular order, and at a diftance appear not unlike a regiment of foldiers following their commander; their legs are very long, of a fcarlet red, and they have very long necks, the plumage of various colours, but their heads are like fcarlet, their bodies are of different colours, beautifully variegated, and their wings fcarlet; it is in every refpect a moft beautiful bird; they exceed in height a tall grenadier, with his cap on his head, yet their bodies are not much bigger than that of the fwan: there are alfo black geefe of the ordinary fize, and this kind are no where elfe to be met with, and are preferable in tafte to any of the other geefe. As for wild ducks, their variety is incredible, and to defcribe their different kinds almoft impoffible. I cannot, however, pafs over two of them without notice, which I thought the moft extraordinary; the one is called the fcarlet-duck, from the colour of its feathers, which are fhaded by other beautiful coloured feathers, and has upon its head a large tuft of feathers refembling a crown, intermixt with all the colours of the rainbow; it is very large, and delicious eating; the other is the yellow-duck,

whofe

whofe feathers are entirely of that colour; thefe are alfo very large and fat and moft excellent eating, and what is very uncommon, they build their nefts on the tops of the higheft trees, and when their young come out of the fhell, they carry them in their beaks to the water : no fowl is more efteemed than thefe, for their delicious tafte, or eafier got, as they commonly betray themfelves by the noife they make, which is heard at a great diftance ; they are always in pairs, and when you kill the one you are fure of the other, as it never leaves its dead mate till you kill it alfo.

Terki, the capital of Circaffia.

On the 20th we weighed from the mouth of the Wolga, under the command of the great admiral Apraxin ; their majefties, the emperor and emprefs, having failed before us for Terki, the capital city of Circaffian Tartary, which is the moft fouthern boundary of his majefty's prefent dominions : this city is ftrongly fortified, and ftands on an ifland formed by the rivers Terki and Buftrow, and is garrifoned by two thoufand regulars and one thoufand Coffacks, who are all horfemen ; the native Circaffians are not permitted to live near the city, but inhabit the country at fome diftance from it. The wind turning contrary, our fleet came to an anchor towards evening, and next day the wind being ftill foul, the whole fleet took to their oars, and keeping as near the fhore as poffible, for there is no coming nearer to it than four or five werfts, becaufe of the fhallownefs of the water, and the whole fhore even to that diftance being overgrown with ftrong high reeds, which makes it impoffible to land any where, even in a canoe. Towards night a favourable gale relieved the poor wearied foldiers, who had rowed hard all day. The wind continued favourable all night ; at one o'clock

in.

in the morning we had heavy rain, with thunder and light
ning. The weather cleared up on the morning of the 22d ;
and as the wind continued in our favour, we failed all this day
in fight of the fhore, and came to an anchor at night near
Labugin, in ten feet water. This day afforded us an amuf- Herrings in
the Cafpian..
ing entertainment, with a kind of fifh of the fize and fhape
of a herring; they fwam and fkipped on the furface of the
water continually, without offering to go down, notwithftanding we purfued and killed numbers of them : we concluded it was their conftant way of living, but having baited
fome hooks with them, we caught a fturgeon and two be-
lugas, which convinced us that they fled to the furface to
efcape the purfuit of the fifh of prey, in the fame manner
as the flying-fifh rife to efcape the purfuit of the dolphin :
thefe little fifh have exactly the fhape and tafte of herrings,
and I am perfuaded they are nothing elfe.

Early in the morning of the 23d, we weighed again, Voyage to
Buttrow..
with the wind ftill fair, and got out of fight of land ; and
in the afternoon our divifion loft fight of the admiral, which
gave us no fmall trouble as we had neither pilot nor compafs
on board, (indeed the reft of the fleet laboured under the
fame inconveniency), and when the night came, not knowing how to fteer, we dropt anchor in eighteen feet water,
and waited the return of day-light. Early in the morning
of the 24th, we got under way again, and about noon got
fight of the land, to the great joy of every body on board,
as it was the only rule for the direction of our courfe ; but
the wind being againft us, we were obliged to have recourfe
to the oar, and rowing along the coaft, which was ftill clofely
covered,

covered with ſtrong reeds, above two werſts from the land,
which made it impractable to land any where on this coaſt,
except in the mouth of a river.   At night a ſignal was made
by our commanding officer, to come to an anchor, which
we did in nine feet water, where we caught very good fiſh
of ſeveral kinds.   At day break of the 25th, by ſignal,
we got under way with the oar, the wind being contrary,
ſtill rowing as near the reeds as poſſible : ſeveral of the gallies ſent out their pinnaces to the reeds, when on firing of a
muſket ſuch multitudes of different ſorts of water-fowl roſe,
that they killed great numbers of them.   At night we came
again to an anchor in fourteen feet water, after a hard day's
labour.   The wind proving fair in the morning of the 26th,
we got early under way, and towards the evening arrived
in the mouth of the river Buſtrow, which flows by the city
of Terki, ſituated three werſts from the ſhore, and here we
found the reſt of the fleet which had kept up with the admiral.

General Wa-
terang's ac-
count from
the Province
of Andreof.   While we were here, his majeſty received accounts from
general Waterang, with the agreeable news that he had defeated and cut to pieces a body of five thouſand men, of
the province of Andreof, and that he had burnt and deſtroyed their capital city, laid the whole province waſte,
and carried off all the inhabitants that he could meet with,
old and young of both ſexes, amounting to many thouſands ;
and ſent them to Aſtrachan under the eſcort of five thouſand
Coſſacks, and fifteen thouſand Kalmucks ; and had beſides
given liberty to ſeveral thouſand Ruſſian ſlaves of both ſexes,
who were then on their way to Terki, to be tranſported
from

BOOK VIII.

1721.

from thence by fea to Aftrachan. For this fignal fuccefs. we had orders to fire three vollies, from all our guns and fmall arms.

I cannot here omit giving fome farther defcription of Circaffia, and its inhabitants. Terki, the principal city, is feated in a very fpacious plain, very fwampy towards the fea-fide, in 43 deg. 23 min. north latitude: it is about three werfts in compafs, well fortified with ramparts and baftions in the modern ftyle, well ftored with cannon, and has always a confiderable garrifon in it, under the command of a governor. The Circaffian prince who refides here, is allowed five hundred Ruffians for his guard, but none of his own fubjects are permitted to dwell within any part of the fortifications. Ever fince the reduction of thofe parts to the obedience of Ruffia, they have put in all places of ftrength, not only Ruffian garrifons and governors, but magiftrates, and priefts for the exercife of the Chriftian religion; yet the Circaffian Tartars are governed by their own princes, lords, and judges, but thefe adminifter juftice in the name of the emperor, and in matters of importance, not without the prefence of the Ruffian governors, being all obliged to take the oath of allegiance to his imperial majefty. The apparel of the men of Circaffia is much the fame with that of the Nagayans, only their caps is fomething larger and their cloaks, being likewife of coarfe cloth or fheep fkins, are faftened only at the neck with a ftring, and as they are not large enough to cover the whole body, they turn them round according to the wind and weather. The men here are much better favoured than thofe of Nagaya, and the women extremely well fhaped, with exceeding fine features, fmooth clear complexions, and

beau-

beautiful black eyes, which with their black hair hanging
in two treſſes, one on each ſide the face, give them a moſt
lovely appearance ; they wear a black coif on their heads,
covered with a fine white cloth tied under the chin : during
the ſummer they all wear only a ſmock of divers colours,
and that open ſo low before, that one may ſee below their
navels ; this with their beautiful faces always uncovered,
(contrary to the cuſtom of moſt of the other provinces in
theſe parts), their good humour and lively freedom in converſation, altogether render them very deſirable : notwithſtanding which they have the reputation of being very chaſte,
though they ſeldom want opportunity ; for it is an eſtabliſhed point of good manners among them, as ſoon as any
perſon comes in to ſpeak to the wife, the huſband goes out
of the houſe : but whether this continency of their's proceeds from their own generoſity, to recompence their huſbands for the confidence they put in them, or has its foundation only in fame, I pretend not to determine. Their
language they have in common with the other neighbouring Tartars, although the chief people among them are alſo
not ignorant of the Ruſſian ; their religion is Paganiſm, for
notwithſtanding they uſe circumciſiom among them, they
have neither prieſt, alcoran, or moſque, like other Mahometans. Every body here offers his own ſacrifice at pleaſure,
for which, however, they have certain days eſtabliſhed rather
by cuſtom, than any poſitive command : their moſt ſolemn
ſacrifice is offered at the death of their neareſt friends, upon
which occaſion both men and women meet in the field to be
preſent at the offering, which is an he-goat ; and having
killed, they flay it, and ſtretch the ſkin with the head and

5

horns

horns on, upon a crofs at the top of a long pole, placed
commonly in a quickfet hedge, (to keep the cattle from it),
and near the place the facrifice is offered by boiling and
roafting the flefh, which they afterwards eat. When the
feaft is over, the men rife, and having paid their adoration to
the fkin, and muttered over fome certain prayers, the women
withdraw, and the men conclude the ceremony with drinking a great quantity of aqua vitæ, and this generally ends
in a quarrel before they part. The river Buftrow is the
fouthern boundary of Circaflia, and the province of Andreof
are their next neighbours, who dwell between the river
Koifu, which rifes out of Mount Caucafus, and the Buftrow.
Thofe people were reduced by general Waterang.

Their majefties having embarked on the evening of the Continuation of the voy-age, and view of Mount Cau-cafus, &c.
26th, the fleet failed early in the morning of the 27th, with a
very favourable breeze, and paffed the ifland of Trenzini, and
foon after we faw land on both fides of us, occafioned by a
peninfula which formed a large bay, upwards of forty werfts
long, and here we had the firft view of the high mountains
of Caucafus, which feem to hide their heads in the clouds.
The mountains of Taurus and Arrarat, are fo contiguous to
the Caucafus, that they appear like a continuation of the
fame mountain, which croffes all Afia, from Andreof, or
Mongrelia, to the Indies. Mount Arrarat is one entire vaft
rock, exceeding even Caucafus itfelf in height, its top being covered with fnow all the year round. It is faid to be
the fame on which the ark refted after the Deluge. The Armenians, who call it Meffina, believe there are ftill fome
fragments of that ark on this mountain, but that by the
length of time they were all petrified; which muft now re-

M m   main

main uncertain, as the mountain is inacceffible from the
furrounding precipices. Thofe high mountains are of great
ufe to mariners in thefe parts of the Cafpian, as moft of
them have very little knowledge of the compafs ; the different appearances they make toward the fea, ferve as an inftruction to the pilots in determining whereabout they are.
But to return to our voyage:—we arrived the fame evening
in the mouth of the river Agrechan, where we anchored
for the night, when we had rain, thunder, and lightning.

By a fignal from the great admiral, early in the morning
of the 28th, we began to land our troops, which was performed with much difficulty. By reafon of the fhoal water,
our gallies could not come within a confiderable diftance to
the fhore, and the men were obliged to carry their arms,
ammunition, baggage, and provifions, a long way in the
water on their backs ; the unloaded veffels were all hauled
up on the fhore, and a ftrong entrenchment thrown up
about them for their fecurity, under the guard of a colonel
and fix hundred men, with all our fick, who were afterwards
reinforced with a thoufand Coffacks from general Waterang's
army. Here a great number of Circaffian and Dageftan
Tartars came to us, with little waggons, horfes, camels, and
oxen to fell, and being well convinced we could not well
proceed without fuch accommodation, they took advantage
of our neceffity, and made us pay what they pleafed to demand for them. I bought a waggon and two horfes for my
baggage, and one to ride on, for which I was obliged to pay
fix times their value.

We remained here till the 4th of Auguft, when we decamped, and began our firft march in Afia: the heat was

fo

fo intolerable, that numbers of our men dropt down by the way, and notwithftanding that, we marched twenty-five werfts this day, and arrived on the banks of the river Sulack at night. On the 5th we marched ten werfts farther up the river, to a place intended to ferry over our army; on our march we were met by the fhafkal, or prince, of Tarku, the chief of the Dageftan Tartars, who was attended by a very grand retinue, and welcomed his imperial majefty into the Dageftan territories, and offered his affiftance to the utmoft of his power; his fubjects, at the fame, brought us all manner of refrefhments for the army. After our army paffed by him in good order, he feemed to be much furprifed at the regularity and fine difcipline he obferved they were under, having never feen any regular troops before; and after feeing our camp formed, he left us feemingly well pleafed. The Tartars brought fuch quantities of grapes, melons, oranges, pomgranates, apples, pears, &c. to the camp, and our people devoured them fo voracioufly, that many were feized with fevers and fluxes; on which no fruit was permitted to be brought into the army. Here we found feveral fmall boats, of which we made two ferries to waft the army over the Sulack.

On the 6th his majefty paft over with his own divifion and fome other regiments, and formed a camp on the other fide, and in the evening the governor of Gorfki, and the governor of Axay, two Dageftan princes, came to wait upon his majefty: the firft brought him a prefent of three fine Perfian horfes, with rich furniture, and fix hundred waggons for the baggage, each drawn by two oxen, befides fifty fat oxen to kill for the army: the latter prefented his majefty

with

with fix fine Perfian horfes, with very rich furniture, and one hundred oxen for the army; recommending themfelves and their country to his majefty's protection. The next day we had fuch a violent ftorm of wind, that it blew down all our tents, and made the river fwell to that degree, that it overflowed its banks, and we were obliged to remove at fome diftance from it; feveral men who were croffing at that time, were drowned in their paffage: our ferries got fo much damage by this ftorm, that we did not get all the army over

General Waterang joins the army.

before the 10th, when we were joined by general Waterang, with his dragoons and Coffacks, and one thoufand of the latter were immediately fent back to reinforce thofe left in the entrenchments, that covered our gallies at the mouth of the river Agrechan. The general brought with him prifoner, the chief of the province of Andreof, whom the emperor caufed to be hanged up the fame day, for an example to others. This irritated the other chiefs of the Dageftans to fuch a degree, that they were determined to be revenged, which brought us into no fmall trouble.

Embarraffed in their march, and fevere punifhment on the officers of the guards.

We began to march again on the 11th, with one half of the dragoons and Coffacks for our advanced guard, and the other half to cover our rear; and went thirty werfts that day, notwithftanding the intenfe heat, which made many of our men drop by the way. When we halted in the middle of the day, we difcovered great numbers of armed men on horfeback riding on the fides of the mountains: his majefty was at that time in the rear, and riding along the army, enquired of the men if their pieces were loaded; and being informed they were not, he gave orders himfelf to load them, ordering, at the fame time, all the officers of his own

divifion

divifion to meet at the head of the grenadier company, where
having met, he harangued and reprimanded us feverely
for neglect of duty; we were then difarmed, and our
fwords, (viz. the field officers, who were at the fame time
generals, and all the captains,) were put all together into a
waggon; the field-officers were ordered to march on foot
in one rank, and the captains were formed in three ranks
behind them, and every officer was loaded with four mufkets
on his fhoulders; in this pofture we marched near two hours
in the moft intolerable heat, when the emprefs being informed of our miferable fituation, came up in her chariot
with the utmoft hafte, and pleaded fo effectually in our
favour, that we were relieved from our heavy burdens, had
our fwords reftored, and were admitted to kifs his majefty's
hand, who told us, that he had only punifhed the officers of
his own guards, becaufe they ought to give a good example
to all the reft of the army.——This was difcipline with a
vengeance.——The poor captain of the grenadiers died the
next day of the fatigue, being a corpulent man, and feveral
others fickened, fome of whom died alfo. We loft feveral
horfes this day by their eating a poifonous herb and want of
water; but none of the camels or oxen were affected, and
I concluded they had not eat any of it.

On the 12th, we reached the city of Tarku, ten werfts; Arrive at
the fhafkal met the emperor half-way, and conducted him Tarku, a de-
to the city; it ftands on the fide of a hill, quite open, with- fcription of
out any walls, and our army encamped on a fpacious plain the Dageftan
below the town. Being now arrived at the capital of Da- Tartars.
geftan Tartary, I fhall endeavour to give fome defcription
of the province and city, from the beft information I could
obtain.

obtain. Their territory reaches from the river Buftrow, their boundary with Circaffia, all along mount Caucafus, as far as Derbent, and they are neither fubject to the Turk nor the Perfian, but are in general governed by the fhafkal, who is their fupreme head : his office is not hereditary but elective. The whole country of Dageftan is divided into fmall diftricts, or lordfhips, each under the jurifdiction of its proper lord, or myrza, who, though hereditary, is neverthelefs not abfolute, but his authority is controlled by that of fome of the chief men among them. All thefe petty lords acknowlege one whom they call fhafkal as fupreme head, to whom they pay their refpect, but not paffive obedience. Thefe people are generally very mifchievous, barbarous, and favage, living for the moft part by robbery and plunder; a great part of their livelihood is for the men to fteal children, not fparing even thofe of their own neareft relations, whom they fell to the neighbouring Perfians, leaving the care of their cattle to their wives in their abfence. They are called Dageftans, from the word *Dag*, which fignifies in their language, a mountain, and are from thence called mountaineers; they pretend to be the defcendants of the Amazons, and firmly believe that Thaleftris, the queen of the Amazons, went from hence to Hircania on a vifit to Alexander the Great, to obtain that favour which ladies, although ever fo defirous of, feldom care to beg. The Dageftans are all Mahometans, ufing circumcifion and all the other ceremonies of the Turks. Their habit is a long clcfe coat, commonly of a dark grey, or black, coarfe cloth, over which they wear a cloak of the fame ftuff; and in winter, of fheep fkins: they wear a fquare cap of a great many pieces fewed together;

their

their fhoes are for the moft part made of horfes hides,
fewed together only at the inftep; the pooreft man
among them is provided with a coat of mail, head-
piece, and buckler, befides a fcymitar, javelin, bow and
arrows.

This city of Tarku, being the metropolis of Dageftan,
contains above three thoufand houfes, and is very full of
inhabitants; the houfes all two ftories high, platformed
at top, ftanding clofe to each other: the women walk
upon them in the cool of the evenings, as the men do in
the ftreets. Every houfe has a garden ftored with all kinds
of delicious fruits, and all well fupplied with fine fprings of
water: as for their women, they are incomparably beautiful,
both in feature and fhape, with a fair clear complexion,
accompanied with lovely black eyes and hair; but as the
men are very jealous, they are always locked up, fo that it
is no eafy matter to get fight of them; and I believe we
fhould not have feen any of them if it had not happened
twice by accident. We had the liberty to go into the city
to buy neceffaries, and were ordered on thefe occafions to
go in ftrong parties and well armed, for we placed no great
confidence in the fidelity of the inhabitants; and being in
town one day with feveral officers, well efcorted, we faw
one of the principal inhabitants going into his houfe, when
we made bold to throng in with him much againft his inclination; but, being informed by our interpreter, that we
were officers of rank, and that we begged the favour he
would indulge our curiofity by fhewing us the infide of his
houfe, he at laft reluctantly confented, and led us into his
apartments; the floors were all covered with very fine Perfian

fian tapeſtry, without any other kind of ornament, excepting
ſome fine mattraſſes, and ſilk quilts, upon which they lie at
night ; they have neither chairs nor tables, but all ſit or lie
on the floor : inſtead of glaſs in the windows, they have
blinds, very curiouſly checkered of plaited reed, through
which they can ſee what paſſes in the ſtreet without being
ſeen within ; the walls and cielings are all white, without
any ornament.   After this he led us into a ſquare court,
divided in the middle by a high wall, which ſeparated his
own apartments from thoſe of the women ; having ſhewed
us alſo his garden, very well ſtored with all kinds of fruit,
he invited us to ſit down with him on a ſofa under a piazza,
and entertained us with coffee, fruits, and ſweet-meats ;
when captain Brunie, one of our company, ſhewed him
a very pretty ſhaving-glaſs he carried in his pocket, and
obſerving he was much pleaſed with it, the captain made
him a preſent of it, which ſeemed to ingratiate us with
him.   After ſome converſation with our hoſt, we begged
the favour of him to let us ſee his women in their dreſs,
only at a diſtance ; to which, though unwillingly, he at laſt
conſented, and went himſelf to their apartments to order
them to get themſelves ready, as we apprehended, and returning preſently, he ſat down again and converſed ſome
time with us. He then went again, and brought out four of his
wives, and eight of his concubines, and placed them all in
a row that we might have a full view of them, in which
poſture he left them ſtanding, and returning himſelf to the
ſofa, he ſat down with us : the ladies, however, ſeemingly
diſpleaſed to be gazed at, at ſuch a diſtance, advanced with
one accord, and ſeated themſelves upon the ſofa oppoſite to

us,

us, at which forwardnefs our hoft feemed not at all pleafed,
and they, not regarding him in the leaft, examined our drefs
very narrowly, and put a great many queftions to us, by our
interpreter, efpecially relating to the cuftoms and drefs of
our women, and how many women were allowed in our
country to each man ; on their being informed that no man
was allowed to have more than one wife, and that the women had the fame liberty as the men to walk abroad and vifit their neighbours; they clapped their hands, and cried
out with emotion, " O ! happy, happy country !" Our
hoft not being at all pleafed with their conduct, ordered them
immediately to their apartments, and they obeyed with much
reluctance. They were all moft lovely creatures, but the
concubines excelled the wives in beauty ; the reafon is ob-
vious, for they are married to their wives by proxy, and the
others they take from choice. After fome fhort ftay we took
our leave, having invited our hoft to come next day and
fee us in the camp; upon his coming we entertained him
very handfomely, and he appeared to be moft delighted with
our regimental mufic ; and he told us at his taking leave,
that as we had fhewn him fo much politenefs and civility,
we fhould always be welcome to his houfe while we ftaid
in thofe parts ; but although we attempted it we never could
again obtain admiffion.

The next view we got of the Dageftan ladies was at the The Dagef-
emprefs's tent ; the fhafkal's ladies, attended by other ladies tan ladies
wait on the
of rank and fafhion, came to wait on her majefty ; they emprefs.
came fo clofe fhut up in coaches that they could not be feen ;
when they arrived at the emprefs's tent, they were feated
on cufhions of crimfon velvet, laid on Perfian carpets, that

N n were

BOOK VIII. were fpread upon the ground, and there they fat crofs-
legged according to their cuftom.   After they were feated,
the emprefs gave orders that the officers fhould be admitted
to fee the ladies, who were, indeed, all of them extremely
lovely; her majefty had ordered, that when one company
of the officers had gratified their curiofity, they fhould retire and make way for others; by which means the vifit of
the ladies lafted till it was pretty late at night, when they
were attended back to the city by her fervants, with abundance of torches, highly pleafed with their reception; and
not only being informed, but alfo feeing how unconfined
our women live, they certainly were as much taken with it
as thofe of our hoft; and I dare fay, if we could have beat
up for volunteers among thofe lovely daughters of the Amazons, their men would now have been left as womenlefs as
they were in thofe ancient times.

Erect a mo-
nument at
Tarku, and
march for
Derbent.

His majefty's manifeftos having been publifhed, not only
throughout Dageftan, but alfo at Derbent, Backu, and
Shamachie; letters were received from Derbent, on the 15th,
with affurances, that the manifeftoes were received with
great joy there, and that they would, with the utmoft pleafure, put themfelves under the emperor's protection when-
ever he arrived there with his army.   Upon this news it was
ordered, that every perfon belonging to the army, from the
higheft to the loweft, fhould bring a ftone of the middling
fize, into the middle of the camp, where a crofs was erected,
round which they were piled up for a lafting memorial, I
fuppofe, and after this divine fervice was performed.   We
broke up on the 16th, and marched twenty-five werfts, in
a fcorching heat, to the river Manas, which afforded us

3   plenty

plenty of water, but we could get no forage, and were obliged to fend our horfes in among the mountains for grafs,
where great numbers of them were taken and carried off
by the Tartars, and among the reft all my three horfes.
When we moved next day, the 17th, general Waterang was
fo good as to order two dragoons to difmount, and yoke their
horfes to my baggage-waggon, but I was, myfelf, reduced
to walk on foot, which was extremely fatiguing in that hot
climate. Madam Campenhaufen, one of her majefty's ladies of honour, obferving me marching on foot before my
company, fent in the evening to enquire the reafon, and
being told my misfortune, was fo kind as to acquaint the
emprefs with it, who was gracioufly pleafed to order her
equerry to give me a horfe with furniture; and his majefty
being informed of my neceffity, gave orders to provide me
with another, fo that I was again mounted, and my fervant alfo, on horfeback : that night, however, I bought two
camels for my baggage, at fifteen rubles each, and gave my
waggon to one of my officers who was in want of one : I
was foon fully convinced of the ufefulnefs of the camels,
who not only carry heavy burdens, but feed where no horfe
can fubfift; and can live feveral days without water, if
they get but a handful of falt in lieu of it. This day we
paffed the river Manas, and at no great diftance from it, the
river Boinack, over a ftone bridge, and encamped for the
night at Old Boinack, having marched thirty werfts, and
come through large fields of cotton and faffron. We loft
this day a number of horfes by heat, fatigue, and want of
forage. It is to be obferved of this country, that the fummer is fo exceffively hot, and all the grafs is fo entirely

withered

BOOK VIII. withered and fcorched up, that the inhabitants are obliged
—————— to feed their cattle with hay, which they provide in the winter
1722. when the country abounds with grafs and pafturage. From
this place his majefty difpatched three Coffacks, with a guide,
to fultan Udenich, who lived at fome diftance among the
mountains, requiring him to fend a deputation in order to a
conference, and defiring him to fupply the army with beafts
of burden, to tranfport our baggage to Derbent.

Sultan Ude-   On the 18th we marched twenty-five werfts, and encamped
nich's cruelty
and its confe- on the banks of the river Nitzi, where the guide returned to
quences. us, with fultan Udenich's anfwer, having his nofe and both
ears cut off, and informed his majefty that they had, in his
prefence, put the three Coffacks to death, in a moft cruel
and barbarous manner: the fultan bade him tell the emperor,
that whoever of his people fell into his hands they fhould
be treated in the fame manner, and as to the defired conference, they were ready to hold it with their fcymitars in
their hands.

On the 19th, the Tartars appeared on the fide of the hill,
about twelve thoufand ftrong, to put their threats in execution; and as we were fufficiently on our guard by the return of the meffenger, the army was immediately under arms
without ftriking their tents, and his majefty marched in perfon toward the enemy with only his own divifion, which confifted of fix battalions, ordering only a part of the army to
follow. Upon our approaching the foot of the hill, we fired
fmartly on each other, without much damage on either fide,
and as they ftood upon a very high eminence, we could not
bring our cannon to bear on them; the emperor perceiving
they kept their ftation without advancing towards us, ordered

dered the dragoons and Coffacks to march round, and attack
them upon the hill, which they did with great expedition,
and as they afcended the declivity we faw them all the
way, but they were not difcovered by the enemy till they were
clofe at their backs, when a great flaughter enfued, and the
Tartars fled with the utmoft precipitation, leaving between
fix and feven hundred men dead on the fpot, and forty were
taken prifoners; among whom were fome perfons of diftinction, and their Mahometan prieft, who had been one of their
principal leaders, and not only advifed but perpetrated with
his own hands, that horrid cruel murder of the three Coffacks, cutting open their breafts while they were yet alive,
and taking out their hearts, and whofe bodies were afterwards found ftuck upon ftakes near the fultan's palace, by
our dragoons who purfued the enemy to the very gates,
which they alfo entered, putting every one they met with to
the fword, amounting to upwards of three thoufand men;
for they had fent away their women and children to the
mountains, before they fat out on this expedition, in which,
befides the flain, the fultan's refidence and fix other villages
were burnt and entirely deftroyed.

In the purfuit, a party of the dragoons had driven twenty Twenty def-
Tartars into a narrow place, from which there was no pof- perate Tar-
fibility of efcaping, and finding themfelves fo clofely hemmed tars.
in, they fell on their knees, and offered, in this fupplicating
pofture, to deliver up their fire arms with the butt ends foremoft, upon which twenty of the dragoons were ordered to
difmount and fecure them; but upon their approach,
thefe defperadoes rofe up and threw their javelins, and
killed every one of the dragoons, and then made fo bold
an attack with their fcymitars in their hands, that they
wounded

wounded feveral more, not giving over till they were every one cut to pieces.

General Romantzof was ordered to march with our fix battalions, to affift the dragoons in deftroying the fultan's refidence, and on our way we were attacked by a body of fix hundred horfe, who were coming from a neighbouring chief to Udenich's affiftance. In their attack they advanced and retired in a very uncommon manner: they were formed only twelve in front, but fifty in depth, following each other with their drawn fcymitars; when the front ranks had made an attempt on our fcrewed bayonets, they wheeled about and placed themfelves again in the rear; having continued to attack us in this manner near half an hour, they thought proper to march off with the lofs of feveral men and horfes killed and wounded. In this attack one of their commanders who had diftinguifhed himfelf with fuperior courage and activity, made frequent attempts and wounded two of our men: general Romantzof obferving him, and feeing me with a rifle-piece in my hand, defired I would endeavour to bring him down, which I did at his next attack, by fhooting him through the thigh, and he tumbled from his horfe, which with his own perfon was immediately fecured. The general was pleafed to make me a prefent of his horfe and furniture, with his fcymitar, bow and arrows; the bridle and furniture were overlaid with ftuds of gilt filver, the handle and fcabbard of the fcymitar, with the fame in filigree work; the horfe I fold for fixty ducats, the fcymitar, bow and arrows, I brought with me to Britain, and ftill have them in my poffeffion. By this means general Romantzof made me fome amends for the horfe and furniture left me by

marfhal

marſhal Weyde, which had been detained from me as I mentioned formerly. This rencounter being ended, we continued our march toward Udenich's reſidence, and found all the way we went, the road ſtrewed with dead bodies, which had been killed by our dragoons in the purſuit ; and among the reſt a youth between eighteen and twenty years of age, whoſe head had been but newly cut off : the beauty of his face and perſon were, even in death, ſo extraordinary, that every one ſtood to look on him as they paſt the corpſe, declaring they had never ſeen any one comparable to him ; but as the admiration of this corpſe retarded our march, the general ordered the body to be removed out of the way. After having marched about fifteen werſts, we were met by the dragoons and Coſſacks on their return, richly laden with plunder; and general Waterang having informed Romantzof that all was over and completely finiſhed, we returned all together in one body, and on our arriving at the eminence where the enemy made their firſt appearance, we found twenty-one of the priſoners hung up by way of repriſal, for the cruel death of our three Coſſacks : one of the priſoners was ſent back to ſultan Udenich, with his noſe and ears cut off, with a letter reproaching him with his ſavage cruelty toward our innocent meſſengers. The prieſt was quartered for his inhuman barbarity.

While this detachment were abſent on that ſervice, lord admiral Apraxin, who commanded the army in chief, had been examining ſome of the priſoners, and aſking them why they had put our innocent meſſengers to ſo cruel a death, they replied that they knew nothing farther about it, but that it was done by their ſultan's orders at the inſtigation:

of

Marginal notes:

BOOK VIII.

1724.

A beautiful Tartar youth ſlain.

Undaunted reſolution of the prieſt.

of the prieſt : the prieſt being thereupon interrogated, very
boldly anſwered, that he would have done the ſame to every
one of our people whom he could have got in his power,
to revenge the treatment the Tartars of Andreof had received from us, whoſe chief we had put to ſo ignominious
a death, and whoſe friends and allies they were; beſides, they
were a free nation, and would ſubject themſelves to no prince
on earth. The admiral then aſked him how they could venture to attack ſo numerous and regular an army, who were
ſo far ſuperior to any force they could raiſe, and all the
aſſiſtance they could expect from their neighbours; to which
the prieſt replied, that they were not at all afraid of our
foot ſoldiers, who were not able to follow them into mountains, and as to the Coſſacks they had been uſed to beat them
often on former occaſions : but what diſconcerted them
moſt was our blue coats, (meaning the dragoons), who kept
ſo cloſe together on horſeback. He then told the admiral
to aſk him no more queſtions, for he was fully determined
not to anſwer any, and that he neither aſked not expected
any favour from ſuch Chriſtian dogs ; upon which he was
taken away. Another priſoner being brought before the
admiral's tent to be examined, he would give no anſwer to
any queſtion that was put to him, on which he was ordered
to be ſtripped and whipped ; but on receiving the firſt laſh,
he ſnatched a ſword from an officer's ſide, and flew with it
towards the admiral, whom he would certainly have killed,
had not the two centries before the tent, run him through
the body with their bayonets ; and even after he fell he pulled
the muſket out of the hands of one of the centries, who
in ſtruggling to wreſt it from him, had a large piece of

fleſh

flefh bit out of his arm by this defperate fellow, who was
t hen foon difpatched. His majefty coming up at this time, ————
he admiral told him that he was certainly come into this
country to be devoured by mad dogs, having never had fuch
a fright before in his whole life: the emperor replied,
fmiling, if the people of this country underftood the art
of war, it would be impoffible for any nation to cope with
them.

The emperor, with a view to keep thefe people in awe,
ordered a fort to be erected on the river Nitzi, under the
direction of baron Renne, lieutenant of the guards, as engineer, and all the Kalmuck Tartars, with fome Coffacks,
were left to cover and protect the works.

The army moved again on the 21ft, and marching all the
way through vineyards and orchards, we came at night to
the river Durback, twenty werfts. Here we were met by
a meffenger, with a handfome retinue, from the ftrong city
of Buku, to congratulate his majefty on his fafe arrival
in thofe parts; recommending themfelves and their city to
his protection; earneftly requefting to be relieved from
Myr Maghmud the ufurper, againft whom they had found
means to defend themfelves the two years laft paft, and be-
feeching the emperor to haften to their relief.

We marched again on the 22d, through orchards and
vineyards, fifteen werfts, when we arrived at a fmall river,
where we found plenty of grafs, having fuffered greatly for
want of it all the way from Tarku to this place; and next
day, the 23d, we continued our route through thefe delightful vineyards, fifteen werfts, to Derbent. His majefty was Arrive at
met half way by the governor and principal citizens, who Derbent.

O o pre-

presented him with the keys of their city, offering, at the same time, to admit his troops into the citadel, to garrison it for the protection of their city, which had defended itself a considerable time against the arms of the usurper Maghmud: this generous offer met a very gracious reception. We marched through the city the same day, under a triple salvo of all their artillery, and encamped on the south side of the town, being now entered for the first time into Persia. We could now plainly see Mount Arrarat from our camp, rearing his summit far above the rest of the Caucasus. The emperor now appointed a governor and three thousand men to garrison the castle, to whom the inhabitants with much joy, gave the immediate possession of, as they were thereby relieved from the fatigues and hardships they had so long undergone, in defending their city against the forces of the usurper. On the ramparts were mounted one hundred iron, and sixty brass cannon, twelve and nine pounders, with large store of ammunition. At a small distance on each side of the castle, stands a high watch tower, from which they can discover the approach of an enemy at a great distance.

Description of the city. The city of Derbent, in the province of Shirvan, lies in 41 deg. 51 min. north latitude, is situated on the shore of the Caspian; the walls are carried into ten feet depth of water, to prevent any one's passing that way; its length from east to west, is nearly five werfts, but its breadth is not proportionable. It is not only the frontier of Persia, lying on its utmost confines on this side, but may with great propriety be called the gate of it, reaching from the mountain into the sea. The city is divided into three distinct quarters;

ters; the caftle, fituated upon the top of the mountain, had always a ftrong Perfian garrifon. The fecond, and principal, reaches from the foot of the mountain to the lower town, which makes the third, and reaches to the fea-fide. This laft, which was formerly inhabited by Greeks, is not now much frequented, being for the moft part converted into gardens, fince the place was regained from the Turks. The whole city is inclofed with a very ftrong wall, fo broad that a waggon may drive along the top of it without the leaft inconvenience, and flanked with fquare towers at proper diftances. The walls are built with large fquare ftones, which appear like a heap of fea-fhells cemented together, yet are hard and durable as marble, and when polifhed look extremely beautiful. Moft of the quarries in the Caucafus, are of this kind of ftone. The houfes are built and furnifhed in the fame manner as thofe of Tarku; the inhabitants are all Mahometans, except fome Jews, whofe chief bufinefs is trading in ftolen children, brought to market here by the neighbouring Tartars of Dageftan; or fome Turkifh or Ruffian captives, which they pick up on fome of their excurfions, which the Jews carry farther into Perfia, and difpofe of.

The mountain above the city, which is for the moft part covered with wood, prefents us with the ruins of a very ancient wall, which, if any credit can be given to the tradition of the natives, had formerly a communication all the way to the Euxine fea, through an extent of country near three hundred werfts in length: this much, however is certain, the ruins of it ftill appear in fome places fix feet high, in others two or three, and in others the track of it is

quite

quite loft. On fome of the adjacent hills are alfo to be feen
the ruins of feveral old caftles, of a fquare form, two of
which remaining undemolifhed to this day, are garrifoned by
the Perfians. The natives in general are of opinion, that the
city of Derbent was built by Alexander the Great, and that
the long wall, which reached to the Euxine, was built by
his order, to prevent the incurfions of the Scythians into
Perfia.

Remarkable
tombs.   Near to our camp we faw fome thoufands of tombs, covered with ftones half round (cylindrical) but exceeding the
ordinary ftature of men, having all of them Arabic infcrip-
tions. The report is, that in former ages, (yet fince the
time of Mahomet), there was a certain king in Media, named
Kaffan, received a fignal defeat in a battle he fought againft
the Dageftan Tartars at this place, and that the bodies of
his officers, flain in the battle, were buried in thefe tombs.
The relation feems not to be altogether fictitious, there being at fome fmall diftance, near the fea, forty other tombs
exceeding thofe in bignefs, inclofed by a wall, which having
each its banner, are faid to be the fepulchres of fo many
lords of the firft rank, and other holy men who accompanied
them: here both Perfians and Tartars, of both fexes, come
to pay their devotions, by kiffing thofe fepulchres, and laying their hands on them while they are at prayers.

Alexander
and Melke-
hatun.   The inhabitants of Derbent have an old tradition among
them, concerning Alexander the Great and Melkehatun, a
widow fultana, in the province of Irvan. On an expedition into thofe parts, Alexander went as his own ambaffador to the city of Berda, where the fultana refided, to demand a furrender of herfelf, her city, and country, to the
difcre-

discretion of the conqueror : Melkihatun being a woman of
curiosity and taste, had some time before procured a picture of Alexander, drawn from the life, so that he had
no sooner presented himself before her than she knew him :
having delivered his message, she desired him to dine with
her, after which he should receive his answer to carry to
the king his master; upon which he was carried into a great
hall, where a table was covered with gold and silver, and
the side dishes of gold plate were full of her jewels. The
great conqueror being seated with the queen, she earnestly
pressed him to eat, at which the great Alexander was very
much surprised, and asked the queen if her table could afford no other victuals than what he saw before him, for these
would not allay his hunger : she said,—" O ! Alexander, I
" thought you could live on nothing else, since for the sake
" of riches, you have laid so many countries waste, and left
" the poor inhabitants to perish for want : you see now, if
" you had all the treasure this world affords, and had no
" victuals, you must perish." Here she ordered a curtain
to be drawn aside, which discovered his own picture, that
hung just opposite to him, thereby shewing him by what
means she knew him; telling him, that notwithstanding he
was now in her power, she would present him with all her
treasure, as she found that riches were his only motive for
ransacking the world; begging, in return, that she and her
subjects might be allowed to cultivate and enjoy their land
in peace. The behaviour and wise discourse of the queen
so pleased the great Alexander, that he granted her what she
could ask or desire, without accepting any of her presents,
except her picture; and after being regaled with substantial
victuals,

victuals, he departed very well fatisfied with the lady and her entertainment. They fay he then proceeded to the province of Shirwan, and laid the foundation of Derbent, and gave order that a wall fhould be built from thence to the Euxine fea, with watch-towers at every mile's diftance, which was accordingly executed. They alfo fay, it was at Derbent where he received a vifit from the Amazonian queen Thaleftris, whofe territories extended from hence to the river Buftro, on the borders of Circaffia.

Thirteen ftore-fhips having arrived at the mouth of the river Millukenti with provifions, from Aftrachan, for the army, we marched thither, fifteen werfts, on the 24th, and found them at anchor. Here his majefty propofed to make a harbour for his fhips on the Cafpian, as there was no other place near Derbent fit for that purpofe, and I received orders to erect a fort to cover it: the dragoons were immediately fet to work to provide fafcines and palifades, and the infantry to break the ground. The firft night after our fires were lighted, we were vifited by creatures called jackals, which howled in a moft pitiful manner; the light of our fires had brought fuch numbers from the mountains, and they made fuch a difagreeable noife in the very front of our camp, that we could get no fleep for that night; and being ignorant what they were, our furprize continued till daylight, when we fhot feveral of them, and found them to be of the fox kind; after this we fired evening guns, which terrified them fo much, that they kept in the mountains. We found alfo at this place a number of fmall creatures, called fand-hares, fomewhat larger than rats; the head, fore-part, and tail, exactly refemble thofe of the lion; their

Jackalls and fand-hares.

4   fore-

fore-legs are very ſhort, and their hinder ones very long, ſo that inſtead of running they jump, backwards or forwards, at a ſurpriſing quick rate, ſpringing full three feet from the ground. We had much diverſion in chaſing theſe creatures, although we could catch but few of them, as they ſoon get into their holes, for they burrow like rabbits : they are very fat and good to eat. This night we loſt above ſeven hundred of our horſes, all of which ſwelled and burſt by eating a poiſonous herb which abounds in theſe parts ; but none of our camels or oxen ſuffered by it, who, upon trial, would ſcarcely ſmell at it. The natives are particularly careful to keep their horſes from feeding where this herb grows, which is only found near the ſea-ſide.

We had ſuch a furious ſtorm of wind on the 25th, from the north, that all our thirteen ſtore-ſhips, with our proviſions, were driven aſhore and ſoon beat to pieces, but the men were all ſaved, and in leſs than three hours there was not the leaſt appearance of any of the wreck to be ſeen, which was all buried under the ſand occaſioned by the ſhortneſs of the waves which ſucceed each other ſo quickly, that the ſands are thereby raiſed to a great degree : the next day it was quite calm, and all hands were ſet to work to dig for our loſt proviſions, and with ſome toil and labour we recovered them ; they conſiſted chiefly in rye meal and flour all in ſacks, and the ſalt-water had not penetrated above an inch into them, and all within that was entirely ſafe ; it was immediately diſtributed to the army, with orders to bake it into bread, and after that to make ſuchary of it. The Ruſſian ſoldiers always bake their own bread, making ovens in the ground wherever they come ; and when

Thirteen tranſports loſt and buried in the ſand.

Suchary bread.

they

they are ordered to make fuchary of it, they cut the loaves,
which commonly are of fix pound weight, into fmall fquare
pieces, and dry them in an oven, or in the fun, by which
they turn fo light, that a man can eafily carry as much bread
as will ferve him twelve or fourteen days, and this kind of
bread is fo hard, that they foak it before they eat it; but
they never make it but on neceffary and preffing occafions.
The Ruffians are fo fond of fuchary, that they always have
plenty of the beft kind of it in their houfes and ufe it in
foups; it eats very pleafant, and will keep above a year.

Two expreffes and an ambaffador arrive at the army.
Two meffengers now arrived in our camp; the one from
the city of Shamachie, and the other from Baku, imploring his majefty's affiftance againft Myr Maghmud, the
ufurper; and very foon after thofe, came other three meffengers, viz. from the Armenians, Melitener, and the
Georgians, who are all of them of the communion of the
Greek church; praying the emperor to fend them fome of
his troops to enable them to defend themfelves againft the
ufurper, as they were fully determined to perfevere in their
allegiance to their rightful fophi; and the next day an ambaffador arrived from the young fophi himfelf, who was
very preffing to have our army advance with all poffible difpatch to his affiftance; offering to give his majefty poffeffion of the ftrong cities of Refht, Shamachie, and Baku.
Upon this we made all the difpatch we could to finifh the
fort and harbour; after which we intended to fet out upon
this expedition. Having fo many hands continually employed on the works, the fort was finifhed on the 5th of
September, which confifted of four baftions, furrounded by
a moat, into which water from the river was led; and a

5   covert

covert way palifaded ; a captain with 200 regulars, and
300 Coffacks, were put into it for its defence.

Our army was in readiness to fet forward next day, when,
to our great furprize, a Turkifh ambaffador arrived from
Shamachie, informing the emperor that they had taken
poffeffion of that city, and that it was by the orders of the
grand fignor his mafter, that he came to fignify to his majefty, the umbrage taken by the Porte at the progrefs he
had made in thofe parts ; and likewife to defire him to withdraw his forces; and if the emperor fhould refufe, to declare war againft Ruffia. Upon weighing this matter duly,
his majefty did not think proper to proceed, as he did not
choofe, at this juncture, to have any rupture with the
Turks; more efpecially, as he was then at fo great a diftance from his own country with the flower of his army;
he therefore immediately refolved to return back, fo that
this was the utmoft limits, for this time, of our Perfian
expedition, and the provinces which had now fo earneftly
fought our affiftance, were afterwards obliged to put themfelves under the protection of the Turks.

All thefe troubles and diforders at this time in Perfia
were occafioned by the indolence and floth of Shah Huffein,
their king, whofe only enjoyments were the pleafures of his
haram, (or feraglio,) fuffering his eunuchs to govern at pleafure. This encouraged the Tartars, Moguls, and Arabians,
to make feveral irruptions into his provinces, and they were
only removed thence by the force of money. Georgi-chan,
the prince of Georgia, was governor of the city of Candahar, on the frontier of India, who being informed or apprehending that Myr Weis, the tax gatherer, was endeavour-

P p ing

ing to excite a revolt among the Aghvans, communicated the affair to the court of Ispahan: Myr Weis was sent for, where his fine parts enabled him very soon to make many friends, and at the same time to discover the weakness of a court quite immersed in softness and pleasures. He found means to be sent back to Candahar with some authority; where he was no sooner returned than he assassinated prince Georgi-chan, and forced the Aghvans to revolt. Thus he raised himself to the sovereign power, which he maintained till the died, the court of Persia not being able to reduce him to obedience. He was succeeded by his brother, who was soon assassinated by his nephew Myr Maghmut, son of Myr Weis. It was he that made himself master of all Persia, and drove Shah Huffein from the throne. What became of that prince after his flight, none could ever tell.

The army return.

Our army decamped on the 6th of September, and we set out on our return to Derbent, to the great mortification of those people, who had so long relied on our assistance, whose messengers now left us with heavy hearts, finding all their hopes frustrated, being now left at the mercy of the usurper Myr Maghmut. The Turkish ambassador attended us till we entered again into Dageftan. We passed through and encamped on the north side of Derbent, on our return, to the general joy of the whole army, who did not in the least relish this expedition among such a savage barbarous people. On the 7th the Turkish ambassador had his audience of leave, and went to Derbent, where he remained till he heard we were re-embarked for Aftrachan. We had now left behind us the five hundred men in the small fort on the river Millukenti, and our governor and three thou-

fand

fand men in garrifon at Derbent, and this day marching
fifteen werfts, we refted on the 8th. The heavy dews now
began to fall in the night-time, which rendered it very cold ;
the fudden change from the fcorching heat of the days to
the coldnefs of the nights, made it intolerable. We marched
again fifteen werfts on the 9th, and refted on the 10th, in
the night of which the hills were very thick covered with
fnow, which made it fo exceeding cold, that we heartily re-
pented having left our warm cloaths behind us at Aftrachan,
thinking we fhould have no occafion for them in fo hot a
climate.

On the 11th we marched twenty-four werfts to the river
Nitzi, where we found the fort finifhed by baron Ronne,
for the defence of which we had left one hundred foldiers, and two hundred Coffacks. It was at this place
where we were attacked by fultan Udinach's army, and
we now found they had carried away in the night, the
bodies of their countrymen we had hung up by way of
reprifal for the murder of the Coffacks. A meffenger arrived here from Derbent, to inform us that Udinach, joined
by Perfian Ufmei and fultan Mahmut of Utimifhof, had affembled twenty thoufand men with an intention to attack
us in the night-time, which obliged us to ftand to our
arms all night long, which was bitter cold, and we continued in that pofture till next day at noon, the enemy hovering all the while within fight : however, we moved again,
and made an afternoon's march of twelve werfts, in continual view of the enemy, who endeavoured to attack us
feveral times on our march, but as conftantly fled on our
approach, ftill hovering near us, and took two of our Cof-

facks

facks prifoners, and we took three of their Tartars. The
wind blew fo very hard this day, that we were almoft blinded
with the fand and duft, of which they thought to avail themfelves, but were fruftrated by our vigilance. We continued
under arms all this night, which proved very dewy and cold,
but as we were attacked in the night in fome part or other,
our continual motions kept us in fome heat. Next day feeing the enemy drawn up very near us, we formed and continued all day in order of battle, and remained all the following night in the fame order, and not a man offered to
ftir out of his rank, being attacked this night in almoft
every quarter of the army ; yet we no fooner offered to advance toward them than they fled. We now again loft feveral hundreds of our horfes by that poifonous herb before
mentioned.

On the 14th we marched twenty-four werfts in conftant
view of the enemy, who ftill kept fkirting the mountains,
every now and then attacking us with fmall parties, on
which occafions we took two more of them prifoners, but
were obliged to continue all this night alfo under arms,
without either pitching our tents or lighting fires, by which
means officers and men were reduced fo low by. continual
marching, watching, and cold, that our whole army, were
become very feeble and unfit for duty. On the 15th, notwithftanding the low ftate to which we were reduced, we
marched to Tarku, twenty-five werfts, and before we got
there the enemy difappeared. We difpatched two trumpe-
ters, attended by two Coffacks, to acquaint the fhafkal with
our approach, but when we advanced near the city, we
found them lying murdered on the road ; their cloaths and
horfes

horfes were found in the poffeffion of feven Dageftan Tartars belonging to Tarku, whom we apprehended and quartered them in the city in the prefence of the fhafkal and the inhabitants, and hung up their quarters in the moft public places for an example to others. His majefty upbraided the fhafkal in fevere terms, both for the murder of his meffengers, and his treachery in joining and conniving with his enemies to annoy his army : the fhafkal in his own vindication affured his majefty that he was innocent of what had happened, but that his brother, and two of his own fons, had put themfelves at the head of a difaffected body of his people, and rifen in rebellion againft him ; and as he had now fecured them, he entreated his majefty to take them, and the reft of the malcontents, and do with them whatever he pleafed : they were accordingly all delivered over to us, and fent as prifoners or hoftages to Aftrachan.

We marched again on the 16th, ten werfts from Tarku, without the leaft moleftation : on our way one of the prifoners brought from Tarku, fnatched a fabre from the fide of one of our Coffacks, with which he very near cut off his right arm, but, upon his endeavouring to make his efcape, was fhot through the head by another Coffack who was attending him. Refuming our march on the 17th, we went twenty-feven werfts; but our guide led us quite out of the road, into fenny and marfhy ground quite over-grown with reeds, which occafioned great confufion in the army, and obliged us to return in a very dark night to extricate ourfelves. Our guide being fufpected of treachery was put in irons, and being found guilty, he was hanged next morning.

The

The new
town of
Swetago-
Kreil.

The 18th, we marched twenty-five werfts to the banks of the Sulack, where the river Agrechan feparates from it. Here we found a plain beautiful fpot of ground on both fides the river; the country overgrown with large tall trees and excellent pafturage, which enticed his majefty to build a new and well fortified town at this place to keep the Dageftan Tartars in awe, and I had orders to lay a plan before him. The plan confifted of five baftions, and two demi-baftions next the river on the fouth-fide, with ravelins and a palifaded covered way; on the north-fide were fix baftions, alfo with ravelins and a palifaded covered way; the two fides to communicate by a bridge in the middle over the river. The emperor approved the plan, and all hands were immediately fet to work under my direction in chief, with fix engineers under me to carry on the work: when the works were laid out and the ftreets regulated, a number of hands were employed in felling timber for building houfes, fo that fortifying and building went on at the fame time. His majefty named the new city Swetago-Kreft (or Holy-Crofs), and appointed general Waterang commander in chief of the army which was to be left for the protection and accomplifhment of the works; the army confifted of 7000 dragoons, 5000 regular infantry, and 6000 Coffacks; in all 18,000 men.

Fort at the
river Nitzi
deftroyed and
revenged.

At this time an exprefs arrived from Derbent, which informed his majefty that a body of 10,000 rebel Perfians had attacked our fort at the river Millukenti, and that the garrifon had made fuch a vigorous defence, that the enemy were obliged to retire with the lofs of 600 men; and that the other fort, at the river Nitzi, had been furprifed and

taken

taken by fultan Udinach, who had quartered all the garrifon, and crucified the officers on the fame fpot of ground where we formerly executed his people: the exprefs alfo brought intelligence, that fultan Udinach was no fooner informed of our army's being gone to the river Sulack, than thinking himfelf in perfect fafety, he had brought all his people down from their retreats in the mountains, and that they were then enjoying themfelves in great fecurity in the vallies. The emperor now loft no time in difpatching a body of light horfe, confifting of 10,000 Coffacks, and 15,000 Kalmuck Tartars, who went with fuch expedition, that they came upon them living in the utmoft fecurity; put feveral thoufands of their men to the fword, the two fultans Udinach and Maghmut, very narrowly efcaped, leaving their women, children, and cattle, a prey to the vanquifhers, befides their flaves, the whole amounting to feveral thoufand of both fexes. Among the flaves were four hundred and thirty-feven Ruffians, of both fexes, who were now left to inhabit the new city of Swetago-Kreft; the emperor allowed the captors two rubles a head for the Ruffians; the reft were fold; as the Coffacks and Kalmucks ferve the emperor in his wars, no purchafe no pay, having only bread allowed them while they continue in fervice, all the prifoners and booty they take is their own, to difpofe of as they can to the beft advantage. When the remaining prifoners, on this occafion, were offered to fale, there were found among them upwards of two hundred Georgian flaves, all Chriftians of the Greek church; for thefe an agreement was made with the captors at ten rubles a head, which her majefty, the emprefs, paid for their redemption;

and

BOOK VIII. and they were likewife left to people the new town. The
——————— reft of the Coffacks who were not employed, and the Kal-
1722.   muck Tartars, were now fent home to their own country
through Circaffia and the deferts of Aftrachan, richly provided with flaves and cattle of all forts, having made a profitable campaign of it.

The army re-   His majefty was now preparing to move homewards, and
embark at A-
grechan, and   I had accommodated my affairs to ftay in this place, but I
the provifions received orders to attend the emperor to Aftrachan, and to
for the cap-
tain's galley leave the direction of the works to lieutenant-colonel
loft, a ftarv-
ing voyage.   Brunie, as engineer in my abfence, which I obeyed with
great pleafure; and as I had neither fold my camels, nor
horfes, the general kindly took upon himfelf to difpofe
of them to the beft advantage. We marched, on the 1ft of
October, thirty werfts, along the banks of the river Agrechan, to the entrenchments that protected our gallies, and
on our arrival, we found them all out and ready at anchor
to receive us. We embarked the fame evening, and the fleet
lay there all night; the next morning, a boat coming from
the fhore with provifions for the ufe of my galley, funk
before fhe could reach us; the men were faved, but every
bit of the provifions loft; I fent immediately to the admiral a report of our misfortune, and defired a fupply of
provifions; and he returned for anfwer, that he could not
fupply us, as the reft of the gallies had little enough for
their own fubfiftence. Makarof, his majefty's fecretary, being then on board with me, was much furprifed at the anfwer; faying, that a fmall fhare from each galley could not
have been miffed, and that, from fo many, would have been fufficient for us. The fecretary advifed me immediately to make

6

the

the beft of our way to Aftrachan, without any regard to the admiral's fignals, offering to be anfwerable for the confequences if I fhould be called to an account for it; which advice I was determined to follow whenever I met with a favourable wind to put it in execution.

The 2d in the afternoon, the fignal was made to weigh, and the weather being quite calm, we rowed along fhore till it was dark, when another fignal was made to anchor; the next day it being ftill a calm, we rowed till night, and while we lay at anchor, a furious ftorm arofe, which beat the fhort waves fo violently againft our galley, that fhe fprung a leak, and notwithftanding all our exertion with the pumps, the water gained fo faft upon us, that we expected fhe would very foon go down; I run down to the cabin to fee what water was under its floor, and upon entering there, I heard a noife of water below the fecretary's bed, and immediately called the carpenter to take up the boards, and then we difcovered the leak, which was a hole fo big that I thruft my hand through it; we got it immediately ftopt, and the pumps then foon cleared the veffel to our great joy: feveral of our gallies were loft in this ftorm, but moft of the people faved.   When day-light appeared, we faw four gallies funk at a fmall diftance from us, with their mafts only above water, and men hanging by them, where they remained till the boats went and brought them off.   Three gallies were fo deeply loaded, that they funk and all the men perifhed.   On the 4th, the ftorm being abated, and the wind favourable, the fleet failed all day; but the two following days, being quite calm, we were obliged to have recourfe to our oars again, and row along fhore, which was very mortifying to the poor foldiers, who were by this time reduced to very fhort allowance. The fecretary and I diftributed to them what little provifions and brandy we could fpare, which went but a fhort way among fo many men.

The 7th, having a favourable wind, we not only made all the fail we could, but likewife applied to our oars, and by this means we foon left the fleet out of fight, and continued under fail all night; but it being calm in the morning, we were obliged to row, notwithftanding the miferable condition the poor foldiers were reduced to by hunger: two of them died this day, more for want of food than ficknefs: at noon the wind began to blow frefh, which relieved the foldiers from the oars, and we continued failing all that night, but I had loft three more of my men. We had a fair wind all day of the 9th, and made the beft ufe we could of it till we ran a-ground in the evening, but with the affiftance of a warp-anchor, we got her towed off again without the leaft damage. This little obftruction to our voyage greatly difheartened the poor ftarving men, and two more of them died that night ; and the furvivors were more like ghofts than men, and were now reduced fo low that they could no longer handle the oars or fails, and even begged leave to eat their dead companions : from this, however, as we failed with a fine breeze, we got them perfuaded to refrain, in hopes that one day more would bring us to the mouth of the Wolga. On the 10th, the wind ftill favoured us, till in the evening we happily fell in with a fifhing-boat with plenty of fifh, and the poor ftarved men fell to eating them fo voracioufly, that they had not patience to broil them ; fo that I was obliged to fet off the boat for fear of the men

killing,

killing themfelves; but as the fifhermen had given us a bag of fuchary, or bifcuit, it was divided in fmall fhares among them, which, with the broiled fifh, a little refrefhed them; and the joyful information that feveral provifion-fhips were lying at the mouth of the river, greatly revived their fainting fpirits: I kept one of the fifhermen on board for a pilot, and ordered the boat with the fifh to follow us, in cafe we fhould have farther occafion for them. We continued to fail all night, but four more of my men died this night, who certainly would have been eaten by their companions, had we not been provided with plenty of fifh. The 11th, in the morning, we got into the mouth of the Wolga, where we found ftore-fhips full of all forts of provifions, and of which I had what we wanted, by giving a receipt; yet I loft three more of my men before I got on fhore, fo that I had fourteen in all ftarved to death on the voyage, and nine more died of too great plenty after we came on fhore. Here we waited the arrival of the fleet, which was on the 14th, in the evening. Admiral Apraxin's galley being the firft that entered the river, he enquired what galley that was on fhore; and on being informed, he ordered me to come on board his galley. Secretary Makarof went with me, and when we got on board, he had a long conference with the admiral in his cabin, and then I was called in and received his commendations for what I had done, and was difmiffed; but from the caution he gave me not to mention what had happened, I had reafon to believe he was afraid this proceeding of his might come to the emperor's ears.

Q q 2

On

On the 15th, the fleet proceeded up the river to Aftrachan, and on our arrival, were faluted by all the artillery of
the city, to the inexpreffible joy of the whole army. We
debarked the next day, and were put into quarters of refrefhment, of which we ftood in great need. One of our
hofpital fhips, with 360 men, had been caft away upon
the coaft of Turkiftan, or Turkomania, on the eaft fide of
the Cafpian ; of which number only one enfign, a prieft,
and feven men returned to give the difmal account : the
reft had all either died ·or been made prifoners by the
Tartars. We loft on this deftructive expedition, above
one third of our whole army, not in battle, but by ficknefs
and fatigue.

At this time an exprefs arrived from Refht, the principal city of the province of Gilan, upon the fouthernmoft
coaft of the Cafpian, defiring his majefty to fend them a
fufficient number of our troops to defend them againft the
ufurper Myr-Maghmut, and offering to put their ftrong city
into our poffeffion. His majefty fent a colonel and two
engineers with one thoufand men to their relief, by fea to
Refht ; but at the time of their landing, the ufurper being
near the town with a numerous army, the inhabitants were
afraid to admit our troops into the town ; our troops
therefore, were obliged to entrench themfelves near the fea-
fhore. On receiving intelligence of this, general Lewafof
was fent with four thoufand more men to join them, and
on their arrival, the inhabitants admitted them into the
city ; the general immediately added feveral outworks
to ftrengthen the place, and we remained in full poffeffion
of

of the province, without the leaft difturbance from the ufurper.

General Lewafof at his fetting out, had orders to call at Baku, and leave a garrifon there of two thoufand men; but he came too late, for the citizens being difappointed of the fupport they hoped for from our army, when we were at Derbent, were obliged to fubmit themfelves to the obedience of Myr-Maghmut, and they refufed to admit our troops.

It may be proper to obferve here, that the jealoufy which the march of our army into thofe parts, had excited in the Turks, and the umbrage they had taken at it, was afterward adjufted by our ambaffador at Conftantinople, where it was mutually agreed that the Turks fhould keep Shamachie; that Armenia, Melitener, and Georgia, fhould remain under their protection; and that the emperor, if he chofe it, might fubdue all the provinces bordering on the Cafpian fea.

His majefty being now determined to make all his con-quefts in future by fea, without running the rifque of ruin-ing an army with marching again by land, gave immediate orders to build a fufficient number of fhips of burthen, and finding our former gallies too fmall for any diftant expedi-tion, gave likewife orders to build a number of double gallies of forty oars, to contain above three hundred men each; and having fettled all his affairs at this place, he left General Matufkin here to command the army in chief, and ordered the fix battalions of his own body guards to attend his perfon to Mofcow. We left all our gallies here, and proceeded in open boats up the river Wolga, fo that inftead

7

of

of enjoying any reſt in this place, we were again put to intolerable hardſhips; and we who had the honour of being the body guards of this indefatigable monarch, underwent greater fatigues, harder duty, and ſeverer puniſhment for neglect of it, upon all occaſions, than any of the reſt of his army.

BOOK

B O O K   IX.

Progress up the Wolga to Czaritza.—The ghost there.—A short history of the Cossacks.—Stephen Ratzin's rebellion.—Ordered to survey the Caspian sea, on which he proceeds to Jaick and Yembo.—Island of Kula, and Turkistan Tartars.—Gulf of Iskander.—River Oxus and the Usbeck Tartars.—The gulf of Carabuga. -River Daria.—River Ossa. Gulf of Astrabat.—Provinces of Terebat and Massenderan —Gulf of Sinsili and city of Resht.—Difficult path of the Pyles.—The rivers Ardefchin and Linkeran, and the famous naphtha oil-pits.—The river Cyrus, or Kur.—The city of Baku.— City of Shamachie. City of Derbent.— The river Sulack.—Gulf of Agrechan, Island of Trentzeni and city of Terki.—General Description of the Caspian sea.—Watch tower on John's island —General Matushkin's marriage. to the widow in tears.—Contest among the Kalmucks, and expedition against them.—Description of their kibbets.—A battle with the Kalmucks.—Some odd customs among them. The Baranetz, or Lambskin.—Returns for Moscow up the Wolga.—A narrow escape from the ice.—Proceed by land. A cruel robbery in the woods.—A remarkable discovery of a town, with an account of it.—A wild girl taken in the wood.—Arrival at Moscow.

THE emperor set out from hence on the 5th of November ; for the first three days some soldiers were put on shore to tow the boats against the stream, who were relieved every hour ; the 8th, having a favourable wind from the south, we went under sail for four days. On the 11th, we met the ice in large sheets floating down the river, and two of our battalions being then in the rear, I asked, and obtained leave of brigadier Kartzmin, under whose command they were, to make the best of my way, and with much toil and labour reached Zornayar on the 16th, a fortified town with a numerous garrison. The river being

com-

completely frozen over this night, I was obliged to draw my boat on fhore, and had the good fortune to be the only officer of our divifion frozen up at an inhabited place. His majefty, with four battalions, was ftopt forty werfts above us, and brigadier Kartzmin, with the other two, was ftopt forty werfts below us, and could not reach Zornoyar by land till the 19th. His majefty preceeded by land to Czaritza, and we remained at Zornayar, till the Kalmuck Tartars came over the river on the ice to take up their ufual winter-quarters in the defart: they covered a road with earth over the ice for their cattle to pafs on, their horfes, for want of fhoeing, as well as their other cattle, being equally unable to fet their feet on the bare ice.

We now bought horfes of the Tartars at a very cheap rate, and fet forward on the 17th of December through a barren defart country, without meeting a fingle houfe in all our way, being obliged to lay in our tents for four fuccef-five nights in very cold weather, and in want of every ne-ceffary: we arrived at Czaritza on the 21ft at night, which is five hundred werfts above Aftrachan. When the emperor left this place fome time before, with the other battalions, to make the beft of his way to Mofcow, he left orders for our two (being thofe of Ingermanland and Aftrachan) to remain here for the winter; which orders we received with great pleafure, as we found very good quarters, and notwith-ftanding the numerous garrifon of foot and Coffacks, we had every thing we could wifh for in great plenty.

The ghoft there.

One day when I was dining with the governor, he enter-tained us with a long ftory about a ghoft that was frequently feen walking the ftreets at night, and had continued to do fo

for

for some years past, bestowing a found beating on any person who offered to disturb it, but did no other harm.   I
mentioned my surprize that no body had attempted to seize
this ghost, as it could certainly be no other than some person who took pleasure in frightening the people.   The governor, who was a very credulous man, replied with some
warmth, " It was very perceptible I was a foreigner, who
" seldom believed any thing."—I told him, that he ought
not to take offence at what I had said, for if he would give
me leave I would secure the ghost the first time it walked the
streets again, which he granted with a sneer.   When I came
home to my lodging, I asked one of my serjeants if he had
heard any thing of a ghost in town ; he told me he had seen
it frequently, and if I was curious he believed I might see
it that same night : on which I ordered him to pick out
half a dozen stout fellows, and attend with them at my
lodging, and send some others to look out and bring me
word when it appeared.   About eleven o'clock at night,
information came that it was walking in the next street to
that I was in ; upon which I sent the serjeant with three of
the men to meet it, and ordered him by all means to seize
it, and went myself with the other three to follow it in case
it should attempt to return back ; but it met the serjeant
without offering to return or escape ; and upon being seized,
threw two of the men under his feet, yet they held him fast
till I came up ; when, presenting a pistol to his breast, he
begged to save his life, and confessed himself to be one of
the Cossacks belonging to the garrison.   I carried him immediately to the governor, who was so much ashamed for
having allowed himself to be so long imposed on, and so

R r   enraged,

enraged, that he threatened to hang the fellow; but as he
had not been guilty of any other crime, except that of frightening people, he came off with a fevere whipping, after he
had ftood fome time with his white fheet about him, as a
fhow to the people of the town.

Having had frequent occafion to mention the Coffacks,
employed both in our armies and garrifons, I fhall endeavour to give fome fhort account of their origin.   They
were at firft no more than a band of free-booters, compofed
of a wild barbarous rabble, moftly boors, from the provinces of Polifh Ruffia, Volhinia, and Podolia.   Having left
their native habitations, they fettled themfelves on fome
iflands in the river Borifthenes, below Kiovia, where they
fubfifted by robbery and plunder.   They acquired the name
of Coffacks from their agility, the word *Coffa* fignifying as
much in the Polifh language: they were particularly remarkable for their dexterity in paffing between the great
number of fmall iflands, fituated in the mouth of the Borifthenes: their piracies early became terrible to the Turkifh
gallies on the Black-Sea, and they grew formidable to Na-
tolia itfelf, when they not only plundered Trebifond and
Sinope, but even the fuburbs of Conftantinople did not
efcape them, and they returned in fafety to their habitations
with their prifoners and plunder.

The fame of their exploits againft the Turks gained them
fuch reputation with the Poles, that Stephen Batori, prince
of Tranfilvania and king of Poland, confidering that thefe
Coffacks might be of great ufe to the crown of Poland, not
only againft the incurfions of the neighbouring Crim Tartars, but alfo might ferve as a confiderable addition to the

ftrength

strength of the Polish army, which consisting for the most part of horse, would be rendered more formidable when augmented by so considerable a number of foot, resolved to put these vagabond soldiers into good order and discipline; which he effected by granting them very considerable privileges, and putting them under a general of their own, called by them hetman, who had the power of naming his own officers. Having thus reduced them into one body, he gave them the city of Techimerof, on the Boristhenes, with all the territory belonging to it, which they made their capital magazine, and residence of their hetman; and by this means, all that tract of desert country which extends itself along the Boristhenes, from Bar, Braclaw, and Kiow, to the Black-Sea, became a populous country, filled with towns and cities, and is now called the Ukrain *. As this body has been of very great service to the crown of Poland, by securing its frontiers on that side against the incursions of the Crim Tartars : so, after some time, it proved very dangerous, having several times taken arms against the republic, which was occasioned by several Polish lords, whose boors (their vassals) could never be well secured as long as the Cossacks enjoyed their privileges, represented them to the king as dangerous to the republic, by reason of the great numbers of peasants that daily ran over to them. It was resolved to build a fort at a place called Kudak, on a point of land formed by the influx of the river Swamer to the Boristhenes, which was chosen from its situation, as a proper place to bridle the Cossacks, being at no great distance from the place of their ordinary rendezvous. The Cossacks, how-

* Ukrain, in the Polish language, signifies *frontier*.

R 2

ever, penetrating the defign of the Poles, were refolved not to fuffer the bridle to be put over their heads; and having defeated two hundred men who were left to fee the fort perfected, under the command of a colonel, they affembled a confiderable body of forces, to prevent the Polifh general in his defign; and from that time there were divifions and perpetual wars between the Poles and the Coffacks. During thefe troubles, great numbers of the Coffacks retired, with their families to the river Don, or Tanais, and fettled between the Don and the Wolga, where they fubfifted a long time by their piracies on the Wolga.

In the year 1653, being greatly oppreffed by the Poles, they joined the Ruffians, who, in the year following, with their affiftance, took the cities of Smolinfko and Wilna; fo that it was chiefly owing to the valour of the Coffacks, that the provinces of Smolinfko and Severia with the palatinate of Kiovia, were annexed to the Ruffian empire, and which were all confirmed to them by the treaty of peace in 1666, made at Oliva. About that period the Coffacks in general put themfelves under the protection of Ruffia, and are ftill diftinguifhed by the Ukrain and Donfki Coffacks, the former of which ferve moftly on foot, the latter all on horfeback. It was the Donfki Coffacks who were employed on our expedition at this time, and were put in garrifon in all our frontier towns, and are in regular pay, and forage allowed them for their horfes. They have now left off robbing, except when they are fent into an enemy's country, then all the booty they make is their own, as alfo the prifoners they take, whom they may fell or retain as their flaves.

2

The

The Coffacks in general are tall, ftrong, well fet, and re- BOOK IX· markably active; they are liberal even to profufion, placing no great value in riches, but are great lovers of their liberty, which they look upon as a thing ineftimable: they are hardy, indefatigable, brave, but great drunkards and very treacherous. Their chief employment is hunting and fifh- ing, yet they apply themfelves both to agriculture and arms; their language is a dialect of the Ruffian and Polifh tongues, but more fmooth and agreeable than either; they pro- fefs the Greek religion in the fame manner as it is efta- blifhed in Ruffia.

A very dangerous rebellion was raifed in the year 1669, when Alexis (his prefent majefty's father) was emperor, by one Stephen Ratzin, a Donfki Coffack by birth; who, ob- ferving a certain difpofition in the Nagayan Tartars inha- biting the kingdom of Aftrachan, occafioned by the heavy oppreffions they groaned under from the mifmanagement and avarice of the Ruffian governors in thofe parts, to fhake off the Ruffian yoke, he gathered a confiderable party, and being affifted by a great number of the Donfki Coffacks, marched at their head againft the city of Aftra- chan, which he befieged and took, after a fmall refiftance. From thence he marched toward Cafan, threatening not only that city, but the fouthern Ruffia with a moft dreadful in- vafion; and his army increafed prodigioufly by the vaft number of Tartars that flocked to his affiftance. But in- ftead of improving this opportunity to his advantage, he abandoned himfelf to idlenefs and all manner of excefs and debauchery, by which the Ruffians had leifure to affemble their forces and ftop his career; in which they were fo ex- peditious as to arrive at Cafan before he could lay fiege to

the

1712.

Stephen Rat-
zin's rebel-
lion.

the place, and having thus cut off all communication with the country thereabout, from whence Aftrachan and the adjacent parts are fupplied with corn, the rebellious army was foon reduced to fuch great diftrefs, by want of fubfiftence, that the Tartars being apprehenfive of their approaching danger, for the moft part deferted their leader; notwithftanding which, the Coffacks ftood it out bravely, refolving to maintain their ground againft the Ruffians; for which purpofe they entrenched themfelves under the walls of Aftrachan. The Ruffians feeing the defperate refolution of the Coffacks, thought it more advifeable to reduce them, if poffible, to obedience by fair means, and a promife of free pardon for all that was paft, than by force of arms, which had the defired effect; for Ratzin finding his Coffacks wavering, and being flattered with hopes of forgivenefs, by fome of his friends in the emperor's court, furrendered himfelf to the mercy of czar Alexis Michaelovitz, the next year. His party being thus deprived of their head, readily embraced the offer of pardon; but Ratzin not long after found himfelf extremely miftaken in his hopes, for he was carried into the great market-place, before the caftle in Mofcow, and there, in the midft of an infinite number of fpectators, affembled to fee the tragical exit of a man, whom not many months before they had confidered as their moft dreadful enemy, he had firft his arms cut off, then his legs, and laftly his head. Ever fince that period, the Coffacks have been kept in ftrict order and difcipline, being for the moft part employed in garrifoning the frontier towns, in which they never exceed one third, and being all horfemen, they are employed out upon parties to keep the neighbouring

bouring Tartars in awe, the Ruffian foldiers only doing
duty in the garrifons.

Early this fpring, when we were in hopes of going to
Mofcow, we received orders to return to Aftrachan, there
to remain in garrifon till the return of general Matufkin,
who had received his orders to proceed to Baku, with a force
to reduce that city : accordingly we moved with our two
battalions, on the 2d of April, from Czaritza down the
Wolga, and arrived at Aftrachan on the 8th, where
we found the general embarking his troops to fail on
his expedition againft Baku. At the fame time I got
very unexpected orders to go all round the Cafpian Sea,
to furvey and found it, and to lay down, in a chart, all
the iflands, rivers, creeks, and bays, with the different foundings, and for this fervice had one of the ftrongeft new
built gallies, of forty oars, carrying two eighteen pounders
in her prow, twenty-four fwivels, and three hundred men;
attended with four boats, two of eight oars, one of ten,
and another of twelve, each boat carrying one fwivel gun;
and two fub-engineers were appointed for my affiftants.

My firft care was to guard againft the misfortunes which
was fo fatal to the laft galley I commanded in the Cafpian,
by laying in a plentiful ftock of provifions, and my old
friend, the Capuchin, fent me a prefent of one cafk of very
good red wine, one of white, a quarter cafk of brandy,
and feveral kinds of preferved fweet-meats; fo that the
good man was never tired in fhewing his gratitude, for the
fmall favour I had done him, in his paffage down the river.
The general with his army fat out on the 15th, and we
went down the river on the 18th of April, and got to the

4   mouth

mouth of the Wolga next morning; from thence proceeding eaftward, we paft in very fhallow water along the coaft

fo overgrown with reed, that we were obliged to keep at five
or fix miles diftance from the fhore, in from ten to twelve
feet water; and in all the way for eight days time, we could
find no place to land even one of our fmalleft boats. We
faw two little iflands in our way, but we could not come at
them for reed; but we killed a great number of fea-fowl,
that have their nefts in thefe iflands, and had plenty of fifh
and fowl all the way. We failed or rowed as the wind permitted, but came to an anchor every night, that nothing
might efcape our obfervation.

to Jaick. On the 26th, we arrived in the river Jaick, the mouth of
which is one hundred fathoms broad, and eighteen feet deep;
we went to the town of Jaick, which ftands about one mile
up the river, is well fortified, has a ftrong garrifon of Ruffians and Coffacks, to keep the Kalmuck and Nagayan Tartars in awe, and to prevent them from attacking each other,
as they live in perpetual enmity. The Nagayans inhabit all
the country from Aftrachan to the Jaick, all along the fea-
coaft, two hundred and fifty-five werfts in extent; and the
Kalmucks poffefs that vaft tract of land, from Saratof and the
great defert of Beriket, and that tract to the fouth of the
Jaick, all along the fhore to the river Yembo, which is ninety-three werfts from this place. We ftayed only one day at
Jaick, and provided ourfelves with frefh meat and water.
Being informed by the governor that there was a large gulf
to the eaftward of this place, to the river Yembo, but too
fhallow to admit our galley, I fent one of the engineers
with two of the boats, to go round and furvey it, and join

us

us again on the oppofite point, for which we proceeded immediately, and failing fouth, we anchored on the 30th, between the ifland of Kulala, and the point of the main, in
fix fathom water, in view of the mountains of Karagan,
and from hence we had a clean and deep fhore. At this
place begin the territories of Turkiftan, or the Turkumanian Tartars. During our ftay here, waiting thereturn
of the engineer, we laid in plenty of wood and water, and
diverted ourfelves with fowling and fifhing : we caught here
a beluga upwards of fix yards long, and thick in proportion ; from the roe of which we made excellent caviar,
which lafted us above a month. Our engineer, with the
boats, joined us again on the 10th of May, who reported
that in the furvey of the bay, he found only from five to
eight feet water ; that the whole fhore was fo covered with
reed, that they could only land at the mouth of the river
Yembo, which was both broad and deep.

We left the ifland of Kulala on the 11th, on our way to
the gulf of Ifkander, where we arrived the 20th. All along
this coaft there is a great depth of water, fo that we could
land with our galley on any part of it. A great number of
fmall rivers fall into the fea from the mountains, but we
could not learn their names, although I attempted to get
information by fending the twelve oared boat, with an officer and twenty-four men, and an interpreter to fpeak with
the people on fhore : but they no fooner came near enough,
than the Tartars let fly a volly of arrows at our people,
who returned the falute with a difcharge of their mufketry,
and we fired one of our great guns from the galley at them,
which made them retire towards the mountains in great

S s   hafte.

hafte. They always appeared in great parties, on horfeback,
well armed, and we faw feveral of their hords, or camps,
at a diftance, which they move at pleafure, and wan-
der from place to place, for thofe Tartars have no fettled
abode: they continued to attend us every day in great parties, to watch our motions, out of the reach of our guns,
and they difappeared entirely on our arrival in the gulf of
Ifkander, which is one hundred and eighty-four werfts from
Gulf of the Ifle of Kulala. In this gulf which is, from eaft to weft,
Ifkander. thirty werfts in length, and eighteen broad, we found, near
the fhore, from five to fix fathom water, with a clean
ground, and exceeding good anchorage; it would be one of
the fineft harbours in the world, as both fides of the entrance are extremely well calculated to erect forts upon, for
its defence. It lies in 43 deg. 20 min. north; feveral fmall
rivers fall into it from the mountains.

River Oxus   We left the gulf of Ifkander on the 26th, and proceed-
and Ufbeck ing along fhore two days in good depth of water; we arrived
Tartars. in the river Oxus, being ninety werfts from the gulf. This
river is both large and rapid, and is about a mufket-fhot
broad at its entrance. Here we found a few unarmed Tartars, who fold us fome fheep, and informed us that feveral
hords of Turkumanian Tartars were encamped on the banks
of the river, a little way above, and that the Ufbeck Tartars encamped on the other fide, this river dividing the two
nations. We had hitherto feen nothing but fine weather,
intermixt with calms and light breezes; but this night we
had a dreadful ftorm of wind, attended with rain, thunder, and lightning, which obliged us to run the galley half
a werft up the river for fhelter, where we anchored in the
middle

middle of the ftream, not daring to venture on either fide for fear of the Tartars, having the Turkumanians on the north, and the Ufbecks on the fouth, hovering at a diftance. The ftorm lafted till next day at noon, when we left the Oxus, and failing along-fhore in deep water, with a clean bottom, attended by parties of the Ufbeck Tartars, who obferved our motions at a diftance from the fides of the mountains. We paffed by two fmall iflands covered with trees (called the Lebajee iflands), where we took in wood, and killed a number of fea-fowl.

The 2d of June, we arrived at the gulf of Carabuga, one hundred and five werfts from the river Oxus; the in- let of the gulf is about two werfts broad, and at one werft within is an ifland, where we landed with our galley, and encamped the people to refrefh themfelves on fhore, and get our veffel cleaned : from hence I difpatched the two affiftants, in the largeft boats, to furvey the gulf; direct- ing them to proceed along the oppofite fides till they fhould meet, and then return to the ifland : in the mean time, I founded all round the inlet, and had from five to fix fa- thom water; but a few werfts within, we could not reach the bottom; I could obferve no current here either in or out. The gulf, from north to fouth, is feventy-five werfts, and fifty from eaft to weft, deep water, a clean bottom, and the fhore fteep, all round the gulf; it is furrounded with high mountains; two large rivers (the Morga and Herat) fall into it from the eaft; the entrance is formed by two narrow necks of land, and might be eafily fecured and fortified; and this ifland, which is two miles in circumfer- ence, would ferve for a protection to the fhipping. As there

The gulf of Carabuga.

is

is no tide in the Cafpian, fome people have alledged that the
waters of the fea find a paffage by this gulf, which made
me curious to examine it more particularly, but I could
not find the leaft reafon for fuch a conjecture.

Having enjoyed ourfelves very agreeably under the cooling
fhade of the trees in this hot climate, without the leaft apprehenfion of any danger from the Tartars, we took our
departure from Carabuga on the 22d, and coafted along
fhore for fix days, in very hot weather, without the fmalleft
breeze of wind, which made it intolerable for the poor foldiers, who were obliged to row all the way, and anchoring
every night, we had continual flafhes of lightning, and
thefe fometimes accompanied with dreadful loud claps of
thunder, which are very frequent in this country during the
fummer.   We were every day attended along the fhore by
numerous parties of the Ufbeck Tartars, who feemed very
jealous of our intentions, which obliged us, as often as we
wanted to fend afhore for frefh water, to fire our great guns
at them, which kept them at a diftance, 'by which means
we fupplied ourfelves.

River Daria.   One hundred and forty werfts fouthward from Carabuga,
we entered the mouth of the famous river Daria on the
28th; it lies in 39 deg. 15 min. north latitude.   It is here
where the gold fand is wafhed down from the mines in the
mountains, and here where the unfortunate prince Alexander Bekewitz, a few years ago, with an army of 3,000
men, were treacheroufly maffacred by the Ufbeck Tartars,
as I mentioned before.   I now faw the place where the fort
had been erected, on a narrow neck of land, oppofite to the
mouth of the river, and which forms a fpacious harbour
capable.

capable of containing a number of ships of burthen, as there
is from three to four fathom water clofe to the fhore, on a
clean bottom with good anchorage; fo that it was a great
pity the prince fuffered himfelf to be over-reached by thefe
treacherous Tartars. If this poft had been maintained,
which might have been done without any manner of danger, it would, in procefs of time, have been a moft glorious acquifition towards enriching the Ruffian nation. I
intended to have gone fome way up this river; but as the
Tartars had taken the alarm at our appearance here, and
were already come from their camp in formidable bodies, I
was obliged to lay afide the defign and leave the place; and
paffing two bays and three iflands, called the Goat Iflands,
we came to an anchor at one of the iflands for the night,
where we landed, faw a number of goats, and killed five of
them.

The next day, being the 29th, we arrived at Minkiflack, River Offa.
on the north-fide of the river Offa, or Orxantes, fixty werfts
from Daria. This river divides the Ufbeck Tartary from
Perfia, is both large and deep, and fhips may ride at anchor here in great fafety. Here we were glad to find people dwelling in houfes, for we had not feen a houfe from the
time we left Aftrachan, except at Jaick. We found the
people of Minkiflack both civil and kind: they live after
the Perfian manner, whofe fubjects they are, and we got
all forts of refrefhments at a very cheap rate, and were afterwards no more honoured with an efcort of Tartars. From
Minkiflack we proceeded along a clean fhore, in deep water,
where we could have landed with our galley on any part
of the coaft, and where abundance of fmall rivulets fall in-

to

to the fea, and the country, abounding with villages, is over-
grown with a great variety of fruit-trees.

The 4th of July, we arrived at the inlet of the gulf of
Aftrabat, one hundred and fifty werfts from Minkiflack : we
entered and anchored within the gulph. The city of Aftrabat ftands on the river Naren, which falls into the gulf
thirty werfts from the inlet; the gulf itfelf is forty-fix werfts
from eaft to weft, and has two and a half fathoms of water
over all; Aftrabat is fortified with high and thick walls,
flanked with towers, and is a place of great trade. This
makes the fouthern extremity of the Cafpian fea, and lies
in 36 deg. 50 min. north lat. This province, with the
neighbouring provinces of Terebat, Maffanderan, and Gilan, produce abundance of raw filk, coffee, faffron, and
cotton; their filk is efteemed the beft in all Perfia, and by it
they carry on a great trade to different parts, efpecially to
Ruffia, where a filk manufactory is eftablifhed at Mofcow.
This country abounds with the moft delicious fruits of all
kinds, efpecially their grapes, which are furprifingly large.
In coafting the country from hence, we made very particular enquiries of the inhabitants concerning fome whirlpools,
laid down near this fhore in fome old maps, but we could
neither hear or difcover the leaft appearance of any fuch thing.

In paffing the provinces of Terebat and Maffanderan, we
faw a moft delightful country, abounding with plantations
of mulberry-trees, and watered by a great number of rivers,
whofe banks were full of houfes, and wherever we landed
the people fhewed us the utmoft civility, furnifhing us moft
chearfully with whatever we wanted at an extraordinary
cheap rate.   9

On

On the 18th, we arrived at the gulf of Sinfili, one hundred and feventy werfts from Aftrabat; we went through
this gulf in four fathom water, fixteen werfts to the city
of Refht, the capital of the province of Gilan, which ftands
at the mouth of the river Kifilofein: the gulf extends
eighteen werfts from eaft to weft; the city is fquare, and
fortified in the fame manner as Aftrabat, with ftrong walls
and towers.

General Leewafof was now governor, with a garrifon of
5,000 men: they were employed at this time in building
a citadel of five baftions to command both the town and
harbour; but as their principal engineer, captain Sager,
had, after a fevere fit of ficknefs, loft the fight of both his
eyes, and they were in want of one to fupply his place, the
general defired I would leave lieutenant Hartman, one of my
affiftants, to be engineer, which I agreed to at the lieutenant's own requeft, as I had now not fo much occafion for
him as formerly. They had loft a confiderable number of
their men by ficknefs, very common in hot climates. Provifions were both fcarce and dear here at prefent, as the
rebels had plundered and laid wafte the whole country as
far as Baku, and what they had, both for the fupport of
the inhabitants and garrifon, they were fupplied with from
Aftrachan. The raw filk, of which the inhabitants had great
quantities on their hands, for want of fale during the troubles, they fent to Aftrachan in the tranfports which had
brought the troops to Refht, and they had provifions in return for their filk.

Several werfts above the city there is a road hewn through
high mountains into Perfia, called Pyles, in which only
one

one single camel, or horse, can go at a time, following each
other. This road is made in steps cut all the way for the
beasts to travel in; every man leads his own horse, holding
the reins loose in his hand for fear he should make a false
step, by which it would fall down a high precipice into the
river Kisilosein, which runs at the bottom with a rumbling
noise; the other side of the road is over-hung with dreadful rocks, which appear as if they would tumble down upon the traveller, which renders it a very dismal passage. If
it should happen by accident that travellers should meet, it
is impossible for either to make way, for which reason there
is always one sent before to prevent its happening.

The rivers
Ardeschim]
and Linke-
ran, and the
famous naph-
tha oil-pits.
    Having stopt two weeks at Resht, we sat out again on
our way northward, coasting a clean deep shore, and passing by the river Ardeschin, we arrived at the river Linkeran, on the 4th of August. Not far from this river stands
the famous mountain Barmach, remarkable for the oil called
naphtha, which issues from it in thirty different pits, all
within the compass of a musket-shot of each other: the
pits are some two, some three fathom deep, into which the
people descend by steps; the oil is of two kinds, brown and
white: the brown is of a strong disagreeable smell, and
much the most plentiful, as it is found in twenty-seven of
the pits; it is used for burning in lamps, in dressing of
leather, and for several other purposes; the white, which is
only found in three of the pits, has a pleasant smell, is the
most valuable, and is used as an infallible remedy in strains
and bruises; as the oil rises from the mountain in the pits,
it is heard as the bubbling of a boiling pot; it is carried from
hence to a great distance. I bought several jars of each
kind,

kind, and carried with me to Aſtrachan, where it proved to be a very deſirable commodity. At this place we had another violent ſtorm of wind, but taking ſhelter in the river, we lay very ſafe : we thought ourſelves fortunate in being at the mouth of a river in both ſtorms, as they are not eaſily weathered in this ſea, where the ſhort waves breaking in ſuch quick ſucceſſion upon the veſſel, require a ſtrong ſhip to withſtand them.

On the 18th, we arrived at the river Cyrus, or Kur, which is joined by the river Araxis, and is the moſt conſiderable river on the weſtern coaſt of the Caſpian, into which it falls through five different channels. We proceeded for the city of Baku, where we arrived the next day, juſt after General Matuſkin had got under way on his return to Aſtrachan. Baku had ſurrendered after a ſhort bombardment, and brigadier Knez Baratinſki was left governor of the city, with a garriſon of four thouſand men. Baku lies from Reſht two hundred and fifty-five werſts; it is very ſtrongly fortified with three walls within each other, each with towers, and which form three diſtinct diviſions of the city; the innermoſt ſtanding on the higheſt ground, by way of a citadel, commands the reſt : it is mounted with a number of braſs cannon. The governor with his garriſon, took poſſeſſion of this part; the outer wall is well ſupplied with iron cannon, the gates were ſtrongly guarded by detachments from the citadel. At ſmall diſtances from the city, ſtand three high watch-towers, built on eminences, from which they can diſcover the approach of any enemy, by ſea or land, at a great diſtance. At the ſouth end of the city, there is a large bay formed by a peninſula, which ſtretches fifteen

The river Cyrus, or Kur.

The City of Baku.

T t   werſts

BOOK IX. werfts to the fouthward, and forms a very fpacious commodious harbour, where fhips can load and unload clofe to the
1723. gates of the city, in four and a half fathom water, fafe
from all winds except the fouth, and from that too they are
fecured by fome fmall iflands, upon which they feed fheep
and goats; by which means this harbour is, without difpute,
one of the moft commodious for trade, in all the Cafpian;
City of Sha- efpecially with Shamachie, which is reputed to be the largeft
machie. and moft populous city in thofe parts, and is only three days
journey from hence. At Shamachie there are factories from
all the eaftern nations, which occafions that city to be much
reforted to from all parts.

City of Der- We ftayed only three days at Baku, and proceeding along
bent. the coaft in deep water, paft by feveral iflands and rivers,
and came to an anchor before Derbent on the 26th at night;
but as it blew a frefh gale at eaft, and there is no fafe landing-place near this town, I could not go afhore. From
Baku to Derbent is ninety Englifh miles by land. We proceeded next morning along the coaft, and arrived on the 2d
of September, in the river Sulack; and I went the fame
evening, in the twelve-oared boat, fifteen werfts up the river,
to the fortrefs of Swetago Kreft, or Holy Crofs, where I
found the fortifications furprifingly advanced, and wooden
houfes built on both fides of the river in regular ftreets,
agreeable to the plan, and fo numerous that the whole army
were now lodged in them. The wooden bridge over the
river was alfo finifhed, with two draw bridges, one at each
end, fo that an eafy communication was opened between
the two fides of the river. The troops here were in good
health and high fpirits, and kept up a weekly correfpondence

ence with the garrifons of Derbent and Terki in Circaffia;
neither of which had been molefted by the Dageftan Tartars fince we left them.   A number of hands were now employed here in making bricks to face the works, and for
building houfes.   This fort promifes fair to be an effectual
check upon the irruptions of the Dageftans into the Ruffian
territories, in which they ufed to do much mifchief, and
carry off great numbers of the inhabitants into flavery.
The multiplicity of the works going forward at this time,
requiring another engineer, I left my other affiftant,
lieutenant Brackley, here; and having given fome farther
directions about the plan of the place to lieutenant colonel Brunie, who was chief engineer, I laid in plenty of provifions in the galley, which was brought up to the town, to
ferve us on our way to Aftrachan.   I waited on general Waterang to receive his commands, and take my leave of him,
and having likewife done fo of all the reft of my acquaintances, we dropped down the river Sulack to the fea.

On the 16th, we coafted along fhore, in fine deep water, Gulf of
and reached, on the 17th, the extremity of the peninfula, iſland of
which forms the gulf of Agrechan, and came to an an- Trenzeni,
chor in the evening, between this point of high land and Terki.
the ifland of Trentzeni, oppofite to the city of Terki in
Circaffia, in fix fathom water.   This gulf is forty five Englifh miles from north to fouth, and twenty from eaft to
weft.

The ifland of Trenzeni is the largeft in the Cafpian fea,
and notwithftanding its fine harbour, there are no inhabitants upon it ; nor indeed are any of the other iflands inhabited, excepting that there are a few fifhermen's huts to

be

be feen on fome of them on the weft coaft, but none on the eaft; they are in general ftocked with cattle, fheep, and goats. And now as all the coaft from hence to Aftrachan had been founded on our former expedition, I judged it needlefs to coaft it again, fo that we took our departure, from Trentzeni on the 18th, and fteering our courfe north for Aftrachan, we arrived at the mouth of the river Wolga on the 2.;th of September, having been gone five months and fix days on the fervice : the diftance from Trenzeni to this place. is one hundred and ninety Englifh miles.

General de-fcription of the Cafpian fea.

The Cafpian fea, in its utmoft length from Jaick, which is its northern extremity, and lies in 46 deg. 15 min. north latitude, to Aftrabat, which is its fouthern extremity, and lies in 36 deg. 50 min. is 9 deg. 25 min. which makes fix hundred and forty-fix Englifh miles, at fixty-nine miles to a degree. The breadth of the Cafpian is various; its greateft breadth to the northward. from eaft to weft, is between the gulf of. Yembo and the mouth of the river Wolga, and is two hundred and fixty-five Englifh miles; the broadeft part to the fouthward is from the river Orxantes, on the eaft fide, to the river Linkeran on the weft, and is two hundred and thirty-five Englifh miles. Its whole circumference, including gulfs and bays, is three thoufand five hundred and twenty-five werfts. The coaft of the Cafpian, from the point of land forming one fide of the gulf of Agrechan, on the weft, to the river Kulala in Turkumania, oppofite to it on the eaft, all round by. the north, is low, flat, and marfhy, overgrown with reed, and the water fhallow; the direct diftance, from that gulf to Kulala, is one hundred and feventy Englifh miles ; on. all.the reft of the coaft from

Kulala

Kulala, by the fouth, and back to the gulf of Agrechan, BOOK IX. the country is mountainous, with a bold fhore and deep water, as has generally been taken notice of in the courfe of the furvey.

1723.

Near the mouth of the Wolga, on the ifle of Ivan,) or John's ifland,) ftands a tower, where a guard is conftantly kept, who muft obferve every day whether any increafe or decreafe happens in the waters of the fea, but they have not yet been able to difcover the fmalleft difference ; from which circumftance it is certain that there is neither flux or reflux in the Cafpian; and what makes it the more furprifing, is that in the fpring, when all the ice and fnow melts, and pours down from the mountains, and all the large rivers and innumerable leffer ones are fwelled to fuch a degree that they overflow all their banks, and which all fall into this fea like a deluge, yet neverthelefs it even at thofe times is not in the leaft raifed by it, fo that it remains a great myftery what becomes of all the water that perpetually falls into it from the clouds and rivers. The water is as falt as that of the ocean, except near the mouths of the rivers, where it is brackifh by the mixture of fo much frefh water from them.

Watch tower on John's Ifland.

I muft acknowlege this was the moft pleafant jaunt I ever had in my whole life : we had always plenty of provifions on board, befides taking and killing fuch abundance of fifh and wild fowl of various kinds, that we could fcarce make ufe of them all ; and during the whole voyage, notwith-ftanding the violent heat, we had only feven men fick. I fhould have found it ftill more agreeable could we have con-verfed with the Turkumanian and Ufbeck Tartars; which would have enabled me to give fome account of them ;

but.

BOOK IX. but the Tartars in general, although they have no fixed
—————— habitations, are very jealous of admitting any ftrangers
1723. into their country.

On the 25th of September, we got up to Aftrachan,
where I waited on General Matufkin with a report of my
proceeding, and prefented him with a draught of the Cafpian fea, and gave another to governor Wolinfki, who had
formerly been ambaffador to China, and who was afterwards
fent ambaffador to Perfia; on both which occafions he defired I might be permitted to go with him, but it was refufed,
although I earneftly petitioned for leave. On his return
from his laft embaffy, he was married to the princefs Na-
refkin, the emperor's firft coufin, being the daughter of
his mother's brother, and was at the fame time made go-
vernor-general over the kingdom of Aftrachan.

General Ma-
tufkin's mar-
riage to the
widow in
tears.

General Matufkin, after the taking of Baku, was promoted to the rank of lieutenant-general, and was at the
fame time major of the firft regiment of guards, and in
great efteem with his majefty. He was an old bachelor
when he married a beautiful buxom young widow, whofe
firft hufband, major general Glebof of the dragoons, had
been concerned in the late troubles with the czarowitz, for
which he was condemned, but died in prifon, and his eftate
being confifcated, the widow was reduced to very low circumftances. General Matufkin, who was appointed judge
on that trial, was folicited by the mournful widow, who
implored him on her knees, bathed in tears, to commiferate her unmerited fufferings, being now reduced to the
utmoft mifery and want. In this fupplicating pofture, fhe
fo captivated the old bachelor, that he directly made her

an offer of himfelf, and all he had for her relief, which
the widow joyfully accepted, on which the general applied
to the emprefs to procure his majefty's confent. When the
affair was mentioned to the emperor, he was much difpleafed at the general's feeking to match himfelf with the
widow of a rebel, offering him at the fame time any other
lady he fhould pitch upon ; but the general told him that
it was impoffible for him to love any other woman, and
humbly befeeched his majefty to grant his requeft, otherwife
he would lofe one of his moft faithful fervants : being feconded by the emprefs in his application, his majefty became
at laft curious to fee this widow, who had made fuch an
impreffion on the heart of the old fpark ; and when fhe
was introduced to the emperor, he declared he was not at all
furprifed at the conqueft fhe had made, and not only gave
his confent, but honoured their marriage with his prefence,
attended by the whole court. The lady ever afterwards
went by the name of the Widow in Tears.

There happened at this time, a great confufion among
the Kalmuck Tartars, occafioned by the death of the cham's
eldeft fon, who left five fons ; the eldeft of whom, with
two others, were born of a concubine, and the two youngeft of the beft beloved wife : the eldeft, whofe name was
Dafan, claimed the right of fucceffion, in confequence of his
feniority, which was a good title, notwithftanding his mother was a concubine ; the two youngeft, born of the wife,
and whofe names were Dunduambu and Batu, claimed in
right of the marriage, and were favoured by the old cham,
their grandfather, and by his fecond fon, Shurundunduck, their uncle, who threatened prince Dafan with deftruction to himfelf and his hord, or clan, which confifted

Conteft among the Kalmucks, and expedition againft them.

fifted of feven thoufand men, if he offered to difpute
the fucceffion with prince Dunduambu. They were at
that time prevented by the old cham, but he dying,
prince Shurundunduck told his nephew, Dafan, that he
was determined Dunduambu fhould fucceed his grandfather
in the fovereignty, and if he would not fubmit peaceably, he
fhould be compelled to do it. But finding their threats had
no effect upon the prince, they began to affemble an army
of twenty thoufand men, which obliged prince Dafan, with
his two brothers, and his whole hord, to retire near to Aftrachan, and he with his brothers came into the city, begging
to be protected againft the ufurpation of his younger brother, offering at the fame time to fubmit his claim to the
decifion of his imperial majefty. Upon this the general
and governor held a council, with the principal officers of
both the army and garrifon, in which it was refolved to
fend fome troops for their protection; the governor intending to go himfelf to reconcile the contending parties, if
poffible.

This being the refolution of the council, governor Wolinfki defired me to go with him on this expedition, to
which I anfwered that it was not my turn, but if he would
procure an order from the general for my going, I would
certainly go with great chearfulnefs; and accordingly, on the
20th of October, I received an order to embark with four
hundred men of our two battalions, one hundred dragoons,
and four field-pieces, to proceed up the river to the place
appointed for the rendezvous by prince Dafan; the governor propofing to follow immediately with fome more
troops, fent me before to fatisfy the impatience of the
prince.

On

On the 22th, we arrived at the defert of Beriket, fixty
werfts above Aftrachan, where we pitched our tents, but
it being intenfely cold, Dafan provided us with fixty kibbets, which is the name of their tents, which are both
warm and large, having a fire in the middle, and a hole
at the top to let out the fmoke; they are twenty-four feet
diameter, and capable of being enlarged or contracted at
pleafure; they are all round, the fides being made of a kind
of checkered wicker-work, and the crofs fticks neatly jointed
for folding together or extending: when they erect a kibbet,
they join as many of them together as will make a circle,
of the dimenfion they choofe, and having fixed the outfide,
which is fix feet high, they raife with their lances a round
board, three feet diameter, with a hole in the middle of it,
and fmall holes all round the edge; the large hole ferves
for their chimney, the fmall holes receive the ends of fo
many ftrait rafters, and the other ends being fixed to the
fides, the roof is formed, which is both ingenious and
pretty: having thus erected the frame of the kibbet, they
cover it over with thick felt, more or lefs according as the
feafon is cold or warm, beginning at the bottom and proceeding to the top, where they place a krine, which they
can turn at pleafure againft the wind, to prevent fmoke.
The kibbet is furprifingly warm, and withftands wind and
rain better than a houfe, and they are erected with greater
eafe in and lefs time than we could fet up an officer's tent.
Prince Dafan, with his hord, was encamped at two werfts
diftance from us, and fent us feveral cattle and fheep
for provifions to our party: he fent alfo a jar of fpirits

U u   diftilled

distilled from mares milk, for the officers, which was as clear as water but strong, and of an agreeable flavour.

On the 23d, we were reinforced by a detachment of two hundred men from our battalions, and three hundred and fifty Coffacks, which made us now a body of one thousand and fifty strong. By this opportunity I received a letter from the governor, telling me that he would join us himself in two or three days, but not a word of orders how we were to act, in cafe any exigence should require it ; being the fenior officer I took the command of the whole till the governor should arrive. On the arrival of this reinforcement, prince Dafan fent more cattle for their provision, and a fufficient number of kibbets for their accommodation. This evening we received intelligence that Shurundunduck, and his nephew, Dunduambu, were encamped with an army of twenty thoufand strong, oppofite to Zornayar, which being upwards of one hundred and fifty werfts from

A battle with the Kalmucks.
us, made us conjecture it would take fome time before they could come up with us ; but we foon found our miftake, for we were alarmed very early in the morning of the 24th by the breaking up of prince Dafan's camp, and feeing his people coming towards us in the utmoft confufion. On this I drew up our men in all hafte, and ordered the dragoons and Coffacks to mount and go to prince Dafan's affiftance : we foon faw Shurundunduck's army advancing, which obliged Dafan and his people to take refuge in our rear, whom I perfuaded to difmount fuch of his horfemen as had fire-arms, and to bring as many of his men as had bows and arrows, to fight on foot as we did, and I fent fome officers

5

and

and ferjeants to draw them up in order: with thefe we formed a fquare towards the river, and fecured their baggage and cattle in our rear.   The enemy being advanced in the form of a crefcent, and within gun-fhot of us, made a halt to confult the mode of their attack.   Dafan was in the utmoft perplexity, and begged me to keep them at a diftance with our great guns and fire-arms, affuring me if we did not, they would rufh in upon us with a very fudden and furious attack, and throw us all into confufion.

On this emergency, I was very much at lofs how to act, having no orders, and advifed with the reft of the officers; when it was agreed to fend an interpreter with a drum, to inform them of his majefty's troops being there for the protection of prince Dafan, who had entirely fubmitted the decifion of his claim to his imperial majefty, and that it was expected they would do the fame, being equally fubject to the emperor; and as the governor of Aftrachan was hourly expected, who might fall upon ways and means to reconcile their differences, they ought to wait his arrival.   The meffenger was fent, and brought back an anfwer: —That they knew very well Dafan had procured Ruffian troops to protect him from their juft refentment; but as they were a free nation, they would do themfelves juftice, without fubmitting to the arbitration of any perfon whatever, and that they were determined to attack their brethren at all hazards, notwithftanding our troops, and if we interpofed in their behalf, and fhould meet with any difafter, the blame would lay at our own doors.

Having returned this anfwer they began to advance in a femicircle, intending to furround us, on which I ordered the

U u 2   field-

field-pieces to be fired among them, and then loaded with
grape-fhot: all this time they avoided coming near our troops,
but bent their whole force againft their own countrymen,
which obliged me to form a front againft them, both to the
right and left, and then began to play on them with grape-
fhot and fmall-arms, which made great havock amongft
them, and their horfes not being ufed to the thundering
noife of fire-arms, became unmanageable, and threw their
whole body into the utmoft confufion; on which our dragoons and Coffacks, feconded by prince Dafan's men, attacked them with fuch vigour, that they foon gave way on
all fides and fled, while we plied them with the field-pieces
as long as they were within reach.

We had two dragoons killed in this action, and feven
wounded, and five Coffacks killed and feventeen wounded;
five of our foldiers were wounded with barbed arrows; but of
Dafan's men, there were three hundred and feventy-four
killed, and upwards of five hundred wounded. Our dragoons and Coffacks returned from the purfuit with fixty-
three prifoners, and Dafan's men took fome hundreds;
we could not afcertain the lofs of the enemy in this fhort
action, but it muft have been very confiderable. In the
evening, when all was over, governor Wolinfki arrived,
and I acquainted him of the tranfactions of the day: he was
much pleafed with the meffage that had been fent to Dunduambu and Shurundunduck, and efpecially that we were
not the aggreffors in the action, nor had fired upon them
till we were actually attacked. He faid he would have come
come up fooner, but he did not imagine they would have
made an attempt in defiance of our troops, but fince they
                                                    had

had done fo, he would now confider them as rebels, and
make an example of them as fuch.   He then gave orders to
hang all the prifoners, (who amounted to fome hundreds),
and Dafan's men executed the orders with great fatisfaction.
Among the prifoners was Dunduambu's greateft favourite
and principal counfellor, whom Dafan put to the moft cruel
torture imaginable, and he had no fooner expired under the
torment, than they divided his body in four, and ftuck up
the quarters on fo many pofts, and his head on another.

The governor, judging from what had happened, that a
reconciliation would now be impracticable, advifed prince
Dafan, with his two brothers, to retire with their people
under the cannon of Krafnayar, where they would be fafe
from any attempt of their enemies, as it was impoffible that
our troops could remain any longer in the field in that advanced cold feafon, there being at this time a great fall of
fnow, which they immediately agreed to.   We broke up
our camp on the 25th, but we had fcarce marched five
werfts, when the enemy made their appearance in the fame
manner they had done the day before, and fent a meffenger
to the governor, to let him know they were fenfible he intended to carry their enemy out of their reach, which they
were refolved to prevent, let the confequence be what it
would ; neverthelefs, if the governor could prevail on Dafan to agree to a partition of the fovereignty with Dunduambu, on reafonable terms, they were willing to hold a
conference with him on that head.   It was directly agreed
that five chief men from each party fhould meet in the
middle fpace between the two armies, where they conferred
together above three hours, without being able to come to

an.

an agreement, and then they returned each to their own party. The enemy having obferved that Dafan's party, during the conference, were tranfporting their wives, children, and cattle over a branch of the Wolga, now fet upon Dafan's men with a moft furious attack, and numbers were flain on each fide before we could come up to prevent it, as the enemy ftill avoided coming near as much as poffible; but upon our horfe engaging them, and our firing with our cannon and fmall arms brifkly upon them, they retired quite out of fight. Our dragoons returning from the purfuit, brought back twenty-five prifoners, who affured us, that Shurundunduck was retired towards Zornayar; on which the governor fet out for Aftrachan, leaving orders with me to fee prince Dafan, and his Kalmucks, all over the river, and fafe under the cannon of Krafnayar, where I arrived the 30th: but the prince finding his cattle could not fubfift in fo narrow a diftrict, divided the hord, and diftributed them among the numerous iflands formed by the feveral branches of the Wolga, where they were to remain in full fecurity till his majefty's pleafure was known. I fet out on the 3d of November, having prince Dafan, and his two brothers, under my convoy, and arrived at Aftrachan that evening, where we found every neceffary accommodation provided for their reception.

Some odd cuftoms among them.

On this expedition I obferved fome peculiar cuftoms among the Kalmucks, which I cannot omit mentioning. As I attended the governor into Dafan's tent, we found the prince and his two brothers, with their principal men, feated in a circle round the fire, having a large iron pipe, filled with tobacco, which they handed about from one to another, each

each taking one pull, filled his mouth as full of smoke as it would hold, and keeping the smoke a confiderable time in their mouths, they at length blew it out at their noftrils; immediately after this they all parted without fpeaking one word; this we underftood to be the conclufion of a confultation among them.

As they are great lovers of horfe-flefh, which they prefer to every other kind, and obferving we were no admirers of it, prince Dafan entertained us with the flefh of a fucking-foal, both roafted and boiled, and I muft confefs I never eat any thing more delicious. In mentioning this Tartar nation before, I faid they paft the winter in the defert of Aftrachan; but I was now informed that the greateft part of them live in the defert of Beriket, towards the rivers Jaik and Yembo, bordering on the Turkumanians.

The fmall-pox is as much dreaded among the Kalmucks as the peftilence amongft us: when any of them are feized with it, they immediately break up their camp and fly, leaving the fick perfon in one of their worft kibbets with a killed fheep, part of which is roafted and part raw, and a jar of water and fome wood for fire; if they recover they follow the hord, which feldom happens, for they almoft all die for want of attendance.

They live but four months at moft in the deferts, and they inhabit a moft pleafant country all the reft of the year; their way of life exactly refembles that of the old patriarchs, their whole occupation confifting in the care of their flocks and herds, fifhing, and hunting. When they go upon an expedition, every one takes a fheep with him for his provifion, and three horfes which he rides alternately; and

and when any of them fail, they kill it and divide the flesh, putting pieces of it under their saddles, and after riding some time upon it, they eat it without any farther preparation; this, in their estimation, is the best way of dressing it; they generally return from their excursions with only one horse, having eat all the rest.

Baranetz or lamb-skin.

I had both heard and read of an herb that grew about Aftrachan, called baranetz, or lamb-skin, which was alledged to grow upon a single stalk in the shape of a lamb, and which when ripe was covered over with hair, or wool, and that it consumed all the grass that grew near it, and that when taken off, it served for fine fur for caps, or lining cloaths; but as there is no such herb, I was at a loss to conceive how such a mistake could arise: however, on enquiry, I was informed, that the baranetzs, or lambs, are cut out of the sheep's bellies, a little before their lambing-time, their skins being then in their greatest beauty, with the hair lying in short, smooth, pretty curls, and of different colours, as dark and light greys, black and white; the dark grey are the most valuable, and are sold as high as ten shillings sterling a piece, and the black at five; the light grey and white at half a crown. This branch of trade is very profitable to the Nagayan Tartars, as the Indians, Persians, and Russians, buy all they can produce. I bought by commission for count Bruce and general Le Fort, of the best kind, to the value of two hundred rubles.

Returns for Moscow up the Wolga.

I had orders from general Matuskin to go as soon as possible to Moscow, to deliver my report of the Caspian sea to the emperor; but as there is no possibility of travelling by land to Saratof, I was obliged to wait till the river Wolga

9   was

was frozen.   On the 8th of January, I set out from Aftrachan in fledges on the ice, in company with feveral others,
for Mofcow, making in the whole a party of twenty men,
all well provided with arms; but as it rained very hard, we
went but ten werfts to Saliterdwor.   The rain continuing the
two following days, the ice became fo weak, that fome of
the horfes fell in feveral times, and it was with much difficulty we faved them from being drowned; fo that we could
only travel eighty werfts in the two days, and were obliged
to lodge both nights on the ice, in the middle of the river,
as there was no poffibility of getting afhore for the water.

On the 11th, it being froft, we went fifty werfts, but
one of our horfes dropt through and was drowned: this
night, however, we refted in fafety on fhore.   The next
day proved rainy, and we could only go forty werfts, but
paft this night alfo on fhore.   On the 13th, although it
was frofty, the ice was fo much rent in feveral places, that
it was with much difficulty we could get the horfes over the
openings; one of them broke his leg, which obliged us to
fhoot him; and after travelling forty werfts, we were forced
to ftay all night on the ice.   The next day it rained, and
the ice became fo full of rents, that we were often put
to hard fhifts to extricate ourfelves: two of our fledges
and horfes fell in, which we faved with great difficulty.
At noon we went on fhore to refrefh the horfes, and went
to a fifher's hut at a fmall diftance to get fome fifh: in this
interval a party of fifty Kalmuck Tartars, all in armour,
furrounded our fledges, where we had left all our fire-arms
excepting three; with thofe we had, cocked in our hands,
we ran in hafte to the fledges, and fecured the reft of our

X x   arms,

arms, the Tartars looking at us with surprize. Their myrzaj, or commander, came up to me and offered me his hand, saying, in broken Ruffian, that he knew me since the action with Shurundunduck: we gave him a dram, and he went away with his party. They are not to be trufted, for the Tartars will rob where they can do it with fafety; this accident determined us to be no more without our arms on our journey. We travelled this day forty werfts, but would not venture on fhore all night for fear of the Kalmucks, who were encamped thereabouts. On the 15th, we reached Zornayar, forty werfts, where we refted on the 16th; and as our horfes had now brought us three hundred werfts, without relief, no other horfes being to be had all the way, the men taking provifions and forage with them to ferve them on the road, their hay being all twifted for the eafier conveyance, we returned them for Aftrachan, with a certificate to the governor, at the defire of our conductors, of the lofs of two of the horfes, as they belonged to government.

On the 17th, being provided with frefh horfes, and having procured ropes to pull out the horfes and fledges in cafe they fhould break through the ice again; the day proving rainy, feveral of our horfes fell in, but were faved; having a rope faftened to each of them; and at night we reached Stupingar, fixty werfts, and the next day, notwithftanding it was hard froft, feveral of our horfes fell in: we travelled feventy werfts, and refted the night on fhore. On the 19th, we went feventy werfts, and at night reached Czaritza, where our two battalions wintered laft year. Here we got frefh horfes, and next day got to Dubofka, fixty werfts,

in.

in rainy weather ; here we were again fupplied with frefh
horfes, and reached Belekli, feventy werfts.   On the 21ft,
we found the ice fo much weakened by the rainy weather,
that we were in continual danger.   We got to Kamufinka,
feventy werfts, on the 22d; and here getting frefh horfes,
we could only travel eighty werfts the two following days
under fuch conftant rain, that the water was now a foot
deep over the ice, fo that we paft the dangerous rents with
the utmoft difficulty, and for the night of the 24th, we
took up our quarters on a woody ifland, making a large
fire to dry ourfelves.

On the 25th in the morning, we had got but a fhort way
from the ifland, before we found the ice fo full of large
rents, that it was impoffible for us to proceed farther upon
it, and in endeavouring to make the fhore, feven of our
fledges fell in through the ice, and five of our horfes were
drowned : the reft we faved with extreme danger to ourfelves, as the ice was continually yielding and breaking under us, till at laft after every effort with poles and ropes,
we got all fafe to the land; but our fledges and baggage
lay fix hours in the water, and muft have been loft but for
the lucky affiftance of a party of men who were paffing
this way, by whofe help we got them pulled out, and in
about half an hour afterwards, the river broke up with a
thundering noife, and nothing but water was to be feen ; fo
that we had a very narrow and miraculous efcape.   We
fortunately were near a wood, where we made large fires to
warm and dry ourfelves, being near perifhed with wet and
cold ; and what augmented our mifery was the perpetual rains
pouring day and night down upon us.   Such a rainy fea-

fon

fon in the time of winter, and the breaking up of the Wolga, had not been known in the memory of man. By the overturning of my fledge, I loft a whole fuit of Tartarian armour, a blunderbufs, a pair of brafs barrelled piftols, a filver-hilted fword, a little trunk in which was my pafs, and an order to fupply us with horfes on our way, and fome money for my travelling charges.

The three following days, we dragged our fledges with much toil over the fands, and having travelled two hundred and twenty werfts, we reached Saratof on the evening of the 28th : this place is one thoufand werfts up the Wolga, from Aftrachan. We ftaid here four days to dry our baggage, which had all been moft thoroughly wet ; I got my baranetz, or lambfkins, fo carefully dried and dreffed, that they looked as well as ever. The governor gave me another pafs, and an order for horfes, in place of that I had loft ; and as this is the firft place from which we could travel by land, we left the river Wolga, and proceeded acrofs the country on a hard beaten road of fnow, being now quite in another climate, where winter appeared in its full rigour. The governor informed us that the roads were peftered with robbers, on account of the very bad crops laft fummer, and advifed us to be on our guard.

We left Saratof on the 2d of February, and travelling fixty werfts, arrived in the evening at a fingle houfe in a wood ; and next day, after a journey of fixty-three werfts, through one continued wood, we came again to a fingle houfe, but when we were within three werfts of it, we faw feveral fledges before us attacked by robbers, and carried off ; we made all the hafte we could to go to their affiftance, and

before

before we got up, the robbers had made off into the wood,
with the horfes and fledges loaded with merchandize : we
found nine men ftripped naked, and three foldiers who
had been their efcort, killed befide them. We took both
the living and the dead with us to this houfe, where
we found only a boy, and enquiring of him for the people
of the houfe, he faid they were gone to a fair fixty werfts
off, and were not to come home that night. As we conceived ourfelves to be in a very dangerous place, we barricaded
the court-yard belonging to the houfe, and kept a very ftrict
watch, placing a centry at each corner ; having our fire-
arms in readinefs, we kept ourfelves very quiet. One of
our company whofe appointment it was to watch the motions of the boy, obferved him at three o'clock in the morning, go to the back door and open it, but being clofe behind him, found the boy talking to a man without, in a
very low voice ; two others of our company getting behind
him, pulled the fellow into the houfe, and faftened the door ;
the ftripped travellers no fooner faw him, than they unanimoufly agreed that this fellow was one of the gang who had
robbed them ; upon this we tied him neck and heels, and
upon our looking out at the back door, we difcovered a
number of men at a fmall diftance, upon the fnow, waiting
as we imagined, for intelligence, but on our firing a few
fhot among them, they retired into the wood. We then
proceeded to examine the fellow we had taken, who faid he
was the landlord of the houfe, and was well known to be
an honeft man, and had no connection with thieves or
robbers, and threatened that he would make us repent the
injury we had done him in his own houfe ; but as all thofe
                                                      who

who had been robbed averred that he was the chief of the gang, and had himself killed one of the soldiers, we determined to carry him and all that were in the house, with us; and accordingly set out.

On the 4th, travelling sixty-four werfts, we came to Penfe, a fortified town, with a strong garrison, where we delivered up our prisoner to the governor, and the plundered merchants, on their examination, declared that he was actually the ringleader of the gang; upon which the governor ordered him to be put to the torture, to make him confefs where the reft of his companions were to be found; but he was fo obftinate, that he would not anfwer any of the queftions that were put to him. On which two of the robbed merchants propofed to go in fearch of them, if the governor would fend a fufficient force to take them, if found, alledging they might be eafily traced by the track they had made through the fnow, in going into the wood: the governor readily confented, and ordered fifty dragoons, and as many Coflacks, to mount and attend them. The next day in the evening, they returned with twenty-three robbers, and the fledges and horfes belonging to the merchants; they were found in hutts in a thicket of the wood, not above three miles from the before mentioned houfe. This wood runs eaft and weft feveral hundred werfts in length, and its narroweft breadth, where we croffed, is one hundred and fixty werfts, without any inhabitants.

A remarkable difcovery of a town, with an account of it.

I was here informed by the governor, that about fix months ago, a large village, or town, had been difcovered by its own inhabitants, who fent a deputation to the emperor for that purpofe. This town lies two hundred miles weft from

from Penfe, and at the fame diftance from any other inhabited place; it is fituated on the fide of a lake in the middle of this great wood, and confifts of above two thoufand
families; they gave the following account of themfelves.——
In the very troublefome times, after the death of czar
Iwan Wafilewitz, the tyrant, to the reign of czar Michael
Feodorewitz, (his prefent majefty's grandfather), a great
number of robbers had affociated themfelves and committed
great ravages over all the country; their leader, or commander in chief, was a degraded colonel, and an experienced
officer; their depredations were fo audacious, that czar
Michael Feodorewitz found it neceffary to fend large detachments of the military againft them, but the robbers
commonly attacked thefe parties by furprize and defeated
them. The czar on this offered a very high reward for the
heads of their leaders, and a free pardon to all the reft. The
chiefs being apprehenfive that they fhould one day or other
be betrayed by their followers, came to a refolution to make
a general plunder, once for all; which they did, and carried off large quantities of corn, horfes, cattle, all forts of
labouring utenfils, and all the women they could meet
with, and retired into thofe inacceffible woods, where they
fettled, cleared, and manured the ground, and lived ever
fince; governed by their own laws, without ever after mo-
lefting, or having the fmalleft intercourfe with any of their
remote neighbours.

I was alfo informed, that a wild girl, about eighteen years
of age, had been lately taken in the neighbourhood of this
town. A woman who lived here, alledged, fhe was her
child, faying, that about eighteen years ago fhe was going
through

through the wood to fee a fick fifter of her's: being then big with child fhe was feized with her labour-pains, and was delivered; and as fhe was then in extreme agony, fhe did not perceive by what means her child was conveyed from her; but hearing the common report that a wild girl was frequently feen in the wood, fhe always faid it could be no other than the child fhe had loft.

Many attempts had been made to catch her, but to no purpofe, fhe being fo nimble-footed that none could overtake her. When the emperor heard of it, he fent orders to the governor to raife the people of the country, and furround that part of the wood where fhe had been obferved to frequent, and fet up their nets with which they ufed to catch the deer, and in this manner fhe was taken without receiving any hurt; the girl was immediately fent to Mofcow, under the care of her fuppofed mother, where I afterwards faw her. She was of a fwarthy complexion, and I was told fhe was much overgrown with hair; fhe was very fhy of being feen, and always fitting in a dark corner, trembling with fear when any body approached her. It was generally fuppofed fhe had been fuckled by a bear, but how fhe fubfifted all the time afterwards muft remain a fecret till fhe learns to fpeak and gives the account herfelf.

On the 7th of February, having obtained an efcort of twenty Coffacks to conduct me to Saranfki, ninety werfts, and my travelling companions intending to continue here fome time, I left Penfe, travelling all the way through one continued wood, which made it very dangerous on account of the many robberies and murders committed on the road, and arrived at Saranfki on the evening of the 8th, without

any

any moleftation. All the way, however, we went, we met
many real objects of compaffion, wearing the vifible marks
of hunger and famine in their countenances, occafioned by
the failure of the laft year's crop, which drove many to
feek relief by plunder. After this I travelled through a
well inhabited country, without the leaft danger, and came
to Arfama, one hundred and twenty werfts; from thence
to Murvin, one hundred and twenty; and from thence to
Wolodimer, one hundred and twenty more; and from
Wolodimer, one hundred and eighty werfts, to the city of
Mofcow, where I arrived on the 22d of February. From
Saratof to Mofcow it is eight hundred and fifty-fix werfts
by land; but following the courfe of the river, it is one
thoufand feven hundred and eighty.

At this time great preparations were making for the
emprefs's coronation, at which ceremony all the great men
and grandees of the empire had been fummoned to appear.
General Matufkin, and governor Wolinfki, with the two
battalions of guards I left at Aftrachan, were ordered to repair to Mofcow with the utmoft expedition, and arrived five
weeks after me; which, if I had known, would have
faved me a very troublefome journey befides a great expence.

The day after my arrival in Mofcow, I waited on prince
Menzikof, who ordered me to attend him to his majefty,
and after waiting a quarter of an hour in the antichamber
I was called in, and found there, his majefty, attended by
the duke of Holftein, admiral Apraxin, chancellor Golofkin, and the princes Galitzin, Dolgoruki and Romadonof-
fki. The emperor examined the chart of the Cafpian fea,

Y y   with

with its gulfs, bays, and foundings, very narrowly; afking me a great many queftions, efpecially concerning the river Daria, of which I prefented him with a draft at large, with which he feemed very much pleafed, as the drawing exhibited the fituation of that river, which appeared to be well calculated for a fort and fafe harbour, fecure from any attempts that could be made by the Ufbeck Tartars. His majefty then gave the duke of Holftein a fhort account of prince Békewitz's unfortunate expedition to that place; adding, that if he had had patience till he had been well fortified and fettled, and not fuffered himfelf to be over-reached by the treacherous infinuations of the Tartars, by this time he might have been fully mafter of that valuable river, with all the gold mines; but as he was now in full poffeffion of the provinces on the oppofite fide of the Cafpian fea, he ftill intended to fettle a colony at that place, and to erect forts along the banks of that river, toward the mines, for their protection; and the forts could be eafily fupplied with provifions from the neighbouring provinces, without having any dependence on the Ufbeck Tartars for them. From all this difcourfe, I apprehended I fhould be again fent to thofe parts very much againft my inclination. After I had given an account in what forwardnefs the fortifications of Swetego-Kreft, on the river Sulack were, and of our expedition againft the Kalmuck Tartars, I was difmiffed, being ordered by prince Menzikof to attend the duke of Holftein's levee while he remained in Mofcow.

B O O K   X.

The duke of Holftein.—The fall of baron Shafirof.—The captain endeavours to get his difcharge.—A dignified troop of chevaliers.—A defcription of the cathedral.—Proceffion to the coronation of the emprefs.—Coronation ceremony.—Proceffion to the church of St. Michael.—Proceffion to the church of the Refurrection.—Dinner in the hall of folemnities.—New mode of promotion.—The captain obtains his furlough.—The captain leaves Mofcow.—A Swedifh colonel at Riga fufpected of having fhot Charles the XIIth of Sweden.—The captain embarks for Scotland.—Puts into Erd-holm, a Danifh harbour and fort.—Defcription of the harbour.—De-parts for Elfingohr.—Driven into Marfirand difmafted.—Quarrel between Carnegie and his mate.—He arrives in Scotland.

HIS royal highnefs Charles duke of Holftein, was the only fon of the eldeft fifter of Charles the XIIth, king of Sweden, whom that monarch intended for his fuc-ceffor; he was now betrothed to the princefs Anne, the emperor's eldeft daughter; his highnefs was in the 25th year of his age, of the middling fize, well proportioned; his lips were thick, and his tongue large, which occafioned a defect in his fpeech; in attending, when very young, his uncle, the king of Sweden, a winter's campaign in Poland, where the cold was very intenfe, and feeing the king endure it with fo much indifference, the prince was afhamed to complain, till at laft his toes were fo feverely froft-bitten, that they began to mortify, and he was obliged to have fome of them cut off; the prince was very affable, and of a chearful difpofition, fond of all kinds of diverfions. He was now lodged in the Inoifemfka Slaboda, (or quarter of foreign-

Y y 2   ers),

BOOK X. ers) : all manner of diverſions were here practiſed for his
amuſement ; he was much pleaſed with the Engliſh country-
dances, and as I was pretty well acquainted with them, I
was always next to his highneſs at thoſe entertainments.

1724.

I had the good fortune to be ſo much in his favour, that
he aſked if I wiſhed to enter into his ſervice. I replied, that
I would accept the honor with great pleaſure if I could obtain my diſcharge from the emperor's : his highneſs ſaid he
would ſpeak to prince Menzikof about it, which he did next
day, and the prince told him that his majeſty would grant
it at his deſire, notwithſtanding his intention to ſend me on
an expedition over the Caſpian ſea, to fortify and ſecure
the harbour at the mouth of the river Daria ; which information put a ſtop to all my hopes. This diſappoint-
ment made me reſolve to get out of this ſtate of ſlavery at
any rate, from which it was impoſſible for any one that
was ſerviceable to extricate himſelf with honour.

The fall of
baron Sha-
firof.

On my return to Moſcow, I had the mortification to hear
the diſagreeable account of the fall and diſgrace of my former benefactor, baron Shafirof, the vice-chancellor, in
whoſe ſuite I was a year at Conſtantinople, where he was
an hoſtage, and afterwards ambaſſador ; he was without diſpute one of the ableſt miniſters in the whole empire, very
high in the eſteem of the emperor, who always employed
him in negotiations of the greateſt importance. The baron's
misfortune was occaſioned by his endeavouring the ruin
of prince Menzikof, which at laſt ended in his own. When
his majeſty ſet out on his expedition to Perſia, he appointed
prince Menzikof regent of the empire in his abſence: by
the aſſiſtance of baron·Oſterman, the prince diſcovered that

5   the

the vice-chancellor had embezzled large fums out of the public revenue, and that he had concealed two hundred thoufand ducats in fpecie, befides jewels to the value of feventy thoufand ducats, the property of the late Knez Gagarin, whofe daughter was married to baron Shafirof's fon. When prince Gagarin was executed, it was made death to any perfon who fhould conceal his effects, and the baron himfelf publifhed the decree; the baron alfo ftood charged with feveral other crimes, for all which he was condemned to be beheaded, and was fo near fuffering the fentence, that his neck was on the block, when the fentence was mitigated to perpetual banifhment into Siberia. Ofterman fucceeded the baron in the office of vice-chancellor; baron Shafirof had raifed him from a low degree, and was afterwards rewarded with ingratitude; he was by birth a German, from a fmall town belonging to the duke of Mecklenburgh, of mean parents, and the baron paffing through that country, engaged him as a fervant; in this fervice he fo ingratiated himfelf with his mafter, that he raifed him by degrees to the office of fecretary in chancery, and as fuch he was fent as fecretary to count Bruce to the congrefs at Aland; where he conducted himfelf with fuch addrefs, that he was appointed the count's colleague, in which fituation he behaved with much haughtinefs: yet, after betraying his mafter and benefactor, he fucceeded him as vice-chancellor, and after the death of count Golofkin, he was promoted to the office of high-chancellor: but when the emprefs Elizabeth afcended the throne of Ruffia, Ofterman was banifhed to Siberia, there to bewail his former ingratitude, meeting with the reward due to all ungrateful perfons.

In

BOOK X.

1724.
The captain
endeavours to
get his dif-
charge.

In the beginning of March, I prefented a petition to the college of war, in which I reprefented my fervices for thirteen years in their army; that the fituation of my own private affairs in Scotland, where I had not been for twenty years, now required my perfonal prefence to regulate them; and defired my difcharge from this fervice for that purpofe. Prince Menzikof and the other generals feemed furprifed at my requeft, telling me that his majefty had fignified his pleafure to give me one of the regiments that were then under the command of general Waterang, at Swetego-Kreft on the river Sulack; from this I faw plainly that it was determined to fend me once more over the Cafpian to the river Daria, to lead a fad life among the Ufbeck Tartars: I told them it was impoffible for me then to accept the honour his majefty meant to beftow on me, as the fituation of my affairs would not fuffer me to remain longer in their fervice; and the board then abfolutely refufed to grant my difcharge. I now urged to them the privilege promifed by his majefty to all foreigners, that they were not to be detained in the fervice againft their own inclination; to this they replied, that they did not look on me as a foreigner, but as one of themfelves; to this compliment I only anfwered by a low bow, and retired.

As I had received a promife from his majefty before we fet out on this expedition into Perfia, that upon our return he would give me leave to go and fee my friends, I now laid my cafe before the duke of Holftein, who advifed me to prefent a memorial to the emperor the next day, at eleven o'clock, when he would be with him; which I accordingly did, and had for anfwer, that my difcharge could not be granted, but that I fhould get a fur-

lough

lough for one year, to go and fee my friends, and fettle my
affairs ; at the expiration of which it was expected I fhould
return. Upon my accepting thefe conditions, I received
his majefty's order to prince Menzikof, to grant me a furlough : upon my producing the order to the war office,
they demanded that count Bruce and general Le Fort fhould
become fureties for my return, which I refufed, telling them
that the furlough his majefty had granted me was fufficient, which 1 infifted upon ; on this the office forced
me to give an obligation under my hand, to return at the
end of the year, which they conceived in the ftrongeft terms
they could exprefs, and gave me the alternative, to fign it,
or remain where I was : the matter being fo far fettled, they
told me that as foon as the emprefs's coronation was over
I fhould receive my difpatches.

The city of Mofcow was now vaftly crowded with foreigners as well as natives, where all people of rank, belonging to this great empire, were obliged to attend, every
one endeavouring to out-do another in grand equipages, fo
that nothing now was minded but affemblies, balls, mafquerades, and grand entertainments, fuch as had never before been known in this part of the world. Yet every body
was much furprifed that neither the grand duke, nor his fifter
the grand-duchefs, the children of the late czarowitz, were
to be prefent at this folemnity, but were left unnoticed at
Peterfburgh.

To aggrandize the coronation, a troop of chevaliers, or A dignified
horfe-guards, were raifed, mounted on fine horfes ; lieute- troop of chevaliers.
nant-general Iagufinfki commanded them as captain ; major-
general Mamonof, as lieutenant ; brigadier-general Le-
wentof,

3

wentof, was cornet; the quartermafters were colonels, the corporals lieutenant-colonels, and the fixty troopers were all captains. Their coats were green cloth, the waiftcoats fcarlet richly laced with gold; on their breafts and backs the emperor's arms in embroidery; their cartouch cafes were of crimfon velvet, with cyphers embroidered in gold; their grenade pouches and belts of crimfon velvet and gold; their fword hilts gilt, and white cockades in their hats; their holfters and piftol-cafes ornamented with cyphers in gold, laced and fringed with the fame; the bitts of the bridles, breaft and crupper-leathers, were covered with maffive gold, and their kettle drums and trumpets were filver, with the emperors arms in emboffed work of gold and filver.

Defcription of the cathedral. The cathedral in which the ceremony of coronation was to be performed, was richly adorned and illuminated with a number of branches in form of crowns, and a very large one in the middle of fine filver of exquifite workmanfhip; they were all full of wax candles gilt. The fteps to the altar, and the pavement of the church to the throne, were covered with rich tapeftry wrought with gold; in the middle of the church was a canopy of crimfon velvet, adorned with the arms of Ruffia, viz. an eagle, fable, with an efcutcheon on its breaft, of St. George killing the dragon, and all round it was the ribbon of the order of St. Andrew, and on the two fides were the arms of the kingdoms of Cafan, Aftrachan, Siberia, &c. the canopy was embroidered with gold raifed-work, with rich fringes, ribbons, tufts, gold lace, &c. it was fupported at the four corners with pillars covered with red and gold filk. Under this canopy was the throne; the fteps and pavement of which were covered

with

with crimfon velvet, on which were placed two elbow chairs for their imperial majefties, which glittered with precious ftones, and a long table covered with cloth of gold, which hung down to the ground : their ufual feats in the church were covered infide and out with cloth of gold, and the bottom was covered with red velvet trimmed with gold; a place was made near the throne, for the royal princeffes, adorned with tapeftry and cloth of gold, with an eagle of gold embroidery fparkling with jewels.

Her imperial majefty prepared herfelf for her coronation, by three days fafting and prayer, and the people had notice given them by the fecretary of the chancery, preceded by an officer, with kettle-drums and trumpets.

The 7th of May, the day appointed for the grand coro- Proceffion to nation, eight battalions and four companies of grenadiers tion of the of the guards were, early in the morning, drawn up in the emprefs. kremelin, or fort of the palace; our grenadiers lined the road from the palace to the cathedral, oppofite to which was St. Michael's church, the burying-place of his ma- jefty's anceftors ; the road between them was lined by two battalions, and the road from the cathedral to the gate of the kremelin was lined by the other fix battalions ; and from the gate to the monaftery of the Refurrection, the burying place of the princeffes of the czarian family, was lined by the regiments of Le Fort and Buterfki, who fup- plied the place of four battalions of our divifion then at Peterfburgh.

At nine o'clock in the morning, the clergy met in the church, and read prayers for the profperity of their imperial

Z z ma-

majefties, and then went in their pontificals, and joined the procefſion, which began at ten in the following order.

1. One half of the horſe-guards.

2. The emprefs's pages, and their governor.

3. The deputy-maſter of the ceremonies, Williaminof, with his mace.

4. The deputies of the provinces.

5. The brigadier-generals, ⎫
6. The major-generals, ⎬ in pairs by ſeniority.
7. The lieutenant-generals, ⎭

8. The two great heralds at arms of the empire, Pleſhof and count Souffe, both in habits of crimſon, and gold embroidery, with the imperial eagle wrought upon them, with their ſtaves in their hands.

9. The grand-maſter of the ceremonies, Shubarof, with his mace.

10. Knez Demetri Galitzin and baron Oſterman, privy-counfellors, carrying, on two cuſhions, the imperial mantle, which was of cloth of gold lined with ermine; the claſps were ſet with many large brilliants; and on the mantle was embroidered, in relievo, the imperial eagle.

11. Knez Dolgoruki, a privy-counfellor, carrying on a cuſhion the globe, which was of fine gold, with a crofs on the top of it ſet with diamonds, rubies, ſapphires, and emeralds: this globe was much admired, as being the workmanſhip of ancient Rome.

12. Count Puſhkin, a privy-counfellor, carrying on a cuſhion, the ſcepter, enamelled and adorned with diamonds and rubies, with the imperial eagle at the top; the ſame

that was ufed at the coronation of the ancient emperors of
Ruffia.

13. Count Bruce, a privy-counfellor and mafter of the
ordnance, carrying the crown, which was immenfely rich
with brilliants, feveral of which were very large, befides
fine oriental pearls of an extraordinary fize and an even
water; among the other precious ftones, of various colours,
in this crown, there was a true oriental ruby of uncommon
luftre as large as a pigeon's egg, and fuppofed to be
the richeft that has yet been known; this fupplied the place
of a globe on the top of the crown, and the crofs was all
covered over with brilliants.

14. Count Tolftoi, grand-marfhal, with his ftaff in his
hand, on the top of which was an imperial eagle of maffive
gold, and an emerald as big as a hen's egg.

15. His imperial majefty, Peter the Great, fupported by
prince Menzikof and knez Repnin.

16. Her imperial majefty, Catherine, led by his royal
highnefs the duke of Holftein, and attended by the high
admiral count Apraxin; and the high chancellor count
Golofhin; her train was borne by the princefs of Menzikof,
the duchefs of Trubetzkoi, the countefs of Golofkin, the
countefs of Bruce, and general Butterlin's lady; they were
followed by twelve married, and twelve unmarried ladies,
clad in robes, and walking in pairs.

17. The married ladies were; four lieutenant-generals
ladies, viz. Jaguzinfki, Matufkin, Dolgoruki, and Kura-
kin; eight major-general's ladies, viz. Gunther, Zernifhof,
Balk, Le-Fort, Trubetzkoy, Ufhakoff, Romanzof, and Cir-

kafki;

kafki; thefe were followed by twelve young ladies of the
firft quality, in pairs.

18. The colonels, and other military officers, and thofe of
the national nobility fummoned to attend, all walking in
pairs.

19. The other half of the horfe-guards clofed the proceffion; during which, all the bells in Mofcow rang, which
was accompanied with the mufic of the drums and trumpets.

Coronation ceremony. The proceffion having entered the cathedral, the regalia
were placed on a long table fet there for that purpofe; and
the duke of Holftein having led the emprefs to the throne,
retired to his place, and the emperor led her to her feat,
attended by prince Menzikoff and knez Repnin, and the
counts Apraxin and Golofkin, and the ladies who bore the
train; their majefties being feated, the archbifhops and other
prelates alfo fat down, but the gentlemen and ladies ftood
during the whole courfe of the ceremony: when the anthem was fung, the emperor ftood up, and taking the fcepter from the table, ordered the great-marfhal to call the
archbifhops and prelates, enjoining them to proceed to coronation. The archbifhop of Novogorod then addreffed the
emprefs thus : " Orthodox and great emprefs, moft gracious
" lady, may it pleafe your majefty to repeat the creed Atha-
" nafian of orthodox faith, in the prefence of your loyal
" fubjects."——The emprefs having repeated this creed,
kneeled down on a cufhion, and received the archbifhop's
benediction, and after prayers were faid, her majefty ftood
up, and two archbifhops took the coronation mantle, and
prefented it to the emperor, who put it on the emprefs,
with-

without laying the fceptre out of his hand ; their majefty's then kneeling down, the archbifhop faid prayers, at the conclufion of which their majefties rofe up, and the emperor, taking the crown, placed it upon her head, but ftill held the fcepter himfelf ; the archbifhops then pronounced their benediction in the name of the Father, Son, and Holy Ghoft, and put the imperial globe into her majefty's hand.   This being done, their majefties took their feats and received the compliments both of the clergy and laity, while the choir fung their ufual anthem for their profperous reign; at the conclufion of which there was a general falvo from all the artillery, and the bells of the whole city were rung.

This done, their majefties being conducted from the throne with the fame ceremonies with which they afcended, they proceeded to the foot of the altar, and from thence to their ufual feats; and during the liturgy her majefty took off her crown, which was committed to the charge of the fecretary of the cabinet; and after the prayers for the communion fervice were fung, the emperor led her majefty, who was dreffed in the crown and imperial mantle, along a walk of fcarlet velvet, doubled, and tapeftry wrought with gold, to the fanctuary, where fhe kneeled on a cufhion embroidered with gold, where two bifhops attended with the holy oil in feparate veffels, and an archbifhop anointed her on the forehead, breaft, and hands, in the name of the Father, Son, and Holy Ghoft; other archbifhops wiped off the oil with cotton, and the archdeacon attending with the holy facrament, faid aloud, " Approach with piety and faith."——Upon which fhe received the confecrated bread from the archbifhop, with a little warm wine; two arch-priefts of

the

the cathedral carried a gold bafon, and an abbot held a gold ewer full of water to wafh, and two other abbots held the napkin for her majefty to wipe her hands. This done, their majefties retired to their feats, and there was a fecond falvo from the guns, and ringing of the bells in the city. At the clofe of the fervice, the archbifhop of Plefkow made an harangue, in which he mentioned the rare virtues of the emprefs, and fhewed how well fhe deferved that crown which fhe had now received from God and her hufband ; and concluded with a congratulation to their majefties in the name of the ftates of the empire.

Proceffion to the church of St. Michael. When this office was over, the duke of Holftein went to attend the emprefs to the church of St. Michael, to which fhe walked much in the fame order as fhe came from the palace, but with her crown and mantle on, and under a rich canopy, fupported by fix major-generals on poles of maffive filver, on each of which were eight eagles of filver gilt, with crowns, &c. and tufts of folid gold, hung to gold twift ; the fcepter and globe were carried before her, and her train borne up as before ; prince Menzikof walked behind the emprefs, fupported by Printzenftein, chancellor of the exchequer, and Plefkof, prefident of the chamber of finances, each carrying a purfe of fcarlet velvet embroidered with gold, in which were medals of gold and filver, which the prince threw away among the populace in the way to church ; when her majefty arrived at the door, an archbifhop met and walked before her with a crucifix ; while the litanies were finging, the emprefs went and paid her devotions at the tombs of the emperor's glorious anceftors ; at her leaving this church, there was a third falvo of the guns

and

and bells, with kettle-drums and trumpets; and the joyful
fhouts of the people rent the fkies.

From hence her majefty went in a coach drawn by eight
horfes to the monaftery of Wofnefinki, or the Refurrection,
the place of interment for the ladies of the imperial blood :
fhe was attended

1. By one half of the horfe-guards, and their officers.

2. Twenty-four valets on foot, marching four a-breaft;
their coats were green faced with fcarlet; their waiftcoats
fcarlet fpread over with gold and filver lace; their hats
laced with gold, and the hilts of their fwords gilt.

3. Twelve pages in green liveries, the facing and veft of
cloth of gold, fcarlet filk ftockings with gold clocks, and
their fword-hilts filver gilt.

4. The emprefs in a moft magnificent coach, drawn by
eight horfes, with four running footman before, richly dreft,
and twelve chamberlains and other officers of the court
magnificently dreft, marching on both fides of the coach.

5. Twelve heydukes alfo on both fides of the coach, at
a proper diftance from the chamberlains, clad in green coats
and fcarlet waiftcoats richly embroidered with gold, with
the emperor's arms and cyphers, the fleeves fringed with
gold, and turned up with fcarlet velvet; their fcarlet velvet
caps were edged with green velvet and gold twift, with a ftar
of gold embroidery, with a tuft of an apple of filver; on
the fides were two filver eagles, and two herons of filver,
with a plume of red and white feathers behind; inftead of
a belt they wore two filver chains, faftened to a ftripe of
fcarlet velvet with gold twift; the hilts of their fabres were
large and gilt; their boots, which were of Morocco leather,

were

were adorned with buttons, and other ornaments, the work of the goldfmith.

6. Lieutenant-general Lacey rode behind the coach, with two heralds at arms, and threw gold and filver medals among the populace, which were carried for that purpofe in purfes by the proper officers.

7. Six negroes dreft in black velvet edged with gold, in-ftead of fcarves and bracelets, they had ornaments of red and white feathers, and they had plumes of the fame in their turbans, which were faced with muflin; their collars were of filver marked with their majefties cypher.

8. His royal highnefs the duke of Holftein in a coach and fix, with rich blue liveries.

9. The counts Apraxin and Golofkin, in one coach and fix, with their fervants in rich liveries.

10. Two coaches and fix, with the ladies of the firft rank.

11. The other half of the horfe-guards clofed the procef-fion, and in their paffing by were faluted with the points of our fpontoons, and colours pointed to the ground, the mufic playing and drums beating till they were paft.

At the monaftery, the emprefs was handed out of the coach by the duke of Holftein; her train was borne as be-fore; and having performed her devotion at the tombs of the ladies of the imperial family, in that monaftery, fhe returned to the palace, and was handed by the duke of Hol-ftein to her apartments where the emperor expected her, and where they paft fome time while the fervice was getting ready in the hall of folemnities.

Dinner in the hall of folem-nities.

This hall, for its largenefs and ornaments, is one of the fineft in Europe, and the windows being proportionably large makes

makes it very light; the roof refts on one fingle pillar in the middle, the cornices and pedeftals are of fine work in plaifter of Paris; all the wainfcotting is of curious workmanfhip, and three feet in height; all round was hung with crimfon velvet and rich cloth of gold; the floor was covered with Perfian carpets of extraordinary fize and beauty. Round the pillars a table was fet, with vefiels of gold and filver, adorned with precious ftones and pearls; the table where their majefties were to eat was fet upon a raifed floor, covered with fcarlet velvet, laced with gold, under a canopy of the fame, bordered round with deep gold fringe; the table, where the duke of Holftein was to eat alone, was at a little diftance from the other in the middle of the hall; and at fome little diftance below that was a table for the ladies, alfo in the middle of the hall; and on each fide were long tables, one for perfons of the firft quality, particularly thofe who had affifted at the coronation; another for the prelates and principal clergy who had officiated on the fame occafion; at the lower end of the hall was a theatre for the mufic. Their majefties, and the duke of Holftein, were ferved in gold plate, the other three tables in filver.

When every thing was ready, the company moved for the hall, and entered in the following order:

1. The mafter of the ceremonies.

2. The two cup-bearers, and count Apraxin, who officiated as carver during the feaft.

3. The great fteward, followed by the grand marfhal.

4. The emperor, and his two fupporters.

5. The emprefs, led by the duke of Holftein, and fupported as in the former proceffion; the train of the impe-

rial

rial mantle being borne by the five ladies beforemen-
tioned.

6. The principal ladies of quality, both of the court and
empire, with her majesty's maids of honour.

7. The other persons of distinction both sexes, clergy
and laity.

When their majesties were under the canopy, an arch-
bishop said grace, and then the whole company placed themselves according to their rank. At every course the grand
marshal gave orders to the master of ceremonies to go with
the officers and order it : all the officers in waiting stood
at the hall door, from the first to the last, to receive the
dishes, which they carried up to the table in the following
order :

1. The grand marshal.

2. The great steward.

3. The chief carver.

4. The officers who carried the services, who were all
colonels ; each dish was guarded by two gentleman of the
horse-guards, with their carbines.

5. The master of the ceremonies.

The great steward ranged the dishes, and took them
off, every time bending the knee, and all the others who
waited on their majesties with plates or glasses, served them
on the knee : they eat and drank out of gold, and the
pyramids of sweetmeats were served up to the royal tables
in gold plate ; the duke of Holstein was also served in gold,
by officers of the first rank.

There were at the same time before the hall, oxen and
all manner of fowls roasted for the populace, and on a

ftage erected there, were fountains of red and white wines
running for them to drink.

Before the court rofe from table, prince Menzikof diftributed to every perfon of rank and diftinction, who had
affifted at the ceremony, a large medal of gold reprefenting
it ; and then their majefties returned to their apartments
in the fame order they had entered, and the officers in waiting, with thofe of the horfe and foot guards, filled the tables,
and when the repaft was over, we returned to our refpective
quarters. The whole night was fpent in great rejoicings,
by fire-works, illuminations, bonfires, drums, mufic, and
ringing of bells; the ftreets fwarmed all night long with
crowds of people. The three following days, the emprefs
received the congratulations of all the foreign minifters,
and the deputies of the provinces.

On the fourth day, her majefty gave a very grand entertainment, and in the evening was exhibited a magnificent
fire-work, reprefenting the emperor placing the crown on
her head, with this motto, " From God and the Emperor;"
the city was again completely illuminated, and univerfal joy
difplayed itfelf in every form.

The whole concluded by a general promotion at court, A new mode
and in the army and navy, in the Venetian manner, by bal- of promotion.
lotting, and this was the mode ; a white iron box was
made with three apertures, and a round opening before, to
admit a man's hand; the three apertures were painted
white, red, and black ; the white for advancement, the red
was againft it, and the black denoted incapacity. The box
was covered with fcarlet cloth, and every perfon qualified
to ballot, had a little ball of white leather given him, which

he could put into either of the apertures without its being observed. Brigadier Knez Ufupof, a major in the guards, was to ftand the ballot for a major-general, and all the officers of the guards, being eighty-four in number, were fummoned to give their fuffrages; but when the boxes were examined, there was found thirty-two to twenty-three againft him, and twenty-nine, declared him incapable. His majefty was very much furprifed at this, as knez Ufupof was well known to be a very brave officer, and one who had always obferved ftrict difcipline, which was thought the real caufe of his having fo many enemies; on this the ballotting was entirely laid fide, and promotions went on according to the ufual form.

The captain obtains his furlough.

I had now once more an offer of preferment made me, but as I conceived it intended to detain me in the fervice, I begged to be excufed accepting any till after my return from Britain; but finding prince Menzikoff, at the inftigation of count Bruce, very much bent for my ftaying, I laid my cafe in fuch ftrong terms before the count, that he at laft confented and fpoke of it to the prince, who at length granted my much wifhed furlough on the 27th of May. I received the pay and forage money due to me from the regiment, but could not get the two years pay that was due to me as engineer, and which amounted to twelve hundred rubles, but was told the money appropriated for the payment of that fervice was at Peterfburgh, and I muft go there to receive it; which if I had done, would have effectually put a ftop to my journey. I empowered major-general Le Fort to receive my pay, and fell my houfe and furniture in Peterfburgh, and to remit me the money to Scotland; but

but a ftop was put to it till my return, and at the expiration of my furlough, every thing I had left there was feized,
fo that I had no reafon to boaft of any advantage I reaped
in Ruffia, after thirteen years fervice.

Their majefties left Mofcow on the 27th of May, on
their journey to Peterfburgh, and I fet out the 28th. I arrived at Novogorod the 7th of June, from thence croffing
the lake Ilmen, fifty miles, to the river Solon, and twenty
miles up that river to Sultza by land, from thence by
Plefkow and Petzora, two ftrong fortified towns, I got to
to Wenden in Livonia, on the 15th. This place had formerly been a place of ftrength, but its fortifications now
lay in ruins ; and on the 17th, I arrived at Riga, which
is one thoufand thirty-fix werfts from Mofcow. Field marfhal Knez Repnin, governor of this city, arrived two days
after me. I immediately waited on the governor, and fhewed
him my pafs, and notwithftanding our former difference, on
my having refufed the offer he made me of being his aid-
de-camp, he behaved very civilly to me, and offered me his
table while I ftaid in that city. I lodged with colonel Berens of the artillery, who married a niece of the countefs
of Bruce.

The colonel took me to the cathedral, and pointing out
a mark on the wall, four feet and a half from the ground,
told me that the waters of the Dwina, at the breaking up
of the ice laft year, had rifen to that mark, and overflowed
the whole city ; and that there happened to be a wedding
celebrating in a wooden houfe without the town, near the
river, which was quite full of people, and by the fudden
                                                    rifing

6

BOOK x.
———
1724.
A Swedish
colonel at
Riga fufpect-
ed of having
fhot Charles
the XIIth
of Sweden.

rifing of the water, the houfe was overturned in the height of their merriment, and every perfon drowned.

As I was dining at an ordinary one day, with feveral of my acquaintances, there happened to be at the table a Swedifh colonel and a lieutenant-colonel, who was born dumb, and had been a great favourite with the late king of Sweden. While we were at dinner, the governor's aid-de-camp came in, and addreffing himfelf to the Swedifh colonel, ordered him in the emperor's name to leave Riga immediately, otherwife he would be proceeded againft as a traitor. The Swede immediately getting up from the table, quitted the room, pale and trembling. On our enquiring into the reafon of this fudden order to the colonel, we were informed that he was fufpected of having fhot the late king of Sweden, in the trenches before Frederickfhal. It feems that fome of the company had by figns, made the dumb lieutenant-colonel underftand the affair, on which he ran after him with his fword drawn, and, but for the interpofition of the aid-de-camp and fome others with him, he would certainly have killed the colonel, who was fafely conducted over the river Dwina, which divides Livonia from Courland, and was followed by his fervants and baggage. It was obferved that while he refided in Riga, large remittances had come to him from Stockholm, which made it generally fufpected that he had been highly bribed to commit the regicide. The colonel made hafte to get into Poland, intending to pafs through that kingdom into Turkey, where he was well acquainted, having attended the king of Sweden all the time that prince refided in Bender ; but as

he

he was no more heard of, it was generally thought he had
been murdered in Poland.

I had propofed travelling by the way of Berlin, but now
finding the fhip Ifabella, bound for Montrofe, John Carnegie, mafter, I took my paffage with him, who undertook
to lay in a ftock of frefh provifions. The fhip went down
the river the 28th of June, and I followed the next day,
attended by many of my acquaintances to fort Dunamand,
where I went on board, and that evening we dropt down
to the mouth of the river. We failed on the 30th of June,
with a fair wind, and paft the iflands of Runen and Oefel,
but the wind turning againft us toward night, I began to enquire into the ftate of our provifions, which confifted of falt
beef, peas, barley, bifcuit, and bad beer. The mafter pretended that in the hurry he had forgot to lay in frefh meat,
which was a great difappointment to me, as I never could
eat falt meat, but for the kind concern of colonel Berens's
lady, who, without my knowlege, had fent plenty of all
forts of provifions on board, which fufficiently made up the
mafter's deficiency. The wind continuing foul we bore
away for the ifle of Gothland, and on the 2d of July, we
paffed the town of Wifby : in paffing along the coaft of this
ifland, I obferved a number of churches with fteeples, not
above a mile diftant from each other. We endeavoured to
make the ifle of Oeland, but could not fetch it, and after
beating three days to little purpofe, I perfuaded the mafter
to come to an anchor at the Iunfer Sheren, near the coaft
of Sweden, where I went afhore with four men in the boat,
at fome fifhing huts, but finding no body in them, and
paffing a little way into a wood, we came to a number of
people

people of both sexes, burning limeftone, and an old man shewed us the way through part of the wood, to a village, where I bought two sheep, some fowls, eggs, and butter, and returning to the veffel, we got under way again; but the wind continuing unfavourable, we made little progress. On the 8th, after a hard gale of wind, with the sea breaking over us all day long, and meeting a Dutchman, who had lost his main-mast in a gale, we got sight of Oeland. On the 9th, the wind turned in our favour, which lasted till ten o'clock next morning, being then near the island of

Puts into Erd-
holm, a Da-
nish harbour
and fort.

Bornholm; but the wind fuddenly changing, we were forced back again, which obliged us to run into the harbour of Erdholm. On a fignal, a pilot came on board, who more through defign than ignorance, run the veffel on a rock at the entrance of the harbour, fo clofe to the fhore, that the military who ftood there, faw diftinctly all our motions on deck, and although they knew our diftrefs, and boats were in plenty by them on the fhore, not one of them offered to advance one ftep to our affiftance. When our warp anchor was putting out, the governor obferving that I was better at directing than working, concluded from thence that I was a paffenger, although I was clad in feaman's cloaths, fent his adjutant off in a boat, offering to bring me on fhore with my effects, which I readily accepted, and coming up to the governor, we knew each other, being formerly acquainted both in Flanders, and at Copenhagen when the Ruffian army was there; but before I would enter into any converfation, I pleaded fo effectually with him for affiftance to get the veffel off the rock, that he fent boats fufficient to take in as much of the cargo as lightened her

enough

enough to get off, fo that fhe did not fuftain the leaft damage: fhe had fcarce got into the harbour, before fuch a
heavy gale came on, as would have beat her to pieces had
fhe remained a quarter of an hour longer on the rock; fo
that the faving of this fhip and cargo was entirely owing
to my acquaintance with the governor.

This harbour belongs to Denmark, and is one of the
beft in Europe; it has an entrance from the fouth and
one from the north, both commanded by forts; they are juft
broad enough to let one fhip at a time pafs with eafe. It
is of a round form, and large enough to contain two hundred fail of fhips; and fo deep, that they can lay clofe to
the fhore. It is of great convenience to the king of
Denmark for his fhips in war time, as they can enter
in at one fide and go out at the other. The ifland itfelf
is an entire rock, without either earth or fand; yet the governor and officers in garrifon, have tranfported earth
enough from the ifland of Bornholm, four German leagues,
to make gardens for themfelves.

Colonel Hirfhnach was the prefent governor, and had
his own regiment in garrifon here: they are in a manner
fecluded from the world, as no fhips ever come in here but
through ftrefs of weather or foul winds. There were at
this time in the harbour, thirteen fhips, Dutch and Englifh,
but they are fometimes a year or two, without feeing a fhip;
in fummer they frequently vifit, and are vifited by their
neighbours in Bornholm, feveral of whom were now here;
and dancing and card-playing, the only diverfions the place
afforded, went forward: fometimes in a fine day they went
in boats to the rocks, (which are in great numbers about

B b b

the

the ifland), to gather feathers or down from the nefts of the wild ducks, of which the governor makes about four hundred dollars a year.

As the Danes at this time were apprehenfive the Ruffians intended an attempt on Holftein, in favour of its duke, the governor would not fuffer me to go near either of the forts, feeing from my pafs that I was only on furlough ; but when I had fatisfied him that I did not intend to return to the Ruffian fervice, he conducted me to both himfelf, when I readily admitted an apology for his prudence from the defencelefs ftate in which I found them ; he told me he had often, in vain, follicited for an engineer to put them in a refpectable condition, and now afked my opinion on what was neceffary to be done for their better defence, and faid he had often folicited for an engineer to be fent from Copenhagen, in vain. As they were much out of repair, I told him it would require the attendance of an engineer for fome time, to put them in a ftate of defence. The governor then propofed my entering into the Danifh fervice, affuring me I would be very acceptable as an engineer, as they were fo ill provided, and affured me that he could eafily procure me a company in his own regiment, with a pretty girl into the bargain. This I found afterwards to have been concerted with captain Fifher, a fuperannuated gentleman of the regiment, and his fpoufe, who was to refign his company in my favour if I married his daughter, a genteel pretty girl at the age of eighteen : as they knew the fhip was to fail with the firft fair wind they propofed my fuffering the veffel to depart without me, with affurance that I could not be long without another opportunity, if their propofal

did

did not meet my approbation; but as I did not incline to be
buried alive in such an out-of-the-way place, I excused myself in the best manner I could.

The 21st of July in the afternoon, all the wind-bound
ships sailed out of the harbour with a fair wind; our
boat being left to carry me on board; the governor and the
rest of his company conveyed me to the fort, where taking leave of them, I went on board, where I found good
store of fresh provisions laid in by the governor and Mrs.
Fisher. Having no guns on board, I saluted them with
seven muskets, which was returned by five guns from the
fort. In passing Bornholm, a Danish man of war spoke to
us, and enquired if we knew or had heard of a Russian
fleet at sea; from repeated enquiries of this kind, it was
evident they expected an invasion of Holstein, as the emperor
had demanded the restitution of that dukedom, in very strong
terms, for his lawful prince. Passing the island of Muin
the 22d, and anchoring next day before Copenhagen, we
arrived on the 24th, at Elsinghor. Here the master went
ashore to clear out at the custom-house, where I accompanied him, and was brought before the governor to shew
my pass, to whom I delivered a letter from governor Hirsh-
nach; the governor detained me to supper, when he asked
me a multitude of questions relating to Russia; and understanding by the letter I brought him, that I was not to return again to that service, he urged me much to follow
that gentleman's advice, and engage myself in the king of
Denmark's, which he observed would be easier obtained,
as I had then several relations of rank in that service: to
which I answered that he might see from my pass that I

was

was not difengaged from the Ruffian fervice ; and as there
was an appearance of a rupture between the two nations,
fuch a ftep might prove of the moft dangerous confequence
to me, which he could not refufe to admit, if the rupture
fhould take place. It is to be obferved that the Danifh
army is chiefly compofed of foreigners, and the Danes and
Norwegians are employed in their navy. Here I met with
Mr. Pritzbaur, a captain of horfe, with whom I had been
intimately acquainted in Mecklenburgh ; he informed me
two of my relations were then at Copenhagen, viz. general
Dewitz and colonel Arenfdorf, a firft coufin of my father's,
and endeavoured much to perfuade me to go with him to
fee them, as I could daily get an opportunity of another
veffel : but as I very much longed to fee my friends in Scotland, I would not confent. However, Mr. Pritzbaur infifted on my making his houfe my home, the four days I
ftayed at Elfinghor.

Driven into
Marftrand
difmafted. . We departed from hence on the 28th, and on the 30th
were overtaken by a violent ftorm, which carried away our
main-maft, with fails, and rigging, and in this diftrefs, with
much difficulty, we reached Marftrand, a town and fort in
Sweden ; here again I met feveral acquaintances, officers
who had been prifoners at Mofcow, who now treated me
with much civility ; feveral Ruffian foldiers who had been
made prifoners by the Swedes, and afterward entered into
their fervice, now earneftly folicited me to intercede with
the governor, to let them return to their native country ; but
he faid it was not in his power to difcharge them, as they
had voluntarily enlifted. It was eight days before we were
in a condition to put to fea again, and we departed on the

7th

7th of Auguft; in two days after we were forced by a contrary wind to run into Hamer found, a place pleafantly fituated near a large wood; the days we were detained here,
we paffed in fowling or gathering nuts. Here the mafter
and his mate quarrelled, and went each with a broad fword
into the wood to fight. A lad called Carnegie, the mafter's
nephew, acquainted me with their defign. I followed them
with my fowling piece, the youth directing me the way they
had gone; we came up with them when they were going to
begin the combat, to which I put a ftop to by prefenting
my piece at them, threatning to fire on the firft aggreffor; and
coming clofe to them, I reafoned them out of their folly,
and returned with them on board, to fight it out over a bowl
of punch, by which means they were fully reconciled again.

On the 14th, we weighed, with a fair wind at eaft, and
paffed by Chriftianfand, and the Neus or Naze, and before
night had loft fight of Norway, and the 17th came in
fight of land, which the Captain took to be at the entrance
of the Firth of Forth, and ftretching to the northward, intending to fetch Montrofe, he paffed it in very foggy weather, and falling in with a fifhing boat, we were informed
we were oppofite Aberdeen. Here I left the Ifabella, and
arrived at Aberdeen in the fifhing boat, after a tedious voyage of fifty days. I fet out next morning for Fife; and
had the pleafure to find my mother, brother, and fifter,
well at Coupar on the 20th, after an abfence of twenty
years.

I got poffeffion of a fmall eftate left me by a grand uncle,
upon which I fettled, and after marrying I turned farmer,
in which occupation I remained fixteen years, till the war

was

Margin notes:

1734.
A quarrel be-
tween Carne-
gie and his
mate.

The captain
arrives in
Scotland.

was proclaimed with Spain, when the government wanted
engineers. I was on this recommended by his grace the
duke of Argyll, to his grace the duke of Montagu, mafter
general of the ordnance, who employed me as chief engineer, at twenty fhillings per day; and was fent to fortify
Providence, one of the Bahama iflands : fo that I once more
launched out into a new world for the fake of my family,
who were by this time become pretty numerous.

BOOK

BOOK XI.

*The captain sent engineer to fortify Providence, and goes out in the Rose
man of war.—Arrives at the island of Madeira.—Waits on the Portu-
guese governor.—Description of the island.—A hard passage to Carolina.—
Misses a fine prize.—A violent storm.—The fortifications at Charlestown.
—Arrive at Providence.—The ruinous condition of fort Nassau—Short
history of the Bahama Islands.—The oppressive practices of governor
Fitz-William.—Governor Tinker succeeds him.—Short account of that
gentleman.—The captain prevails on the inhabitants to carry materials
for building fort Montagu.—Nature of the stone—and mastich wood.
—Description of fort Montagu.—The governor's letter about it.—A
quarrel with lieutenant Stewart.—The captain confined,—and set at liberty.*

THE first of July, 1740, I was appointed chief engineer to fortify the Bahama Islands, at twenty shillings per day. I sat out from Scotland the 8th of August,
and arrived in London on the 16th; and having received
my instructions from the board, I was ordered to go out
with John Tinker, esq; who was appointed governor of the
Bahama Islands, and the Rose man of war, commanded
by Thomas Frankland, esq. was appointed to carry us
there. We embarked the 6th of November, and sailed the
next day from Spithead, where we lay at anchor till the 9th,
and then endeavoured to sail through the Needles, but
were obliged, by a contrary wind, to return again to
Cowes, where we lay till the 12th; when we sailed
through the Needles, having seven vessels under our convoy,
one of which carried stores and recruits for the Bahama
Islands;

BOOK XI.

1740.
The captain
sent engineer
to fortify Pro-
vidence, and
goes out in the
Rose man of
war.

Iflands; but the wind proving contrary, we were forced on the 15th to go into Torbay, and as we were going in we obferved a Spanifh privateer boarding a merchant-man; we immediately put about, chafed, and came up with her at 3 p. m. having fired five chace-guns at her, when fhe ftruck; as we were then under all our fails, with a brifk gale, they let us pafs by them without attempting to come on board, and getting under our ftern, they endeavoured to get away again; on this the captain ordered to fire with fmall-arms at her, and the fellow that was hoifting the fails being fhot, they put out their boat and came on board. She had only a captain and twenty men on board, and two Englifh mafters of veffels, whom they had taken the day before; having fent her lieutenant and twelve of her hands with her prizes for Spain. They feem to have been ill provided with cloaths when they fet out, for we faw none they had but what they had plundered from the Englifh; they had fixty-four pounds in money, were well-armed, with plenty of ammunition and provifions; the Englifh mafters told us, fhe was a prime failor, had fixteen oars, and only for the cowardly fpirit of the crew, it would not have been in our power to come up with her; for they were fo inti-midated, that at every gun we fired, they ftopt their oars to fay their *Ave Maria.* Governor Tinker had a narrow efcape here, for one of his piftols going off by accident, the ball went through his cloaths.

We got into Torbay the next day, where we found the Argyle, of fifty guns, captain Lingen, bound for Ireland, and the Portmahon, of twenty guns, captain Paulet, for Gibraltar; the next day we burnt our prize, and fent the

6 captain

captain on board the Argyle; he was a Genoefe by birth, had formerly been in our Eaft India company's fervice, and as he was well acquainted with our coaſts, we thought it beſt to fend him to Ireland; at firſt he pretended not to underſtand Englilh, but as he happened to be known by the maſter of the Rofe, who had failed with him to India, he could no longer pretend ignorance of the language. On board the Argyle he endeavoured to bribe the guard to let him efcape, which was no fooner difcovered than he was clapped in irons; the reſt of the prifoners were fent on fhore.

We left Torbay the 23d of November, and next day had a gale of wind and a heavy fea, which broke over the fhip and occafioned a great rolling: I had then the lieutenant's cabin, where the ſkuttle was forced in, and the water came in and wetted all my cloaths and bedding, which obliged me to fet up all night: next day we had a violent ſtorm, which made us take in our fails, lower our top-maſts, and drive before the wind. On the 26th, we entered the bay of Bifcay, and were toſſed about by foul winds in that heavy fea for feveral days, and loſt fight of all our convoy; at the fame time a moſt violent epidemic diſtemper raged in our fhip, by which we loſt a number of the men, fo that at laſt we were forced to bear away for England again, and arrived at Falmouth the 5th of December.

Here we found the Argyle and Port-Mahon windbound, but none of the fhips that had been under our convoy were heard of. During our ſtay here, we fent our furgeon and feveral of the people afhore fick, and got another furgeon and nine feamen out of a merchantman; and our

C c c

yawl,

yawl, in going afhore for water, was ftaved to pieces, and
one of the failors dangeroufly hurt, and four of our people deferted : we paffed our time agreeably enough on fhore
at this place, having frequent balls and affemblies till the
17th, that we put out to fea again, and had very boifterous
weather for nineteen days fucceffively, which increafed the
diftemper among the people.

Arrives at the ifland of Madeira.   On the 5th of January we made the ifland of Madeira ;
but as no body on board had ever been there, except the
mafter, he infifted it was the ifland of Porto Sanéto, which
lies fifty-one eaft from Madeira ; and depending on his
judgment, we ftood away to the weftward, and failed two
days without difcovering land, but finding our miftake,
were obliged to return, and arrived at Madeira on the 9th,
towards night.   The next day we were carried afhore by
the Portuguefe in their boats, none of our own people durft
venture on the great furf, which is almoft continually on
the landing-place here even in calm weather.   This is a confiderable advantage to the Portuguefe, who carry every thing
on board and afhore at Madeira.   The method they take
in landing is this, they keep themfelves very dexteroufly with
their oars on the top of a high wave, which carries them
a great way on fhore, where a number of men ftand ready
and pull the boat out of the reach of any fucceeding wave.
In going on board they put the paffengers and goods into
the boat on dry land, and the boatmen feat themfelves ready
with their oars in their hands, and a fufficient number of
men run with the boat and pufh her upon the top of a
wave, and fo go off without the leaft difficulty.   I could

6.   not

not but be furprifed to fee with how much dexterity this was BOOK XI.
performed †.

When we came afhore, I accompanied governor Tinker 1741.
to wait on the governor of the place; who was faluted by Wait on the
a numerous guard, and afterwards conducted by two gen- Portuguefe
governor,
tlemen towards the Portuguefe governor, who received us
on the top of a high outer ftair, and carried us into a large
hall; Mr. Tinker, with his retinue, being feated on one fide
of the room, and the Portuguefe gentlemen on the oppofite, the Madeira governor took his feat directly facing
Mr. Tinker, and after exchanging a few words in a very
ceremonious manner, we went away, efcorted with the fame
formalities as we had at entering. We dined with Mr.
Baker, the Britifh conful, where the Portuguefe governor
came after dinner to return governor Tinker's vifit, which
was as fhort and as ceremonious as the former; and here
ended all the intercourfe between the two governors. We
went next to fee their churches and monafteries, conducted
by an Irifh prieft; next day, we dined with Meffieurs Scott,
merchants, and afterward walked up the fouth-fide of the
hill, where we faw a number of pleafure-houfes, but particularly that belonging to the providore, where there were
three artificial flats below each other in front, with water-
works and flower-pots, prettily laid out, although fmall. Defcription
All the fouth-fide of this ifland is an entire mountain, co- of the ifland.
vered with vines, interfperfed with houfes, and orange, le-
mon, and other kinds of fruit-trees; the north-fide of

† The fame method is practifed at Deal, in Kent, when the furf is heavy
on the beach, which often happens.

C c c 2 the

the mountain is not inhabited, but referved for pafturage for their cattle; the inhabitants dwell all along the fouth-fhore, and the bay is commanded by two forts, well fupplied with cannon. The laft day of our ftop, here, we dined with Mr. Chambers, and fpent the evening with Mr. Gordon, both merchants; from the latter I bought feveral pipes of wine, at eleven pounds five fhillings the pipe, which I fent in a fnow to South Carolina; they put an anchor of brandy into every pipe, that goes abroad, both to ftrengthen and preferve it.

A hard paf-
fage to Caro-
lina.

On the 13th of January we went on board, and failed in the night, when the captain's French cook jumped overboard and fwam on. fhore; we had now loft nineteen men in all fince we left Spithead; the next day we had a violent ftorm, and fuch a heavy fea, that the waves broke over the quarter-deck in fuch a manner that the people could not ftand to their duty, and every bed and hammock in the fhip were foaked with water. The diftemper began to rage more and more among us; the governor, captain, and moft of the officers were fick in bed. All this occafioned a lownefs of fpirit over the fhip; the ftorm continued all the 15th, during which we were in a moft difagreeable fituation in our wet clothes. On the 16th, the ftorm abated, but the ficknefs increafed, very few who were feifed efcaping with life, fo that the corpfe of fome one or other was every day committed to the deep. The 17th, we paft near Teneriffe, and the ifland of Palma; and the 18th, we got into the trade-wind, when we fteered due weft; as by this means the fhip's crew were relieved from their toilfome labour: the fick were all brought upon deck, the fhip was
tho-

thoroughly cleanfed, by which the ficknefs very much abated,
and the men were encouraged in all forts of diverfions,
thereby to keep them in perpetual motion. We chafed
feveral fail, but when we got up with them they proved to
be either Englifh or Dutch. On the 31ft, we were be-
calmed in lat. 24. 51. north, and faw a great number of
tropic birds; and this day five more of our people, and a
negroe belonging to the captain, died.

February the 3d, we had a ftrong gale, with fuch a Mifs a fine prize.
tumbling fea as made the fhip roll away her fore-top and
top-gallant mafts, which came down upon deck with all
their furniture; after this we had tolerably good weather.
On the 16th, in the morning, in lat. 30. 46. we chaced a
fhip and got up with her at ten o'clock; fhe hoifted Dutch
colours and ftruck on our firing; on coming clofe up to
her, the captain ordered the mafter of her to come on
board, but they pretended not to underftand him; our
lieutenant, with twelve men in the fhaloup, were fent on
board to examine her papers, who reported, that fhe was
a Dutch fhip from Curacoa for Amfterdam, loaded with
dollars and tobacco, and had four French gentlemen paffengers: we were unanimoufly, however, (except governor
Tinker) of opinion, that if fhe were ftrictly examined fhe
would prove a lawful prize, and the captain feemed determined to fecure her; Mr. Tinker endeavoured to diffuade
him, by infinuating the trouble and expence feveral captains
had brought themfelves into by carrying Dutch fhips out of
their courfe; captain Frankland afked my opinion: I told
him, that if it was my cafe, I would not carry her out of
her courfe, but would go along with her till I had narrowly

exa-

BOOK XI. examined her: and as I underſtood both the French and
Dutch languages, I offered my affiſtance; but the governor
ſo intimidated the captain, who was but young, and this his
firſt voyage as a commanding officer, that he let her paſs
without farther enquiry, to the diſſatisfaction of the whole
ſhip's company, as we had afterwards certain information of
her ſafe arrival at Cadiz, with one hundred and thirty
thouſand pounds ſterling on board.

A violent
ſtorm.

On the 18th, at ſix in the morning, in latitude 31 deg.
13 min. we met with a terrible hurricane, attended with
heavy rain, thunder, and lightning; it carried away our
fore-maſt ſails and all over board, after that our main-top-
maſt, and at eight o'clock our mizen-maſt; and as their
maſts had got under the ſhip, they were faſtened to her
bottom by the wet ſails being thereby in great danger of
foundering; at the return of every heavy ſea the ends of
our broken maſts and yards ſtruck her bottom with ſuch
violence that it was a miracle they did not make their way
through. All hands were ſet to work to clear away
the rigging, which, when performed, a high wave at laſt relieved us from that incumbrance; and in this pitiful ſituation
we were toſſed up and down the remainder of the day, and
all the following night. The next day the weather being
a little ſettled, we hoiſted our main-ſail and ſet up jury-
maſts; we went under theſe till the 26th, when we ſaw a
ſhip not far from us, ſtranded on a ſand-bank, and a ſmall
ſchooner ſailing along the coaſt; on our firing a gun to
bring the ſchooner to, the maſter came on board, and informed us we were at Cape Roman, to the northward of
Charleſtown, Carolina; he piloted us to Charleſtown bar,
where

where a pilot from the town came on board. I went in the schooner to Charleftown, where I found this city in a deplorable fituation, the one half of which had been laid in afhes by a dreadful fire, and the ruins were ftill fmoaking: a vaft quantity of merchandize, to a very confiderable amount, was quite confumed. Our fhip lying without an opportunity to get over the bar, was driven out to fea by a land-breeze, which carried away her jury-maft ; two veffels were fent out to her affiftance, but it was the 2d of March before fhe got over the bar : in the time they were driven out to fea, both the mafter and gunner died. We found here the Phœnix, captain Fanfhaw, and the Tartar, the honourable captain George Townfend, both twenty-gun fhips, ftationed at this place, and our ftore-fhip, who had pufhed through the bay of Bifcay, made a good voyage to Providence, where fhe landed her recruits and ftores, was returned here. The fnow alfo arriving from Madeira with our wine, I fold the half of mine, by which I had the other half free.

The gentlemen of the council and affembly, and others of Charleftown, fhewed us a great deal of civility during our ftay here, with daily entertainments and balls. The 23d we faw their militia reviewed, which confifted of fix companies of one hundred men each ; the officers appeared all in uniforms, and the men performed their exercife furprifingly well; the review concluded with an elegant entertainment and a ball at night. The next day I went with governor Tinker, and the captains Townfend and Frankland, by invitation, to colonel Vander.Duffen's plantation, where we fpent fome days very agreeably ; after

our.

our return to town, we went to view Johnfon's fort, which ftands two miles from the town, and commands the paffage into the harbour.   At our arrival the governor was faluted with eleven eighteen-pounders.   This fort is a triangle, badly executed, mounted with twelve fix-pounders; below it is the fea battery mounted with thirty guns, nine, twelve, and eighteen-pounders : on our departure we were faluted with eleven nine-pounders. Upon a point of land at the fouth end of the town, ftand Broughton's battery, which commands both Cooper and Afhley rivers, and is mounted with forty-five guns, nine, twelve, and eighteen-pounders; and betwixt Grenville and Craven baftions, upon the cur-tain along the bay fronting Cooper river, there are one hundred and thirty guns of different fizes, the carriages of feveral of which were burnt in the late fire. There was but one brafs mortar of eleven inches, and eight cohorns, all the reft having been fent to general Oglethorpe, on his ex-pedition againft St. Auguftine.

Governor Tinker finding it would be yet a confider-able time before the Rofe man of war could be fit to go to fea, defired Commodore Fanfhaw to fend the Tartar to carry us to Providence; which he complied with, and we went on board on the 10th of April.   We ftruck feveral times going over the bar, but received no injury from it ; we had a pleafant paffage till the 19th, in the evening, when fitting after fupper, and all very chearful, we were alarmed by the call of breakers, by one of the people ; captain Townfend immediately ran upon deck, and ordered the helm a lee, which was inftantly done, and the fails were fhifted with great regularity and expedition, not a

voice

voice was heard but the captain's; and when the ship was
about, one might eafily have thrown a ftone from the ———
ftern upon the rocks of Abbaco: it happened very luckily
to be fine moon light.   Mr. Buckle, the lieutenant, who
was then in bed preparing himfelf for the night watch,
upon comparing his reckoning with the pilot's, apprehended we were twenty leagues to the weftward of the ifland
of Abbaco ; but the ftrong currents that run here occafioned the miftake. Next day captain Townfend loft a very
fine black boy, who coming up with a kettle of boiling
water, fell with it, and fcalded himfelf in fuch a manner,
that he died foon after, to the great regret of his mafter.

On the 21ft of April, juft as we had got over the
bar at Providence, a fudden ftorm of loud thunder and
lightning, with a prodigious heavy rain, burft upon us,
with fuch a terrible noife, that we could not hear the
falute of the cannon of the fort, although we were oppofite to it, which fome people confidered as very ominous.
On our landing we were met on the fhore by great numbers of the inhabitants, convened to congratulate their new
governor on his fafe arrival on the ifland, expecting, as they
expreffed themfelves, to live under a milder government
than they had experienced under the arbitrary power of
their late governor.

Captain Laws, who commanded a floop of war ftationed
at this place, and who had loft his rank by accepting the
command of the floop, expecting our arrival, and to fhun
his being under the command of a junior officer, went
a few days before our arrival to Jamaica, and left his
ready-furnifhed houfe (one of the beft in the town) for

my ufe, having paid his year's rent (at twenty pounds fter-- ling per annum), of which there was nine months to come, for which I was certainly much obliged to him; it had alfo a garden with a large grove of orange trees.

There was an independent company at this place, con- fifting of one hundred and fifty men, of which the gover-- nor is captain; with three lieutenants, the oldeft of whom was John Howel. Mr. Howel was now prefident of the Bahama iflands; he had formerly been a furgeon to the pirates, and upon an act of grace, he purchafed the lieute- nancy, and was alfo furgeon to the company, and colonel of the militia for the fake of the title. The fecond lieu-- tenant was William Stuart, who was major of the militia; this gentleman acted in a double capacity, having purchafed the furgency from the former; but the governor made him part with the furgency to James Irving, who came with us from Charleftown. The third was William Moone, who came from London in the ftorefhip with the recruits; Mr. Moone had no commiffion, but acted under the governor's warrant a confiderable time, in expectation of one; of which he was at laft difappointed by the arrival of Patrick Dromgole, a nephew of the former governor's, with a commiffion for third lieutenant, which was a very great hardfhip to Mr. Moone. The only people of note here, were chief juftice Rowland; James Scott, fecretary and clerk of the admiralty; John Keowin, provoft marfhal; Chaloner Jackfon, collector; and Mr. Smith, the parfon.

The ruinous condition of Fort Naffau. Upon viewing fort Naffau, I found it in a very ruinous condition; the barracks, which were built of wood, were ready to tumble down, and there was no other building within

within the fort; the powder magazine was a houfe which ftood at fome diftance from it, expofed in fuch a manner that any body might fet fire to it. I found no more than fixteen guns, mounted upon very bad carriages; the reft were all fcattered up and down, and fome buried within high water mark in the fand, fome of which were fpiked up, others rammed full of ftones and fand; the carriages trucks and fhot were alfo difperfed, fo that with much difficulty I collected them together: the inhabitants had made ufe of great part of them for ballaft in their veffels. Having got them all collected in one place, I drilled thofe that had been nailed up, cleaned the whole from ruft, and proved them by firing, I had now fifty-four guns of fix, nine, twelve, and eighteen-pounders, fit for fervice, and mounted them on the new carriages which came out of the ftore-fhip from England. My greateft difficulty was the want of mafons, of whom there was not one in the place, which obliged me to commiffion fome from the northern colonies; but all I could get were two bricklayers from Philadelphia, who knew nothing of mafonry. So that I had the trouble of teaching them and fome of the foldiers, to form, cut, and lay ftones; and as no labourers were to be got without finding them in provifions, which were not to be procured here, as the inhabitants themfelves lived principally on tortoife and fifh, (any kind of flefh-meat being a great rarity,) I was obliged to fend to New York for provifions. The former governor, as well as the prefent, had provided a quantity of lime; fo that my next concern was to provide ftone for a new fort. The harbour is formed by Hog Ifland, which is three miles in

length,

length ; and as the enemy in attempting to deftroy this fettlement, had commonly landed at the eaft end of the harbour, within three miles of Naffau, I refolved to build my
new fort at this place, as the moft effential to prevent fuch
infults in future, where, as the entrance is not a gun-fhot
broad, the harbour would be fufficiently fecured.   The ifland
of Providence is twenty-feven miles long, and eleven broad,
and is fo entirely furrounded by innumerable funken rocks,
that it is impoffible for any fhips to land, except in the harbour ; and if an enemy were to land in boats, it would be
impoffible for them to get through the underwoods, without
cutting a road through them.   There are no inhabitants on
any of the other iflands, excepting Eluthera and Harbour-
Iflands.

The departure of the honourable captain George Townfend, on his return to Carolina, on the 16th of May, left
this place very lonely; the officers and feamen being commonly on fhore, had greatly enlivened it while they remained.
In the mean time, that I was providing materials for building the fort, I made it my bufinefs to enquire into the firft
fettlement, and the nature of thofe iflands; and the following particulars are what I collected.

The Bahama Iflands are fome hundreds in number, but
the far greateft part are very inconfiderable ; they are fituated
between the 22d and 23d deg. north lat. they were originally difcovered by the Spaniards, and St. Salvadore, now
called Cat-Ifland, was the firft land Columbus fet his foot on
this new world, which was in the year 1493, and where are
ftill to be feen the ruins and foundations of their chapels
and other buildings ; for their firft fettlements were here, till

the

the natives, who wore plates of gold upon their lips, being asked by signs whence it came, pointed towards the south-west; and thefe iflands came to be deferted for the mines of Mexico and Peru. The cruelty exercifed by the Spaniards over thefe poor people, both during their ftay amongft them, and afterwards from Cuba, exceeds all imagination, they having trained up dogs to hunt thofe unhappy people as their proper game; and this cruel fport they followed till they had entirely deftroyed all the inhabitants.

About the year 1607, thefe iflands were again difcovered by captain William Sayle (afterwards governor of Carolina), and granted by king Charles II. to fix of the proprietors of Carolina, viz. the duke of Albemarle, lord Craven, fir John Carteret, lord Berkeley, lord Afhley, and fir Peter Coleton; but as people are more defirous to obtain grants of land than careful to improve them, they have been very much neglected ever fince. Several lawlefs people at that time had taken poffeffion of Providence, which lies in 25 deg. north latitude, to which they were encouraged by its very commodious harbour; and being joined by feveral pirates, they fubfifted by their depredations on the coafts of Cuba which they called *buccaneering*: befides this they enriched themfelves by the frequent wrecks happening upon the Bahama banks. Thefe practices naturally exafperated the Spaniards to the refolution of deftroying thofe buccaneers, and the proprietors in all that time took no notice of their iflands, but let them live as they pleafed, till the year 1670, that they appointed Mr. Collingworth to be governor; but, after his arrival, in endeavouring to reform them, they

feized

feized and fhipped him off for Jamaica, not being willing
to fubject themfelves to any government.

 In 1677, the proprietors appointed Mr. Clarke to be their
governor, but he fared infinitely worfe than his predeceffor;
for the Spaniards, jealous of every Englifh colony, landed in
Providence, where they feized the governor, burnt all the
houfes, deftroyed the ftock, and took all the inhabitants they
could catch, the reft hiding themfelves in the woods; they
carried off Mr. Clark in chains, and afterwards tortured
him to death, and then roafted him.

 When Mr. Lilburn was governor, in the year 1684, the
Spaniards again furprifed the place, deftroyed all their improvements, carried away a number of the inhabitants with
the fame barbarity as before, and left thofe that efcaped in
a miferable condition, difperfed in holes and in the woods,
without any manner of government till 1687. They re-
affembled and renewed their fettlements, and chofe Mr.
Bridges, a prefbyterian minifter, for their governor, under
whom they lived three years. The lords proprietors fent
out Mr. Jones to be their governor in 1690, who oppreffed
and tyrannifed over the inhabitants with a very high hand,
in which he reckoned himfelf perfectly fecure by the affiftance of Avery the pirate, who commanded a fhip of forty-
fix guns, and one hundred and twenty ftout feamen; but,
in his abfence, the inhabitants put the governor in prifon,
and chofe Mr. Afhley for their prefident, till Mr. Jones could
be brought to his trial: but upon the return of the pirates
from a cruize he was by them fet again at liberty: after which
he behaved much worfe than before, and imprifoned all

                thofe

those he fufpected; defiring the pirates to carry them off
the ifland and make away with them.

Thefe proceedings coming to the ears of the proprietors, they fent Mr. Trot as their governor, to fupercede Jones, in 1694, and immediately releafed the imprifoned inhabitants; he alfo allowed Jones to go off the ifland without a legal trial, to the no fmall grief and vexation of the inhabitants: he likewife fuffered Avery the pirate, who changed his name to Bridgeman, to fhelter himfelf and his crew at Providence: their fhip, called the Fancy, was voluntarily loft, and the effects which they had pirated from the great mogul, were landed and fhared, with which they fettled upon the ifland, till a proclamation againft pirates obliged the governor to fummons them before fuch a court of juftice as he had in Providence: but, for want of power, and the pirates being now joined with the inhabitants, he durft not try them, for fear of being himfelf murdered, for he had often mutinies during his government. The inhabitants, after this joined, and built a fmall fort, and planted it with twenty-two cannon, to protect themfelves againft the frequent invafions of the Spaniards, and alfo built a town of one hundred and fixty houfes, which they called Naffau.

In 1697, Mr. Jones was fucceeded by Mr. Webb, as governor, who continued in it two years, and in that fhort time found means to render himfelf fo obnoxious to the people, that he found himfelf obliged to fhip off his effects and go to Penfylvania; from whence, without the knowledge of the proprietors, he deputed one Elding, a mulatto, to fucceed him, in 1699; by virtue of which deputation, he had the affurance to act as governor, notwithftanding he

was

was a perfon of a moft infamous character : but by keeping up a correfpondence with a new fet of pirates, who frequented the Bahamas, he, by their affiftance, maintained himfelf in this government two years, till

1701, the lords proprietors appointed Mr. Hafket, governor; who, on his arrival, profecuted and confined Elding, with feveral others, under pretence of enforcing the laws againft pirates and their abettors. In this the inhabitants thought Mr. Hafket acted with too great feverity, and too much regard to his own intereft, and not having ftrength to fupport his authority, they, in open rebellion, in about five weeks after his arrival on the ifland, feifed and confined him in irons a clofe prifoner fix weeks; but being prevailed upon to fpare his life, they put him on board a ketch in the harbour, with ftrict orders to the commander to carry Mr. Hafket to England, from whence he came; and chofe one Lichtwood, who was one of their accomplices, for their prefident and deputy-governor in his room. Lichtwood continued in his office about two years, till the French and Spaniards, in 1703, when they were at open war with England, furprifed the ifland fo completely, that they found the inhabitants feafting with their prefident, and their neglected fort without any garrifon. The enemy deftroyed the fort, fpiked the guns, burnt the town and church, plundered the inhabitants, fome of whom, and fome negroes, hid themfelves in the woods, and carried their deputy-governor, with many others, prifoners to the Havannah. Shortly after this, thofe formidable enemies returned again, and carried away all the inhabitants and negroes they could

find,

find, the few who efcaped fled to Carolina and Virginia, leaving the ifland entirely defolate.

It was afterwards for fome years the refort of pirates only, who made it their general rendezvous : they dug holes in the ground in the woods, and hid their ill-gotten treafures there, where they remained, as many of them were killed or died at fea ; and fome part of their depofits are now and then occafionally difcovered to this day.

Soon after this defolation, the proprietors appointed Mr. Birch to fucceed Mr. Harket, as governor ; but on Mr. Birch's arrival at Providence, and finding the ifland quite deferted of inhabitants he returned. From this time the lord's proprietors have not concerned themfeves in thofe iflands, but gave up their right in them to the crown, having met with nothing but expence and trouble while under their direction.

The king was folicited by the merchants of London and Briftol to fortify thofe iflands, as a fecurity to their trade ; and, in compliance with their requeft, his majefty (George I.) appointed Mr. Wood Rogers, their governor, and fent him out with an independent company of one hundred men, with a large quantity of all kind of ftores to fortify the place. On Mr. Rogers's arrival, in 1717, the pirates voluntarily furrendered themfelves to him, and accepted the benefit of an act of indemnity which had been paft, and have ever fince been the principal inhabitants of the ifland. Under the moderate governments of Mr. Rogers, and his fucceffor, Mr. Finney, the people found themfelves happy, and many families came and fettled here, befides many Palatines, who, by their induftry and improvements upon

E e e   their

their plantations, furnished the markets with all forts of provisions.

After Mr. Finney's death, Richard Fitz William, efq. was appointed governor, in 1733, who brought an addition of fifty men to the independent company, with a large quantity of all forts of ftores, and an engineer (Mr. Thomas More), to fortify the place; but his fudden death prevented him from making any great progrefs in the work. The governor exerted fo arbitrary and tyrannical a power, that the beft of the inhabitants, and all the Palatines, withdrew from the ifland, forfaking their fine improvements, to fhelter themfelves in other parts, where they were fure to meet with better ufage. The governor's agents for putting thofe oppreffive fchemes in execution were, lieutenant Stuart, one of the council; James Scott, judge of the admiralty; and one Archibald, his fervant, who ufed to knock down any one who dared to refufe to enter into the governor's meafures: on which three of the moft confiderable inhabitants found means to get to London, where they entered a complaint againft the governor before the king and council. They were Mr. Colburgh, collector Jackfon, and Mr. White; their petition, too long to be here inferted, contained many charges of a very extraordinary nature againft the governor.

In confequence of which, Mr. Fitz William was fome time after ordered to return, to make his defence; and, after a tedious and expenfive trial, he loft his government, and was fucceeded by John Tinker, efq. who, upon his fetting out, was determined to make the people eafy and happy under his government; and to turn out all Mr. Fitz William's favourites, efpecially thofe who had advifed and affifted him

in

in his oppreffions; of which he made a beginning at Charles-town with his fecond lieutenant, William Stuart, who was there at our arrival, whom he obliged to difpofe of his fur-gency to James Irving, lately arrived from Guinea in a fhip with flaves; and when Mr. Tinker arrived at Providence, he turned out the two lieutenants, Howel and Stuart, the one from being lieutenant-colonel, the other major, in the militia, and appointed two of the chief inhabitants in their room. James Scott was difplaced from being chief judge, and Mr. Rowland was re-inftated; with many other changes, to the great joy and fatisfaction of all the inhabitants, who now expected to enjoy their own in fafety.

John Tinker, efq. had formerly been factor to the South-Sea-Company at Panama, and afterwards appointed, by the African Company, governor of Cape Coaft, in Guinea.

The council at Providence, at this time, confifted only of three; the lieutenants Howel and Stuart, and John Snow, the governor's fecretary: the ufual number is fix. To fupply this deficiency, the governor propofed to captain Frankland and me to be of his council, which we both declined; but we both accepted to be chofen members of the affembly, which confifted of twenty in number, and of which James Scott was the fpeaker; fo that collector Boothby, and Mr. Thom-fon, one of the inhabitants, were appointed to be of the council.

In the mean time I was employing myfelf in providing ma-terials for erecting fort Montagu, on the eaft point of the har-bour, three miles from Naffau. As the lime which the two go-vernors had provided was at too great a diftance, I made lime upon the fpot. I found great inconvenience in providing ftone,

The captain prevails on the inhabit-ants to carry the mate rials for building Fort Mon-tagu.

which

BOOK XI. which was to be carried from the woods on the heads of the

────── negroes ; and as they could not carry a stone of any size, it

·1741. would have proved an endless work, there being no such
thing as a wheel carriage in the island. Mr. Bullock, one
of the inhabitants, arrived here on the 8th of June, from
the Havannah, where he had been some time a prisoner,
who assured us that the Spaniards were fitting out two men
of war, of 80 guns each, and three large gallies, full of men,
to make a descent on Providence. Upon this I took the opportunity to lay the defenceless state of the island before the
assembly; assuring them, that if they would supply me with
materials, I would, in a short time, put the east side of the
harbour in a posture of defence, as that was the place where
we had the most to fear, having always been the enemy's
landing place : to this request they unanimously agreed, and
ordered all their vessels and boats to bring me a sufficient
quantity of stones of proper sizes for erecting the fort, and
also a number of mastich trees, for pallisades. This very
soon enabled me to employ all my own hands upon the building, which I carried on with the utmost dispatch and diligence.

Upon the 10th of June the governor laid the foundation
stone, in the presence of the principal inhabitants, and named
the fort Montagu, and the sea battery, Bladen's Battery.

Nature of the All the stone on this and the adjacent islands is of so soft a

stone. nature, when raised from the quarries, that we could cut
and shape them into any form with very little labour ; and
after they have been some time exposed in the open air, they
turn hard as flint, with this excellent property, that in firing
into the walls, the ball lodges as in a mud wall, without

4   making

making the leaft breach; this I proved by feveral fhot from
an eighteen-pounder. I found no fmall difficulty in getting
frefh water for the mortar; I was at firft fupplied by a fmall
pool of rain water, but when that was dried up, I had recourfe to digging a well through this foft rock; and getting
as low as the level of the fea, we found water very frefh, by
the fea water having filtered through the ftone, and left its fa-
line particles behind. We found afterwards that the farther
we dug from the fea, the water proved to be fo much the
frefher. The mafters of veffels provided themfelves with fil-
tering ftones, which contained feveral gallons, to rectify their
fpoiled water on board. The maftich wood, which the in- And maftich
habitants delivered for palifades, was as hard and heavy as wood.
iron; I was obliged to form them while the wood was green,
for when they are fully dry, there is no poffibility of working them. The inhabitants affirmed to me that they would
laft above a century: they are fo hard that a mufket-ball
makes no impreffion on them; they affured me they were
proof againft fwivel fhot, but this I did not think proper
to try.

Fort Montagu and Bladen's Battery were finifhed the A defcription
latter end of July, 1742, and mounted eight 18, three 9, of Fort Mon-
and fix 6 pounders. Within the fort is a terraffed ciftern, tagu.
containing thirty tons of rain water, and fo contrived as to
receive all that falls within the fort, with a drain to carry off
the fuperfluous water; there are barracks for officers and
foldiers, a guard room, and a powder magazine, bomb proof,
to contain ninety-five barrels of powder; two of its fides are
clofe upon the fea, and the two land fides are well fecured
by maftich pallifades.

When

BOOK XI.   When the fort was finifhed, I invited the governor and
——————   principal inhabitants to it, and then delivered his excellency
1742.   the keys thereof, under a difcharge of all the cannon. The
the governor and the inhabitants were now extremely well
pleafed to confider themfelves in a condition to repel the
invafion of an enemy, as the back door through which the
place had often been furprifed, was now fhut up; and in
this good humour the governor wrote the following letter to
the duke of Montagu.

New Providence, Aug. 28, 1742.

" My Lord,

The gover-
nor's letter
about it.

" I fhould have prefented my duty to your grace much
" fooner, but waited till captain Bruce had finifhed the fort,
" which I have taken the liberty of calling by your grace's
" illuftrious name, as a mark of refpeЄt and veneration due
" to your grace's perfon and merit. It is fituated fo as to
" guard the eaftern part of this ifland very fecurely, and is
" as ftrong as any thing of its fize can be : and I muft do
" the gentleman who has the direЄtion of thofe works, the
" juftice to fay, I believe the public money was never more
" frugally or more juftly adminiftered; which is a proof of
" your grace's excellent judgment in the choice of men. He
" is now engaged about the other works, at fort Naffau;
" and as he propofes to lay before your grace, and the board
" of ordnance, the abfolute neceffity there will be of ereЄt-
" ing a ftrong redoubt, in order to complete the well-forti-
" fying of this ifland, a farther fum of money will be want-
" ing than the fixteen hundred pounds already allowed;

7   " which

"which will be foon laid out in raifing the old fort from
"the ruinous condition it lies in now. I think, by the
"neareft eftimate we can make, there will be ftill wanting
"two thoufand five hundred pounds; which, when your
"grace is pleafed to compare with the mighty fum that Mr.
"Moore's plan would have taken to put in execution, I hope
"this will be thought a trifle; efpecially when the ill confe-
"quence of fuch a place falling into an enemy's hands, is
"taken into confideration. We may fet them at defiance
"if thefe works are all completed in the manner propofed;
"becaufe I am perfuaded this will then be the ftrongeft pof-
"feffion in Britifh America: always fuppofing a proper
"garrifon will be eftablifhed, which cannot be lefs than three
"hundred men. Fort Montagu requires an officer and fifty
"men for its ordinary guard; your grace will fee the im-
"poffibility of doing the common duty with only one in-
"dependent company, our whole force at prefent.

"I have prefented a memorial to the board, praying for
"a fupply of powder and fmall arms, which, I hope, will
"not be thought unreafonable, when it fhall appear fifty
"barrels were fent to general Oglethorpe before he went to
"St. Auguftine, and two mortars, which have never been
"returned, and now I believe he has ufe enough for them.

"I have alfo intelligence, that if the Spaniards fucceed at
"Georgia, they will fall upon us next. I humbly afk par-
"don for this freedom, and only beg your grace will be
"pleafed to take the Bahama Iflands and their governor
"under your protection.

"(Signed)   J O H N.   T I N K E R."

BOOK XI.

1742.

At

BOOK XI.
━━━━━
1742.
A quarrel
with lieute-
nant Stuart.

At the delivery of the before mentioned materials by the inhabitants, it was hinted to me, by way of friendly advice, to ſtate the ſame to the government's account, as that could not be looked on as a breach of truſt; but as I was deter-mined not to enter into any unlawful ſchemes, I rejected the propoſal. A club had been inſtituted to meet once a week at a tavern, and at our third meeting, which happened ſoon after this friendly propoſal, a diſpute aroſe between me and lieutenant Stuart; and when his excellency ſaw the diſ-pute beginning to grow warm, he abſented himſelf; on which, averſe to any farther altercation, I went home. Next morn-ing, at day break, looking out at my window, I ſaw Stuart riding paſt, armed with ſword and piſtols; I aſked him where he had been ſo early in the morning, accoutred in-that manner; he replied I had certainly forgot that I had given him a challenge the night before; I told him I could remember no ſuch thing; but ſince that was the caſe, as he ſaid, I would immediately put on my cloaths, and attend him wherever he pleaſed; obſerving to him my ſurprize how he came to paſs and repaſs under my windows, knowing I was aſleep in bed, without either calling or ſending to ac-quaint me with his deſign: he then replied, ſince I did not remember my giving him a challenge, he had nothing to ſay, as he did not intend to have any quarrel with me; that it was great folly for people to involve themſelves in needleſs dangers; and wiſhing me a good morning, he went home.

The captain
confined.

About three hours after, as I was walking along the bay, in my morning dreſs, with half of a ſtick in my hand, ſplit down the middle, and had got oppoſite the governor's win-dows,

dows, Stuart came up with me, and knocked me down; upon recovering myfelf, I hit him with the edge of my half ftick fuch a blow, that it laid his cheek open from his ear to his mouth; on which judge Rowland, and feveral of the inhabitants, who had been witneffes to Stuart's treacherous infult, came and parted us; and, upon my fervant's bringing me my fword and piftols, we were both fecured by the guard, and had fentries placed at our doors: there I remained a prifoner for a fortnight, without the governor's enquiring into the merits of the cafe, or offering to give me the leaft fatisfaction for the infult I had met with in his view; but he was every day with Stuart, who feemed to me to be only detained a prifoner by way of a blind.

As the workmen could do nothing without I fhewed them daily how to proceed, it in courfe put a ftop to the works, which occafioned a very loud clamour among the inhabitants, who had contributed fo much towards getting thefe works expeditioufly carried on; on which the governor fent for me, and propofed an accommodation between Stuart and me; who, he faid, had offered to acknowledge his fault, and afk my pardon in public, and in as ample a manner as I fhould think fit: but I told the governor that as I had been in a manner affaffinated in his own fight, I could not but have expected to have been redreffed by him; inftead of which I had been punifhed by two weeks confinement; and as I was fatisfied there was no fafety for my perfon, I fhould be obliged either to leave the ifland, or put a ftop to the works till farther orders from England. Upon this the governor propofed, that fince he had certain intelligence of the determination of the Spaniards to invade this ifland, I fhould

And fet at liberty.

BOOK XI. proceed to put the place in a pofture of defence; and he
——————— would engage his word and honour, fince nothing elfe
1724. would fatisfy me, that as foon as fort Naffau was finifhed,
he would order Stuart to any place, out of the ifland, I pleafed
for my fatisfaction, upon condition I fhould make no attempt againft him till then; to which conditions I agreed,
and proceeded with the works again with the utmoft diligence; but never without my fword and piftols, thereby to
prevent my being attacked again in fuch a villainous manner.

B O O K

B O O K XII.

The treatment of two privateers and their owners.—Letter from lieutenant Moone.—Letter from a friend.—Letter from lieutenant Dromgole.—Division of the quick-silver.—The captain applies again to the assembly to bring the materials.—The assembly withdraw the governor's salary.—Letter from lieutenant Moone.—Another from Charlestown.—Letter from governor Glen.—Produce of the Bahama islands, and the adjacent sea —Observations on St. Salvador and the Bimini islands.—The inhabitants of Providence.—Description of fort Nassau—Cost of both forts.—The captain leaves Providence.—Arrives at Charlestown.—His report of the strength of Charlestown.—A visit from a Cherokee king.—Captain Frankland's rich prize.—A short description of Carolina.—The captain sails for England.—Arrives at London.

IN the month of September a rich Spanish register ship and settee were brought in by John Sibbald, of the George schooner, and William Dowall, of the Joseph and Mary sloop, both privateers from Philadelphia; the captains of the privateers were recommended to Mr. Tinker's protection by governor Thomas, of Philadelphia, and several considerable merchants of that place, their owners. A few days after the prizes were brought in, a flag of truce arrived from the Havannah, sent by the governor and royal company there, to redeem the register ship, whose cargo amounted to one hundred and fifty thousand pieces of eight, prime cost at Cadiz, besides some valuable private trade, not belonging to the royal company, computed at thirty thousand pieces of eight; the settee was loaded with quick-silver, wine, and

F f f 2   other

other goods. As governor Tinker was empowered by the owners to bargain for the prizes for their account, he agreed with don Pedro de Leftrado, who came from the Havannah for that purpofe, to deliver him the regifter fhip and her cargo for ninety thoufand pieces of eight; and the private trade, and the fettee were referved for the owners of the privateers, don Pedro having only orders to redeem the royal company's effects. So the Spaniards gained fixty thoufand pieces of eight by the cargo, befides the value of the fhip, which was a fine new one, built in the river Thames, and taken by the Spaniards in her firft voyage. As the money for the purchafe was to be procured at the Havannah, don Pedro returned in the flag of truce for that purpofe, accompanied by John Snow, the governor's fecretary, and feveral Spanifh prifoners, captured by captain Frankland.

In the mean time, the privateers' men were encouraged on fhore with rioting and drinking, thereby to run them in debt ; and as none of them would go on board to do the work, the captains and officers of the privateers were obliged to do all the neceffary duty on board the veffels, themfelves. The captains applied to the governor to order the people on board to their duty, but all in vain ; inftead of that, they were encouraged to infult and affront them on all occafions. At length don Pedro Feron arrived from the Havannah, with thirty chefts of pieces of eight, each cheft containing three thoufand ; which he delivered in full payment for the fhip and cargo, and got poffeffion of her, after all the private trade was taken out. With don Pedro Feron came another don, with plenty of money, to purchafe the private trade, and the privateers were to efcort the regifter fhip to

2   the

the Havannah; but the captains could perfuade very few of the men to go on board, which obliged them to hire feamen at very extravagant wages, their people on fhore being encouraged to fpend liberally, that they might take none of their prize money away with them, and they departed for the Havannah on the 8th of February, 1743.

On the return of the privateers, the captains were determined not to enter this harbour again, and came to an anchor at a place called Salt Keys; they came both on fhore to demand their money, which was in the governor's cuftody, and likewife the fettee, and private trade; but his excellency told them he would oblige them to fhare here, as their people owed confiderable fums to the inhabitants of Providence; which debts the captains offered to pay, and faid when that fhould be done, they hoped to have liberty to depart for their proper port. But a party of drunken fellows, inftigated by fome interefted perfons, took a pilot and his boat, and went on board the two veffels, and brought them into the harbour, upon a pretence that the captains had a defign to deprive them of their prize money, which they ought now to prevent, affuring them, at the fame time, they would come to no harm thereby, as they were to be fupported by the leading men of the ifland. On this they went on board, confined their officers, brought in the veffels, and threatened to cut the officers in pieces if they did not fhare the prizes immediately.

On this the captains went to the governor, and reprefented their cafe to him, and begged his protection againft fuch a dangerous mutiny of the people; and that he would order them on board to do their duty, not doubting but as

foon

foon as they got fober, they would behave as they ought. The governor then told them he had been petitioned by Mr. Ellis, to whom they were in debt, and the whole body of the inhabitants, to have every thing fhared here, which, in juftice to them, he could not refufe. Upon this the captains fhewed the governor the articles figned by all the men, of both veffels, obliging themfelves to fhare no where but at Philadelphia ; and affured him that moft of them had families there, who had been fupplied by the owners upon the faith of thefe prizes; and that many of them were indentured fervants, whofe half fhares belonged to their mafters, fo that it was impoffible for them to confent to the diftribution here, not knowing what debts they owed at home ; but they were willing and ready to pay what debts the people owed in this place, although they underftood they were very confiderable.

The governor told them, fince they would not give their confent to the fharing, he would order it to be done ; on this the people were advifed to conftitute James Irving their agent, with an allowance of 5 per cent. and, when that was fettled, his excellency fent twenty chefts of dollars, being fixty thoufand pieces of eight, to Mr. Irving's houfe, to be divided amongft the people ; which the agent did in fuch an arbitrary manner, that the officers, if they offered to make the leaft remonftrance, were treated with the utmoft indignity ; of which they frequently complained to the governor, who as often replied, that " he would not concern himfelf with their private quarrels ;" his ufual reply to all complaints on fimilar occafions.

Mr.

I

Mr. John Snow, the secretary, now returned from the Havannah with several English prisoners in exchange for the Spaniards he carried there, and twelve more, whose discharge don Pedro Feron complimented me with, in return for some little civilities I shewed him while he resided here ; of the twelve, ten were masters of ships, and one a surgeon. Mr. Snow brought with him four chests of dollars (or twelve thousand pieces of eight), as it was reported, for the governor, and a purse with one thousand quadruple pistoles, a gold hilted sword, a gold-headed cane, gold buckles and buttons, besides many other valuable presents ; and as the chests with the money could not be brought privately on shore, it was given out that the governor had sent rials in exchange for the dollars ; but every body saw through this thin pretext, for it was very well known there were not so many rials on the whole island ; besides, there was at this time above one hundred thousand dollars in the place, as the Spaniards had brought plenty with them to purchase the private trade and naval stores.

When the officers of the privateers, who had ventured their lives for this prize, found they could obtain no justice, they petitioned his excellency, that now, since the money was shared, he would be pleased to let them depart with the settee and her cargo, with the private trade, which he promised to do upon his word and honour ; but they were detained from time to time, under various pretences, till the people had spent all their shares, which were four hundred and fifty dollars a man ; and which they did in a very short time, by gaming and throwing it away as fast as they got it. They were again encouraged by their agents to petition

the

the governor, that the quick-silver, and other goods on board the fettee, and the private trade, might be fhared alfo; which was accordingly ordered to be done.

The captains finding there was no end of thefe fingular proceedings, got the ten chefts of money referved for the owners, as their one third fhare of what was divided before, hired the Englifh failors, which came from the Havannah, to man their veffels, and failed from hence, leaving all the reft of the property behind. Captain Dowall fpringing his main-maft, was obliged to return here to get it repaired, and thought it prudent to take whatever fhare they pleafed to give him, rather than run the rifque of lofing all. The poor failors, when their money was all gone, curfed and damned this government ; but they foon found to their coft, now all their money was fpent, that inftead of being courted as formerly, they were thrown into jail, and very exorbitant fees exacted from them. Some were relieved by the humanity of their fhipmates, who had a little money left; and two of them, who were bricklayers, I redeemed, by paying their debts, and employed them on the works, where they continued till they were finifhed. Some of the foldiers having got money on this occafion, it was hinted to them, that whoever could pay one hundred dollars, might have his difcharge ; on which feveral did purchafe it at that price.

Dr. Irving now began to build a fine new houfe, and, thinking every thing he did was lawful, went to the fort and ordered feveral of the labourers to go to his houfe to dig a cellar. The overfeer would not allow any of the people to leave the works, without an order from the engineer ;

Irving

Irving took the tools out of the men's hands, and ordered them to be carried to his houfe. The overfeer, in endeavouring to prevent it, was miferably beaten, and had his head cut in feveral places; he came to me, all covered over with blood, to complain of the hard ufage he had met with; I fent him, in that pickle, to judge Rowland, to enter his complaint againft the aggreffor; but he was no fooner before the judge, than Irving followed, who beat the overfeer again, before the judge's face. As foon as I heard how the poor man had been abufed, in a place where he ought to have found protection and redrefs, I went directly to the governor to feek redrefs, but was anfwered with his ufual cant, " that he would not concern himfelf with private quar-" rels:" however he fent for Irving, who was no fooner in his prefence than he threatened death and deftruction to any one that durft prefume to enter a complaint againft him; which fo nettled the governor, that he fent him prifoner to the fort; telling him, at the fame time, that it was not for the complaint laid againft him, but for the want of that refpect due to his perfon; upon which explanation I left him; but, upon an application from Scott and Stuart, Irving was fet at liberty.

In the evening, as I was fitting in company with the parfon, the collector, lieutenant Dromgole, and feveral others, my fervant came and told me, before the company, that Dr. Irving, and one Cuthbert, were fwearing death and revenge againft me and my overfeer; and that they were waiting for me with loaded piftols before their door, which was next to mine, and by which I muft necceffarily pafs in my way home. This alarmed the company; fome advifed me to fend for

G g g

the

the guard; others, that I fhould ftay where I was all night: but, finding me determined to go home, they offered to efcort me, for which I thanked them kindly, and told them, that as I well knew all bullies to be cowards, I would make my way, attended by my overfeer alone; but, as it was clear moon light, and they could fee as far as I went, they might ftand at the door till I paffed thofe bravos, that they might bear witnefs of what might happen. We proceeded with cocked piftols in our hands, and coming to Irving's door, he thought proper to fculk behind it; I ftood fome time there, and finding all quiet, I went very peaceably home to bed. This being told the next day, with all its circum-ftances, to the governor, he only replied in his ufual ftyle, that " he had nothing to do with private quarrels;" for if one was killed, he would hang the other.

About this time, a fcene of confufion and diffenfion began to take place in the ifland; and the fudden death of Mr. Hodges, the chaplain of the garrifon, gave rife to a variety of fpeculations.

Two days after which, I received a letter from lieutenant Moone, of which the following is an extract.

" Fort Montague, July 7, 1743.

" Sir,

" In a conference I had with governor Tinker, the 3d
" inftant, wherein part of the difcourfe rolled upon fome
" quarrels and divifions which happened lately amongft fome
" gentlemen in Naffau, the governor intimated, that they
" were to be thrown into the public fcale, as if he was to
                                                        " be

" be anfwerable for them ; which he feemed much exafpe-
" rated at, and occafioned the following declaration : that
" he would not, for the future, interpofe in any of their
" quarrels, for if one was killed, the other fhould be hanged ;
" and then he would be quit of two troublefome perfons.
" I give you this hint by way of caution, which feems to be
" levelled at one of us. The fudden and unexpected death
" of our minifter, Mr. Hodges, on the 5th inftant, though
" his cafe was not dangerous, is matter of great fpeculation
" amongft the inhabitants of this ifland. That the great
" God may blefs, protect, and keep all honeft men out of
" the hands of their enemies, is the fincere wifh of

(Signed)   W. MOONE."

The little cordiality that had for fome time fubfifted between the governor and me, and the ticklifh fituation in
which I found myfelf, began to make me entertain very
ferious thoughts of quitting the ifland ; and the invitations
which I had repeatedly received from feveral of the colonies
on the continent, made it neceffary for me to give an inti-
mation of my defign to his excellency ; at the fame time
taking occafion to acquaint him, that I was far from confidering myfelf in a ftate of abfolute fafety, and that if any
accident happened to me, I had the greateft reafon to believe
that a very ftrict enquiry would be made into the authors of
it. That there was fome foundation for this apprehenfion,
will appear from the following letter, which was fent to me
by a very particular friend.

" Fort

　　　　　　　　　　　　　　　" Fort Naſſau, Auguſt 10, 1743.

　　　" Laſt week I had ſome diſcourſe with governor Tinker
" concerning your intention to leave this government, as ſoon
" as the money allowed by his majeſty for fortifications,
" ſhould be expended ; upon which the governor replied,
" that the engineer, nor nobody elſe, ſhould leave this iſland
" without leave ; and that he would order his officers to
" ſtop you, if you attempted it. However I told the go-
" vernor I did not apprehend how that could be put in ex-
" ecution, confidering that you were independent of this
" government, and anſwerable to the board of ordnance
" only. The governor then replied with great warmth and
" earneſtneſs, that he was king in this government ; and if
" he gave orders to kill any man whatſoever, his officers
" were to obey him, without enquiring into the cauſe
" thereof. This I hint to you by way of precaution, that
" you may be upon your guard ; I have likewiſe acquainted
" Mr. Moone with the purport of the letter, ſince I find
" he intends to leave this government by the ſame oppor-
" tunity."

　　　One of the complaints againſt the late governor, was his
forcing the inhabitants, by way of puniſhment, to make three
lime kilns ; Mr. Scott, his agent, now wanted me to buy
this lime of him at a very exorbitant price ; I told him I
was willing to take it by meaſure, but not otherwiſe, and
that I would pay him the price I gave governor Tinker for
his, which was ſix pence per buſhel, which he could not
refuſe ; but being nettled becauſe I would not give him the
　　　　　　　　　　　　　　　　　　　　　　ſum

sum he demanded for the whole, without measure, he acquainted Mr. Fitz William thereof; Mr. Fitz William wrote to Mr. Tinker about it, who shewed me the letter, in which he threatened and abused me in a very injurious manner, for not giving the price he demanded. Upon my declaring I would resent it, his nephew, lieutenant Dromgole, begged me not to write, as he was certain the matter had been wrong represented by Scott, and that he would write and explain the matter to his uncle; of which letter the following is a copy.

" Providence, Dec. 11.

" The 9th instant captain Bruce, our engineer, paid Mr.
" Scott for your lime, at six pence per bushel, according to
" Scott's agreement with him, which is the same price was
" allowed to governor Tinker for his; you have both been
" greatly imposed upon in the making of it, because the en-
" gineer made all the lime for building fort Montagu at less
" than half a rial per bushel, and charged the government
" no more. Mr. Scott, upon receiving your letter, and see-
" ing what you had wrote to the governor on that head, re-
" fused, for some time, to take the money from the engineer;
" but as I wrote you before in a former letter, that by the
" carelessness of your good attorney, the half of your lime
" was stole and washed away by the great rains, which I
" heard governor Tinker and Mr. Scott say from their own
" mouths, before ever the engineer touched it, otherwise it
" would have turned out very much to your advantage;
" and I beg leave to tell you that I am extremely sorry that
" governor Tinker shewed him your letter, because you
" have threatened to make captain Bruce smart if he did

" not

" not comply with your demands ; befides, you have treated
" him with fo much indignity and contempt, that he has
" conceived a juft refentment againft you for it, which
" makes me dread the confequence. Perhaps you may ima-
" gine he was fome little theorift, fent out by the board of
" ordnance ; if fo, you are greatly miftaken, for he is one
" of the beft engineers in his majefty's fervice, and a gen-
" tleman of long experience in the army ; has weathered
" eighteen campaigns, and, I believe, has built more forts
" than all the reft of the engineers on the Britifh eftablifh-
" ment, and is a man of the ftricteft honour and integrity ;
" but will not pocket an affront of any man, by what name
" or title foever dignified or diftinguifhed. Captain Bruce
" has been one of the beft friends I met with fince my arrival
" in Providence ; therefore a difference of this fort muft
" give me no fmall concern, and hope you will write to
" captain Bruce to apologize for it."

PAT. DROMGOLE."

Divifion of
the quick-fil-
ver.

As the quick-filver was to be divided among the people in
fhares, I had bought twenty-eight fhares from the officers
and fome few of the men, who went home in the privateers,
who left me a power to receive them from Mr. Irving, their
agent ; each fhare was a cag and a half, and each cag
weighed one hundred weight ; fo that I had forty-two cags
to receive. When the time for the divifion came round, I
applied for thefe fhares, but could only get eight cags out of
the forty-two I had a right to receive ; and the agent fent
me word that the reft had run out in the cellar by the burft-
ing of the bags in the cags ; but if I would fend empty
bottles

bottles to put it in, he would weigh up as much as amounted
to my fhare; when the bottles were fent, he told my fervant ————
to come for it the next day. Mr. Keowin, the provoft marfhal, then attended, at my defire, to receive it, and was
told by Mr. Irving that as he had not received it by weight,
he would not deliver it on thofe terms, and fince it had
made its way into the cellar, he might go and gather it up
himfelf. Upon Mr. Keowin's going into the cellar to look
for it, there was none to be found. Mr. Irving had pre-
vioufly taken care to gather it up in jars, and convey it by
negroes to his own houfe in the night time, which all the
people in the neighbourhood offered to prove. When a
complaint was made to the governor, he faid that as the
quick-filver had burft the bags, and was run into the cellar, he could not in juftice defire Mr. Irving to deliver it,
as it might have made its way to the Antipodes for ought
he knew. At the fame time, I had feveral cags run out into
my own cellar, taken up without lofing an ounce. This
abfurd and barefaced injuftice in the governor, was a matter of great furprize to all the inhabitants.

The money allowed by government for fortifying this The captain
place being all expended, I intimated it to the governor, and applies again
to the affem-
told him I intended to go to Charleftown till a frefh fupply bly to bring
materials.
of money could be obtained from England, to finifh what
was begun; but he replied, that as a war had been proclaimed againft France, I could not leave the ifland till fort
Naffau was finifhed; for which he would advance his own
money, and be anfwerable for fo doing to the board of
ordnance. I told him I would not accept his money, without an order from England; but if he would take upon
him

him to pay the tradefmen and labourers himfelf, I would direct the work till it was completed. This he agreed to, and I forwarded the works with the utmoft diligence. As the affembly was fitting at this time, I had recourfe to them again for their affiftance, thereby to put it the fooner out of the enemies power to annoy them; to which the affembly unanimoufly confented, and affeffed every taxable in the ifland to furnifh his quota of the neceffary ftone and timber for finifhing the work; yet notwithftanding this went much againft the grain with the triumvirate, they could not well, in the prefent fituation of affairs, refufe their affent, fo that it was affirmed by the council.

The affembly withdraw the governor's falary.

The agreeable profpect the inhabitants had formed to themfelves of living happily under Mr. Tinker's government, and which they had built upon the fair beginning he made, in turning out his predeceffor's evil counfellors, by whom they had been fo grievoufly oppreffed, induced the affembly, on the governor's arrival, to appoint him a yearly falary of two hundred pounds fterling; but now finding their expectations fo effectually difappointed, the affembly declared that they were unable to continue the governor's falary any longer; and finding themfelves oppofed in this affair by Mr. Scott, their fpeaker, they voted him out of the chair, and chofe Mr. Florentine Cox in his place; on which the governor diffolved the Houfe of Affembly; and that he might mortify them more effectually, he appointed James Scott one of his council, and made him chief-juftice, treafurer, naval officer, ftorekeeper, &c. thereby to enable him to revenge himfelf upon the inhabitants.

The

'The three domineering gentlemen now joined, and for their own account built a new floop, and had the vanity to call her after their own ufual diftinguifhing title, the Triumvirate.

The bad ufage I had hitherto met with, made the governor fufpect me of being inftrumental in his lofing his falary, as alfo that I fent complaints againft him to England ; but I declared I neither did the one nor the other ; at firft indeed I did my beft to perfuade the affembly to fettle that falary upon him, but as foon as I learned they were determined to with-hold his falary, I withdrew myfelf from the affembly, and went no more near them ; fo that I acted neither pro nor con in that affair. Upon this Mr. Moone wrote me the following letter, dated Fort Montagu, December 30.

" The 27th inftant I waited on governor Tinker, to know
" his commands. As foon as I was feated he told me he was
" furprifed that I did not dine oftener at his houfe, and that
" I kept company with perfons difaffected to his govern-
" ment ; which could be pointed at none but you, Mr.
" Cox, and captain Petty, becaufe of our being frequently
" in company when I go to town. I told his excellency I
" did not know what he meant by difaffected perfons, un-
" lefs he would include every body who fhewed a juft re-
" fentment for injuries received from their neighbours, in
" defiring a redrefs of grievances. All the anfwer the go-
" vernor made me was that he hoped it would be in his
" power to hang up two or three of them very foon.——As
" a farther confirmation of the truth of this affertion, Mr.
" John Thompfon, one of the council for thefe iflands, af-

H h h " fured

" fured me, before his brother Richard Thompfon, and fe-
" veral of the inhabitants, that governor Tinker had ex-
" preffed himfelf lately in the fame manner, in council, in
" threatning that he would hang up fome of the inhabit-
" ants ; and confirmed the fame with an oath.   It is there-
" fore incumbent upon us to be upon our guard, left we
" fhould be among the number of the profcribed.   His dif-
" folving the houfe of affembly at this time, becaufe they
" would not continue his falary, is a fignal inftance that he
" prefers his own private intereft to the public good.

(Signed)   W. M O O N E."

An opportunity foon after offered itfelf for his excellency's gratification in hanging people : a foldier was condemned and executed for ftabbing his ferjeant; and two
negroes belonging to captain Laws, of the navy, formerly
ftationed here, who were at work for their mafter in the
woods, cutting brazilletta, and being ill ufed by an overfeer
appointed by Mr. Scott, one of them fired a fowling-piece
at the overfeer, and lodged fome fhot in his fhoulder ; for
which he was hanged, and his innocent companion was alfo
hanged, to bear him company.

At the time of thefe tranfactions I received the following
letter from lieutenant-governor Bull, of South Carolina, dated
Charleftown, June 22.

" As it has been determined by the government here, that
" a new magazine, capable of holding 500 barrels of pow-
" der, fhould be built in Charleftown ; and as his majefty
" has no engineer in this province, upon the Britifh eftab-
" lifhment, confequently none with whom I can advife, or
" who

" who can be affiftant to me in the erecting fuch a work ; I, BOOK XII.
" by the affembly of the province, am defired to apply to —————
" you for a plan thereof, in brick building, and which I   1745.
" requeft you will favour me with, together with fuch other
" directions as you fhall judge proper. I doubt not but
" this favour will be gratefully acknowledged by the go-
" vernment here.

(Signed)   W. B U L L."

In compliance with this requeft I fent a plan and profile,
and fuch directions as I thought neceffary, in two weeks
after the receipt of that letter, by a floop that failed from
hence for Charleftown ; but not hearing of its being delivered, I defired lieutenant Moone, who left this the beginning of September for Carolina, in his way to London,
to enquire if the plan had been delivered, who wrote me
the following letter.

" Charleftown, September 14, 1744.

" Thanks to the Supreme Being, I am now out of the Another from
" power of the governor of Providence, and his triumvi- Charleftown.
" rate. I have enquired about the plan of the powder ma-
" gazine, which was received and laid before the council ;
" the reafon why the receipt was not acknowledged, I find
" to be occafioned by the governor's arrival, and the lieu-
" tenant-governor's retiring into the country about the time
" it was fent. They all wifh for you on account of their for-
" tifications, and have wrote to you fome time paft on that
" head, which, I prefume, you have received advice of.

H h h 2   " I pre-

" I prefume the triumvirate go on as ufual, Jehu
" like.

                (Signed)   W.   M O O N E.

I never received the letter Mr. Moone alludes to, nor two
others written by the new governor, which Mr. Tinker took
care I fhould not ; but I received his third letter, as follows :

                " Charleftown, October 9.

Letter from governor Glen.

" As there are fome works to be carried on for the better
" fortifying of Charleftown, at the expence of this province,
" and as there is, at prefent, no perfon here that is thought
" properly qualified for giving advice and direction in that
" matter, the affembly did recommend it to me to write to
" you, to defire the favour of your affiftance : I have al-
" ready written twice upon that fubject, and hope by this
" time you are embarking for this province, where I fhall
" endeavour that you fhall meet with a kind reception. The
" affembly have agreed to give you three hundred pounds,
" money of this country, as the expence of your paffage,
" and have likewife come to a refolution to make you a
" handfome prefent for your trouble, provided you arrive
" here within a month after the date of this letter.

            (Signed)   J A M E S   G L E N."

It is worthy of obfervation, that Mr. Tinker, at his firft
arrival in Providence, behaved fo fmoothly and civilly to all
ftrangers, that it was foon fpread over all America how
happy the people now lived under his mild government;
which report enticed feveral people of fubftance to come, at
                                    dif-

different times, from the Continent, Bermudas, and the
Leeward Iflands, with an intention of fettling here, being
drawn hither by its fertility and wholefome air ; but upon finding how the inhabitants were oppreffed, they returned from
whence they came, and fpreading the report wherever they
went, deterred others from coming to this place ; befides,
all our privateers intended to have made this place their
general rendezvous ; but the treatment Sibbald and Dowall
met with, prevented any from coming near us. And even
captain Frankland, who was ftationed here, would not venture to bring his prizes into this harbour, but fent them to
Charleftown, to be condemned and difpofed_of ; which very
much mortified our governor, who now found by his endeavours to grafp all, he loft all. It is very much to be
lamented that thofe fertile and valuable iflands fhould lie
uncultivated for want of people, which are capable of maintaining many thoufand families with eafe ; but it will ever
be the cafe, while the governors are fuffered to tyrannize
over the inhabitants, as nobody that can do better, will ever
come to fettle here, and, of confequence, they muft remain uninhabited.

To convey fome idea of the value of thofe iflands, I fhall
endeavour to give the following account of them from my
certain knowlege.

The Bahama iflands enjoy the moft ferene and the moft
temperate air in all America, the heat of the fun being
greatly allayed by refrefhing breezes from the eaft ; and the
earth and air are cooled by conftant dews which fall in the
night, and by gentle fhowers which fall in their proper
feafons ; fo that as they are free from the fultry heats of our
other

other fettlements; they are as little affected with froft, fnow, hail, or the north-weft winds, which prove fo fatal both to men and plants in our other colonies; it is therefore no wonder the fick and afflicted inhabitants of thofe climates fly hither for relief, being fure to find a cure here. The fame caufes which conduce fo much to the health of man, contribute greatly to the quick growth of plants and vegetables; which here is furprifing, for the feeds of limes flung carelefsly into the ground without any culture, become, in two or three years, fhrubs or little trees in full bearing.

All the iflands vary in their extent; while fome exceed a hundred miles in length, others are very inconfiderable; the principal are the Bahamas, Lucayos (or Abaco), Harbour-Ifland, Eluthera, St. Salvador (or Cat-Ifland), Exuma, Yumeta (or Long-Ifland), Andros, the Bimines, and Providence, which lies near the centre of the whole, in lat. 25 degrees north, with a fine harbour, which has fifteen feet on its bar at low water, and is formed by Hog-Ifland, which is three miles long, and now fort Naffau commands the weft entrance, and Montagu the eaft.

All thefe iflands are covered over with wood, as indeed is all America, but with this effential difference, that here the trees themfelves fufficiently pay the labour of cutting them down, exclufive of the benefit which refults from clearing a fertile foil; for not to mention the maftich tree and other timber fo ufeful in building houfes, mills, &c. here are Madeira, mahogany, and cedar, all ufed in fhip building; befides vaft quantities of curious woods, as prince-wood, yellow-wood, box, naked-wood (moft beautifully veined

5   and

and marbled), lignum vitæ, black and red iron-wood, ebony, manchinelle, black feney, dog-wood, pines, palmettos; and many dying woods, as log-wood, brazilietta, green and yellow fuftick; they have likewife trees of valuable bark, which are no where elfe in fuch quantity and perfection; among which are the cortex eluthera, or wild cinnamon, growing in fuch abundance that they exported annually between fixty and feventy tons to Curafoe, and the other Dutch fettlements, where it is made ufe of in diftilling cinnamon waters; the cortex Winterania, a fweet-fcented bark, which is alfo carried to the Dutch, and by them tranfported to the Levant, where the Turks burn it for perfume and incenfe. The wild vines are in great plenty in the woods, and when cultivated, are as good as any I ever faw; here is alfo the myrtle, from which the green wax candles are made.

They have tamarinds equal to any in the world; the Lucca olive, as well as the wild kind; oranges (fweet, four, and bitter), lemons, limes, citrons, pomgranates, plums, fugar apples, pine apples, figs, papues, fapodylles, bananas, fowerfops, water and mufk melons, yams, potatoes, gourds, cucumbers, cod and bird pepper, guavas, cafava, plantains, prickly pears, oil of caftor, fugar, ginger, coffee, indigo, cotton preferable to that in the Levant, and tobacco; Indian wheat, Guinea-corn, and peas: befides thefe all the roots of Europe grow wonderfully quick, and to a furprifing fize. The flowering fhrubs and other plants are fo aromatic, that they perfume the air to a great diftance.

Their wild fowl and birds are, the flamingo, fometimes to be met with in flocks of two or three hundred; it is a tall bird, fix feet high, of a moft beautiful plumage, being red

all

all over the body, with black wings ; they are excellent eating ; wild geefe, ducks, pigeons, and green parrots in great
plenty ; befides whiftling ducks, Mufketo hawks, tobacco
doves, crab-catchers, galdings, droffels, mocking birds, and
humming birds.

The fea hereabouts abounds with fifh unknown to us in
Europe ; thofe of prey are crocodiles, alligators, fharks, dol-
phins, fword-fifh, fea-devils, fpermacæti-whales, grampufes,
porpoifes, feals, nurfes, and fnappers ; thofe for food are,
the king-fifh, jew-fifh, hog-fifh, pork-fifh, mutton-fifh,
rock-fifh, Margaret-fifh, cuckold-fifh, coney-fifh, angle-
fifh, bill-fifh, hound-fifh, gar-fifh, parrot-fifh, blue-fifh,
fucking-fifh, tang-fifh, trumpet-fifh, porjes, grupers, jacks,
hynes, old wives, grunts, fkate, fchoolmafter, breams, ten-
pounders, ftingers, ryfpree, mullets, fenets, baracuda, fhip-
jacks, albecores, rainbow, threfhers, mackrel, hedge-hogs,
pilots, fhads, pilchards, failor's choice, fquirrels, and ca-
valy ; many of thefe are excellent eating, but fuch as feed
on the copperas banks are poifonous, affecting the joints of
thofe who eat them with itching pains, and the diforder
goes off by rubbing the parts ; the method ufed to diftin-
guifh the fifh is by putting a fpoon, or piece of filver, into
the water in which it is boiled, which turns black if the
fifh is poifonous. They make plenty of oil from the nurfes,
feals, &c. and a beneficial whale fifhery might be eftablifhed here, as that fifh comes in great numbers to wean
their young among the iflands, and feveral have been thrown
afhore, full of the fpermacæti ; there is likewife found in
the fhore much ambergrife. Their fhell-fifh are conques,
perriwinkles, coneys, fogers, wilkes, cuckolds, craw-fifh,
lobfters, crabs ; they have alfo the land-crab, and many
forts

forts of tortoifes, of which the hawk-bill is the moft valuable for its fine fhell, and the green kind for eating; the
greateft number of which are taken at the Bimini iflands.
There is alfo ambergrife found in confiderable quantities on
thefe fhorcs.

There are no animals which can be faid to be peculiar
to thofe iflands, excepting the guana, which is found in
great numbers on Andros, which lies five leagues fouth-weft
from Providence; it is a fmall creature, with fhort legs, and
a fhort tapering tail, fomewhat refembling the lizard or al-
ligator, and is about two feet in length; it is efteemed delicious eating, and is taken in great plenty by the people of
Providence.   On fome of the other iflands are numbers of
wild hogs, fheep, and goats, which are produced from a
breed left there by the inhabitants; and from which they
are now fupplied with frefh meat when they go to cut dye
woods, or rake falt at Exuma, of which they export yearly
many fhip loads to our northern colonies on the continent.

In fhort, it is their own fault if the inhabitants want any
of the neceffaries of life: they have horfes, cows, fheep,
goats, hogs, and all forts of poultry, and have grafs all
the year round; but they neither fow nor plant more than
is neceffary for maintaining their own families; whereby
one of the moft fertile parts of our Weft Indies is neglected
for want of cultivation.   They depend on their cargoes of
falt, mahogany plank, dying wood, tortoifes, fruit, &c.
which they fell to great advantage; and likewife upon the
fhipwrecks, which happen frequently upon thofe extenfive
banks; all which make them carelefs in improving the na-

tural produce of that fertile country which, were it once well
peopled, would foon be in a flourifhing fituation.

The greateft inconvenience they have here is from the
plague of numerous vermin, or infects, which torment
them both night and day; as bugs, cock-roches, mufquetos, flies, fand-flies, ants, and trigers: the laft kind are
no larger than a mite, and are very troublefome to ftrangers;
they get through the foles of people's feet, and lodge between
the fkin and the flefh, where they lay their eggs and breed,
if not timely prevented, which is done by picking them out
with the point of a needle, at which the negroes are very
dexterous; and care muft be taken to get out the bag (as
they call it) with the eggs, and then they fill the wound
with tobacco or fnuff; but if they are fuffered to remain,
they caufe moft intolerable itching pains, and great fwelling
in the legs, which are often attended with danger to the
life.   The ants are alfo very troublefome, by creeping into
the houfes and beds, and require care and attention to keep
them from the victuals, efpecially fugar, of which they will
carry off a great quantity in a night's time.   The mufquetos
and fand-flies come in great fwarms in the evening from the
woods, and people are obliged to drive them off with fmoke
round their houfes all night long: this inconvenience is
chiefly occafioned by their not clearing the ground from
thofe thickets of underwood; an inftance of which we experienced at fort Montagu, where I cleared away all the
wood within cannon fhot, and there, by that means, was
happily delivered from the infects both by day and night.
The governor took the example, and cleared to a confider-
                                                        able

BOOK XII.

1744.
Obfervations
on St. Salva-
dor and the
Bimini
iflands.

able diftance from his own houfe, and feveral of the inhabitants were beginning to do the fame.

The Bahama iflands, in general, are more conveniently
fituated for annoying the Spaniards in time of war than
any of all our other fettlements, efpecially two of them.
The firft is Salvador (or Cat-Ifland) the eaftermoft of the
whole; it lies clear of the bank, and furrounded by the
ocean; is moft conveniently fituated for intercepting the
outward-bound trade of Old Spain; lies between the 24th
and 25th degrees of north latitude; is 45 miles long by 7
broad, 28 miles from Eluthera, and 90 from Providence.

The next is the Biminis, 105 miles weft from Providence,
120 north from the Havannah, and only 60 from the continent of Florida; by which it has the full command of
the gulph, through which all the homeward-bound trade of
the Spanifh Weft Indies muft pafs : in war time this would
be the moft advantageous ftation in all Britifh America.
The harbour is formed by two iflands; the weft, and principal entry is from the gulph, and only a quarter of a mile
broad, where, and all within, it has only ten feet at low
water, and eighteen at high water; it is fecured by rocks
on the north, but firft-rate fhips can ride clofe to the weftern
fhore, free from all winds; the eaft entry is only for boats,
and is dry at low water; thefe entries are only two miles
diftant from each other, but the harbour it fix miles in length
from north to fouth, and could contain all the privateers of
America.   The Spanifh homeward-bound fhips generally
take in their wood and water here; and here the people of
Providence catch moft of their tortoife, and are frequently
taken, and carried prifoners to the Havannah.   The ifland

is twelve miles long and two broad. It was the general
opinion if two or three floops of war had been ftationed at
this place when general Oglethorpe befieged St. Auguftine,
they would effectually have prevented the Spaniards from
fending their gallies from the Havannah, with men and ammunition to their relief, and the place muft have fallen into
that general's hands, as the Spaniards were in great want of
both at that time, and muft have furrendered. This harbour might be eafily fecured by a fmall fort with a fea battery, as the entrance is fo narrow : it lies in 25 degrees north
latitude. The Bahama ifland lies 48 miles north, and Andros 60 fouth, from this ; but none of all thefe valuable
iflands are inhabited, excepting Providence, Harbour Ifland,
and Eluthera.

The inhabit-
ants of Provi-
dence.
    The inhabitants of Providence, Harbour Ifland, and Elu-
thera, confifted at this time of Englifh, Scotch, Irifh, Ber-
mudians, mulattos, free negroes, and flaves ; their whole
number were

Heads of families, – – – –	310
Women and children, – – –	689
Negro, male flaves, – – – –	426
Black women and children, – –	538
The independent company, officers included, –	100
Harbour Ifland and Eluthera in all, – –	240
Total inhabitants of the Bahamas,	2303

white and black men, women, and children ; which might
maintain more thoufands, than they have hundreds.

Fort

Fort Naſſau and Sea Battery were finiſhed the latter end
of December, which I rebuilt almoſt from the foundation, as
I found, them in a very ſhattered ruinous condition : I found
it neceſſary to add a new baſtion in place of an old ſquare
tower, and built in it the powder magazine and gunner's
ſtore, each of them to contain 300 barrels of powder ; and
under the eaſt curtain three large ſtores, or caſemates, and
a gate, all bomb-proof ; above the gate an arched apartment for the governor, with a view of the whole town and
harbour ; upon each point of the baſtions are ſentry boxes
of ſtone ; through the weſt curtain is a ſally port and caſemates, alſo bomb-proof, before which is the ſea battery ;
and the whole is ſurrounded with palliſades of maſtich wood,
eight inches ſquare, and three inches diſtant from each
other, eight feet above ground, and two feet ſunk in the
rock, well ſecured above and below with rails and braces.
As there were formerly no buildings within the fort, except
barracks of wood entirely decayed, I built new barracks of
ſtone to contain ſix hundred men, and a ſuitable ſet of apartments for officers ; likewiſe a kitchen and bake-houſe, with
two ovens, above which are apartments for the chaplain,
ſurgeon, gunner, and armourer ; within the fort is a well
with freſh water, and one before each gate within the palliſades. The whole is mounted with fifty-four pieces of
cannon, 6, 9, 12, and 18 pounders, all on new carriages,
beſides twenty-ſix braſs mortars, two of which are of 7
inches, twelve of $5\frac{1}{4}$ and twelve of $4\frac{1}{4}$ inches, mounted on
new beds.

The finiſhing of both thoſe forts coſt government no
more than four thouſand pounds, whereas a former eſti-

9   mate,

mate, for the fame thing, came to twelve thoufand, two hundred fifty-four pounds nine fhillings and ten pence three farthings; but as I happened to come here at a time when war was declared, and we were threatened with an invafion, and being then expofed to the infults of an enemy, the inhabitants very frankly provided materials for their own fecurity, which, with the other frugal methods I took, faved the government feveral thoufand pounds; but I was ill rewarded for this my faithful and dangerous fervice.

When all was finifhed, the governor and I attefted each other's accounts, and I gave him a bill on the board of ordnance for two thoufand and four hundred pounds he had laid out toward finifhing thofe works, and he gave me, at the fame time, a certificate of my having performed and finifhed all the works neceffary to be done in the ifland of Providence, which I gave in to the board of ordnance on my arrival in London.

As Mr. Tinker was confcious how far he deferved complaints to be entered againft him, he fent his fecretary, John Snow, by the way of Jamaica to London, to foreftall any complaints that might be entered there againft him; but he might have faved himfelf both the trouble and expence, for I neither mentioned, nor intended to mention, his name in London, knowing that a redrefs of grievances is not eafily obtained.

While I was preparing for my departure for Carolina, captain Jelf, of the Swallow floop of war, with his officers, arrived here in a boat; he had been fent from Charleftown with two brafs mortars, and a quantity of bomb

8   fhells,

shells, that had been lent to general Oglethorp in his expedition to St. Auguftine, and his fhip was caft away on the rocks of Abaco : what furprifed me was, his having the fame pilot on board that came with us in the Tartar man of war, under whofe conduct we very narrowly efcaped being wrecked upon the very fame rocks. Captain Jelf had intended to carry me with him to Carolina, but was now very glad to take his paffage with me in a floop I had hired.

When every thing was ready for our departure, and as I was informed that Stuart's floop was to go to Abaco to bring what could be faved from the wreck of the Swallow, I fent my overfeer with an open letter to him, demanding his attendance at Abaco, to give me fatisfaction for the treacherous infult I had received from him : he fent me word that he would go to the governor and afk his leave, and foon again returned me for anfwer that he could not obtain it ; upon which I wrote to the governor, and reminded his excellency of the infult I had received from Stuart, and the promife he gave me, upon his word of honour, to order him, as foon as the works were finifhed, to attend me ; and as his floop was going to the wreck, I hoped he would perform his engagement, as this gave us a proper opportunity to decide that affair ; but Mr. Tinker gave me an abfolute refufal, well knowing himfelf as much in fault as the other : on this, I wrote again to Stuart, telling him that I knew he had a law-fuit depending at Charleftown, which would foon require his prefence there, and that I would wait five or fix months for him ; to which he replied, he would attend me there. Thefe requifitions I had determined to make in as public a manner as I could, and tranfacted them be-

fore

fore captain Jelf, and his officers, collector Boothby, and
captain Cox, that he might not have an opportunity to

deny facts; yet, notwithstanding Stuart's friends and attornies at Charlestown represented the necessity of his per-
sonal appearance there, as the whole success of his law-
suit depended on it, and his own repeated assertions that
he was just coming over, he never made his appearance all
the five months I stayed there, and thereby lost his cause,
which was matter of diversion at Charlestown, where captain Jelf and his officers had made the reason of his not
appearing as well known as it was at Providence, and
was afterwards revived by Boothby and Cox.

On the 5th of January I went on board the Pelham sloop,
a new vessel built of mahogany, by Florentine Cox, who
also commanded her, and we sailed the same day, with captain Jelf and his officers, and arrived next day at Abaco,
where the wreck lay. We were detained several days in col-
lecting the crew of the Swallow, who were dispersed over
the island; and with the addition of their number (120)
we were sufficiently crowded in the Pelham. Stuart's sloop
recovered the mortars and shells, and the guns, anchors,
sails and rigging belonging to the Swallow, which were all
sold at Providence; and, as I was credibly informed by
letter, were afterwards sold to the Spaniards. We had fine
weather and a pleasant passage in the Pelham, attended daily
by a number of sharks. Captain Cox, a native of Bermudas, who are esteemed the most dexterous fishers in the
world, caught upwards of a score of them in a day: his
method was by hanging out a rope, with a noose at the
end of it, through which he hung a piece of beef; when
the

the fhark approached the beef, it was pulled forward through
the noofe, fo that the fhark in purfuit of it was flung by
the tail, which is large and broad, and in that manner was
pulled on board. Some of the fharks were fo large, that
when their tail was even with the gunnel, the half of their
bodies were under water; we cut thefe over-grown ones
through the middle, and let them drop into the water again,
where they were foon torn to pieces by their voracious companions, which afforded us diverting amufement; but as
the young are good eating, we brought them on deck, and
cut them up for the people, who were thereby plentifully
fupplied with frefh provifions, which was a fortunate circumftance, as we had not provifions for fuch a number;
but it is a common faying, that a Bermudian will never
die for want at fea, if he is provided with fifhing tackle.

In the evening of the 21ft of January we arrived before Arrive at
Charleftown.
Charleftown bar, and as it was then growing dark, low
water, and blowing hard, we did not think it prudent to
venture over the bar; but two of the Englifh feamen belonging to the Swallow informing captain Jelf that the Irifh
failors on board, who were the greater number, had entered into a combination to fecure us, and carry the veffel
to Auguftine, made us attempt to get over the bar. We
were no fooner on the bar than fhe ftruck, and thumped
eighteen times with fuch violence that every fhock lifted us
from our feet; but as the tide was then beginning to flow,
it was with no fmall difficulty we got her about again, and
put out to fea, but fo leaky that it required our utmoft efforts to keep the veffel from going down. We fired frequent guns of diftrefs, which prevented the mutineers from

K k k

at-

attempting at that time to enter upon the execution of
their project. Captain Jelf, in the midst of our confusion,

and under favour of the darkness, had sent off his officers in
the boat to the commodore to inform him of our danger ;
and by day-break next morning two long boats were difpatched full of men, well armed, to our affiſtance ; and a
twenty gun ſhip was ſent down to the bar to be ready to
follow us in cafe of need. This armament quite confounded the mutineers, and we were no fooner within the
bar, than they were all fecured in irons on board the man
of war, and we got at laſt fafe to Charleſtown on the 22d,
chiefly owing to the ſtrength of our veſſel, otherwife we
muſt have periſhed ; but ſhe was very much ſhattered by
the many ſhocks ſhe got on the bar. The diſtance of Providence to this place is 7 degrees, or 420 geographical
miles.

Here I met a kind reception from the governor, council,
and aſſembly, who defired that I would, without lofs of
time, proceed to furvey the place, and give my opinion
touching what I thought was farther neceſſary to be done
for their greater fecurity and defence. After I had taken
a full furvey of the place, and had examined the nature of
the morafs that lies before the town, and founded Hog Iſland
Creek, I gave in the following report.

Report of the
ſtrength of
Charleſtown.   " As this town is built on a point of land, and furrounded
" on the eaſt, fouth, and weſt fides by Cooper and Aſhley,
" two large navigable rivers, which render thoſe three fides
" ſtrong by nature, yet I obferve that all that has hitherto
" been done toward fortifying this place is all toward thoſe
" rivers ; whereas the north fide of the town, toward the main

                4   " land,

" land, is neglected and left open, expofed to the infults of
" an enemy, who, by the nearnefs of the woods, might at
" any time furprize the town. This place is fubject to
" the fame danger by fea; for although the bar is a great
" fecurity, and fort Johnfon commands the ufual paffage
" to the town, yet as there is another paffage at Hog Ifland
" Creek, of greater depth of water than is upon the bar it-
" felf, and an enemy may pafs that way without being ex-
" pofed to the guns of fort Johnfon, or to thofe upon the
" curtain-line next the river, they may by that means get
" behind the town, where it is altogether defencelefs, and
" make themfelves mafters of it.

" I am therefore of opinion that a canal ought to be
" cut at the free-fchool, fix or eight fathoms wide, and
" eight or ten feet deep, from the one marfh to the other,
" it being only 120 fathoms in length; this would prevent
" a furprize by land. In the next place, to prevent a fur-
" prize by fea, a fafcine battery ought to be erected at
" Rahte's point, being the only proper landing place, and
" another battery at Anfon's houfe, each of fix or eight guns
" of the largeft fize, to command the paffage through Hog
" Ifland Creek, fhould an enemy attempt to pafs it; befides,
" Rahte's point might be flanked by the guns of Craven's
" baftion, as well as by thofe at Anfon's houfe; and after
" that paffage is thus fecured, it would be neceffary to erect
" a large battery upon the marfh oppofite to the town,
" part of which is folid and firm, and what is not may be
" made fo by driving piles; this battery fhould be in form
" of a horfe-fhoe, mounted with thirty pieces of cannon
" of the largeft fize, which would not only command Re-

K k k 2   " bellion

BOOK XII. " bellion-road, but alfo both channels (that of Johnfon's
———— " Fort and Hog Ifland) by which the keeping up of John-

1745.   " fon's Fort will become needlefs, more efpecially if the bat-
      " tery begun at the point near Granvill's baftion was finifh-
      " ed, and that will alfo render Broughton's battery need-
      " lefs.

      " In the next place I am of opinion that it would be very
      " neceffary to erect a regular fort, with four baftions, upon
      " the neck of land between the workhoufe and free-fchool,
      " which would not only cover the town, but command both
      " rivers; and it would be a confiderable addition to the
      " ftrength of fuch fort if it were furrounded with pallifades,
      " which, in cafe of an attack, might be lined with negroes
      " either from the town or country : no danger could arife
      " to the inhabitants from their being entrufted with fire
      " arms, fince they would be immediately under the eye of
      " their mafters, and they would have no accefs to the fort,
      " or any communication with the works, but within the
      " pallifades alone, where they would prove a great annoy-
      " ance to an enemy.

      " The more I confider the fituation and circumftances of
      " the place, the more I am confirmed in opinion of the
      " utility and neceffity of a fort or citadel, as the town is
      " quite open on that fide to the incurfions of the Indians ;
      " two hundred of whom, by approaching in fmall parties
      " through the woods, might do great mifchief in one
      " night. Your country negroes are quiet at prefent, but
      " they have not always been fo ; and their late attempts at
      " Antigua, New York, and Jamaica, may be fufficient warn-
      " ing to any country, where they are fo numerous, to pro-

" vide againſt accidents, and confider of a force that may
" be turned againſt them ; the town negroes alſo will be
" more faithful when they know it is impoſſible for them
" to eſcape if they ſhould miſbehave. I could mention
" many more advantages that would ariſe from fortifying
" this important paſs; for there is no doubt but there are
" people in all towns, who, on the approach of an enemy,
" would wiſh to be as far removed from the danger as poſ-
" ſible, who, knowing there is no eſcaping, will do their
" duty ; beſides, it will greatly encourage every man to
" exert himſelf when his wife, children, and moſt valuable
" effects are in a place of ſecurity. I might likewiſe take
" notice that within this fort there might be houſes for the
" governor, the council, and aſſembly ; and barracks for
" officers and ſoldiers, beſides work-houſes, priſons, maga-
" zines, arſenals, ſtore-houſes, &c. It is therefore my opi-
" nion that no enemy we may expect in this part of the
" world would venture to attempt this town, knowing of
" ſuch a ſtrength, till they had made themſelves maſters of
" this fort ; and as that could not be attacked but on the
" land ſide, two or three hundred men would defend it,
" unleſs in the event of a general aſſault.

" I have prepared two plans of a fort, which I herewith
" lay before you ; the one of four regular baſtions, the other
" of two baſtions, with a raveline before the curtain, to-
" ward the continent, and two demi-baſtions next the town.
" My not laying before you an eſtimate of the charges of
" ſuch works, is owing to my being an entire ſtranger to
" the prices of materials and labour ; but it may be eaſily
" computed by gentlemen converſant in building, as I
                                        " have

" have annexed both the quantity and quality of the feveral
" works that are neceffary to be done.   But in cafe this
" government fhould find the expence of erecting fuch a
" fort to exceed their expectation, and be thereby deterred
" from putting it in execution ; then my next propo-
" fal is to cut a moat, or ditch, with a curtain line from
" Craven's Baftion to the work-houfe, ftrengthened in the
" middle by a baftion, and a demi-baftion next to Afhley
" River, by which means the town will be inclofed on the
" land fide from one river to the other, and this may be done
" with fods."

A committee of fome of the members of the council and
affembly were appointed to make an eftimate of thofe works:
and as an entire want of ftone in this country obliges them
to build their works of ftrength with brick, and they have
no lime but what they make of oyfter and other fea fhells,
together with the very high price of labour, they found the
execution of thofe plans would amount to a confiderable
fum ; and as their treafury, at this time, was not in a condition to fupport the charge, they were of opinion that they
fhould endeavour to negotiate a loan from England at three
per cent. or obtain an act of parliament to enable them to
raife one hundred thoufand pounds of their own currency, by
iffuing paper notes, and to petition that an able engineer
might be fent from London to execute thofe plans, as they
did not choofe to truft the execution of them to colonel
Baile, their prefent engineer, alledging he had already run
them into great expence in erecting works of no fignifi-
cation. They preffed me very earneftly to ftay with them
by offering to double my pay, and to fhew me other favours.

vours. I obferved if they had applied to me when I came
out to Providence, I could have carried on their works at
the fame time ; but as that opportunity was now paft, it
was at prefent out of my power to comply with their requeft, without an order from the board of ordnance. Befides, as thofe gentlemen were very dilatory in their deter-
minations, and in a bad underftanding with their governor,
I fhould have met with great difficulty to pleafe both parties. However, as they feemed moft pleafed with my laft
plan, as the eafieft and cheapeft, at the defire of governor
Glen, I gave full inftructions to colonel Baile how it was to
be performed, and recommended him to the committee for
the execution of it, with affurances that they might fafely
truft him. The two batteries at Rahte's Point, and Anfon's
Houfe, for the fecurity of the paffage through Hog Ifland
Creek, were begun. The gentlemen of Charleftown made
me a prefent of fifty guineas, alledging that as I was only on
my way to England, and not come there with any intention
to ftay and ferve them, they could not make me the return
they intended to have done, if I had come with a defign of
being ferviceable to them in putting my plans in execution.

We had a vifit at this time from a war captain, or Indian
king as they called him, with about one hundred Cherokee
Indians in his retinue, under pretence of renewing his alliance with king George ; but the real object, I believe, was
to receive the cuftomary prefents. They come all naked on
thofe occafions, and return well clad ; they are well fhaped,
generally of an olive colour, with their faces painted in many
different ways, according to their different ideas of conveying
ter–

terror to their enemies. Some have one fide black, and the other red ; others with four different colours ; their heads were adorned with all forts of feathers, intermixed with down, by way of powder ; they cover their nakednefs with a fmall piece of fkin, or leather ; they are excefIively fond of fpirits, which they will drink till they are quite drunk. Their camp was a mile from the town, to which they returned every night, and after a week's ftay, being all new clad, and receiving the cuftomary prefents, they decamped, and returned home. I omitted to mention that their king, or chief, with two of his principal officers and three women, were new clothed before they made their public entry into the town ; then the chief with his two nobles were brought in ftate in a coach drawn by fix horfes, to the council chamber, where they made their fpeech, which confifted in a very few words, affuring us of their fteady attachment to the crown of Britain : after the ceremonial part of their vifit was ended, they fhook hands with every one in the room, took their leave, and were conducted back to their camp, in the coach that brought them ; they were neither painted nor adorned with feathers, as the reft, but were decently clad in blue cloth, and each a gold laced hat, with which they feemed very well pleafed.

Captain
Frankland's
rich prize.

Captain Thomas Frankland brought in here a very rich French prize, whofe principal loading confifted in piftoles, a few chefts of dollars, and a great deal of wrought gold and filver ; the quantity was fo great, that the fhares were delivered by weight, to fave the trouble of counting it ; fo that piftoles were now feen in Charleftown in greater plenty than the dollars had been in Providence, which could not

but

but be very mortifying to governor Tinker, who was thereby deprived of the profits accruing from her condemnation, confidering captain Frankland was ftationed there; but he met with this mortification in general, as no privateer would ever enter with their prizes into the harbour of Providence after the treatment that Sibbald and Dowall had met with. After all the cargo was taken out of this prize, and the veffel was to be put up to fale, the French captain told captain Frankland that if he would engage to reward him handfomely, he would difcover a hidden treafure to him, which no one knew of but himfelf. Captain Frankland engaged to reward him very generoufly, and he did difcover thirty thoufand piftoles in a place, where no one could have thought of finding any thing. The French captain afterwards told governor Glen, that captain Frankland's generofity confifted only in one thoufand piftoles; a poor reward, he faid, for fo great a difcovery. Captain Frankland made another very accidental difcovery: he had taken into his own fervice a brifk little French boy, who had belonged to the French captain, who, having a walking ftick of no value, one of the failors had taken it from him: the boy lamented his lofs fo much, that captain Frankland ordered fearch to be made for it, to return it to the boy: the ftick was brought to the captain, who feeing it of no value, afked the boy how he could make fo much ado about fuch a trifle. The boy replied brifkly, he could not walk like a gentleman, and fhow his airs without a ftick in his hand; upon the captain's going to return him the ftick, he gave him a tap on the fhoulder with it, and finding fomething rattle in the infide of it, withdrew to a room by him-

felf,

felf, and taking off the head of it, he found jewels (according to the French captain's report) worth twenty thoufand
piftoles ; who had given the ftick to the boy when he furrendered, in hopes of faving it, as no body would take notice of fuch a trifle in a boy's hand. Upon the whole, fhe
was a confiderable prize to captain Frankland.

About the fame time, captain Jofeph Hamer, of the
Flamborough man of war, brought in here a Spanifh prize,
with fuch a quantity of dollars on board that he fhared
twelve thoufand for himfelf.

A fhort de-
fcription of
Carolina.

Carolina is now fo well known, that I need not give a
defcription of it ; yet I cannot omit mentioning that it is,
in general, very low and flat, the foil being, for the moft
part, fand interfperfed with fwamps and marfhes, which
yield great plenty of rice, with which they have carried on
a confiderable trade ; but as the demand for it was leffened
by the war, the inhabitants turned their thoughts to the
culture of indigo, and have brought that article to confiderable perfection. They have abundance and variety of
fruits ; but their oranges and vines are frequently blafted by
the north winds ; mulberry trees grow here in plenty to
great perfection, fo that they might eafily breed a number of
filk worms, which would add a very beneficial branch to
their trade. The face of the country is covered with wood ;
their live oak, which is an evergreen, is, in my opinion,
preferable to Englifh oak for fhip-building ; their pines
grow to a prodigious fize, fit for any mafts. Their woods
abound with all kinds of venifon and wild fowl, efpecially
turkeys and fummer ducks ; the latter came from the interior
parts of the country, fince the planting of rice ; they are

ex-

extremely beautiful, and are kept about gentlemen's houfes as a rarity. Whilftling birds are here in great variety, of
which the mocking bird is the moft entertaining ; they
come in numbers out of the woods, and are fo very tame
and familiar that they perch on the houfe tops, and on the
trees before the windows, efpecially when they either hear
mufic or finging, to which they liften with great attention,
and afterwards repeat the notes. I took feveral of them
and the fummer ducks to bring with me to Britain, but in
fpite of all my care they died at fea.

The Rofe and Flamborough men of war having got their
orders in the latter end of May to fail for England, and
take fuch merchant men as were ready to fail under their
convoy, I took my paffage with captain Hamer in the Flamborough. I put a quantity of quick-filver, mahogany plank,
dyeing-wood, and cotton, on board two of the merchant fhips
for London, in equal proportion, not being able to get
thofe goods infured here. The one was afterwards taken
in the Englifh Channel, and carried into St. Malos ; the
other arrived fafe at Cowes in the Ifle of Wight. We failed
from Charleftown on the 1ft of June, with five merchant
men under our convoy ; and after two days fail in fine weather, with a fair wind, we left the five fhips under our convoy in the night, and made the beft of our way homewards,
with very pleafant weather. We paft to the northward of
the Azores, or Weftern Iflands, and one evening we difcovered three fail to windward, bearing down upon us. In
the morning one of them, which was a prime failor, having left the others at a very confiderable diftance, came
pretty near up with us, and perceiving her to be a fhip of

BOOK XII.

1745.

The captain
fails for Eng-
land.

L l l 2   war,

war, captain Frankland made the fignal to put about and meet her; which fhe perceiving, immediately made back to her conforts, and we proceeded on our courfe again, and faw no more of them; nor did we fee any more fhips till we got into the Channel, where we met a large man of war and a frigate, under Dutch colours. On hailing them, they told us they were from Helvoetfluys, bound for the Mediterranean, to cruize againft the Algerines, and at parting they faluted us with nine guns, which we returned by the fame number. In the evening we got into Plymouth harbour, followed by two merchantmen, a Dane and a Dutchman, who both informed us that the fhips we had hailed were French; that the man of war was the Elizabeth, who had a little before had an engagement with the Lion, and that the frigate in company had the Pretender's eldeft fon on board, which our captains would not believe, but regarded as a mere fable; but the event afterwards evinced the truth of it. After one day's ftay in the Sound we failed for the Downs, and arrived off Dover the 25th of July, when, according to our fhip's reckoning from Carolina, we had failed five thoufand two hundred miles. I went afhore at Dover, and got to London on the 27th.

Arrive at
London.

On my arrival I found every body in the utmoft confternation upon the news of the Pretender's fon being landed in the north of Scotland, at a time when both the king and army were abroad, which afterwards brought the nation to no fmall trouble and expence. After I had delivered my report and accounts to the board of ordnance, and fettled my own affairs, I was ordered to repair to Hull, where the magiftrates had petitioned the board to fend them

4   an

an engineer to direct them how to carry on their fortifications, which they were at this time repairing at their own
charge. I arrived at Hull on the 8th of October, where I
found people of all ranks induſtriouſly employed in deepen-
ing and clearing out their moats and forming their para-
pets; next day I attended lieutenant-general Jones, deputy-
governor, the mayor and aldermen, round the ramparts; I
was ſurpriſed to ſee the great progreſs they had made in ſo
ſhort a time, and to as good purpoſe as if they had been
directed by an able engineer. At their deſire I left them
further directions how to proceed for the better defence of
the place; and having received a great many civilities from
them, I proceeded, in obedience to my orders, to join the
army under marſhal Wade.

On the 15th I arrived at Doncaſter, where the Dutch
troops had joined us; on the 18th the marſhal reviewed the
army, and broke up the camp on the 21ſt to proceed northward; the Dutch behaved on the march as if they had
been in an enemy's country, robbing, plundering, and
abuſing the country people; the particulars of their behaviour are too ſhocking to relate. On the 31ſt we arrived at
Newcaſtle, where we encamped in very cold, bad weather;
and here receiving intelligence that the rebels had beſieged
Carliſle, we broke up to march to its relief, leaving near
one-fourth of our army ſick in the hoſpital.

On the 18th of November we got to Hexham in North-
umberland, in extreme cold weather, which march, with
the ſudden tranſition from a warm to a cold climate, entirely ruined my health, being ſeized with a rupture and
an aſthma, which diſabled me from ſtanding the hard fatigues

BOOK IXI. tigues of a winter campaign. We were informed here that
——————— Carlisle had surrendered to the rebels, on which we marched
1745.   back to Newcastle, where we arrived the 22d. The weather was now become so intensely cold, that the army could
not pitch their tents, so they were quartered in the town
and adjacent villages. In this situation we received intelligence that the rebels had marched for Wales, which made
us leave our warm quarters, and march southward. On the
6th of December we reached Ferrybridge, from whence we
sent our sick to Doncaster, and our horse and dragoons to
join his royal highness the duke of Cumberland, and we
arrived at Leeds on the 11th, where we were informed the
rebels had returned back for the North, on which our army
marched back again.

F I N I S.

www.ingramcontent.com/pod-product-compliance
Lightning Source LLC
Chambersburg PA
CBHW022021110726
47901CB00006B/1611